Karin Baine lives in [   ]1, two sons, and her out[   ] Her mother and her g[   ] books inspired her lov[   ] becoming a Mills & Boon author. Now she can tell people she has a *proper* job! You can follow Karin on Twitter, @karinbaine1, or visit her website for the latest news—karinbaine.com.

Sue MacKay lives with her husband in New Zealand's beautiful Marlborough Sounds, with the water on her doorstep and the birds and the trees at her back door. It is the perfect setting to indulge her passions of entertaining friends by cooking them sumptuous meals, drinking fabulous wine, going for hill walks or kayaking around the bay—and, of course, writing stories.

Also by Karin Baine

The Single Dad's Proposal
Their One-Night Twin Surprise
Their One-Night Christmas Gift
Healed by Their Unexpected Family
Reunion with His Surgeon Princess
One Night with Her Italian Doc

Also by Sue MacKay

Taking a Chance on the Single Dad
The Nurse's Twin Surprise
A Fling to Steal Her Heart
Reclaiming Her Army Doc Husband
The Nurse's Secret
The GP's Secret Baby Wish

Discover more at millsandboon.co.uk.

THE SURGEON
AND THE PRINCESS

KARIN BAINE

CAPTIVATED BY
HER RUNAWAY DOC

SUE MacKAY

MILLS & BOON

First Published in Great Britain 2021
by Mills & Boon, an imprint of HarperCollins*Publishers*
1 London Bridge Street, London, SE1 9GF

The Surgeon and the Princess © 2021 by Karin Baine

Captivated by Her Runaway Doc © 2021 by Sue MacKay

ISBN: 978-0-263-29759-1

MIX
Paper from
responsible sources
FSC® C007454

This book is produced from independently certified FSC™ paper
to ensure responsible forest management.
For more information visit www.harpercollins.co.uk/green.

Printed and bound in Spain
by CPI, Barcelona

THE SURGEON
AND THE PRINCESS

KARIN BAINE

MILLS & BOON

With love for my lovely editor, Charlotte,
who is worth her weight in gold! xx

CHAPTER ONE

'ROBO-PRINCESS. PART MACHINE, part fairy-tale heroine.'

Georgiana could almost hear her squad now, as they'd sat joking around her hospital bed after her amputation. It had been their way of trying to cheer her up. The army way, with dark humour disguising their concern and love for one of their own.

She missed her team and the close relationships she'd forged. Since her op, she hadn't had a chance to catch up with them again. More from a sense of shame than lack of opportunity. She didn't want them to pity the person she'd become.

Back then Georgiana had laughed along with the teasing, convinced it was only a matter of time before she'd be back with the others in some capacity as their medic. Now the nickname felt more like a cruel joke. She was neither warrior nor princess. Simply a one-legged failure at both.

There was no way she could go back to the army now, when it was taking all her strength just to live her life unassisted. As for the princess bit—well, she'd never seriously considered that as a career. More of a curse bestowed upon her at birth, being next in line to the throne of Bardot, a small kingdom sandwiched between Liechtenstein and Switzerland that the rest of the world neither knew nor cared about.

The sound of her much-missed squaddies in her head was replaced with the steady thud of her pounding the treadmill. A reminder she was almost back on her feet, even if only one of them was real. At least they were both moving in sync now, so she was no longer walking like an inebriated penguin. Balance was a tricky thing to achieve with only one leg. One and a half if she counted the remaining scarred stump.

She watched herself in the full-length mirror of her home gym. The wounds on her face had faded but she still saw them there, ugly and gaping, like the ones all over her body. Reminders of what she'd gone through and lost.

The explosion rang deafeningly in her ears once more. The safe walls around her were blown away, replaced with clouds of dust and debris, and she was back there. Clawing the dirt out of her mouth and eyes. Trying to stand and falling. Then she was screaming, 'Medic down!' while tying a tourniquet around what was left of her leg, injecting herself with morphine and waiting as her team leader called a Medevac to fly her to hospital.

Georgiana increased her pace, closed her eyes and tried to outrun the past. It didn't work. Nothing did. Even coming back to Bardot, separating herself from that army environment she'd been encompassed in during rehabilitation, hadn't lessened the pain of what had happened and what it meant for her future. Especially knowing if she'd simply accepted her position here instead of trying to distance herself from the toxicity of the establishment, she'd have remained in one piece.

These were the thoughts she failed to block out day by

day in her recovery. Neither the increased heavy pounding of her body on the treadmill nor her laboured breathing could drown them out.

She grabbed the headphones hanging over the handrail and somehow managed to wrestle them on without missing a step. Those tiny, wireless buds were all the rage these days but her old-fashioned padded ones blocked out more of the world. So she was cocooned, safe, surrounded by the familiar music blasting in her ears. It helped her push through the pain barrier, both physically and mentally. If she was to get back any resemblance of her old life she had to keep going. No matter how much it hurt.

Unfortunately, her damaged body couldn't quite live up to the promises she'd made to herself. This was her new normal and she hated the powerlessness over her physical self. She wasn't a quitter, she'd proved that to progress as far as she had in military life. There had been no exceptions made for her, no special favours called in, she hadn't wanted that. She'd worked as hard as any other recruit. Sometimes harder, to prove that she wasn't simply a pampered princess. Well, she had been until she'd made a stand against the life she'd been born into. Swapping it for something more fulfilling.

Now that she'd been forced to leave that much-wanted military life she was lost again. With no true direction or sense of self when everything had been taken away from her. The danger of being back in the palace was that she'd get dragged back into that superficial existence of personal appearances and mentions in the tabloids. It was that world that had killed her brother, Freddie, and she wanted to do something more substantial and meaningful with her life. She simply didn't know what that was any more. Not while she was like this. Half the person she used to be.

Georgiana slowed her speed for the cool-down phase of her workout and pulled off the headphones. As she stepped back down onto the gym floor, her good leg was trembling with the exertion of her punishing exercise. It knocked her a little off balance and she had to reach out for the nearby chair to steady herself, before collapsing into it, taking the weight off her unsteady prosthetic leg. She'd suffer for this later, knowing the pressure of the prosthesis rubbing on what was left of her lower limb would leave the skin raw. Not that she would feel sorry for herself when she was lucky to still be alive.

'You really shouldn't be so hard on your body.' A critical masculine voice startled her and she reacted as she would with anyone who dared to trespass on her private training session.

'Who are you and how did you get in here?' She stood up so she wasn't at such a disadvantage against the tall, broad figure walking towards her. Squaring up to this stranger wearing only her racer-back gym top and shorts exposing her prosthetic leg wasn't as intimidating as she wanted since it didn't halt his progress towards her.

She was trying not to freak out but wished she hadn't dismissed all the staff in the vicinity. Her fight back to recovery wasn't a spectator sport for anyone, including security or whoever this was. It wouldn't be the first time they'd had an intruder at the palace, thankfully there out of curiosity rather than for any malicious reason. That didn't make a possible similar situation any less concerning.

He didn't look like a tourist who'd walked in off the street, dressed in an immaculate charcoal-grey suit, complete with silver silk tie and real leather shoes. She prayed he wasn't a journalist either. That would almost be worse than someone simply wanting a selfie with a member of the royal family. Her army training had taught her how to defend herself but it was something she hadn't put into practice since her traumatic injury and she didn't want to test it now.

'I'm Edward Lawrence. I was here for a consultation with your mother regarding her riding accident. Sorry for the intrusion. I just happened to see you in here as I was on my way out.'

'And you wanted a closer look at the freak show?' She didn't bother introducing herself. He didn't deserve to be on the receiving end of social niceties if he couldn't observe them himself.

He frowned as though he didn't quite understand her meaning and she waited, arms folded, until the penny dropped.

'Goodness, no. I was taking an interest merely from a professional point of view. I'm a consultant spinal surgeon and physical rehabilitation is one of the specialities at our mobility clinic.' He reached into his inside pocket and produced a business card for Move, a private clinic, presuming she'd accept it as proof of his credentials. His name did ring a bell.

'I haven't been home in quite a while but I remember a Dr Lawrence here as an older, more distinguished gentleman.' One who would've knocked before walking in. He'd been a tall man but with a thinning silver pate and a bushy moustache. A contrast to the sun-kissed swoop of hair this guy was sporting, blond with a matching golden smile on his handsome, clean-shaven face.

'That was my father, a GP. He's retired now.'

If she'd wondered how someone who would've looked more at home running barefoot across a beach with a surfboard under his arm had wangled a gig at the palace, now she knew. Nepotism. Regardless of whatever capacity her family had acquired his services, it was nothing to do with her.

'Yes, well, neither you nor your father have any right to be in my personal space so I'd appreciate you leaving.' She attempted to show him out with a wave of her hand, uncomfortable at being exposed to anyone like this.

Since returning home she'd purposely avoided contact with the outside world so her current state would remain unknown or at least a mystery to those with an insatiable appetite for royal scandal. Unveiling her broken body was something she wanted to do at her own pace, if at all. By barging in here uninvited he'd stolen some of that power from her and now she just wanted him gone.

Yet again he showed a blatant disregard for common courtesy by failing, not only to leave, but to apologise. 'By overexerting yourself you're putting your body under more strain. You could be causing more damage. Surely you have some sort of exercise plan drawn up with a physiotherapist?'

His whole lack of manners and apparent knowledge of her circumstances disoriented her. If he knew who she was or had been taken by surprise by her injury he gave no indication of it. His focus remained on how she was potentially abusing her body. Perhaps he was who he purported to be after all. An expert.

'To put your mind at ease, I completed my rehabilitation at a professional residential facility. I'm quite capable of continuing my recovery at home. On my own.'

'Georgiana—I hope I can call you that—' Mystery

solved. He knew exactly who he was dealing with and presumably had some idea of how she'd come to be in this position.

He didn't wait for a reply. 'Recovery is an ongoing process best served by remaining in contact with medical professionals. It's a guess but I suspect you haven't attended any follow-up appointments since leaving the centre?'

The truth burned her skin. 'Look, you obviously know who I am, so you'll understand why I'm not keen on continuing my recovery in public. I've got everything I need here. I'm fine.'

He gave her gym equipment a cursory glance. 'No offence but this looks like it's been commissioned by an interior designer, not by anyone who knows what they're doing.'

She should've been offended by the comment. He had absolutely no right to be in her private gym, much less mock it. However, she could see his point. It was the most expensive gym furniture on the market but she had wondered if it had been chosen primarily for decorative reasons. Rehabilitation wasn't meant to be pretty, but the area that had been commandeered for her recovery had been set up before her return. She'd had no input and there had been no consultation with regard to her individual needs. Most likely because her mother didn't trust her judgement over an outsider's on the matter. As a result, she'd been greeted with a room befitting a princess with a gym habit rather than a wounded soldier.

The full-length mirrors she needed to watch her gait were gilded with golden frames. The walls were brilliant white, the floors bleached oak. Perfect for a glossy magazine photo shoot. While she enjoyed the anonymity provided by being in the farthest corner of the palace, it was stark with no natural light coming in. A window wouldn't have gone amiss.

There was a crystal chandelier hanging from the ceiling, dappling the plump, upholstered armchairs with teardrops of artificial light, but none of the aesthetics were of particular benefit to her. Although, the upside of the space here was that everyone knew to leave her alone. Except for the nosy doc who'd know for the next time he happened by.

'I'm grateful my parents made the adjustments for me.' That was diplomatic. She was thankful and she knew they wouldn't hesitate to provide her with anything she might need. It was the atmosphere around the place, silent accusations and the air thick with recriminations, that was more difficult to live with. A matter that was no one's business outside the family.

'It's fine for a normal home gym but you need specialised equipment. We have everything you'd need at our medical facility, including hydrotherapy pools.' He was tempting her. With the pool idea, not his good looks and charm.

She'd used water a lot to strengthen her core during her rehabilitation and missed that feeling of weightlessness. Sometimes she even managed to forget the physical part of her that was missing when she was swimming, but it wasn't as though she could tuck a towel under her arm and head to the local swimming baths any time she wanted.

'It's a very kind offer but, as I've told you, I want to keep my appearance and recovery private for now.' Ed could see she was wavering. He hadn't expected it would be an easy task to convince her to accept help, but he'd promised her mother he'd at least try. If there was the slightest opening in her defence, he was willing to take advantage of it for her own good.

'We could arrange completely private sessions. You have my personal guarantee on that. If you decide you want to avail yourself of any of our other services, our physios or counsellors, that will be on a strictly confidential basis too. A lot of our clients are in the public eye, so we're used to being discreet. It's one of the reasons your mother came to me for her consultation.' Along with his father putting his name forward when she contacted him for his valued opinion on her condition.

Apparently, she'd had an ulterior motive in having a home visit. The queen had been insistent she didn't want Georgiana to know she was interfering but it was clear she was worried about her daughter. It wasn't any of his business what was going on but there was a blatant lack of communication between mother and daughter. A parent should be able to demonstrate concern for a child without fear of losing them. It was the close bond he had with his own parents that had saved their family. Even if it sometimes felt as if he'd sacrificed his freedom to keep everyone together.

Meeting Georgiana himself, he could understand her mother's reticence to be seen as interfering. She was a force to be reckoned with. Defensive and self-assured, and someone who could totally do this on her own if she had to. It simply made sense to use the services available to aid a faster recovery process. If only her body language didn't scream, 'Stay away from me if you value your life!'

Despite her obvious disability she still had that in-built alertness that came with being a soldier. One false move and he had no doubt she'd battle anyone or anything that threatened her. She certainly looked like a warrior, as well as having that defensive attitude that emanated from her in waves. Her slight frame was toned with defined muscles that would put most people to shame. Eyes blazed with green fire in her heart-shaped face, her defiant chin tilted upward. The flowing brunette locks he'd seen in newspaper features had been shorn into an edgy cut. One side of her head was shaved close to the scalp, while the other was choppy and non-conformist. He wouldn't be surprised if she'd done it herself in a fit of pique. It made her look like the rebel she was reputed to be. The addition of a prosthetic right leg only added to that intimidating impression of someone who was not to be messed with.

Georgiana Ashley was unlike anyone he'd ever met, though he'd come across many other wounded veterans unwilling to appear helpless or weak by accepting help.

'Even if I did agree to scoping the place out, there's the small matter of leaving here unnoticed. It's impossible. I'm sure you've witnessed the crowds of tourists and press assembled outside waiting for a glimpse of life beyond the palace gates.' She clutched her hands to her heart in mock dramatic fashion. Ed was sure the deprecating humour was an attempt to undermine the high esteem the family name drew rather than making fun of those who looked up to them.

'You are the country's main tourist attraction.' He couldn't help adding fuel to the fire and wasn't surprised to receive her narrow-eyed glare in response.

'My point exactly,' she said, letting him get away with the insolent comment that could have seen him lose his head a few centuries ago.

'If you were serious about attending the clinic, I'm sure we could find some way to get you there.'

'I don't see how, unless you've got an invisibility cloak on you.' She turned her back on him to retrieve a garish set of pink headphones from the treadmill, losing interest in the conversation. Clearly underestimating the heights of his own determination.

'If you're serious, I could sneak you out in my car. No one seems interested in my comings and goings. It shouldn't be too hard to smuggle you out under cover of darkness. That way you could be sure to have the facilities to yourself too, if you attended in the evening.' It might sound like the plot of a farcical movie but Ed was a problem-solver and this seemed the easiest way out of her predicament. If she wasn't simply making excuses.

'Are you joking?' It did manage to grab her attention again and when she faced him, he could see the trace of a smile on her lips.

'I never joke about my work,' he replied in complete seriousness. This wasn't about having a little excitement in his life. Goodness knew he had his hands full already, taking care of his parents and his little brother.

'You would actually try and sneak me out?' She was openly laughing at him now but he didn't care. He would do whatever it took to get her to agree to some sort of aftercare. Not only had he made a promise to her mother but, having spoken to Georgiana, he knew she needed this. A space away from the pressures of her life here and somewhere she could be comfortable in her own skin. To reach the limits he knew she could be capable of now he'd seen her in action. It was their job at the clinic to encourage patients back to full health physically and mentally. Shutting herself off completely from the rest of the world wasn't conducive to that recovery.

'Sure. It's not as if I'd be kidnapping you. If we got stopped, I'd expect you to say as much. I'm not getting locked up for attempted regicide or treason or whatever trumped-up charges they'd come up with.'

'What are we talking here? A blanket over the head or full trench-coat-and-moustache disguise?' At least she'd stopped scowling at him as the idea seemed increasingly to amuse her. It shouldn't be this hard for a person to leave their own home.

'Wear what you want. I'm not your stylist.' He shrugged, unwilling to make such a big deal of things that she might become wary.

'You have no idea, do you? I mean, why should you? You can just swan around the place as though you've every right to be here simply because your father got you this job.'

'That's not—' His father had mentioned his name for the consultation but he was sure his reputation and experience would have secured the queen's trust in him regardless.

'It must be nice to go where you want, do as you please, with no one expecting anything from you.' She was unleashing some of her frustration on him. It was good, he supposed, for her. Except she knew nothing about his life or the demands upon him. He had no more freedom than her, the princess imprisoned by her own privilege.

If she had the first clue about his situation, she'd never accuse him of having any sort of liberation from family. Not now and especially not when he was growing up. As the eldest of his six siblings, including a brother with spina bifida, he'd shouldered a lot of responsibility. That family loyalty hadn't lessened with age. Most of his brothers and sisters had moved on or married and started families of their own. Things most people took for granted when they pictured their future. Not Ed. He'd stayed close to home, remained in that role of carer, so now he was the one looking after their elderly parents and checking in on his kid brother. That didn't leave room for whatever fun and games Ms Ashley seemed to think he got up to. It had already cost him a relationship of his own.

'That's a lot to assume about someone you don't know.' He was the one getting defensive now.

'We're taught in the army to make quick, detailed assessments of every situation.' She looked him up and down. 'I stand by every word I said.'

Ed bit the inside of his cheek lest he say something he'd later come to regret when he was locked away in a tower somewhere as punishment. 'Thankfully, my offer isn't conditional on your knowledge, or lack thereof, about my personal life. So, if you could set aside whatever preconceived notions and ill-judged prejudice you have against me and focus on yourself, you'll see how you could benefit from our state-of-the-art facility.'

'Uh-huh, and what's in it for you?' Georgiana stripped off her shirt, so she was standing there in only her black sports bra and shorts. He knew it was a move to make him uncomfortable and at the same time display her own confidence. It worked on both levels but he wasn't a man to give up easily.

'Nothing except the satisfaction of giving someone else the best chance of a full recovery. It's what I do.' He knew he sounded glib but he didn't think sincerity was going to do him any favours with her. Those barriers she'd put up weren't coming down any time soon and he could tell straight away she wasn't the sort of woman who'd respond to a softly-softly approach.

She rolled her eyes as she patted a towel around her neck and her décolletage where perspiration from her workout was glistening on her pale skin. If they'd met at a gym or anywhere other than a royal palace, he would never have believed her to be a princess. He was just as guilty of having preconceived notions of her before meeting. Of course, he'd seen and heard mention of her in the press but assumed the stories were either fiction or she was simply another rich kid feigning rebellion. Now he knew different. Georgiana was very much her own person.

He watched as she hooked her thumbs into the waistband of her shorts, tugging them down slightly so the flat plane of her impressive abdominal muscles was visible. It showed she was a hard worker, motivated in the hardest of circumstances to keep up her fitness regime, and boded well for her future despite her life-changing injury.

She cleared her throat and he lifted his eyes to meet her querying gaze.

'If you don't mind, I'd like to shower and change in private.'

'Yes. Sorry.' He bumbled around, trying to avert his gaze and regather his composure.

'Close the door on your way out.' She was ending the conversation and the meeting without agreeing to anything. Ed had to admire her tenacity. It could be the very thing to get her back to the person she used to be. If that was different from the woman standing before him now, he had no idea.

'She's going to be okay, by the way. In case you were wondering.' It occurred to him she hadn't referenced the reason he was in her home in the first place.

'Who?' She looked genuinely puzzled as to who or what he was referring to. It said a lot, nothing good, about her relationship with her mother. Either she didn't care or there had been a complete lack of information shared with her about the accident. Perhaps even both. The concept was alien to someone who was constantly in contact and, indeed, worried about his own parents. His family was always foremost in his thoughts.

'Your mother. Very badly bruised after the fall from her horse but no long-term damage,' he reminded her, in case the details had slipped from her memory during the course of their discussion.

'Oh,' was all the response she mustered. He couldn't help but wonder what had caused their relationship to become so strained. Especially at a time when she would need the support of her family more than ever. He didn't know how she'd got this far without them.

'Anyway, I've checked all the scans and X-rays to put her mind at rest and she's going to be fine,' he assured her again. Although nothing in her tone suggested it had caused her any concern thus far.

If Georgiana, by any miracle, did agree to attend the clinic, he'd be advising her to seek the services of one of their counsellors. In case the psychological trauma had in some way caused this apparent lack of empathy towards the very person who'd come to him for help. Families were a complicated business and no one knew that better than he did.

'I never doubted it. Now, if you don't mind…' She dismissed him again with a nod of her head towards the door. Clearly, social etiquette wasn't as important to her as it was to her mother. Unless this was another side effect from her accident. Sometimes patients had no filter after such an ordeal. She'd been through a lot and he was prepared to make allowances for someone he really knew nothing about. He could only hope she would do the same for him, since he didn't seem to be making a great first impression.

'You have my number should you decide to use our clinic. Goodbye, Miss Ashley.' He turned to take his leave, only to have a pair of shorts land on top of his head.

Unwilling to give her the satisfaction of going back to confront her, clad now only in her underwear, he pulled them off his head and kept walking.

She really didn't know him at all if she thought he wasn't up to a challenge.

CHAPTER TWO

'LET ME TAKE that in for you.' Georgiana reached out to take the silver tray from the maid she'd just startled in the hallway.

'Are you sure, miss?' The wide-eyed girl looked at the tea tray and back at Georgiana, unsure about what to do in the circumstances.

She was a new face, not one Georgiana had seen before being deployed. It was difficult to tell if she was worried her employer's daughter couldn't manage the task without falling over or if she was afraid of letting someone else do her job.

In the end Georgiana made the decision for her and took the tray off her hands. 'I want to check and make sure Mother is okay.'

That seemed enough to ease her conscience and she gave a little curtsey before scuttling off downstairs. It was difficult to get used to being waited on hand and foot after being self-sufficient for so long in the army. From the outset of her return Georgiana had done her best to put an end to that kind of attention and intrusion from the staff by insisting she be left alone. Other than those she ran into in the halls, or in the kitchen when she was on a snack hunt, she rarely had any interaction. It was her way of keeping perspective even though she was living in a palace with servants available at the ring of a bell.

She knocked lightly on her mother's bedroom door.

'Come in.'

Georgiana opened the door with her elbow and slowly backed into the room, careful not to upend the tray. If she made a scene here, it would only prove to her mother she was incapable of the smallest of tasks. Months ago, she could only dream of being able to balance a tea tray without spilling anything. Sheer determination and the stubborn streak she wished her poor brother had inherited had got her to this point. Hopefully, it would be enough to see her through this and back to the life she'd made for herself away from this fake reality. She believed it was better for her mental health if she was able to live independently from her parents again, where she was able to think for herself and not under pressure to live the way they wanted her to.

'I thought I'd come and see what the consultant said.' She couldn't be sure if it was guilt or anger that had kept the man and his comments in her thoughts while she'd changed.

'Georgiana, you shouldn't be carrying that. Where did that girl go? I wish Lise had never left. At least she knew how to do her job properly.' Her mother shifted up the bed, struggling to sit upright but somehow still managing to look regal in her nightgown.

'I sent her away. I wanted to bring you your tea.' She placed the tray across the patient's knees and arranged the pillows behind her until she was sure her mother was comfortable.

'You shouldn't be doing that in your condition.'

'I'm not pregnant, Mother, and I don't have a condition. I've had an amputation and I need to adjust to it, not pretend it hasn't happened.' This was the kind of thing she usually tried to avoid—a pity party thrown in her honour. She didn't want one and she didn't deserve one. It was her parents' refusal to accept what was going on before their very eyes that had resulted in Freddie taking his own life. If the family had pulled together, faced the future united and been honest to themselves and the rest of the world, he might still be here.

'You shouldn't be pushing yourself too hard.'

Where had she heard that one before?

'I'm not. I'm only bringing you some tea,' she said with a smile, trying to give her mother the benefit of the doubt that she was truly worried about her daughter's health and not wrapped up in how her disabled daughter would look to the staff.

'We have employees to do that, dear.'

'So, Mr Lawrence says you're going to be okay. That's good news.' Georgiana pulled over a chair and sat down, her muscles beginning to ache after her workout.

'Oh, you saw him?' There was a sparkle in her mother's eyes at the mere mention of the handsome consultant. Georgiana could admit the dashing Edward Lawrence was something of a head turner because it would be a long time before she acted on any attraction to the opposite sex. If ever. Especially if it was someone so rude and pushy as the aforementioned visitor.

A memory of her attempt at having the last say popped into her head. The absolute gall of him to take her shorts with him as some sort of trophy. It went to show the difference between him and his distinguished father. He wasn't embarrassed at all by her undressing in front of him. It certainly hadn't hastened his exit as she'd intended.

'Hmm… He stopped by the gym. Where did you get him from anyway? He seems very full of himself, if you ask me.' She was still smarting after their encounter. Primarily because he seemed to think he knew her body better than she did.

'His father retired a few years ago but he came very highly recommended. Edward has a lovely bedside manner.'

'I'm sure he does,' she muttered, not having had the same experience.

'He can be very discreet, if that's what you're worried about, darling.' She gave a pointed look towards Georgiana's prosthetic. It was difficult to admit that her mother was correct in her assumption that having him see her was what had bothered her.

'I think you might need to talk to him about boundaries. Surely he shouldn't be free to wander around here snooping on the rest of us if it's you he's here to see.' If he wasn't intimidated in the slightest by her, admonishment from the monarch might take him down a peg or two. His ego could do with some deflating.

'I—I'll have a word with him. Did he say something to upset you, Georgiana?'

'He…uh…'

It wasn't so much what he'd said to her, more the way he'd said it. All superior and cocky. Although she knew if she said that, she'd sound like a petulant brat and her mother didn't need more reason to treat her like a child. It was one of those things she'd simply have to deal with and move on.

'Not exactly. He said I was welcome to use the gym

equipment at his clinic. In his opinion it's better than the stuff I'm using at home and could speed my recovery.' When she said it out loud it seemed so straightforward. That was what she wanted, wasn't it? To get back to normal as soon as possible. Perhaps if anyone other than the laid-back Mr Lawrence had offered, she wouldn't have been so against the initial idea. Now she was beginning to wonder if she'd let her personal opinion of the man in question cloud her judgement. If she stripped away the personality traits that made her dislike him on sight and focused on the professional interest, she could see they both had the same goal in mind. To get her back to her fighting best.

'That's good, isn't it?' Hope was written all over her mother's face that this was somehow the answer to all their prayers. As though some high-grade gym equipment would restore her to the woman she was before her injury. For once Georgiana and her mother were in complete agreement about what they wanted.

'Have you completely lost your mind?'

Ed glanced up from his laptop to find his business partner, Giles Winhope, sitting on his desk. 'You got my message, then? I'd appreciate it if you kept the details between us. I promised full confidentiality.'

'And you didn't think to consult me before you agreed to this?'

'You were on board with our other royal appointment. I didn't think it would be a problem.'

'You wouldn't,' Giles muttered as he sorted Ed's paperwork into a pile and rounded up the assortment of dirty coffee cups he hadn't got around to washing yet.

Okay, he had a casual approach to housekeeping, but

he gave everything important in his life his full attention. It was no reason to accuse him of being unprofessional.

'It's one thing having royal approval from the queen, but agreeing to sneak her daughter in here isn't exactly standard business practice.'

Ed had been as surprised as anyone when Georgiana had called. He'd extended the invitation but he hadn't expected to hear from her after their meeting unless it was to demand her shorts back. In hindsight it was possible he'd taken them home with him so she would have reason to speak to him again. Even if it was to threaten him with the police. Except she hadn't mentioned them at all during the short phone call, sticking only to the salient points.

'I'd like to take you up on your offer of using the facilities at your clinic. In private. Pick me up tomorrow night at seven o'clock.' She hadn't given him the chance to speak, much less remind her that he wasn't one of her servants. He had promised to transport her in relative privacy but he wasn't at her beck and call. Something he'd point out to her at the first opportunity. He had family commitments, which came before everything else.

'To be honest, I never thought she'd agree. It was her mother who thought she needed some extra encouragement.'

'It's going to be a circus around here. Are we going to have to get extra security to accommodate our new client? A press room? Souvenir stalls?' Giles's main concern was always money. He and Ed were polar opposites but that was what made them such good business partners. Ed was the heart and soul of the clinic while Giles was the money man. Neither minded admitting their strengths and weaknesses because between them they made it work. Along with the other consultants, doctors, nurses and assorted staff they employed.

When the call had first come in for Ed to have a consultation at the palace, Giles had been over the moon because it added a certain gravitas to their reputation. Those who moved in the same aristocratic circles as the Ashleys would know they were the best at what they did now they had royal patronage. That prestige added financial value to the team. It was the thought of having to pay money out to oblige Georgiana that was causing him to come out in a sweat.

If Ed was a cruel man, he'd continue to let Giles think their finances were about to take a massive hit. Fortunately, he wasn't.

'Ms Ashley wants to remain incognito. No staff, no press, no other gym users when she's here.'

'How are we going to manage that? That will seriously damage our appointment book.' That was Giles's speak for losing income.

'I said we'd open exclusively for her at night. I'm a keyholder, I can arrange it, don't worry.' It was on his head since he was the one to suggest the move without proper consultation with the rest of the team.

'How are you going to manage that along with your other personal commitments?' Giles arched an eyebrow in disbelief that he could make this work but Ed wasn't one to shirk his responsibilities.

He had surgery days at the local hospital as well as his work here at the clinic and just as many demands on him at home. The only time he'd let anyone down was in his personal life when he'd failed to carve out enough time and energy to save his relationship with his ex, Caroline. He'd thought he could settle down like anyone else but when she'd left him he'd realised there was only room for one family in his life. It hadn't really been a choice for him, when he'd always be there for his parents, but it still hurt.

Worse than his own heartbreak was knowing he'd caused Caroline so much pain in the process. She'd done nothing wrong except get involved with someone who couldn't give her everything she needed. Ed had sworn then not to get into another serious relationship and repeat the same mistake.

He regretted not being there for Caroline as much as everyone else in his life but it made it easier to manage his other commitments now he was single.

'That's up to me to figure out. This is a done deal, Giles. I'm on my way to pick her up now. I'm simply doing you the courtesy of letting you know what's going on.'

'After the fact...'

'I didn't get much notice myself, to be fair, but she needs this. It's what we do.' He grabbed his car keys off the desk and shrugged on his jacket. There was no point in picking holes in things now, when he'd made arrangements. He simply needed Giles gone before he brought Georgiana here.

'So, you're doing chauffeur and personal trainer?' Giles shifted himself off the desk with a sigh of resignation. This was happening whether he liked it or not.

'I'm not sure how much input she's going to want from me or anyone else with regard to her training, but she doesn't want anyone to know she's attending. That makes me chauffeur, escort and bodyguard, I guess.'

They both headed for the exit. Ed decided against turning the lights off since he'd be back within the hour.

'Are you sure you can manage this on your own?' Giles asked.

Ed thought about the fearsome Georgiana, who looked permanently ready to go into battle, and shrugged his shoulders. 'I guess we'll find out.'

Georgiana checked her watch for the umpteenth time. He was late. Every extra second she waited here, the more her stomach somersaulted and her breathing quickened.

It had been weeks since she'd been beyond the palace gates and if Mr Lawrence didn't get here soon there was every chance she'd change her mind about doing this. She supposed it wasn't a big deal to him; she doubted anything was. To her, though, this could be the start of her new life. Or the first time her secret might be exposed to the outside world.

She texted him.

Where are you?

Since the initial phone call to confirm her attendance, she'd kept contact limited to text messages with instructions of when and where to pick her up. Though she was keeping her nocturnal visit quiet from the public, she was keen to keep it from those inside the palace too. There was no way they'd agree to her leaving without security. Whether Edward didn't realise the risks they were taking, or he didn't care, he'd gone along with the plan. Which entailed smuggling her out under the noses of security and the staff. The logistics of which were not easy and only added to her swelling anxiety.

I'm here. Out the back. Where we arranged.

She'd got him security clearance, citing a medical consultation so he wouldn't seem suspicious turning up here. The plan was for her to slip out the back unseen and he would drive her out, leaving security none the wiser. It was very cloak and dagger but she'd rather do it this way than go through formal procedures to authorise the visit.

She'd dressed down, in dark clothes so she didn't draw attention to herself. With a baseball cap pulled low, she crept out into the courtyard where Edward was waiting for her.

He was standing with his hands in his pockets staring up at the night sky. His profile was romantically lit by the moon, defining his strong jaw and the sparkle of his eyes. He'd ditched his tie and his shirt was open at the collar. Clearly it hadn't occurred to him to keep up appearances once he'd clocked off work.

Her breath hitched in her throat but it was due to the thrill of sneaking out, nothing else. The last time she'd done anything like this was with Freddie when they were kids. He'd been the bad influence then and she should've encouraged that independent streak instead of trying to tame it along with everyone else. If they'd all simply let him be who he was without imposing stupid restrictions on him he might still be here.

The crunch of gravel under her feet drew Edward's attention, a genuine smile on his face appearing when he saw her. Thinking about her brother and all the time they should have had together made her too sad to return it. She was angry Freddie wasn't here to make jokes at her expense and be the light during the darkest time of her life. At least, the darkest one since her dear brother had ended his life.

That hadn't been the official cause of death but she

knew, as did her parents, that he'd killed himself rather than continue living a lie. The tragedy of that being that they were still living that lie to save face. That betrayal of Freddie's memory had proved the final straw and the turning point in her own life. Determined not to end up in the same position as Freddie, forced to be someone she wasn't, Georgiana had joined the army. It was the best decision she'd ever made but she hadn't counted on being injured and forced to return home, in a more vulnerable position now than when she'd left.

'You're late,' she snapped, unwilling to let him see any weakness in the tears she was holding back at the thought of the injustice done to her and Freddie. Edward's smile narrowed by the second.

'Only by fifteen minutes. I had to run things by my business partner before I left. This was a bit last minute, you know. I do have a life away from here.' Apparently, it was his turn to vent some irritation and she knew she deserved it. Georgiana found it reassuring that she could ruffle his feathers as much as he could hers. She might've disturbed him on a date or a night out with the lads. Whatever counted as a life for a single man in his late thirties.

'Let's go before someone spots us.' She went to open the back door of his car but Edward hovered beside her.

'You're getting in there?'

'I'm not about to climb into the boot.' She rapped her knuckles on her lower leg, letting the hollow sound explain the reason why.

'Oh. Yes. Sorry.' Thankfully he went to retrieve something from the boot so she was able to get into the back seat unseen. Although she'd mastered the art of walking again, things such as climbing into the back of a car could be tricky. Ungainly. She didn't want him to see her struggling and feel sorry for her. It was much easier to deal with those who either pretended not to notice her disability or who didn't care about it. People she'd found were few and far between.

'If you want to lie down, I've got a blanket I can put over you.' He came back with a tartan picnic rug and a box of files.

'Do you do a lot of this, Mr Lawrence?' She couldn't help but tease in an attempt to cover her own unease at the situation. The occupational therapist had helped her deal with transferring her body weight in and out of seats during rehab, but this was the first time she'd done it in front of a relative stranger. That slight struggle to manoeuvre herself into the small space reminded her of her limitations and it wasn't something she relished.

'Not often, no.' He didn't rise to the bait. It obviously took more than gentle teasing to embarrass him or else he did have a habit of entertaining random women in the back of his car.

The thought of which suddenly made her black hoodie and sweatpants combo too warm against her skin. It didn't help when he covered her with the blanket so she couldn't be seen from outside.

'I'm going to set some of my files on you to help cover the fact there's a body under there.'

There was a gentle pressure as he weighted her down with paperwork, then she heard the door slam when he was finished. The car suspension adjusted to take his weight when he got in the driver's seat and the engine purred into life. It was pitch black under her disguise and claustrophobic. Her hot breath came in gasps, increasing the temperature and her unease as they drove off.

There was that same trepidation she used to experience before going out on patrol with her unit, not knowing what lay outside the safety of the compound. Sure,
this wasn't a life or death situation but the adrenaline
rush and fear of the unknown brought back memories
of that horrific day. Perspiration coated her skin and she
was doing her best to quell the panic threatening to reveal her to the outside world. She was seconds away from
whipping the blanket off and winding down the window
to gulp some fresh air.

'Are you all right back there?' As if he'd sensed her
discomfort, Edward's voice filtered through her claus-
trophobia to provide a grounding reassurance. He was a
medical professional; he knew what she'd been through
and if there was the slightest chance she was freaking
out he'd be the first to call a halt to this.

She took deep, long cleansing breaths and visualised
the freedom afforded her outside the gates. No prying
eyes, whispered conversations or sympathetic stares. It
was enough to steel her through the next leg of the journey.

'I'm fine.' Her muffled voice didn't project as well
as she'd hoped.

If he had any doubts about her state of mind or what
they were doing, he said nothing and kept driving. She
suspected he was leaving it down to her to make the crucial decisions. It made a nice change not having someone
taking over and telling her what was in her best interests.

The car slowed, she heard the electric window go
down and muffled voices outside. He'd reached the security gate where they were probably giving the visitor
and his car another sweep before he left the palace.

Georgiana held her breath, illogically thinking they

could somehow hear her as they walked around the car. Every footstep, every pause in between, convinced her she was about to be rumbled. Then she heard a double thump on the roof, some more deep muttering before the car set off again.

''Bye,' she heard Edward call cheerfully and she could imagine him waving to the guards on the way past.

As soon as the electric window whirred back to life, she was able to breathe again.

'You really should up the security around here,' Edward said for her benefit.

'I'll look into that.' She hoped he could tell she was rolling her eyes at him under here. 'Can I come out yet?'

She hated being literally kept in the dark. Not knowing what was going on around her, blind to the surroundings and relying on someone else to keep her safe.

'I'll do a few laps around these side streets and make sure no one is following us first.'

'Okay.' She'd forgotten it wasn't simply about getting out undiscovered but also dodging any press lurking around. Crawling out of the back of a car really would get her in the headlines and in everyone else's bad books.

Patience. It was something she'd had to have a lot of recently and didn't come easily to her. She wanted to be back to normal *now*. Not when her stupid body was ready. She didn't want to think about what would happen if her physical self never caught up with her determined mind.

The click of the indicator and the car slowing brought her back to the present.

'I think it's safe for you to come out now. You can stay in the back if you want or sit up here in the passenger seat like a commoner.' Edward's sarcasm was a welcome distraction from her own thoughts and worries.

'Do you think I drove around Afghanistan with a chauffeur?' she snarked back, throwing off her coverings.

'No. I assumed you travelled with your golden carriage and horses.'

'They don't work so well in the desert and tend to draw attention.'

Edward waited with the engine idling for her to join him in the front of the car. She was grateful he didn't get out to offer her a hand, preferring to manage on her own.

The cold night air went some way to regulating her body temperature again, so she was relatively comfortable for the remainder of the journey.

'I thought we should go in the back door to avoid detection,' he said, pulling up outside the clinic. It wasn't too far from the palace, making the whole escapade easier.

'This must be a novelty for you.'

'What?' It was all new to her—sneaking around, getting out of the palace and being around someone who wasn't family or military.

'Using the tradesman's entrance. I imagine you're used to red carpets and the smell of fresh paint everywhere you go.'

'You mean you haven't been redecorating to an appropriate standard for my arrival? Tut-tut.' Getting out of the front of the car was slightly easier so she wasn't as defensive as she was earlier. In fact she was almost beginning to enjoy her time out with the consultant. He wasn't as annoying when not telling her what to do or making out he knew what was best for her. How long that would last now they were in his territory, she had no idea.

'As I said, this was late notice or, you know, we would've held a reception for you.' He countered her sarcasm with some of his own and opened up the clinic, leaving Georgiana to get out of the car on her own.

She wondered if this was how he behaved around most women or if this was just for her. He looked like a door opener, a 'take a woman's hand and help her out of the car' gentleman. She thought more of him for sparing her blushes and realising she'd hate him to do that for her. That courteous gesture in other circumstances wouldn't have bothered her but these days it simply reminded her she couldn't do the simple things on her own.

Given their short history there was a possibility he was just rude in keeping his back to her until she managed to get back on her feet.

'How did your partner take the news about me using this place out of hours?' She wasn't so obtuse she didn't realise this was unorthodox and the clinic wouldn't get the publicity they'd probably otherwise prefer. Edward had mentioned being late because of their meeting and Georgiana hoped she wasn't the cause of any fallout.

Now she paused to think about it, having her here would be more of a headache than a bonus to their business. It made her wonder why on earth Edward had suggested it. Especially when she'd taken him for the type to avoid any hassle that could impede his freedom.

'He's fine with it. As long as I'm the one putting in the extra hours to accommodate our new guest.' He flashed her a smile as he let her into the premises to show her he didn't mind. It only served to make her feel worse about the way she'd treated him thus far when he was going out of his way to accommodate her.

They'd come to a compromise over her use of the equipment so there was no misunderstanding over their roles here. She wasn't going to be a paying client, thus

Edward wouldn't have any input into what she was doing. There would be no doctor/patient relationship. This was a favour.

Whatever his reasons, it was difficult for her to believe anyone could be so altruistic. She'd been through so much, trust wasn't something she gave easily. Life with her parents had made her guarded and her injuries had made her even more so. In the army she'd been forced to rely on others, at times put her life in their hands. She'd had to do the same with the hospital team who'd saved her after the blast. This was different and Edward was still virtually a stranger. Surely, she was right to be wary?

She could thank him, tell him not to put himself out on her account but that made it sound as though she owed him something.

'Good. I wouldn't want any disgruntled staff selling me out to the papers to get the clinic some publicity.' She walked on in, doing her best to exude that self-entitled, regal air despite her current outward appearance.

'No. You have my word on that score. Privacy is very important here. Now, let me give you the tour.' The sincere comment combined with his unflinching eye contact made her believe him. That unwavering blue-eyed gaze also caused the hairs to stand up on the back of her neck. For a moment she was lost, swimming in that azure sea without a care in the world. Then he rested his hand on her elbow to gently guide her and jolted her back to the present.

Etiquette around members of the royal family included a 'no touching' rule. One she should be enforcing right now. Except it had been a long time since she'd felt that human connection. In hospital she'd detested being poked and prodded and having her limbs manipulated. No control over her own body. Being back home she'd been so focused on getting better, in private, she'd starved herself of basic human interaction. It was nice to have someone touch her so casually without it being a big issue.

CHAPTER THREE

'WE'VE DONE EXTENSIVE research on the best equipment for someone living with a disability.' Edward was proudly showing off the fitness machines in the shiny gym but his last word was a slap across the face to Georgiana.

She still thought of invalids being those who'd suffered a serious stroke or a spinal-cord injury. Even other people who'd had amputations, but not her. Despite the permanency of her loss she continued to see her situation as a temporary problem she could solve with a lot of hard work. Other people might call it denial but she knew it was her mental strength that would get her back to her physical peak along with the training.

'A lot of this I already have at home.' She picked up one of the dumbbells from the bench with ease. The weights and resistance bands were crucial to strengthening her upper body so she could support those weaker areas during exercise.

'I know, and I'm not saying you should stop your home training. The extra work you do here is to supplement that. We have the arm cycles, for example. There are the free-standing machines you can use with or without seats depending on how much you rely on your wheelchair.'

'I don't need a wheelchair.' She'd hated that thing from

the very first moment she'd been pushed around in it like some helpless infant. The one thing it had done for her was to spur her on to her first milestone: to be able to get out of it. Some didn't have an option but knowing she could walk on her own if she worked hard enough had been a powerful motivator. Sure, there were some days she was in pain, when it would be easier to give in and use it for getting mobile. On those bad days she'd use her crutches so there was some support but she still had to work at it.

Edward held his hands up. 'Hey, there's no judgement here and absolutely no shame in using them. A lot of our patients are wheelchair users. Wearing a prosthetic leg places additional stress on the body and you do what you need to in order to stay mobile. I'm simply advising you on the options available.'

Georgiana knew she was being testy but the chip on her shoulder about being seen using one of those things came directly from her mother. They were both aware it marked her out as different when it was possible for her to pull on a pair of trousers so no one would know she wasn't whole.

'I appreciate that but I won't need anything to do with a wheelchair.' It had been difficult enough coming back from rehab to find her parents had adapted half the house for a wheelchair user. As though it was going to be a permanent feature. Well, she'd showed them, putting in the effort to ensure she didn't have to use one longer than necessary. Now the ramps that had been installed for her benefit slowed her up when she had to adjust her balance every time she walked up or down one.

'I'm just giving you the standard tour. Take or leave whatever is or isn't applicable to your specific needs.'

He appeared unfazed by the news and Georgiana was miffed by his indifference. It was a huge achievement when someone transitioned back onto their feet and an acknowledgement of that would be nice. Perhaps he was so used to dealing with patients at every level of rehabilitation it wasn't as big a deal to him as it was to her.

'I see you have the heavy boxing bag. I suppose that's for core work.' And relieving frustration, as long as she didn't overbalance in her enthusiasm to punch things.

'Yes, and the speed bag can be adjusted so you're reaching overhead and challenge your range of motion.'

'Hmm. Maybe I'll take up boxing. We're always encouraged to get involved in competitive sport. I like the idea of punching people in the face.' They championed sport to improve fitness but also to give patients a new area of their lives to focus on and work towards. That competitive spirit gave a boost to those who might otherwise want to give up. She wasn't going to be one of those people lying in bed all day feeling sorry for herself, but neither did she want to be on a stage celebrating what had happened to her.

Boxing, however, was a skill she could carry through with her as another defence for when her sardonic repartee failed to get people like Edward Lawrence to back off.

'I'm not sure that's the spirit of the sport. Remind me never to get on the wrong side of you.' Without his jacket she could see the impressive bulge of his biceps straining the cotton shirt and she knew she'd be no challenge to him. Yet she appreciated that he didn't think of her as a fragile doll.

'I do have military training...' She gave him what she hoped was an intimidating glare, although her Cheshire cat impression might have undermined the overall effect.

'I'll bear that in mind,' he said with a grin to match hers. 'Especially when I tell you about the glider here. Yes, it's designed for wheelchair users but I think it does help build the oblique, core, back and arm muscles.'

She pursed her lips to prevent a further tirade about why it wasn't suitable for someone who could get around perfectly fine. He knew that now but he obviously had more to say on the subject.

'Go on…'

The worried frown lines evened out across his forehead when she let him off the hook. 'You can pull up a seat and just work out the arms on this one. It's a great way to improve strength and cardio. Plus, it can strengthen your shoulder orbit muscles.' He demonstrated the machine, pulling and pushing the levers, which she could see were replicating rowing and cross-country skiing motions for the upper body.

She had a rowing machine at home but she had to take off her leg to keep the air flow on her limb and prevent sweating. This glider would certainly complement the exercises she was already doing for her arms. By combining both gym workouts she'd hopefully improve her overall fitness. Edward certainly looked fit. She was mesmerised by his thick, tanned forearms pumping the levers back and forth. That was the level of strength she aspired to. Her fascination wasn't in any way an objectification of the man himself.

'It looks…er…good.' She cleared her throat and her mind. This man was an aid to her recovery, nothing more. Okay, maybe he was some pretty window dressing in a room dominated by ugly, functional machinery.

'Do you need me to demonstrate anything else or help draw up some sort of plan? I know that's not my particular area of expertise but I have learned a thing or two over the years about strength and conditioning exercises.' He walked over to the stationary bike and though her first instinct was to scoff and tell him she knew how to ride one, a different instinct held her back.

'You can change the gradient here depending on how much resistance you want.' He was talking as he pushed the buttons on the electronic display panel but she was more interested in watching the bulging thigh muscles rippling with his every pedal.

'I know how a bike works,' she snapped eventually, not happy about the physical reaction she was having to the scene before her. It wasn't as though she was unused to being in close proximity to men in their prime. She'd been in the army, for goodness' sake, living and fighting along with the best the country had to offer, and she hadn't had her head turned. Yet she couldn't seem to take her eyes off every flex of muscle and wonder what lay beneath the fabric of his clothes.

'We're supposed to run through instructions for the equipment with all new patients but I guess I'm not an instructor and you're not a patient.'

'No. Think of it more as private rental of the space. I'm not here for the social side.' Even if spending time with him tonight had proved an eye-opener for her.

'I don't suppose you'll be needing an exercise programme customised for you either? That could be arranged along with any of our other services.' He swung his leg over the bike and came to join her again. Georgiana knew he meant well but she'd be more at ease once he left her alone.

She shook her head. 'I have all that from the rehab centre and I'd prefer to adapt things to suit my own body's needs and capabilities. I know my boundaries and how far I can push them.' Cardio and strength training had been her priority since coming home in her effort to get her body back to the way she wanted it. Short of growing her leg back. She didn't need anyone interfering or disrupting her training and slowing her progress.

'Right, well, don't overdo it,' he reiterated, managing to raise her hackles again. 'I'll be working in my office if you need me. Let me know when you're ready to leave.' He pointed to a door down the hallway. Thankfully, it wasn't one of those open-plan, all-glass set-ups, which would have stripped away any illusion of privacy. Once he was secured behind his office door, she was free to do her thing without an audience.

As he made his way off the gym floor, Georgiana followed so she could close the door after him. He caught her off guard when he spun around again. She didn't have time to react and move back, so they were almost nose to nose when he spoke.

'Oh. I was just going to say I didn't have time to show you the pool area. Not to worry. You can't use that without supervision anyway. We'll sort something out for next time.' He seemed to say everything in one breath, then turned away sharply to disappear down the corridor. Leaving her breathless in his wake.

It took her a few seconds and some deep breaths to absorb what had happened. His usual cool demeanour had deserted him momentarily. Almost as though being so up close in her personal space had thrown him as much as her. She had to concentrate to remember what he'd even said. Something about the pool being out of bounds. It didn't matter tonight as she hadn't brought a swimsuit with her, but the pool had been the clincher for her coming here. She missed swimming but hadn't been able to face doing it in a public area with people staring. A situation where she really couldn't hide any more.

Once Georgiana completed the cool-down part of her workout, she longed for the soothing relief of a warm pool to ease her aches and pains. Hydrotherapy was the one thing she'd looked forward to when she'd been in the rehab unit.

When she'd first slid into the water after her amputation, the sense of movement had been a defining moment in her recovery progress. It was then she'd realised she didn't have to be confined to a wheelchair for the rest of her life.

Her physical therapist had helped her see the benefits of exercising in the water. The warm water relaxed her body and allowed her to become vertical without bearing weight on her remaining leg. It made things more bearable in those early days compared to her land-based regime.

She'd done her cardio now on Edward's expensive toys, so she didn't need to do the deep-water jogging while wearing a flotation belt around her middle, which did the same job. Some sense of normalcy would be nice now, where she didn't have to strap on fake body parts and work hard just to walk. Her mood was completely different when she was in the water because she wasn't consumed by anxiety. She was free to enjoy a swim and move unimpeded. Without pain or fear.

A glance down the hall told her Edward was still ensconced in his office as she undertook a little tour of her own. All she had to do was follow the smell of chlorine. Georgiana had only intended to take a look, get a feel for the place, but the water was so inviting. The low-level evening lighting was preferable to the usual fluorescent glare she was forced to endure when swimming. It was calming and the empty pool was calling for her to take a soothing dip.

She could see they had all the hoists and devices for lowering disabled bodies into the water but she no longer needed any of that. The fact she didn't have a bathing costume didn't put her off either. She simply stripped off at the side of the pool, so she was standing in her neon-pink sports bra and mismatched black knickers. It was removing her leg that made her more self-conscious but with no one here to see she had nothing to worry about.

Using the handrail at the side of the steps, she eased herself in. Once she was enveloped in that watery embrace she could finally relax. On her back now, she floated aimlessly, letting her thoughts drift away. The glittering, morphing reflection of the water on the ceiling hypnotised her into a state of calm. Here, it didn't matter about her appearance or abilities. She could just be.

It was only the occasional splash when her constantly swishing hands keeping her afloat slapped the surface that disturbed her reverie. She could get used to coming here to unwind at night. Edward had indicated she'd need supervision but she wasn't one of those helpless patients who couldn't fend for herself. There'd been a time when she had been dependent on lifeguards and physios to make sure she didn't drown but she'd worked hard to get this independence and she wasn't going to give it up now.

Once she thought her hydrotherapy was bordering on being self-indulgent, she rolled over onto her belly and began to swim. There were those who had special prosthetics made to swim with but she was content to be unencumbered for this short time.

After a few lengths she began to tire. Her limbs and lungs were telling her they'd had enough for one day. Regardless of what Mr Lawrence thought, she did listen to her body. She wanted to improve and regain the fitness levels she'd had pre-amputation, not make things worse. At this point she didn't know what that could be but if she overdid things there was a fear of being laid up again.

Those weeks spent in hospital, unable to do anything, followed by relearning basic things such as standing and walking, had been the worst time of her life. It had left her weak and ashamed at being so helpless, relying on strangers to help her carry out the simplest tasks. There was no way she was returning to those dark days.

The clock on the far wall told her it was getting late. As kind as Edward had been in staying on, she didn't want to take advantage. He had work in the morning and there was likely to be someone waiting for him at home. Oddly, the thought of him going back to a cosy domestic scene while she sneaked back into the palace, where her disappearance probably wouldn't have been noticed, bugged her.

She hauled herself up and over the edge of the pool where she'd left her clothes. Unfortunately, she hadn't had the foresight to set a towel within reach. There was a bale of freshly laundered fluffy white towels sitting on the low-level lockers over by the door. She had two options: either put her clothes on over her wet underwear or hop over to get one. There was no point trying to put her leg on first when she was wet. She needed to dry off before she attempted that.

It wasn't that far anyway, and she was used to getting

around on one leg in her bedroom rather than put the blasted thing on and off when she needed to get something.

With the aid of the handrail, she pulled into an upright position and steadied herself. She propelled herself forward, letting her leg take the full weight of her body. It took a few seconds to centre herself again and get her balance. Things like this were tiring and frustrating. Such was her new norm after a lifetime of taking such a basic thing as having two legs for granted. If she didn't believe things like this would get easier she'd have given up a long time ago.

Another hop brought her closer to her target but as her foot landed on the tiled floor it splashed in a small puddle of water and she lost traction. Though she frantically reached out for anything to stabilise her, she was powerless against gravity and landed with a thud.

The pain was excruciating as she hit the deck. When her body landed on the hard, wet surface it literally knocked the breath out of her. Her head had cracked against the tiles too and she lay there stunned, wondering how things had gone so wrong so quickly.

'Georgiana? What the hell—?' Edward's angry voice reverberated around the walls and for a moment she thought she'd imagined it. Until he loomed over her. She groaned out of pain and the humiliation of him finding her lying here.

'I slipped.' She sounded pathetic and knew she looked even more so, sprawled here with her stump on show for the world to see.

'I've been looking everywhere for you. Did you hurt yourself?' He knelt beside her in the puddle of water. The genuine look of concern on his face as he brushed the wet strands of hair out of her eyes made her want to weep. She loathed seeing sympathy on people's faces yet at the same time she was desperate for someone to see, to realise, what she was going through inside. To confide those feelings in anyone meant trusting again and she wasn't ready for that. She could only stay strong if she listened to herself and didn't rely on others for her happiness.

'It's nothing serious. I've felt worse.' The dark humour was supposed to cover her uncharacteristic bout of self-pity but she could sense her chin wobbling and giving the game away. If Ed showed her any more compassion there was every chance she'd fling her arms around him and cry on his shoulder. The whole scene was mortifying and she was tempted to roll over and let the water claim her.

'This is why I told you not to come here alone. For your own safety.' He reached over to grab a few of the towels and covered her body to keep her warm. Oh, yeah, she was lying here in her wet underwear too. Honestly, she didn't think she could've done a better job of humiliating herself if she'd tried.

'I know... I'm sorry.' She hiccupped, fighting the sobs trying to burst out of her throat.

'All you had to do was ask, Georgiana, and I would've come with you.' The words came out on a sigh, so it sounded less of a scolding and more like disappointment in her. That made it so much worse.

'I know... I'm sorry,' she repeated. Really, what more could she say? This was her fault, not his. All because of her stubborn pride.

She tried to sit up but Edward was having none of it.

'Stay still until I've checked you over.'

'I'm sure I'll be fine,' she insisted as he gently felt her head for signs of injury.

'There's no sign of any blood and I don't see any abrasions. Did you lose consciousness at any time?'

'No. I don't feel sick or have any problems with my vision either. I'm pretty sure I don't have a concussion.' She was able to diagnose herself even if he wouldn't take her word for it.

'It doesn't mean you couldn't develop symptoms later. I'll get you an ice pack to stop any swelling developing and you can rest up in my office for a while where I can keep an eye on you.'

'I don't need looking after. I can manage on my own.' She struggled to sit up to prove her point but Ed didn't budge from her side.

'What is your problem? Why are you so against anyone helping you? Or is it just me?'

With his piercing eyes locked onto her, Georgiana had nowhere to hide from his questions. He had every right to be annoyed with her. She'd kept him up all night, ignored his warning about coming here alone and now he was the one left picking up the pieces. That was how she saw herself now—broken pieces of the woman she used to be and someone who could never be repaired. Not that she could voice any of that to him when it sounded so pathetic.

Unfortunately, those emotions she'd been supressing for so long bubbled to the surface because of this one act of kindness. Instead of giving him an answer or a snappy comeback to cover her embarrassment, she burst into messy, ugly tears.

'Georgiana? I didn't mean to upset you. Sorry. Please don't cry.' Ed thought he couldn't feel any worse than he had when he'd seen her lying on the floor in pain. Now he'd made this strong, seemingly fearless Amazon sob into his chest by shouting at her.

She seemed so fragile and vulnerable in his arms and, though he liked having her there, he hated the idea of her being so upset. Georgiana wasn't a woman who showed her emotions easily. Unless it was to express her dislike towards him. Although now he was beginning to wonder if he'd got that wrong about her too.

He should've been keeping a closer eye on her. Instead he'd had his head buried in paperwork for a cause he was having difficulty getting off the ground. If Georgiana had been anyone else here he would've insisted on being involved in their training regime but there was something about her that made him go against all his instincts. He could tell she needed to do things on her own but he shouldn't have let that compromise her safety.

Now she was hurt and embarrassed, desperately trying to cover her leg as though he hadn't already seen it. Naturally it bothered him to see it but from a personal point of view, not for any aesthetic reason. It was an indication of the amount of suffering she'd gone through. Something he'd probably never be able to understand. She was such a strong individual but one slip on a wet tile seemed to have broken her and he knew she'd hate for him to witness it. He had a strong-minded younger brother who was just as determined to manage his disability on his own. Jamie's spina bifida was something he and the family had lived with for his entire life, so Ed knew that sometimes the smallest upset could cause a setback. He was always there to make sure that didn't happen.

'Shh. It's all right,' he soothed, his arm around her, holding her tight to him. 'Everything's going to be all right.'

Georgiana continued to weep into his chest, silently now but with no less sorrow.

In different circumstances he was sure she'd jump on that, demanding to know how things could possibly be all right when she wasn't about to grow her leg back, but for now she seemed content to let him placate her.

Eventually her shoulders stopped heaving with the effort of crying and she withdrew from him.

'I'm so sorry. I don't know what came over me. Shame probably.' She wiped away the tears and offered up a heartbreaking half-smile, trying to dismiss everything he'd just seen.

'There is absolutely no need to be ashamed about anything. Nor do you have to keep pushing me away, Georgiana. I know what your injuries are. I deal with similar every day.' He saw her flinch at the acknowledgement but if that was holding her back from accepting help, they had to address it.

'It—it's something I'm still struggling to accept myself,' she admitted through stuttering gulps of breath.

'I know we haven't got off to the best start, but I'm being honest when I say I want to help speed your recovery as much as I can.'

It was true. This mission might have started as a favour to her mother but Ed genuinely wanted to help Georgiana. He knew the hardship involved for those with mobility issues. His brother Jamie's fight had affected the whole family. That was why he did what he did here. To give every patient, every family, the chance to reach their full potential.

The clinic could give her a boost physically and, given tonight's outburst, she needed a friend to get her through this. Though he was sure she'd never say as much. Her pride and obstinacy had got her this far but there was a chance it could prevent her progressing any further. He recognised something of himself in her. That determination to do everything herself was in line with the responsibilities he shouldered with his family. It was better for him to be on his own dealing with everything than put the burden on anyone else's shoulders.

Perhaps that was why she'd been on his mind since their fraught first meeting. He'd watched her work out to the point of exhaustion, sweat trickling down the back of her neck. Yet she'd carried on because she knew that was what it would take to meet her eventual goal. He was a hypocrite for warning her about burning herself out when he'd have acted exactly the same way.

Not many would've managed his workload, balancing a successful, demanding career while caring for his loved ones. He did because he saw no other choice. At least, not one he cared to entertain. Like Georgiana, he didn't want strangers getting involved and taking over his duties. He managed and though committing his time to her too was going to put further strain on him, he'd do it. Because she needed him. He'd never turn down someone in trouble when he had the capacity to help and potentially change her life for the better with his work here.

Anything else that drew him to her—those troubled brown-green eyes, her fierce spirit and her blatant disregard for anything he said—were extraneous. Yes, the quicker they were able to get Georgiana to the level of fitness and recovery she was happy with, the better. Then he had no need to see her again or keep her on his list of people to care about.

* * *

Georgiana didn't know how long they'd been sitting on the wet floor but it was the most comforted she'd been since her operation. It was probably the only time she'd let anyone hold her, much less see her cry. She didn't know why he was different. Perhaps it was simply because he was there when she was at her lowest or that he didn't shy away from her when she barked at him. Most likely it was because on some level he seemed to understand what she was going through. He wasn't pushing her to talk the way everyone else did.

She supposed he'd seen a lot of people in her situation and she wasn't anything special to him. Yet he was here, pretending this was perfectly normal behaviour. Not for her it wasn't and, regardless of his poolside manner, she knew she'd come to regret this whole scene. This was the opposite of surviving on her own.

'I should get changed. I've taken up way too much of your time. I'm sure you have someone waiting up for you at home, cursing me up and down.' As soon as she withdrew from his body heat she began to shiver uncontrollably.

'I'll grab your things for you. You can change where you're sitting. I promise I won't look.' He was joking around with her, easing the intensity of the situation. It didn't escape her attention that he'd avoided confirming or denying if he had anyone to go home to.

Edward collected some extra towels, her clothes and, to her horror, her prosthetic. Technically it counted as one of her 'things' and he wouldn't think anything of it, but she'd never get used to treating it as casually as any other accessory.

'Thanks.' She took the pile from him and set it beside her, her leg balancing on the top.

True to his word, Edward turned away and put some distance between them. The changing room wasn't far but getting there would've been another humiliation too far.

'We should arrange a proper timetable so we know where we both stand. If you let me know what nights you want to come, I can make the arrangements.' He kept talking as he walked, preventing any awkward silence as she dried and attached her leg.

'I was thinking of coming most nights if that's possible? I know that's asking a lot of you.'

'No. That's fine. Same time? Same exit strategy?' Georgiana could hear the smile in his voice and was glad he was comfortable enough to make fun of her. So many tiptoed around her it was insulting. She'd lost a limb, not her sense of humour or any IQ points.

'As long as you remember to bring your invisibility cloak for me. Oh, you might want to pop a mattress in the back of the car too.' She only realised how that sounded as she pulled her top on.

'Excuse me? I know things have thawed between us but I'm not that kind of guy.' A shocked Edward was peering back at her when she popped her head through her hoodie.

She was certain he was exactly that kind of guy but she was horrified her jokey remark could be construed as some sort of sleazy come-on.

'I didn't mean... I was talking about for in here in case I fell again.' The end of this night couldn't come a second too soon. At this point in time she just wanted to get into bed, pull the covers over her and forget how big a fool she'd repeatedly made of herself tonight.

Silence. Then to her relief he laughed, a deep hearty chuckle that echoed around the room and caught her in the midst of its warm embrace.

'Edward!' she scolded but she was relieved he was teasing her rather than offended by her unintentional advances.

'Ed, please. Edward's so formal. Only business acquaintances give me the full first-name treatment.' He came over and stretched out a hand to help her up to a standing position. Usually she would refuse, to make a point, but they were past that now. She accepted his hand graciously.

'Thank you, Ed.'

'Does this mean I can call you Georgie now?'

'Definitely not.'

He insisted on taking her to his office, stopping to retrieve an ice pack on the way. Georgiana couldn't believe the sight she was greeted with on opening the office door.

'Excuse the mess. I'm working on something.' Ed made an attempt to tidy away the papers littering his desk and the floor but she'd seen enough for the guilt to surface.

'You should've said you were swamped with paperwork. I'd never have dreamed of taking you away from work if I'd known.' Not that she'd given him a chance to explain he didn't have time to entertain her tonight. Looking back, she'd dictated what he was doing and at what time. Perhaps she'd inherited a smidgen of that self-centred streak from her parents after all.

'It's fine. Take a seat. It's just a charity idea I'm working on. Nothing that can't wait.' He pulled a chair over for her and placed the ice pack gently on the back of her head where she'd hit the floor.

Georgiana flinched as the cold compress met the tender area on her scalp. 'What's the charity? Is this something the clinic is championing?'

'No, it's a personal venture of mine. A children's charity for young amputees. New limbs aren't dished out as and when they're needed. There's a budget, a limit on what these kids can have. Generally, that means nothing fancy and it certainly doesn't cover sports blades or water limbs. The government, much the same as my business partner, tends to deal in figures rather than human stories.' He handed her a sheaf of papers with the smiling faces of children beaming out from the stark white sheets of A4.

'These are patients of yours?'

'Some. Others are possible candidates who could benefit from the scheme. Not everyone can afford private healthcare, but I want this available to all. If we can get the funding. I have a list of potential donors but I'm having trouble finding somewhere willing to host a gala dinner where I can present my ideas and secure some business sponsors. Not everyone wants to support a worthy cause if they're not making money from it themselves.'

Georgiana watched disappointment gradually cloud the absolute joy that had been on Ed's face when he was talking about the subject. It seemed such a shame for the whole thing to stall at the start line when such a great idea could do so much good. She'd seriously underestimated this man and his good intentions. It put her to shame when she was in a position of some influence and chose to hide rather than help the less fortunate as

Ed was doing. Although she wasn't ready to put herself out there personally, there was something she could do to contribute and to pay him back for his generosity and compassion towards her. It apparently hadn't crossed his mind to ask her for help or even advice on the subject.

'Why don't I ask my parents if you could host the event at the palace? I'm sure they'd be happy to contribute in some way even if it is just to donate the use of the ballroom for one night.'

'Do you think so? That would be amazing. Thank you so much. I can give you all the information you need to convince them.' He began to scoop up armfuls of papers in preparation.

Georgiana laughed at his childlike enthusiasm, though it was pleasing to see him so passionate for the cause he'd chosen to support. Not many put themselves out for others. Especially when they had a workload as big as he apparently had. 'I'm sure knowing it's your brain-child will be enough supporting evidence for my mother to give the go-ahead. I'll run it past her tomorrow and let you know.'

'Thank you so much. You don't know how much this means to me.' Judging by the width of his smile, she had a fair idea. It also gave her a little glow inside to know she'd contributed to something positive. The first time since her return home.

As they made their way back out to Ed's car, Georgiana had a real sense of making progress tonight. This was the extra push she needed to truly get back everything she'd lost and she was grateful a persistent Ed had stumbled across her in the palace after all.

CHAPTER FOUR

ED KICKED HIS chair out from his desk and stretched with a yawn.

'Did your princess keep you up all night?' Giles was standing in the doorway, grinning at having caught him in a rare moment of visible fatigue.

'Something like that.' He lifted his coffee cup and took a sip only to find he'd let it go cold.

'I don't suppose you're going to admit to taking too much on with this?'

Ed looked enviously at the mug Giles was cradling in his hands, steam curling up into the air and wafting the smell of freshly ground coffee beans towards his nostrils.

'Never,' he insisted, regardless that he was so tired he could have slept where he was sitting. Giles didn't need to know what had happened last night with Georgiana. He'd only worry they'd get sued by the royal family for health and safety violations. Although, he doubted she'd want anyone to know about her tumble when she was embarrassed enough that he'd been there to witness it.

In a way he was glad he had been there, not only to help her, but to provide the emotional support she so clearly needed too.

Besides, it wasn't Georgiana's fault he was so tired

today. What was supposed to have been a brief stop at his parents' house had gone on longer than expected when he'd discovered some loose carpeting at the top of their stairs. He wouldn't have slept at all for worrying if he hadn't taken the time to nail it back in place. If either of them had tripped and fallen he'd never have forgiven himself.

Giles slurped his coffee and Ed was sure he was doing it only to make him jealous. He wasn't the kind of person to make enough for anyone else who might be in dire need.

'It's just that you've been mainlining caffeine since you got here and I'm sure you're wearing the same clothes you had on last night.'

'I'm not but thank you for caring. Late one at my parents' last night.' He was spending more time over at theirs doing little jobs to make sure they were safe. They seemed oblivious to the dangers around them now they weren't as fit or spry as they used to be, but he was the only one who really visited or ran their errands for them. At the end of the day they were his family and he didn't begrudge giving them a helping hand. Though some extra sleep would be nice.

'No problems with your visitor, then?' Giles was doing his best to keep the conversation casual but his continual hovering in the doorway spoke of his concern. Ed wasn't going to jeopardise Georgiana's nights here by confirming there'd been any sort of a problem. They'd had a small incident but he'd take steps to ensure it would never happen again. He wouldn't want her to end up in that situation a second time.

'Nope. Ms Ashley did her workout and I took her home afterwards. Nothing to report.' He couldn't quite meet Giles's eyes but it was only a white lie to save Georgiana's blushes. It had been nice having someone to confide in about his plans for the charity and she was doing him a huge favour in possibly securing a room at the palace for the event. If everything went to plan he'd have a venue for the gala dinner and an exclusive one at that. He couldn't see anyone turning down an invitation to the palace. Including Giles.

'Good, but if you're planning on doing the same this evening you might want to try and wake yourself up a bit. Bags under the eyes don't make a good impression.' Ed couldn't blame him for wanting to cover the clinic's back as well as his concern for his workload. In the past Giles had suggested getting his parents into some sort of community housing to ease his burden but Ed wouldn't hear of it as long as he was able to keep them in their own home. The family home he'd grown up in with his brothers and sisters.

'If you were that bothered you would've brought an extra cup of coffee with you.' Ed crumpled up a piece of paper and lobbed it in his direction. Giles dodged it, spilling only a drop of his precious liquid cargo.

'I thought I'd encourage you to move and make your own to wake you up.' Giles flapped his hand across the steam, wafting the aroma across the room, then walked away chuckling to himself.

Despite the teasing, Ed could see his point. He still had a few hours to put in before Georgiana's session, then he'd be calling in on his parents to see what they needed. This drowsy state he was in wasn't going to be conducive to the rest of his working day.

He gave himself a mental shake and got up out of the chair he'd been too comfy in for most of the day.

'If the pool isn't busy, I'm going to jump in for a dip,' he informed Giles as he passed him in the corridor outside his office.

'Good man. All I ask is for you to remember to put on a pair of swim shorts. It's not adults-after-dark time just yet.'

'Ha-ha. Very funny.' It was unnerving to have Giles making jokes at his expense when it was usually the other way around. More than that, he was unused to this fizzing in his veins with the reminder he was going to see Georgiana again tonight. He couldn't remember acting this way around any visitors to the clinic before. As Giles had said, he'd had more caffeine than was good for him today. Perhaps he needed to detox.

It was such a different atmosphere around the pool in the afternoon compared to the evening. All business and work, despite the happy faces of patients and staff and constant chatter. The bright glare of fluorescent light felt intrusive when being here with Georgiana had given him a new perspective of the place. With only two of them under minimum lighting it had been intimate, no room for all these people here now.

She would've hated to have been surrounded by all this toing and froing and not only because she was hung up on her appearance. Ed knew she remained in denial about what had happened to her. It wasn't unusual for someone who'd had their life and possible future wiped away from them out of the blue. Being surrounded by other people at different stages of their recovery with their trainers would've been too much reality for her to deal with all at once. Yet Ed knew she needed support as much as every other person here. It was simply going to take a different approach to get her to accept that. She'd do much better with a one-to-one than being faced with anything more confrontational. He was picking her up in a few hours so he'd have to come up with something quick before then.

His recreational swim wasn't important compared to the therapies being offered to those using the facilities. Ed was happy to wait his turn at the edge of the pool watching his patients' progress. They all knew him to see and most waved or shouted over at him, unbothered by his presence.

Lots of people were happier to come here than the gym or the physio rooms so there was a positive vibe. Except for whatever commotion was going on in the corner of the pool closest to him.

'Look, Hannah, I'll come in with you. All you have to do is let go of Mummy.' Ellie, one of their young trainers, had immersed herself in the water, uniform and all, in an effort to get her little patient in with her.

'No!' Hannah crawled further up into her mother's embrace, clinging onto her neck like a baby monkey.

The exasperated parent tried to loosen the child's grip around her throat. 'Hannah, you're hurting Mummy now. Let go, please.'

The little girl was one of their new patients. He'd met her when she came in for her initial assessment after losing part of her leg in a car accident. Paediatric amputees were always difficult. It was an adjustment for the child as well as their parents and he could see the frustration on the mother's face when she wanted her daughter to make as much progress as she could.

'Is there anything I can do to help? Hi, Hannah, remember me? Ed?' He slid into the water where the trio were, Hannah still refusing to let the water touch any part of her. She shyly put her head on her mother's shoulder and began to suck her thumb.

'We're introducing her to hydrotherapy today.' Ellie pinked as he interrupted the temper tantrum going on in the shallow end.

'She's not having any of it.' The exasperated mother tried again to prise her off. 'Look, Hannah, the doctor's here. Don't you want to show him what a big girl you are?'

'No!' She wriggled, struggling to get away from the attention on her.

'It's okay,' he mouthed to the mother. 'If she's not ready we're not going to force her.'

Hannah was finding life as an amputee challenging. As were her parents. She was resisting any attempts to get her fitted for a prosthetic leg so they could start helping her try to walk again. So far, she was content to get around under her own steam, shuffling about on her bottom and asserting her independence. Her behaviour wasn't unlike some other remarkable young woman he knew. It was the sign of a strong individual and he knew they simply had to find a new way to get through to her. He'd figure it out. It was too important to the child's future to simply let her slip from their grasp.

Ever since confirming tonight's session with Ed, Georgiana had had that fluttery, fidgety feeling spreading through her body. Other than sitting in with her mother taking lunch, keeping her company while her father was doing her share of royal duties, she hadn't been able to settle.

There had certainly been big changes in her life when an evening training session had her blood pumping. Once upon a time it had been the thought of going out on patrol into enemy territory that had had the same effect.

After the previous evening's events she no longer considered Ed and his clinic enemy territory. Now she could see the benefits, knew what was on offer, she was looking forward to revisiting. She could do without a replay of her damsel-in-distress routine and jump-starting Ed's instinct to protect her. It wasn't in keeping with their usual dynamic where he let her make her own decisions and mistakes without judgement.

Of all the people around her and despite his profession, he was the one she hated to think of her as helpless. Until last night he'd treated her as an equal, as able-bodied, regardless of appearances to the contrary. The worst thing about it all for Georgiana was that she'd found it cathartic weeping into his chest as though she were some delicate flower. For a short while he'd allowed her to let the strong façade slip and be honest with her emotions.

She'd wanted to cry for a long time, to cling to someone who would stroke her hair and let her fall apart in their arms without embarrassment on either side. Now she'd done it and got it all out of her system, she felt cleansed and almost back to her old self. It had been a moment of weakness. Clearly, she'd gone soft since leaving the army.

Tonight, they'd employed the same tactics as last night to smuggle her out. Goodness knew what the staff thought he was doing here, visiting for only a few minutes at a time, but she wasn't about to stop simply to put an end to any potential murmurings.

* * *

Ed had left her alone tonight to complete her workout but she was under strict instructions to find him if she fancied a swim.

Her muscles were crying out for relief and she'd thought ahead to pack a swimsuit this time. It didn't prevent her from hovering outside his door, uncertain if she should go ahead and knock.

In the end, the lure of the chlorine was too tempting to resist. She rapped on the office door. Instead of giving a reply, Ed yanked the door open. He'd been waiting for her.

'Georgiana? Are you ready to leave already?'

It was the shock that left her at a loss for words, not the sight of him with his shirt undone and sleeves rolled up his thick, tanned forearms. She should be used to his casual dress outside professional working hours but it seemed to surprise her every time.

'No. I…uh…not yet. I thought I might go for a swim first, but if you're busy with your charity project I can leave it for tonight.'

'I could probably do with shutting off for a while. I've been trying to find a guest speaker for the gala. Someone to give us some prestige and help drum up some interest in sponsors.'

'Um…hello. Princess here.' It was infuriating, not to mention insulting, that he didn't ask her for help, which he clearly needed. He was the first person she seemed to turn to these days.

'Really? You'd be okay with speaking at the event? I wasn't sure you'd be comfortable enough yet with appearing in public.'

'I'm going to have to do it at some point. It's part of

the job description. Besides, it's for a good cause and I can relate better to the kids you want to help than some reality-TV star.'

'Absolutely. As long as it's not going to be too much for you, that would be absolutely amazing.' Ed looked visibly lighter, not to mention astounded that she was willing to bail him out. She wondered why it was such a surprise that someone would want to reciprocate the kindness he showed towards people every day.

'I'm hoping by the time it comes around I'll be ready to go back into the land of the living,' she joked, but she was already freaking out about what she'd agreed to do. It had been a knee-jerk reaction to knowing he needed assistance and wanting to ease his workload. Like her, he was someone who obviously didn't depend too much on others to get the job done. He was beginning to show her how counterproductive that was at times. Sometimes more could be achieved by accepting a hand every now and then.

'We'll do our best to make that a possibility. Now I can go and have that swim with one less worry on my mind. I'll get ready and meet you outside the changing rooms. Try not to break anything until I get there.' It wasn't the charming smile that was devastating her as much as the words accompanying it.

'You're going in the pool too?'

'Yeah. I did say you'd need someone with you.' He looked concerned that she was querying his decision, when she hadn't considered he would actually be getting in the pool with her.

'But I thought...' She didn't know what she'd thought. It would've been creepy if he'd told her he'd be keeping an eye on her via CCTV. With all her demands for privacy he couldn't very well have drafted someone else in to do the job either. She hadn't really left him with any options since she'd shown him she couldn't be trusted on her own.

He was waiting, listening for her version of their crossed wires, but she wouldn't make a big deal of it. After all, it surely would've been more uncomfortable for both of them if he'd had to sit fully clothed at the side of the pool watching her. 'It doesn't matter. Just don't get in my way.'

'Yes, ma'am.' He gave her a mock salute, at which she didn't even pretend to hide her non-impressed face.

Georgiana was torn between leaving the changing room at all and ignoring his instruction to wait, jumping straight in the pool. There were numerous difficult decisions she had to make on a daily basis now. Such as whether to take her leg off now or poolside.

It was a toss-up between losing her dignity by having to hop across the floor and potentially risk another floor show or removing it in front of him. In the end she opted for walking out with a modicum of dignity. Ed wouldn't consider removing a prosthetic leg to swim anything out of the ordinary in his line of work. She had to keep telling herself that.

'Don't worry, I'm not going to get my stopwatch out.' He was waiting for her as promised outside the changing room. Georgiana would confess to being somewhat distracted by his physical appearance now that he was bare-chested and she could see exactly what he'd been hiding under those restrictive shirts.

Broad and toned just as she'd known he would be. With a smattering of golden-brown hair on his chest, which became darker as it trailed down his torso and disappeared into his blue swim shorts.

'Pardon me?' It was hypocritical of her to be staring at his body, appreciating it from a merely aesthetic point of view when it was the thing she was most afraid of herself. Although her fairly plain black all-in-one was more than he had seen her in lately.

'I mean I'm not assessing your form or treating this as some sort of training session. I'm here strictly to prevent you from hurting yourself again.' He was teasing her. She was getting used to seeing that light in his eye and tilt of his mouth as he baited her. Now she recognised it as the good humour he intended it to be, she didn't rise to it.

'You know you could do that from a distance, fully dressed, right?' In keeping with their new dynamic, she threw a dismissive glance at his swimwear this time. Ed wasn't liable to take offence. He was much too sure of himself to be self-conscious wearing a non-revealing pair of shorts. Budgie-smuggler trunks might have been a very different story for both of them.

'I thought I'd mix business with pleasure.' He gave her a wink and pulled on a pair of swimming goggles. Georgiana was left wondering which category she fell into as he dived into the water, his body a perfect arch as he hit the surface.

With Ed doing the front crawl away from her, she could take her time getting pool ready knowing she wasn't under surveillance. She wasn't quite as impressive hitting the water but it sure felt good to take the pressure off her limbs.

Ed was already on his second lap by the time she reached the deep end but she didn't care. This wasn't a race or somewhere she had to prove she was every bit as good as her previously able-bodied self. She saw this as more of a wind-down, therapy for the mind rather than her body.

She rested her arms on the edge of the pool, kicking her leg out in front of her to keep afloat as she watched Ed's progress. His fitness levels and confidence were evident in every stroke. The pace was more than she could manage now but, as he'd said, it wasn't a competition. She shouldn't envy the ease with which he covered the length of the pool.

Ed popped his head up beside her, removed his goggles and rested his elbows back on the edge of the pool.

'Can I ask you a question?' He rubbed one hand over his head, raking his hair into wet spikes.

'Sure.' As long as it wasn't anything personal. She was becoming more comfortable in his company now he'd seen her at her worst and hadn't run off screaming. It was nice to be around someone who treated her normally. The only thing that could ruin that would be having to talk over any serious, painful personal stuff about her family or what had happened to her.

'You do seem to enjoy the water. How helpful did you find aqua therapy during your recovery period? I mean, I know we use it here, but, personally, did it help you?'

Georgiana could tell his question arose from genuine curiosity rather than simply prying into her private life. It made it easier to answer.

'Yes, but possibly not in the way you'd imagine.' Judging by the raised eyebrows, she decided he wasn't expecting that response.

'Oh? Didn't you find it useful exercise during rehabilitation? I assume they did have hydrotherapy pools at the clinic where you had your after care?'

'Sure. The strengthening exercises were less painful in the water compared to the gym because of the hydrostatic pressure. It's known to improve respiratory function without overtaxing the body.'

'But?'

So far, she got the impression she was telling him something he already knew, since it was part of their programme for their amputee patients.

'It's more about the mindset of being in the water, if that makes sense… When I'm on solid ground the onus is very much on walking or doing everything on two legs, which is no longer natural for me. It's different in the water. I can almost forget I'm not normal now. I no longer need the leg or hoist to swim, float or splash around. You know, have fun.' She flicked her fingers across the surface of the water, spraying Ed, who didn't seem to mind in the slightest.

'It's good to know for future patients that even if they can't manage the exercises or prosthetics, they can still get something out of this.' He was pensive, as if he already had someone in mind, and Georgiana was curious about this person who'd grabbed his attention.

'Glad to be of help. Is this a hypothetical fishing expedition or are you thinking about someone in particular?' It was ludicrous for her to dig for more info as though she were a jealous girlfriend or a patient with a crush. Strictly speaking she wasn't a patient and he probably had some sort of gagging order preventing him from talking about people he treated. It was none of her business and she really didn't know why she was getting all worked up about the idea he could be swimming after hours with another secret visitor.

'A little girl who's having some trouble adapting. Hannah.'

Relief whooshed through her, chasing away her irrational territorial hold of Ed at the thought of sharing her swimming partner. She wanted to give herself a good slap for being so stupid about the whole matter.

'How so?'

A smile played across his lips as he thought about her question. 'She doesn't like being told what to do. Reminds me of someone, but I can't imagine who.'

'Ha-ha. Some of us simply know our own minds. It could be you simply don't know how to deal with a strong independent woman.'

Ed laughed. 'She's four years old but you could be right. Hannah's refusing to wear a prosthetic or go anywhere near the water.'

'And your usual charm offensive isn't working?'

'I know you'll find this hard to believe but, no, it isn't. I must be losing my mojo.'

Georgiana liked that he wasn't afraid to make fun of himself, even if he was frustrated by another patient refusing to fall in line with his usual tried and tested ways.

'Oh, I doubt that. You just have to find a new way of getting her to trust you. She's not going to co-operate until she sees what's in it for her. Everything about life after an amputation is a difficult journey. Even more so at that age, I'd say. She's not going to put herself through any more pain if she can't see the benefit of it. Take me as an example. I didn't want a part of you or this clinic. I had no reason to believe you had anything to offer me of any benefit. Yet, the promise of a swimming pool and some privacy and I'm hiding on the back seat of your car.'

In the end she'd wondered what he'd got out of the arrangement but after seeing him here in a quandary over a little girl, she knew. The satisfaction of knowing he'd done everything in his power to help. Georgiana was grateful for his perseverance and she knew Hannah's parents would feel the same about his personal attention.

'I'm not sure that would be appropriate in these circumstances.' He twisted his body around in the water so he had his back to the wall beside her, kicking his legs out in front. From a distance they would've looked like any other two swimmers taking a rest and having a chat. That was all Georgiana wanted. To be unremarkable.

'You're going to have to work hard to get on her good side, the way you did with me.' Georgiana was becoming increasingly involved in the story, since she knew what a difference it was having her prosthesis. If the child was to experience everything life had to offer it would be in her best interests to take advantage of everything being offered to aid her recovery.

'I'm on your good side? Good to know.' He looked pleased with himself at that snippet of information. Georgiana immediately had the urge to wipe the smirk off his face, lest he think he had won her over so easily.

'For now.' She pushed herself away from the side of the pool, accidentally on purpose splashing him as she kicked out.

'Oh, you're in for it now!' Ed shouted after her, spurring her pace. That sudden competitive edge between them made her heart race that little bit faster too.

The water swirled and moved alongside her as he launched himself after her. Georgiana went to give an excitable shriek, only to inhale a mouthful of water. It went up her nose and down her throat, making her choke. Panic swamped her and she dipped under the water. She lost focus, tried to get herself upright, forgetting she no longer had two feet to steady herself on the bottom of the pool. Now she was gulping the water, splashing desperately in an attempt to keep herself afloat.

Arms caught around her waist, pulling her from the depths, hands holding her fast until she broke the surface and could breathe again.

'I've got you. Just anchor yourself to my waist and take slow, deep breaths.' Ed's face was so close to hers she had nowhere to look but into his eyes, his mouth issuing instructions she was compelled to follow.

She wrapped her arms around his neck, her leg around his middle, which she wouldn't have done in any other circumstances save for the immediate threat of drowning.

She was relying on him saving her, letting him feel her disability for herself. Yet he was calming her, taking her mind off everything that frightened her by maintaining eye contact and syncing her breathing to his. Deep breaths in and out. Until the panic subsided and they were left entwined, her chest heaving against his, their breath mingling, eyes locked. They'd moved on from potential drowning incident to…well, she didn't know what.

Eventually Ed spoke. His voice hoarse as though he were the one who'd inhaled half of the pool. 'Are you okay?'

She wanted to say no, she wasn't okay with any of this. Either proving him right that she couldn't be left alone in here or about this overwhelming urge to kiss him. She didn't know where that thought had sprung from other than their sudden physical proximity. Yes, he was single as far as she knew. Why wouldn't a woman want to snog the face off him? It was the knowledge that she wasn't necessarily someone he'd want to kiss back that stopped her. At least, not any more.

'Yes. Thanks. I lost track for a moment and panicked.

Sorry. I'm all right now.' She attempted to extricate herself from him but he held her fast.

'You've had a fright. Let me——' He started to tread water with her still attached.

'No. I said I'm fine. I'm not an invalid.' With that she shoved hard against his chest so he let go, then swam away. This time she was very well aware of her inadequacies. She'd had them wrapped around Ed's waist.

CHAPTER FIVE

ED TOOK HIS time showering and changing, trying to get his head around what had nearly happened. When Georgiana had begun play-fighting, showing him a fun side he hadn't seen before, all he'd wanted to do was encourage it and indulge his own. It seemed a lifetime since he'd really cut loose from work and his home life and let himself be free.

That burst of spontaneity hadn't come without cost. Both he and Georgiana had put her in danger with their game of one-upmanship. Their lack of judgement nearly causing a catastrophe.

When she'd started floundering he'd cursed himself for putting her in that position. It had left her vulnerable and made him think of the time when she'd been hurt. Her pain, her strength, her courage and subsequent fight to live.

Ed grabbed a towel and dropped it over his head, shutting out the world and leaving him in the dark with his jumbled emotions. What bothered him most about the incident in the pool was the aftermath. When the danger had passed and he and Georgiana were left entwined in the water. He hadn't wanted to let her go. For a brief second he'd thought he'd seen the same hesitation in her eyes.

Something had flared to life between them and he knew it was more than a primitive reaction to holding a beautiful woman so close. He'd wanted to kiss her, and not just some patronising peck on the lips to assure her she was still alive and breathing. Ed had wanted to taste the sweetness and passion of the woman who'd been constantly on his mind since they'd met and drink her in. Until he was the one drowning.

A sharp rap on the changing room door dragged him out of his thoughts.

'Are you still alive in there?' It was Georgiana checking on him, letting him know he'd been lost in his reverie for too long.

'Give me a minute.' He dressed in double-quick time, his hair and skin still damp.

She was leaning against the wall outside when he finally managed to gather his things. He felt guilty about keeping her waiting but at least she'd hung around. Given her reaction to him in the pool, he wouldn't have been surprised if she'd made her own way back home. Perhaps she had no one to call for a lift or no money for a taxi.

He hoped she'd forgiven him for the predatory way he'd surely been looking at her so they could put it behind them. After all, it hadn't meant anything. It couldn't.

'You took your time. I thought you were suffering from delayed shock in there.'

He had in a way.

'No. Just shaving my legs,' he deadpanned and shut the conversation down.

As they stepped out into the autumnal air, Ed was dreading the thought of taking Georgiana home and then going on to his parents' house. Despite the complications, their time in the pool had given him a sense of release. A freedom he wasn't yet ready to surrender.

'Would you like to go for a coffee? There's a place down the road that should still be open.' What was more normal than having a chat over a cuppa? Making small talk in a public area should help erase whatever had almost happened between them.

'Er...' Her eyes darted everywhere but at him. She gave the impression she was uncomfortable at the thought but didn't know how to break it to him.

Ed wasn't the sort of man who refused to take no for an answer. He'd bow out gracefully with what was left of his pride.

'It's not a problem. You want to get home. I understand.' He pulled down the shutter on the door and locked it tight, not wanting to prolong Georgiana's agony any longer than necessary if she wanted rid of him.

'It's not that. We've gone to so much trouble to keep my identity hidden on these visits it seems reckless to stroll into a coffee shop now.'

'Of course. Sorry.' He slapped his hand to his head. 'I'd completely forgotten you're supposed to be incognito.'

He'd stopped thinking of her as a princess or someone he was doing a favour to. Which should've been insulting to a member of the royal family, to completely disregard her heritage or status, but Georgiana seemed delighted.

'Really?'

He took a good look at her. Free from the heavy kohl eye make-up she favoured and her hair soft, no longer spiky with product, she was simply a beautiful young woman to him.

'Really.'

'The truth is I'd love to do something as ordinary as

order a latte and a pastry, but I could do without the circus which would inevitably follow if I was recognised.'

'Get over yourself, Georgiana. You look as much like a princess right now as I do.' He swept his hair back with a toss of his hand and made her laugh, the sound so moreish he wanted to make her do it again and again.

She stuck her tongue out at him, then plonked her trusty baseball cap on her head. 'You know, I do have an adrenaline buzz going on. I suspect it's something to do with nearly drowning.'

'You were never in any real danger. Although I might advise you to wear a life jacket for any future pool shenanigans.' He was glad they were back to their vocal jousting best, any awkwardness consigned to the past. It meant he no longer had to obsess over what had happened or how he'd felt when he'd held her.

'Or perhaps a lifeguard who does evening shifts?'

A surge of something bitter swelled in the pit of his stomach as she floated the idea of another man taking over their secret swim sessions. He didn't like it.

'About that coffee…you might have to change your order to something decaffeinated. Perhaps a milky drink like a hot chocolate to help you sleep later.' To his surprise she linked her arm through his as they walked down the street.

'What? I thought it would look less suspicious if we pretend we're together instead of walking in separately.'

'Not because you want me to pay?'

'Hey, you were the one who asked me out.'

'There's a seat in the corner by the door. Try not to be too princessy until I get back.' He directed her towards a small table for two crammed into the corner of the café.

Georgiana chose to sit with her back to the rest of the shop to maintain a low profile, but it went against all her army training. She couldn't see who was coming in or might be behind her. Blind to anyone who could approach. She'd have to rely on Ed for surveillance as well as security. He wouldn't mind and, strangely, neither did she.

Over these past days he'd proved she could trust him with her life and her secrets. Loyalty was highly prized now that her privacy meant everything.

'One milky, adrenaline-free hot chocolate with extra cream and marshmallows for you and one for me.' A tall glass mug layered with sugary goodness appeared in front of her and she inhaled the comforting aroma.

'All calorie free too, I assume?'

Ed tilted his head to one side. 'I don't think you need to worry yourself on that score.'

There was something in his lowered tone that zapped her right in the danger zone and made her blush. He'd seen most of her, felt most of her pressed up against him, and the reminder made her burn with more than embarrassment. She didn't think he was teasing her. He was missing the twinkle and the smirk she'd got used to when he was doing so. This time she swore his eyes had darkened and his voice got huskier, which only made her hotter.

That moment they'd had in the pool had sent her hurtling away from him for this very reason. These sudden urges towards him scared her. She didn't want to face what it meant when her life was already so complicated.

After her operation, she hadn't dared imagine having feelings for anyone again. Much less someone to be interested in her that way. Ed might tease her but he would never do anything ungentlemanly. Unless she asked him to.

'Two cheese and ham toasties.' The barista-cum-food-warmer set two plates down, disturbing the tense mood around the table.

'I didn't order anything,' she whispered to Ed, afraid of upsetting the member of staff and causing a scene.

'I know it's not your usual haute cuisine, Princess, but I thought you might be hungry after your swim.' Ed unfurled his cutlery from its paper envelope and sawed through his hot toasted sandwich.

Georgiana wasn't sure if hot chocolate and toasties were a food combination she totally approved of but her rumbling tummy made the decision for her.

'I am. Thank you.' It wasn't the best meal she'd ever eaten but the sentiment and company made the evening better than any she'd ever had in even a five-star establishment.

While she delicately cut her sandwich into bite-sized pieces, Ed attacked his with gusto. She noted his large hands, his eager mouth, and had to look away again. Horrified by the hormonal mess she'd become around him lately.

She chewed and swallowed her food but no longer tasted it. At this point she thought it might have been a better idea to have gone home when she'd had the chance.

Ed Lawrence was the wrong man for her on all sorts of levels. Probably. She was just having trouble remembering what those reasons were right now.

After taking a healthy mouthful of his hot chocolate, he'd coated his top lip with cream and melted marshmallow. She was mesmerised by the tongue licking it off and savouring the taste.

Goodness, they must've put the heating on in here because her temperature was spiking.

'Did you get a chance to ask your folks about hosting the gala at the palace?'

'Yes, they agreed. Sorry, I meant to let you know.' Georgiana was keen to have something other than Ed's eating habits and her own libido on her mind.

'That's such a weight off my mind. Thank you. I can hopefully set a date and send out the invitations now. This is actually happening.' He smiled as he shook his head as though he couldn't quite believe it. Despite all the hard work he'd obviously been doing to bring it to fruition.

'Yes, it is. Thanks to you.'

'And you. I thought I'd come to the end of the road. You saved us.'

'My parents aren't going to be present, of course. That's not part of the deal.' She shook off his undeserved praise. It was Ed who'd put his heart and soul, not to mention the extra hours of work, into setting this up.

'Understood.'

'Although, Mother does want to do her bit by bringing in her own caterers and florists for the occasion.' She'd been surprisingly keen to get involved when Georgiana had put the proposal to her. The cynic in her wondered if it was in some way to ease her conscience over her own amputee daughter.

'That's very generous of them.'

'Yeah. To their credit, my parents haven't been pushing me to go back to work yet. Speaking at the gala gives me something to work towards. It will be a test. I'm just holding out for that day when I, and the rest of the world, no longer care about my appearance.'

'I understand you have hang-ups about your prosthetic.

It's a big change for you, but you lost a leg, not your life. What kind of existence are you going to have if you stay locked away from the rest of the world?'

'A quiet one,' she muttered, every inch the petulant child.

'That's what you want? I don't believe someone who has travelled the world and been in life or death situations could be content to rot away behind four walls. What would make you happy, Georgiana?'

'You don't understand. It's not about being happy or content. It's about not feeling any worse.' Someone who looked like an Aussie surfer and ran a successful business would never have her worries.

'So, tell me.' He sat back in his chair, arms folded, waiting for her to unload.

'I joined the army to get away from people staring and talking about me as though I'm not a real person.'

'That's the reason you went into service?' He raised an eyebrow in disbelief at her. She really wasn't explaining herself very well but it was the first time she'd tried to put how she was feeling into actual words.

'Not entirely. I wanted to be someone of worth, to do something I could be proud of and help people where I could.'

'You mightn't be able to go back to that now, but that doesn't mean you can't be an asset elsewhere. You're certainly going to be inspirational for my charity families.'

'I'm sure I'll make a great pin-up girl,' she scoffed.

'I never had you pinned as someone who sat around feeling sorry for herself.' Blotches of red blossomed in his cheeks but it was Georgiana who felt the sting. Was that how he saw her? A spoilt rich girl feeling sorry for herself? After some thought she realised it wasn't an unreasonable conclusion to come to, given her recent behaviour.

'If you have parents who are more interested in public perception than the welfare of their children, you might realise why I'm so fixated on my…imperfection. As far as my mother's concerned, I'm damaged goods. The only way I could ever be right again is if I grew my leg back.' She thought of Freddie, her beautiful fun-loving brother. His perceived imperfection had been his sexuality. Something else to shame their parents.

Just as she couldn't change her circumstances, neither could Freddie. He hadn't been able to live with the disappointment any better than she could. Georgiana's way of coping was to hide away. Surely that was a better option than taking one's life? Depending on who you asked, of course.

'Really? I didn't get that impression from talking to her. She came across as being very proud of you.'

Any form of praise for her parents always darkened her mood.

'I'm sure she managed to give you that impression for the duration of her appointment. Saving face is part of her job description. The reality is somewhat different.' Her mother didn't seem as proud when she was giving her those sideways glances of despair any time Georgiana had her false leg on show. She certainly hadn't been loud and proud about her colourful son either.

'Who do you think suggested I called in on you that first night? She's worried about you but afraid to go anywhere near you and who can blame her? You're a hard person to crack, Georgiana Ashley.'

There was that unpleasant sinking in her stomach again. A sense of betrayal and confusion about what had been going on behind her back dragging her down into despair.

'Is—is that why she hired you? To break me down?' She'd thought their meeting and subsequent forays at the clinic had been a happy quirk of fate. Finding out it was something her mother had orchestrated made a mockery of her and the emotions she'd begun experiencing around Ed.

The odd food combination she'd had along with this nauseating bombshell made her want to vomit.

Ed let out a groan of frustration and scrubbed his hands over his head. 'She didn't hire me for you. Your mother brought me in for a consultation on her back injury. All she asked where you were concerned was to have a chat and make sure you were all right. Everything that happened after that arose from circumstance and opportunity. It wasn't a set-up.'

'Is that what all this was about? Be nice to the poor amputee who's so desperate for company she'll do anything in return?'

'Of course not. I'm not that kind of man, Georgiana. If I was trying to butter you up don't you think I'd take you somewhere more upmarket?' Now Ed was the one all puffed up with indignation, his voice carrying farther than she appreciated.

'I couldn't say. It's not as if I know you.' She leaned across the table to continue the argument in private, hoping to persuade Ed to do the same so as not to draw any attention from bystanders.

He looked as though she'd helped herself to his food as well as hers. His pain so palpable she could nearly feel it.

'I thought we were getting along well.' The laid-back Ed she'd thought him to be was gone, to be replaced with someone prepared to stand against the disservice she was doing him. He got up, walked over to the bin and deposited his rubbish in one short, sharp motion before returning to the table.

Georgiana considered what he'd had to say and the way he was reacting to the suggestion their interaction this far had been a convoluted plot by her mother. It was blatantly obvious how annoyed he was in his tone and his body language. Unless he was an award-winning actor, she'd really insulted him.

She was both relieved and remorseful, even if none of this managed to change her mind.

'If I got that wrong, I apologise.' She was stubborn and defensive but when she was wrong, she admitted it. Something she'd learned was important from parents who would never confess to making mistakes. Apologies and acknowledgement of wrongdoings were vital for closure. Poor Freddie never got his and she doubted she ever would either.

'You did get it wrong. Apology accepted.' The thin line of his mouth relaxed along with his frown. One good thing about a man who didn't sweat the small stuff was that he didn't appear to hold a grudge either. Georgiana wished she were more like him.

Whatever Ed might think, she didn't see what difference she could make to anyone's life when her own was so pathetic the one person who'd befriended her now stood accused of being paid off to do so.

How was such a paranoid, needy loser going to improve someone else's lot? Unless she was held up as an example of what not to become. None of this changed her mind about the situation.

Ed waved a white paper napkin in surrender. 'Truce?'

What choice did she have but to agree to a ceasefire in hostilities when he was the only person she had to talk to?

She took her time finishing her drink, knowing they were going to be locked in the car soon, where she'd be suffocated under that damned blanket and the reminder of failing her public duty.

The door to the coffee shop was thrown open and a young family burst in. Their excited chatter filled the air and took the pressure off her to try and make more conversation with Ed.

'What do you want, Ethan?' The young dad ushered his boisterous son into a booth next to them, followed by his other half, who was pushing a buggy.

'Hot chocolate.' The youngster climbed up on the back of the seat to stare over at Georgiana. She gave him a flash of a smile then pulled her baseball cap down again.

'Sit down, son, and leave the lady alone.' The father tugged him back down, making sure he was settled in a seat before he went to the counter.

The baby started wailing then to be released from its imprisonment, and as his mother was busy trying to pacify her youngest Ethan made a break for it again.

Georgiana couldn't see what was going on behind her but she could guess as draughts of cold air hit the back of her neck.

'Ethan, leave the door alone,' his father bellowed from the other side of the coffee shop.

'Time to go?' Ed suggested and Georgiana nodded her head enthusiastically. There'd been sufficient conflict for one night. She didn't need to be involved in anyone else's domestic.

'Yes, please.' She deposited her rubbish and they made their move to go.

Suddenly there was a blood-curdling scream drawing the attention of everyone in the café towards the door.

'Ethan!' The little boy's mother was screaming just as loudly as her son and it wasn't long before they saw why.

'He's trapped his fingers in the door.' Ed hared off towards the sobbing boy, where the glass door was now smeared with tears and blood.

'We need a first-aid kit now. Now!' Georgiana shouted to the staff. She was straight back into medic mode faced with the emergency.

Ed held the door at an angle so she could ease the boy's hand out of the door jamb. Whatever he'd been up to, he'd managed to get his fingers caught inside the heavy hinged door.

The distraught parents rushed over but she knew it would be best for them to keep their distance until they managed to stem Ethan's injuries.

'We're both medical professionals. If you could phone an ambulance, we'll take care of your son.'

The dad immediately got out his mobile phone and the mum did her best to soothe both of their children while looking close to tears herself.

'It'll be okay, Ethan, baby.'

'They can't get anyone here for a while. All available ambulances have been diverted to a major emergency on the motorway.' Ethan's father relayed the bad news but Ed remained calm as he knelt down beside the boy. 'We'll take him to my clinic down the street. I can help him.'

He motioned Georgiana over and she could see why he was anxious to get the child to the clinic. The large gash running along the back of his hand was bleeding everywhere and so deep she could see exposed bone.

She grabbed a bottle of water from behind the counter, which Ed poured over the wound to clean it. Ethan yelled.

'Sorry, mate, we don't want anything nasty to get in there and cause an infection. Georgiana, can you get a dressing out for me?' Ed was holding the boy's hand up, trying to stem the flow of blood, and left it to her to inspect the contents of the first-aid kit provided by the staff.

She took out a wad of tissues and dabbed the area to dry it off before applying a sterile dressing. The wound was going to need stitching but that would keep it dry and clean until they could get him to the clinic. 'Are you doing okay, Ethan? Let me know if you start to feel sick or dizzy, okay?'

Shock was an important factor to look out for after any injury and particularly in one so traumatic, but Ethan's father gathered him up in his arms and Georgiana knew everyone was keeping a close eye on the boy to make sure he'd be okay.

They must have made an odd-looking procession as they made their way to the clinic premises. Ethan was still holding his hand up but the dressing was soaked with blood and the child was greyer than the overcast sky.

Ed was racing ahead to get the place opened. There was no way Georgiana could keep up with him without her gait giving away her secret. She stayed behind with the pram-pushing mum.

'Don't worry. Ed's a surgeon. He knows what he's doing.' There was no one better to have in a medical emergency.

The young woman nodded but didn't speak. As she was biting down hard on her lip, Georgiana could tell she was afraid of saying anything and breaking down when she was trying to be strong for her son. She had some inkling of what that was like.

'I'll wait out here to direct the paramedics. I'm not great with blood,' the mum finally admitted.

'You'll be better in the fresh air and it's probably not a bad idea to keep the baby out of it all.'

Georgiana managed to give her a reassuring pat on the back before disappearing inside after the others. They'd need as little distraction as possible in there.

Ed had set up in one of the treatment rooms, where bright lights were dazzling and Ethan was perched up on a bed with his arm stretched out.

'Georgiana, I'm going to need your help here.' Ed was sitting in a chair by the bed, carefully unwrapping the blood-soaked dressing from around the boy's hand.

'Okay.' His request caught her unawares as he seemed to have everything under control, but she was pleased he'd thought to include her. That her career history hadn't been completely consigned to the past along with having two good legs.

'If you could clean things up here again, I'm going to give him something for the pain.'

She sat on the bed beside Ethan, armed with the swabs and iodine Ed had provided.

'Hi, Ethan, my name is…Georgie.' It was important to her to draw a line somewhere between her public and private persona.

From the corner of her eye she could see Ed smirk, but this wasn't the time to get into one of their spats. She didn't have to explain her every move to him.

'We're going to get you cleaned up and give you something to take the pain away.'

'Ow!' he cried as she dabbed delicately at his hand.

'I know it hurts but this is all to make you better.'

Ethan buried his head into his dad's chest but let her do what she had to.

Ed turned back with a needle in his hand. 'You're going to feel a little scratch, Ethan, but this is going to take away the pain for you.'

Georgiana held the small hand in place for Ed to inject. It would make it easier to stitch and lessen the chance of infection setting in.

She had no doubt Ed could undertake that or any possible surgery should the need arise. He had that same temperament and skill that would've served him well if he'd chosen to work in a military environment.

'Good boy,' she encouraged when she saw Ethan tense at his advance.

Once the injection had been administered, Ed made sure the wound was clear and the area was numb before he began to suture.

'You'll feel a little tug when I'm stitching, Ethan, but it shouldn't be painful.' Ed pulled the sides of the skin together and closed them with the tiny needle and thread.

'It'll all be over in a second,' Georgiana soothed.

Once Ed had finished suturing, she applied another sterile dressing to cover the site and keep it clean and dry.

It was a revelation to her that she could still be of use in this field. Ed was the lead here but she knew she could've handled this on her own had it come to it. Her medical skills hadn't deserted her simply because her confidence had. What was more, this feeling of being useful in some capacity had given her spirits a lift. Which was more than any well-meaning words had managed from those around her.

She gave Ed credit for getting her to see she didn't

have to resign herself to being on the scrap heap. Even if he'd been harsh in the delivery. Although they both knew she would never have responded to a soft approach.

If this feeling could be sustained, she wanted to capture it now. She could help, she could improve a child's life and she wanted to do it.

Ed gave aftercare instructions and told them to have the stitches taken out at the hospital, with a warning if there were any signs of infection to have Ethan's hand seen sooner. Georgiana waited until the family were on their way home before she approached Ed. Her blood was pumping in anticipation of discussing things with him. Positivity was surging in her veins, giving her a renewed sense of purpose. It was a small step but one in the right direction. One out of the shadows and into the light. Where hopefully a new future was waiting for her and others in her situation.

As they stood outside once more, the excitement over, Ed shut the clinic one final time. Georgiana inhaled a lungful of cool, clean air.

'I'd like to help with Hannah. I'll talk to her for you.' She didn't have time to consider the implications of another commitment she'd made as Ed grabbed her into a bear hug. It was good to be back in her rightful place.

CHAPTER SIX

ED HAD HELD his tongue the whole way back to the palace last night. Afraid to make a song and dance about Georgiana's decision in case she changed her mind in the cold light of day. After all they'd just been involved in a medical drama.

He was sure it had been a long time since she'd been involved in anything like that but Georgiana was on the phone first thing. Literally as soon as dawn broke.

'Hello?'

'Hello, Ed? This is Georgiana.' Her perky voice instantly made him sit upright in his bed so he didn't sound as though he'd been fast asleep only seconds before.

'What can I do for you?'

'I wanted to let you know I'm still available for that chat with Hannah if you can sort something out with her parents.'

'That's great. I'll call them when it's a more reasonable hour.' He yawned, but waking up to the sound of her excitement wasn't the worst thing to start the day.

'Sorry for waking you. I haven't slept much.'

'It was a lot to deal with. I was going to call you anyway to see how you were after last night. You beat me to it.' She'd certainly been on his mind. Enough for Ed to wonder if he'd been dreaming when he'd heard her on the other end of the phone.

'Is it awful of me to say I got a real buzz out of it?'

'There's nothing like an emergency to get the heart pumping, is there? No need to feel bad about it. Ethan's going to be fine.'

'Now if we can do something for Hannah too…'

He liked the sound of 'we'. It denoted a bond as well as forgiveness for omitting to tell her from the start about her mother's involvement.

'Can I ask what prompted your decision to help?' He finally blurted out the question that had been on his lips since she'd mentioned it last night. She seemed in such good spirits and lacking that usual defensive attitude; he was curious about what had brought it about.

'It was Ethan actually. I'd forgotten what it was like to be useful. I thought about what you said and you were right. My army days are behind me but I could have a new path waiting for me. It might take some adjusting but I want to do something other than being a burden to people. I want to make a difference.' Ed could hear the passion in her voice and it was intoxicating. Everything he'd wanted for her. Coming to terms with the end of her life as she'd known it was no small feat but after seeing her in action he knew she had so much more to give.

'I'm one hundred per cent behind you, Georgiana. You know that.' Ed was perched on the edge of his bed now.

'All I'm doing is talking to a little girl. One step at a time. Excuse the pun.' She was laughing at herself. Something else new and positive. Things Ed didn't want to be responsible for ruining.

'Thank you for agreeing to speak to Hannah. I know how much it took for you to agree to do that. I'll arrange a time with her parents and get back to you. Anything after that is totally in your hands, Georgiana.'

She wasn't someone who could be rushed into things. She moved at her own pace and made her own decisions.

Ed was hoping the clinic and he would be a part of any of her future plans.

Meeting a member of the public, no matter how young, brought all sorts of dilemmas for Georgiana. First of all, she'd had to decide if she wanted to make it an official engagement. Which would have entailed informing security, staff and making special arrangements at the clinic.

She'd gone for option B instead. The sneaking-out method.

There had also been the question of what to wear. It wasn't a diamonds and pearls event where she'd be expected to wear haute couture. No, this was worse. In order to get Hannah to relate to her she had to go with something to show off her prosthetic leg.

It was the thought of Ethan and the effusive thanks they'd received from his parents for helping that sealed her decision. She'd donned her usual casual gym kit that she was comfortable in.

Now she was waiting in Ed's office to be introduced to Hannah and her parents. As she paced the floor, her pulse was doing the samba, her skin was clammy and she wasn't altogether steady on her feet. Anyone would think she'd just run a marathon.

To keep herself busy she began to tidy the mess that was supposed to be Ed's desk. It was a curious insight into the man who'd put all this into motion. The dirty coffee cups lying around suggested someone too busy to be bothered with a trivial thing such as washing up at work.

What struck her most was the lack of personal touches in his workspace. There were no photos of family or items from home she'd expect to have crept into an environment where he spent most of his time.

She no longer thought of Ed as some beach bum who drifted through life. He was devoted to his job and patients if Hannah was any indication. With no obvious signs of his personal life, she wondered if this was because of his dedication to his career or something else. He knew a lot about her and she realised she wanted to find out more about Mr Lawrence beyond the job.

She heard voices in the corridor outside, saw the door handle move and her heart leapt into her throat. This wasn't a public event and as far as she knew there were no photographers around to capture the moment but she was just as anxious as though she were on the international stage.

Georgiana stood by the window, creating a space between her and the people about to walk into the room.

'There's someone I'd like you to meet, Hannah.' Ed's voice filtered in first.

Georgiana took a deep breath.

Four more faces entered the room. One familiar and smiling, a little suspicious one and two open-mouthed and staring.

She swallowed down the anxiety threatening to choke her and moved forward with her hand outstretched. 'Hi, I'm Georgiana.'

The woman with the small child clinging to her like a koala was completely still, her gaze fixed on Georgiana.

Ed stepped forward to break the awkward moment of recognition. 'Georgiana, this is Hannah and her parents, Phil and Kate Howell.'

It was Phil who finally shook her hand. 'Pleased to meet you.'

'But you're, you're—' Kate's reaction to meeting a member of the royal family wasn't unusual but this was the first time Georgiana had faced it since her time in the army. She wasn't used to it any more.

Ed discreetly closed the door behind the family. 'Hannah, Georgiana is a princess and she has a poorly leg just like you.'

They'd discussed introductions before the family arrived and she'd agreed that for once her royal status might prove helpful. By all accounts Hannah was obsessed with princesses and happy-ever-afters. Georgiana knew something about one of those things at least.

Although the little girl didn't seem convinced, her eyes narrowed and mouth pouting. 'She doesn't look like a princess.'

The words, though they'd come from a child, still struck her where it hurt most. Out of the mouths of babes, the truth was inescapable. Georgiana was a freak.

'Well, the princess is here to exercise. She wears her ball gowns and tiaras at home in the palace.' Ed was grinning at her and that urge to run and hide gradually died away.

Of course, she didn't look like a princess to a four-year-old who believed in fairy tales. In Hannah's head Georgiana should have long thick glossy hair, a perfect body and always be ready to accompany a handsome prince to a ball at the chime of the bells. She was the anti-princess. Ed, however, would've been perfect cast in the handsome prince role.

'Sorry, Hannah. This is how I am most days but I promise I do live in a palace.' It seemed absurd to be bragging about such a thing when she'd spent most of her life resenting it but, for once, this wasn't about her. When someone was in need, she would work with whatever she had in her kit to make them better. In this situation her heritage might prove more effective than a first-aid pack.

Hannah looked to her mum for guidance. 'Is she really a princess?'

Mrs Howell nodded. 'She really is.' Then she turned and whispered to Ed, 'Should we curtsey or something?'

'That's really not necessary. I'm just here to have a chat with Hannah. I hear you had a big operation the same as mine.' She saw the girl staring at her prosthetic and decided to bite the bullet. Pulling a chair over, she sat down and proceeded to remove her false leg.

Hannah's eyes widened as she removed the protective sock off the end of her stump. Georgiana couldn't bring herself to glance at Ed even though he'd seen her at her most vulnerable. Instead, she addressed the parents, who wouldn't have been aware of the circumstances leading to this.

'I'd appreciate it if you could keep this private. I'm still coming to terms with the injuries I sustained during my time in service and I'd prefer not to have the press hounding me during my recovery.'

'Of course.'

'We read about you joining the army but had no idea you'd been involved in active duty. Much less injured. I'm so sorry.'

It was daft but Mr and Mrs Howell's understanding and compassion made her well up. Usually any display of sympathy angered her, making her feel as though she was a figure to be pitied. Here, though, these people understood the implications and difficulties since they were going through the same with their daughter. They were the first *civilians* she'd shared this with and it was a hugely significant step for her. One that she wouldn't have taken without a push from Ed.

Seeing their honest, thoughtful reaction, she had a lot to thank him for. Perhaps her 'coming out' wouldn't be as bad as she'd feared.

'Why don't you take a seat?' Ed urged them forward and it was something of a relief to all be on the same level with no distinction between abilities or class.

Hannah was squirming in her mother's arms and making unhappy noises until she was set down on the floor. She shuffled on her bottom across the carpet towards Georgiana. Without saying a word she looked at her own stump, then at Georgiana's, comparing the two. She could obviously see the similarities despite the difference in size.

When Hannah reached out to touch her stump it was all she could do not to leap into the air. It didn't hurt, not any more, but that intimate recognition of how her body had changed remained a sore point.

She held her breath as the tiny hand explored the scarred tissue for what seemed an eternity.

'Hannah, you should have asked for permission first. I'm so sorry, Miss Ashley.' The girl's mother went to pull her back but Georgiana put a hand up to stop her.

'It's fine. She's curious, that's all.' There was no judgement being made, only a childish fascination she shouldn't take offence at.

Suddenly the little girl took hold of her hand and tugged it. Georgiana eased herself out of the chair so she could sit on the floor with her, their legs stretched out almost mirroring each other's.

Still holding Georgiana's hand, she placed it on her little stump where her leg used to be. The gesture took her by surprise. It was the connection everyone had been waiting for. A reminder that she wasn't alone. There were so many like her and Hannah, adults and children who needed support.

'Does it hurt?' she asked, when the scars and operation Georgiana had endured seemed too much for someone so young, so small, to have to deal with.

Hannah shook her head.

'You're not much of a talker, huh?' Georgiana didn't blame her for being uncooperative on so many different levels when so many strangers had come into her life uninvited recently. It was her way of keeping some control. The same reason Georgiana was clinging to her privacy.

'Only until she gets to know you, then she never shuts up.' Her father laughed and Hannah stuck out her tongue at him.

'Would you like to see my new leg?' Georgiana used her interest to their advantage and handed her prosthetic to Hannah for inspection. There was no doubt this was surreal, especially with an audience, to be waving about the leg she'd been trying so hard to hide.

Hannah had trouble lifting it off the ground and dragged it over to the end of her stump where it dwarfed her.

'This one's too big for you but I'll show you how it works.' She was sure to have seen videos and leaflets but perhaps it was different when confronted with the real thing. Hannah was playing with her trainer-clad foot, making it comically hop lopsided across the floor.

'We have some more your size, Hannah, if you want to see?' Ed had spotted the ideal opportunity to introduce her to the idea of prosthetics and fetched several samples for her to see.

'Hey! I never got to choose a colour.' Georgiana feigned outrage as the youngster was handed a hot-pink prosthetic. One surely fit for a princess or a lover of fairy tales.

'You should've come to me earlier,' Ed joked, but she'd been thinking the same thing herself. In the space of a few days in his company she was swimming again, treating medical emergencies and meeting people. If only she'd met him sooner her recovery might have been further on than it was currently. He pushed her to the limit without the sort of interference and control she'd feared. Whatever happened from here, she had a lot to thank him for.

This had been such a risk for Ed to take but worth it, judging by the smiles on everyone's faces. Hannah was full of wonder, handling and working out how the prosthetic moved. Her parents were sitting back, letting her explore without interference but seeming relieved. Then there was Georgiana. He hadn't seen her shine as brightly as she was now. Her eyes welling up with happy tears showing how much this meant to her too.

Hannah was responding to her, opening up to the idea of a prosthetic, and that could only bring positive news regarding her future. Georgiana was blossoming right alongside her. He was watching her interact, no longer self-conscious, and it was glorious.

'What's this funny one?' Hannah dumped one of the prosthetics in his lap, demanding his attention.

'This one is for running. It's called a blade. Do you see

how it's curved at the bottom? It's springy too.' He bent down to demonstrate it, much to Hannah's amusement.

'There are all types of ones you can get and having one of these means you can walk on two legs again. Wouldn't you like to do that, Hannah?' Georgiana shifted back up into her seat and proceeded to attach her prosthesis.

Hannah was watching her every move with rapt fascination as her princess stood at full height. Mrs Howell gave a sob. This was such a milestone for them even Ed found himself getting choked up.

'I can make an appointment for you to get fitted for one of your own, Hannah.' He'd make sure to get her in as soon as possible before she changed her mind.

'Since you're here, we thought you could go to the pool with us. I can show you how to swim. Would you like that?' Georgiana had put the idea to Ed and, in turn, he'd suggested it to the Howells. Going to the pool would be a huge step for both her and the little girl, but they hoped in seeing her Hannah would recognise it was possible to still have fun with only one leg.

After considering the proposal Hannah solemnly nodded her head and everyone else in the room breathed a collective sigh of relief.

'Why don't we sit on the edge of the pool? That's okay, isn't it, Hannah?' Georgiana was perched poolside, letting her leg dangle in the water.

Apart from the lifeguard, they were the only people in the pool area, which Ed knew she'd appreciate. After their talk about her insecurities it was a move in the right direction for her to bare herself to these strangers. Even if she was wearing a modest one-piece.

Ed and Mr and Mrs Howell sat down too and Hannah watched them with sceptical interest from her mother's arms.

'Do you want to sit next to me, Hannah?' Georgiana patted the space between her and Ed. After apparently deciding it wasn't a trick, Hannah clambered off her mother and scooted over beside Georgiana. Ed noted she was careful not to go anywhere near the water as she settled in between them.

Georgiana splashed her foot in the pool and Ed did the same.

'Do you ever have water fights, Hannah?' She playfully scooped some water over him, careful not to hit Hannah and upset her.

'Oh, she loves having water-pistol fights with her daddy. Don't you, Han?' Now her mother seemed to get the gist that they were trying to make her comfortable around water and started splashing her feet too.

This time Hannah nodded enthusiastically and shuffled closer to the edge. It wasn't some sort of phobia she had, at least.

Ed flicked some water back and showered Georgiana.

'Hey!' she shouted with good humour and retaliated.

Ed shook the drops out of his hair and scooped the water with his hand to soak everyone this time. To his delight Hannah was giggling at the exploits of the adults. It wasn't long before the poolside was a riot of squeals and splashes with little Hannah in the middle of it all. She was kicking her good leg in the pool, roaring with laughter every time she managed to splash someone.

They didn't push her too far out of her comfort zone, but he and Georgiana did compete in another race. This time without incident and with a cheering squad. It was their way of showing Hannah there was nothing to fear when Georgiana was just as able to swim as he was, even with only one good leg.

Step one was complete. Ed was willing to do whatever it took to get Hannah's hydrotherapy started. Recovery here wasn't a series of tick boxes. It took as long as necessary. With Georgiana's input he was sure Hannah would be back on her feet when she was ready.

'If you don't mind, I'd like to stay on in the pool for a while,' Georgiana said as the Howells got ready to leave.

'Not at all. We've got an appointment with the physiotherapist next. Perhaps we'll see you later.' Hannah's father stopped her from feeling too bad about not seeing them off because she wanted to enjoy some more pool time.

'Call by my office before you go.' It seemed Ed wasn't going to get out either as he waved the family off from the pool.

'You don't have to stay on my account. I promise not to drown or break anything if you have work to get back to.' It was bad enough she monopolised his time at night without doing it during office hours too. She simply wanted some swim time to chill out after her earlier nerves about meeting Hannah and her family.

'It's not always about you, Princess. I have to exercise or I don't get to eat my junk food. For the record, our private session will be coming to an end and I don't know how much longer we'll have the place to ourselves. There will be other patients booked in to use the pool for the rest of the afternoon. You know, if you're not comfortable with anyone else seeing you here.' With that he pushed away to do a non-stop lap of the pool.

'It's fine. I've got over that hurdle now.' What difference was it going to make now if she was joined by other people who were likely more concerned with their own recovery?

She'd barely got the words out of her mouth when they were joined by one of the therapists and her patient. Their privacy was over as the rest of the clinic were granted use of the facility too. Georgiana carried on with her swim as the man was lowered into the pool on the hoist, knowing he'd be every bit as self-conscious as she was, thinking someone might be watching. She did, however, nod an acknowledgement to his anxious family member looking on.

When she'd been having her hydrotherapy sessions she'd done them alone. There were some who had family and friends to support them, but there were plenty of others like her who'd chosen to go through their recovery on their own. Looking back, she could see how much harder that had made things for her mentally. That had been the beginning of her pushing everyone away, rejecting any support. Her time here at Ed's clinic had shown her the benefits of having someone in your corner, shouting their encouragement and providing a sounding board for those struggling with their mobility.

The woman was walking up and down the length of the pool urging on who Georgiana assumed was her husband. Ed had been the one doing that for her lately. Perhaps if she'd had someone like him from the moment she'd been injured she might have found it easier to deal with the events. As much as she hated what her body had gone through, if it hadn't been for that bomb she would never have met Ed and she was grateful every day that he'd come into her life.

The patient was oblivious to the cheer squad as he continued his swim but Georgiana was fascinated. That outpouring of emotion, with no hint of self-consciousness, from the partner in pursuit of her husband's progress was something her family had never displayed even in the most traumatic of circumstances. Until recently she hadn't thought much of it, but now that level of support seemed the most important thing in the world.

Her envious surveillance proved invaluable when she saw the woman falter, a look of sudden distress crossing her face. Georgiana swam in her direction to make sure she was okay, just in time to see her drop to the ground and begin fitting on the floor.

'Ed!' She yelled for help, hoping he could get to her quickly.

His head jerked up to see what had made her call out. Then all hell seemed to break loose.

'She's epileptic.' The husband shouted from the pool, clearly frantic that he couldn't get to her side without help. Ed was swimming so hard towards the side of the pool he didn't seem to be taking a breath between strokes. The woman's body was jerking and twitching uncontrollably, then she just seemed to roll into the water.

Horrific screams echoed around the walls and Georgiana wasn't sure if they were coming from her or the husband as they watched her fall helplessly into the watery depths of the pool. The lifeguard dived in and between him and Ed they managed to haul her leaden body to the surface. They kept her head tilted back to keep her face out of the water so she wasn't inhaling any more water. There was no way of knowing how much had already gone into her lungs or what damage she'd done when her head hit the floor. Georgiana knew from painful experience how hard those tiles were against one's skull. She'd been lucky not to have suffered anything more than an egg-shaped lump but a serious head injury here could have caused a skull fracture or damage to the brain.

Georgiana climbed out and shuffled over on her backside to help pull the woman out as the men pushed her from the pool. Those exercises to strengthen her muscles came into effect as she hooked the woman under her arms and pulled with all her might. She lay her down on the floor and tilted her head back to check her airway as the men scrambled up beside her.

'She's stopped fitting but I don't think she's breathing.' Georgiana couldn't feel a pulse and even with her ear to the woman's mouth she couldn't hear anything.

'She's bleeding too.' Ed pointed out the increasing pool of scarlet spreading out across the once pristine white tiles.

'Starting CPR,' Georgiana called. The most important thing was to get her breathing again. She started chest compressions, putting her hands on top of one another, interlocking her fingers and pushing the heel of her hand hard into the woman's chest.

'I'll get the defibrillator.' Ed took off, barefoot and wet, to track down the essential equipment.

This was the sort of life-saving emergency Georgiana was trained for so she was able to remain calm while the husband was crying and his therapist was shouting about having called for an ambulance.

The lifeguard, who she'd made redundant, made himself useful by covering the patient with towels to keep her warm.

Apparently Georgiana hadn't lost this instinct, this mission to save lives. It was something she didn't want to ever lose when it could prevent a family from the heartache of losing a loved one. She thought of the team who'd saved her. Though she'd lost a limb, she would be grateful for ever that they'd worked hard enough to make sure she had another chance at life.

Ed came rushing back with the portable defibrillator they obviously kept here in case of such events. 'We need to get her dried off and away from the water.'

Between them they made sure it was safe before they deployed the machine.

She heard it whir into life as Ed unbuttoned the woman's blouse and prepared to do his bit to save her too. He ripped the backing off the sticky pads and attached them to the woman's skin on each side of her chest. 'Stop CPR.'

'Stopping CPR.' Georgiana leaned back on her heels and let the machine take over, analysing the patient's heart rhythm. She and Ed waited until the shock had been delivered and instructions were given to continue CPR before they touched her again. They took turns between the shocks being delivered until the woman began to show signs of life. She tilted her head to one side and coughed some of the water out of her lungs.

The adrenaline coursing through Georgiana's veins during the high-pressure event was allowed to subside now she'd successfully done her part of the work. Ed's smile said he felt the same. It was down to the paramedics and the hospital staff now to take over but every joint medical emergency and patient interaction was bringing her and Ed closer together. As well as making her believe she was more than a victim. She still had a purpose, a skill that was needed, even if it was in a very different environment from the one she'd been used to. Her life was changing again but hopefully this time for the better.

* * *

'Maybe for your next appointment you should bring some water pistols.'

'Thanks. I'm sure she'd love that.' Hannah's father scooped her up in his arms as he thanked Georgiana for giving her a reason to return to the pool. They'd stopped by Ed's office as promised to say their goodbyes. Thankfully they'd missed the poolside drama and it was only Ed and Georgiana who were coming down off the adrenaline high.

'Maybe I should've asked Mr Lawrence about that first.' Georgiana laughed.

'That's fine by me. Always happy to take part in a water fight.'

It gave Ed a warm glow because this was going to aid Hannah's progress and was also an indication Georgiana intended on sticking around. He was getting used to having her here.

'Thanks for everything, Miss Ashley.' Mrs Howell went to shake her hand then emotion apparently took over and she threw her arms around her. Georgiana's expression was priceless.

'Any time,' she gasped, through the embrace.

'And we swear not to breathe a word to anyone.' Mrs Howell pretended to zip her mouth shut, making it clear she'd keep her word. This was their secret, their private club to which no one else was invited. Georgiana Ashley was another part of their daughter's recovery process and they wouldn't do anything to jeopardise that.

'You too, Doc. Thanks for setting this up.'

'No problem at all.'

Another round of thanks and goodbyes and suddenly Georgiana and he were alone in the room.

'That went better than I expected,' he said, waving them off before closing the door.

'Yes. I thought she responded really well. Maybe you should buddy up some of the adult amputees with the new patients so they can see what they're working towards.'

'If you're volunteering for future appointments, I'll take it.' It was a long shot but having her around would be a boost for everyone who came through the clinic doors.

He included himself in that bracket when they were already spending so much time together enjoying each other's company. To Ed she fell into neither of the two categories he seemed to divide his time into—work and family. She was a refreshing change from responsibility and being with her gave him some sense of having a life of his own outside those areas.

She glared at him with that 'don't push your luck' vibe and for once Ed knew when to shut up.

'What happens as the children grow? Do they get adjustable legs or do they have to be refitted?' Georgiana was holding up the different samples he'd brought in to show Hannah. Some of which were so tiny it was difficult not to be affected.

She was a compassionate woman so it was natural she should be thinking of Hannah and those like her.

'It's hard for the kids. They're being constantly refitted. There are the sporty ones who really need specially adapted limbs, but it's an expensive business with limited funding from the government. Unfortunately, I don't hold any sway in that department. I can mention it in the right ear but I'm not certain my input will help in any meaningful way.'

'You've been a great help with the charity, and look at how much you've done for Hannah's family.'

She gave him the side eye. 'That was a chat. I didn't achieve anything other than an interest in my leg. I can do that with anyone if I walk down the street in a pair of shorts.'

'You underestimate the influence you have. We have all tried in vain to get Hannah to co-operate and within a few minutes of meeting you she's suddenly engaged and excited about the prospect of a new leg.'

'Not everyone is going to respond to me in the same way as a four-year-old princess-mad little girl.'

'You're a member of the royal family, a soldier and a medic. There's plenty of reason to be impressed by you. You could be a great asset to the team here.'

'What do you mean?'

'You were great with Hannah. She related to you. Saw herself and what she could achieve. None of us have been able to get her near the water or to get fitted for her prosthetic. You could make that big difference to people's lives you wanted by being here. Would you like a job?'

CHAPTER SEVEN

GEORGIANA ALMOST LAUGHED in Ed's face at the suggestion of becoming his employee but the least she could do was hear him out after everything he'd done for her. Before he'd come along she would never have believed she could sit and discuss her prosthesis with strangers as though it was the most natural thing in the world. She supposed it was now. Although talking to one family was very different from revealing all to the nation. The subject of many a nightmare.

'You want me to work here?'

'It's a possibility.'

Georgiana didn't know if the following pause was for dramatic effect or if he was expecting her to shoot down the idea immediately. She wanted to hear more before she did that. When he realised she was listening he carried on.

'You could be a mentor or train as one of our aqua therapists.' Ed was fidgeting with the paperwork, rolling it up into a tube, then unfurling it again, until the ends were curled up like the fallen autumn leaves lying outside.

'This isn't some made-up position you think I need to give my life meaning, is it?' She didn't want to get into the details beyond the title until she could be sure it was more than a vanity project for her.

'No. Absolutely not.' Ed's stern denial and matching frown left her under no illusion that he was deadly serious.

'Good. I prefer people to be upfront with me. I've had enough of duplicitous people.' Life would be so much easier if people were more transparent with their agendas. It could have saved her brother for a start.

'I don't have time to play games with you, Georgiana. You should know by now I'm not someone who will pander to you to make you feel better. Nor would I lie to you.' He reminded her of their first meeting when he was anything but convivial. Ed had been pushy, confrontational but never patronising or sycophantic. She'd met plenty during her royal duties who possessed those particular qualities and Ed certainly hadn't made that list.

'What would it involve? I'd need you to lay it all out for me.' She wanted to believe Ed that she could make a difference in the lives of people who were in the same position as her, but she needed more convincing.

'It could be a long night and that's something best discussed on a full stomach. I'll order some takeaway then I'll take you through everything.'

'Sounds good to me.' So good her heart gave an extra kick at the promise of having dinner with him after office hours.

When the food arrived a short time later, Ed shoved all the paperwork to one side. The only thing greater than his work ethic was his appetite.

'All this comfort food can't be good for you. Not that I'm complaining. It's a long time since I indulged in some fast food.' Georgiana was already salivating with the smell of fried chicken. It wasn't the same when the palace chef attempted to replicate it.

'I usually eat at home with my folks, so these past nights have made a nice change for me too. At least I don't have to listen to stories about the garden exploits of next door's cat or get a list of jobs to do around their house.' He ripped the paper bags open to use as a make-shift plate on top of his desk and proceeded to unpack the goodies.

'I'm the lesser of two evils? Honestly, I'm not sure my conversation is any more stimulating.' She was messing with him but deep down she was touched he was doing this for her. Taking time out from his family to spend it with her. Yes, they were discussing his work tonight but last night had been all about her. Each time he made sure they had sustenance to get through. None of which was in his job description.

'Trust me, it is. It feels as though I actually have a social life when I'm with you.'

'Ah, yes, you said you weren't involved with anyone.' Georgiana was intrigued by the idea of Ed's past loves, probably more than she should be.

For all the time they were spending together she knew virtually nothing about him. It wasn't fair when he knew all her dark secrets, or at least most of them.

'I was with someone for a while—Caroline—but I guess I wasn't putting the time into our relationship that it needed to work.'

Time. That was a word he used a lot, as though he didn't have enough of it. Yet he was always available when she needed him. It raised all sorts of questions about his home life and she hadn't forgotten he'd spoken of personal commitments. She was sure it wasn't a child he was talking about because he would've told her and he wouldn't have been so accommodating if he'd had a little one to get home to.

Perhaps he had a house full of cats to take care of, to feed and to empty litter trays. The image of Ed as a friend to felines amused her, but she hadn't seen one single cat hair stuck to his clothes.

One of the most frustrating things about him was that he was even more guarded than she was about his personal life. If she was to have any thoughts about going into business with him, she needed to know more about the man inside the business suit.

Ed was a good man, hard-working and incredibly easy on the eye. It was hard not to be attracted to him. Even more so the longer she spent in his company.

'Now, where are we eating? Here or on the floor?'

In keeping with the informal nature of the evening she went with the second option. She was loving the fact that he didn't see their time together as a chore or part of his charity work. Especially when he was fast becoming the highlight of her day.

Being with Ed was a taste of normality and she didn't have to pretend about anything when she was with him. Sometimes she wished they'd met under different circumstances. Pre-amputation.

He sprawled out on the floor next to her, his long legs parallel to hers with the parcel of food sat between them.

'You're a homebody, then?' She steered onto the topic of his family to detract from her wandering thoughts as she helped herself to a breadcrumb-coated drumstick.

'More through circumstance than choice,' he said, grabbing a handful of fries. Georgiana had to wait until he'd washed them down with a gulp of cola before he explained. 'I'm the eldest of six. Mum and Dad worked full time and when my youngest brother was born with spina bifida they had their hands full taking care of him. It fell to me to look out for the others because they spent so much time at the hospital for his surgeries and treatment. I guess they got used to me in the carer role. My siblings are married with families of their own but I stayed to take care of our parents. They're getting on in years now. Then there's my little bro, Jamie, who, despite his insistence he doesn't need me hanging around, I like to keep an eye on too.'

It was more about his personal life that he'd shared in the interval before his next bite of food than in the entire time she'd known him. She could see how the implications of his circumstances filtered into every other aspect of his life once she read between the lines.

'Is that what caused the friction between you and your ex?' She could imagine that fighting for his attention against his responsibilities to his family and work could have been demoralising. Yet, he'd been able to find time to fit her in. Perhaps he hadn't been with 'the one'.

Why did that give her a glimmer of heartless satisfaction and where did she rate in his priorities alongside a girlfriend? These were questions that were going to plague her later and she knew why. She liked him. More than she should for someone she'd only known for a few days and she wanted to believe it wasn't one-way traffic. Nothing could come of it, she understood that, but it would be nice if he found her desirable in some way.

'In hindsight, she put up with a lot. Quality time as a couple ended up at the bottom of my priorities. With work and taking care of my family, I was never there when she needed me. Perhaps I should've tried harder, or maybe I'm just not cut out for relationships if I can't give someone what they need from me.'

'Relationships are tricky at the best of times but when you've got complicated family matters going on too it's impossible to make them work. It's not as easy to walk away from family as it is a relationship. I should know. I joined the army to distance myself from mine, yet here I am, back living with my parents. Any chance of suitors is a distant memory.' She consoled herself with another bite of fried chicken. It had been an age since she'd been with anyone and longer still since any meaningful dalliance. She'd had too much going on with her home life and her army career to consider anything serious.

'It's not as though you've moved back into a terraced house where you're all living on top of each other. You live in a palace. Don't expect me to feel sorry for you.'

She mirrored his good-natured grin. Ed wasn't afraid to call her out on things like that. He didn't pander to her and made sure she stayed grounded, not caring she was royalty. However, that insolent comment deserved a suitable reaction.

She lobbed a chip at him, which he managed to catch in his mouth.

'Show-off.'

'Are you going to tell me what caused the rift between you and your parents? It's none of my business but they do seem to genuinely care about you.'

Georgiana couldn't argue with that, despite their differences in the past. They'd gone out of their way to adapt the home for her coming back. Even if she had seen it at the time as resignation that she was changed for ever. At least she'd had somewhere to retreat to when coming to terms with everything. Their actions were only beginning to sink in now her emotions weren't so fraught.

What Ed was asking her to do was spill the family secrets. Something her parents had gone to great lengths to cover up. However, telling him what had happened was more about honouring Freddie than betraying anyone. Her appetite abandoned her as she thought about it all.

'I expect you heard about Freddie's death a few years ago.'

'Your brother? I remember reading about it. I'm sorry. He was very young to have died so suddenly. It was his heart, wasn't it?' There was the gut punch. The story that had been fed to the nation and the one she was about to blow wide open.

'In a roundabout way…' It was heart failure listed as the cause on his death certificate but it failed to detail the circumstances of her dear brother's last tragic hours.

She knew she had Ed's attention when he stopped gnawing on the chicken bones.

'You don't have to tell me if it's too painful.'

'No, I want to. Someone should know the truth.' It was on the tip of her tongue to ask him for his discretion but given his loyalty to her thus far it would've been an insult. Especially when he'd laid his own personal life bare only moments before.

'If this is something I need to sign a non-disclosure agreement for before I hear it, you might want to rethink that idea.' He offered her an out, most likely aware of the significance of the event itself as well as what it was taking for her to confide in him. This story would earn a fortune in the wrong hands. Thankfully, she was aware of how safe and strong Ed's hands were.

'I trust you.' The words almost caught in her throat,

her body trying to hold onto them because she was so unused to saying them.

He wiped his hands on a napkin and sat up straighter. 'I'm listening.'

Georgiana closed her eyes so she could see a picture in her mind of her brother in happier times. It was getting harder to remember Freddie before he succumbed to the darkness hounding him but there he was, smiling back at her. They were physically alike—he was tall and willowy with a shock of dark hair—but that was where the similarities ended.

His wardrobe choices were more flamboyant than hers. He had a wicked sense of humour where Georgiana had been the sensible one of the pair. Trying to keep him out of trouble and usually failing. He had as much trouble accepting their limitations as part of the royal family as she did. Only he'd kept his pain mostly to himself. If she'd known, if she'd been able to help him stand up to her parents and the regime that rejected the idea of a prince who didn't fit in with their ideals, he might be here now calling her Hopalong or something equally inappropriate.

When Georgiana opened her eyes Ed was watching her intently. He held out a hand to hold hers.

'Are you okay?'

She squeaked out an affirmative. With the unexpected physical contact and his eyes full of concern, she didn't think she could hold it together for much longer. So, she got straight to the point.

'Freddie was gay.'

Ed was still holding her hand.

'He never came out to us but we all knew. We all pretended otherwise. A gay prince didn't fit in with tradition, you know?'

'I can see that.' His hand on hers gave her the strength to carry on no matter how tough it was in the retelling.

'He did his best to conform for our sake but he must've been so unhappy.' Her voice cracked as she imagined the pain Freddie had gone through, knowing he wasn't wanted in his truest form.

Ed scooted forward so his knees were bent and he was face to face with her. 'I'm sure that wasn't your fault.'

'I didn't do anything to help. He clearly didn't think he could talk to me about anything or ask for my help. It was an overdose. None of us saw it coming. Afterwards, none of us were allowed to discuss it. Instead of raising public awareness about the issues of mental health or some introspection about what had led him to take his own life, we were supposed to sweep it under the carpet. A tragic accident if anyone asked. They didn't learn anything from Freddie's death and kept on pretending everything was fine. I couldn't take any more.'

'That's when you joined the army?'

'Yes. I wasn't prepared to play along any more. I needed to separate myself from the whole suffocating regime. None of us are perfect but we have a right to be happy. A right to be ourselves. I signed up because I wanted to do something meaningful and make a difference.' She wasn't sure she'd achieved anything except prove she couldn't escape her destiny as part of the royal family.

'I'm sure you did to the men and women you served alongside. You certainly did with Hannah and her family today and I'm sure you will with the rest of our patients. You're an amazing woman, Georgiana.' He was so close to her, saying all the things she needed and wanted to hear, and it was all she could do not to bury her head in his chest and lose herself in his embrace. She'd been strong for so long on her own and Ed was the one person with whom she could let go. He'd take care of her if she asked him to. Goodness knew she was close to doing so.

The office door suddenly burst open and Ed dropped her hand as if it were suddenly something contagious. A tall, owlish man a good ten years younger than him stood staring at them.

'Sorry. I didn't realise you were here. I saw the light on.'

Ed jumped to his feet and helped her into a standing position. 'We were running through a few ideas for the clinic. Georgiana, this is my partner, Giles.'

There was that moment all too familiar to her as he pondered how to react to the introduction. To save any awkward attempt at a bow she stuck out her hand first.

'Pleased to meet you.'

A look of relief flashed across his face as they shook hands. 'It's an honour to have you here. I heard you made quite an impression today. Welcome on board.' Giles was beaming at her. It made her irrationally happy when Ed had made out he was a difficult man to please.

'Thanks.'

'If I'd known you were still around, Giles, I'd have saved you some chicken.' Ed gathered the empty take-away cartons and dumped them in the waste bin.

Giles wrinkled his nose. 'No, thanks. I'm sure we could've arranged a proper meal for our visitor, Ed, if you'd told me we were entertaining.'

Georgiana did her best not to smirk at the glare Giles directed at Ed, promising to have this out with him later.

'It's fine. It's not often I get to eat "normal" food.'

'Yeah, she's slumming it with the common people tonight. Eating with her fingers on the floor instead of silver service in the banquet hall.' It was difficult to tell which of them Ed was teasing, her or Giles, but this time she wasn't the one rolling her eyes at him.

'In that case I'll leave you to it. Lovely to meet you, Ms Ashley.' This time Giles did give a half-bow before he took his leave.

'I don't think I've ever seen Giles quite so awestruck. I think I should keep you around for a while.' Now she knew it was her he was teasing she didn't mind when he was talking about continuing their association. It wasn't a doctor/patient set-up, nor was it strictly speaking a working relationship. The truth was she didn't know how to describe their pairing and that made it something new and exciting.

'Why, thank you. I'm truly privileged.' She also enjoyed the jovial atmosphere they cultivated so easily. Ed didn't alter his personality to suit her. Something rare in her social standing.

'He'll be calculating how much our shares will go up if we have a princess on staff.'

'Well, he seems very charming. He definitely has better manners than you.' Georgiana crumpled up a rogue fries packet left on the floor and tossed it at him but his quick reflexes saw him catch it easily.

'Ouch, and after I pulled out all the stops to impress you.' He clutched his chest as though fatally wounded. This man was too much. Too funny, too pretty and way too much of a complication for her heart to be all of a flutter.

'We've had dinner and annoyed your partner. Is it time

to call it a night?' Regardless of the crush she was having on Ed here, she didn't want to outstay her welcome.

The realisation that was what was happening made her glad he couldn't see her blushes. It wasn't that he'd given her any indication that he saw her as anything other than another project. Apart from the way he'd come to her aid in the pool, bought her dinner, twice, and held her hand earlier. *Oh.*

'I hope not.' Before she could overanalyse his every look and touch as much as her own, Ed came to stand beside her. She was so aware of him now the air between them seemed thick and charged with something new.

'I meant what I said earlier. I'd love you to be a mentor here. If you'd prefer something on a full-time basis I'd be happy to take you on at the clinic if you wanted to retrain in a medical capacity?' His belief in her was intoxicating. He really thought she was capable of anything. Such a contrast to those who'd written her off. Including herself.

'I'll think about it. Tell me more about the charity you're setting up. Other than talking to people and getting funding for prosthetics, what else do you have to achieve?' There needed to be something long term to sustain the momentum.

'I had toyed with the idea of a sports event. There are games held for disabled athletes and wounded veterans but I thought we could have something similar for our kids. Eventually branching out into an international event.'

'That's a brilliant idea.' She thought of all the other people who'd had their dreams stolen from them with the loss of their limbs and who needed something else to focus on rather than the life left behind.

By first bringing Hannah to her attention, Ed had given her a renewed sense of purpose and achievement. To the point where she wanted to continue that work. They could do the same for others by introducing this sports programme.

'It would take a lot of organisation and dedication.'

'I'm sure you're up to the challenge.'

'I hope so. I thought we could get some of our well-known athletes with disabilities to help with motivation or even training.' He produced a list of recognisable names.

Now she'd got to know Ed it was clear he thought much more about others than himself. As if he needed any more brownie points in her eyes. At this rate she'd be starting a fan club for him before too long.

'I might be able to get some veterans on board. I met quite a few at the rehabilitation unit.' It occurred to her that, so far, she wasn't contributing a whole lot to this meeting except for making eyes at her colleague.

'That would be fantastic. The more inspirational mentors we have who've experienced the same struggles as our patients, the more they'll benefit.'

'I'll get in touch with some of my old army buddies and see what I can come up with.'

'If you can get a list of people together who are willing to participate I can show it to Giles.'

'I get the impression he doesn't know that this is happening?' Ed had been careful not to mention any of this in his presence.

'He's aware I have an interest in building a charitable arm for the clinic so I would have to consult him. However, I'd prefer to present it to him as a fully formed plan.' He was already scribbling notes, his mind working overtime on how to make it all work. Georgiana admired his dedication. Among other things.

'If you don't mind me asking, why are you doing this? I mean, obviously it's going to help those families who couldn't otherwise afford to fund these things, but what's in it for you?' It wasn't that she thought he was doing it for accolades or recognition for his altruism, but she was interested to know what drove his passion for it. For her it was a deeply personal issue on many levels.

She could relate to those going through the process of amputation and rehabilitation. Ed was already so in demand to those closest to him—she didn't dare include herself in that group—it didn't make sense why he'd take on another time-sucking task.

'I told you about my brother, Jamie? Well, we were told he'd never be able to walk. I think in the old days they wrote you off if you had any sort of disability. Our mother and father put as much time and effort in with him as they could to stimulate him, did physiotherapy with him. If they'd sat back and accepted his limitations he wouldn't be living a normal life now.'

'It was their dedication that pushed him to break those boundaries they were told to expect.' Georgiana suspected it was also down to their loving eldest son, who allowed that to happen. He'd said he'd practically raised his other siblings. Although he didn't see it as a sacrifice of his childhood since it had allowed his brother to have one too.

'Exactly, and I want these children to have every opportunity to do the same. Make every therapy, each new bit of technology that could enrich their quality of life, available to them. Money shouldn't be an obstacle to a child fulfilling their potential. I'm not in this for me or the clinic. This is for every child who has had a difficult start in life like my brother. Every loving family who wants the best for their babies.' His impassioned speech, coming from so deep within his heart, left nowhere for him to hide his feelings. Eyes filled with liquid emotion and voice wobbly, he was drawing from his own heart-wrenching experience watching his brother's fight.

In that moment she could feel his passion, his pain at being so powerless at the time and a vulnerability in him she would never have expected to find. Ed was a man who loved unconditionally.

'It sounds as though you went through a lot.'

'It was Jamie who went through the operations, the bladder problems and the skin irritation. Everything that comes from living with spina bifida. It was my parents who put the extra time into his physical activity. Taking him to all his appointments so he could reach *his* full potential. Not everyone has such supportive parents.'

'Or such an amazing big brother.'

Ed ignored the praise. 'There are kids with the condition who'll never walk, but some have more use of their legs. We saw some families who either didn't want to, or simply couldn't, give the same time and commitment to their children with extra needs. They're the ones who need the most help in later life. Jamie can get about most days without assistance and lives independently. Everyone should have that chance. The same goes for the children who want to get involved in sports and it's only the matter of money stopping them from fulfilling their potential too.'

'That's all very admirable but you don't have to do it all alone, you know.' Georgiana could see and hear what was driving him to work so hard on the behalf of others, but she worried he was doing it at the expense of his own needs. He'd already lost one relationship over it.

'Says Miss Independent,' he countered with a sardonic smile to make her laugh.

'Yeah, I know, but I've had this really irritating voice in my ear for days now making sure I stop feeling sorry for myself and get out of the house.'

'I'm an irritating voice? Wow.'

'You know I'm joking. Without you I'd still be locked in my room doing my Greta Garbo impression.'

Her 'I want to be alone' motto was becoming more like 'I want to be with Ed' these days.

Ed shrugged. 'I could see your pain but I also understood that need to do everything yourself. It seems easier to do things that way. Then you're the only one who gets hurt.'

She related so much to everything he was saying. They'd both chosen to shut themselves off from the world rather than run the risk of getting hurt again. 'Yeah, but look what we've achieved together. Ethan, Hannah's family and that woman at the pool—we worked as a team to save the day. It doesn't always have to be a bad thing to get help or ask for it. You've taught me that.' The smile on her lips was interrupted by the touch of Ed's as he leaned forward and kissed her.

Eyes closed, heart hammering, she shut out everything around her except the soft pressure of his mouth on hers. It was unexpected but it also seemed natural after they'd been so intimate with their emotions. She sighed into the kiss, enjoying the sensation and excitement of exploring this new development with him.

All of a sudden that delicious pressure was released. She opened her eyes to see Ed had moved back, looking stunned, as if he'd been zapped with a thousand volts of electricity.

A creeping sense of unease made its way through her body. Rather than wanting to make mad passionate love to her, he was pulling away from her.

'Ed?' All her insecurities came rushing back. Why on earth had she thought a handsome, kind doctor would be attracted to a woman with so many obvious issues? He'd probably only kissed her because he felt sorry for her. She hadn't been subtle in her admiration of him.

Georgiana got up, wanting to escape any further humiliation, but Ed was there before her, blocking her exit.

Before she could dodge around him and bolt for the door, Ed was cradling her face in his hands, smiling at her. 'Stop talking.'

This time she did as she was told and let him kiss her as if he meant it. As if he'd been holding back the first time and now he was letting the bubbling well of desire come to a boil. His arms were locked around her now, holding her tight to him as his mouth found hers again and again. Hard and insistent. Soft and tender. Sending her mind and body into a whirl.

She melted against him, let him fold her into his strong frame like the delicate princess she was supposed to be. Except princesses weren't supposed to be trying to rip a man's clothes off, desperate for him to remind her what it was to be desirable.

Ed groaned as Georgiana untucked his shirt from his trousers and slid her hand under the fabric. Searching hands found their way confidently across his abdomen. He sucked in a shallow breath at the intimate touch. It had been some time since he'd last engaged in this kind of fevered display. It felt good. He hadn't been sure that she was attracted to him in any way, yet her playful tongue in his mouth, her apparent determination to strip him of his clothes would suggest differently.

Deep down Ed wondered if she was searching for affirmation she was still attractive when she was so hung up about her altered appearance. In satisfying her craving for male interest, he might've been anyone. For him, though, this moment would only have happened because of the strong, courageous person he knew her to be. From the moment he'd seen her pounding the treadmill, defying those who'd tried to steal her independence, her life and her femininity, he'd been lost. There was nothing he wanted more than to clear the contents of his desk onto the floor and take her right here, right now, but that would cause more damage than satisfaction.

An ill-advised tryst would endanger everything they were working towards. Getting in deeper with Georgiana could only end in tears for a multitude of reasons. For a start she was a princess and he, for the want of a better word, was a commoner. It would cause the sort of scandal she wanted to avoid. She was also vulnerable, not in the right head space for romantic involvement. He'd be taking advantage to continue this. With all their plans, they were going to be spending a lot of time together and there was no room for tension between them. Which was bound to happen when he had so many other commitments. History had told him so. He'd been here before, only this time they were both loners. Making a future together as a couple was impossible.

Yet it was hard to put a stop to something he was enjoying so much. Hard being the operative word.

'Georgiana…we…need…to…stop…before…this…

goes…any further,' he said in between passionate kisses. He slipped a hand around her waist, pulled her in for one last, long, lingering lip lock before letting go and stepping back, breathless and wanting.

'Whoa.' He had to hold onto the edge of the desk until he got his bearings again, the adrenaline rush of having her in his arms and subsequently letting go knocking him off kilter.

'What? What's wrong?' Her dilated pupils and kiss-swollen lips only increased his level of guilt because he still wanted to kiss her.

He should've shut this thing down instead of selfishly prolonging it for his satisfaction. It took all his resolve not to oblige her sweet mouth begging for more.

'Nothing's wrong, it's all so very right,' he said regretfully, 'but that's not why we're here.'

'Right,' she said, blinking furiously, trying to focus.

'Neither of us is in a position to start something. You're going through a lot of life changes and, as I've told you, my home situation is already demanding. It isn't a good idea.' He didn't want anything to compromise the work they'd been trying to do together. Georgiana was helping him so much with the gala, then there was the possibility of her working at the clinic. His libido couldn't be his motivating factor when an inevitable break-up would impact on all areas of his working life. There was no way he'd jeopardise the futures of his patients just so he could have some fun.

'It's no big deal. Just a kiss. It doesn't have to mean anything and it certainly shouldn't impact on our plans here. Let's never speak of it again.' She was trying to make light of it but her eyes held that sadness that came from rejection.

It was difficult to ignore what had happened when he was buttoning his shirt and tucking it back into his trousers, his skin scorched where Georgiana had sought him.

'It'll probably take a few days before I can report back on those veteran guests we talked about. I'll get back to you with details when I can.' She was letting him know she'd be out of bounds for a while, which wasn't a bad thing considering what they'd been up to. At least with some space they might be able to forget it, put it down to a lapse in judgement and leave it in the past.

If only he could forget how she tasted on his lips, felt in his arms and set him on fire everywhere she'd touched him.

'Let's get you home.'

Out of my office, out of my head and out of temptation's way.

CHAPTER EIGHT

'I'D LIKE TO talk to you about something.' Missing the company she'd had at the clinic, Georgiana had taken to sitting with her parents in the evening. Ed had put their nocturnal activities on hold under the guise that he needed to finalise arrangements for the gala dinner. It was probably for the best when there could be no future for them together and she didn't want to spoil the relationship they already had.

Since the incident in his office they'd been careful not to be alone together. As agreed, they hadn't referred to it again. It didn't mean his lips weren't still imprinted on hers or that her brain would let her forget how incredibly hot it had been when he'd kissed her.

'Of course.' Her mother set aside the book she'd been reading and gave Georgiana her full attention. She was out of her sick bed now, a little delicate but well enough to get around indoors at least.

Georgiana cleared her throat, anxiety having taken up residence there and threatening to block her airways. In talking to Ed about his family, telling him to reach out for help, she'd have to do the same. To move on she was going to have to confront the past. With her parents.

Asking them to acknowledge their mistakes in order to help her.

'I've been sneaking off to Mr Lawrence's clinic to use the gym equipment there.' She thought honesty was the best way to begin.

'Oh.' Her mother formed a perfect 'O' with her lips.

'I hope that's all you've been doing.' Her father was frowning at her from his armchair, his newspaper now abandoned on his lap.

This conversation had been easier in her head when she'd been rehearsing it.

Georgiana swallowed hard as illicit images flashed guiltily into her mind of the other thing she'd got up to with Ed at the clinic. 'Not all, no.'

'We don't need any scandal.' He scowled at her, his reaction making her all the more eager to have this conversation.

'Everything's entirely above board. I've been helping him out with a patient, that's all, but it has made me think about everything that's happened since my surgery.' She was building up to say things she'd been holding inside for years. The air in the lounge was thick with anticipation, as though the very walls of the palace were waiting for her to speak her truth. Her parents were silent, listening for whatever she had to say. The clock on the mantelpiece behind her ticked away the seconds and the fire crackled and spat in the hearth, urging her to get a move on.

'We're very proud of you, my dear. Everything you've achieved since coming home is, quite frankly, remarkable.' It was unexpected praise from her father, not known for outbursts of sentimentality, but it wasn't what this was about.

'That's the first time you've said that to me.'

'I'm sure it's not, Georgiana. We are astounded by the progress you've made.' Her mother chimed in but the praise was offset by the cast-upon look on her face. As though she were the one who'd been wronged.

'But you've never said it. That's my point. We haven't actually sat down and had a conversation about how this affects us.'

'I think we're managing fine. You're back on your feet and, with Mr Lawrence's help, I'm sure you'll fully recover.'

'No, Mother, I'm never going to fully recover. My leg isn't going to grow back, is it?'

'Don't be facetious, dear.' Her mother sniffed.

'I'm serious. It's gone and I'll have to wear a prosthetic leg for the rest of my life. There's no point in pretending otherwise. We have to accept that or at least acknowledge it.'

'There's no need for that, Georgiana. We know perfectly well—'

'Then for goodness' sake talk about it.' She cut off her father's scolding, years of pent-up emotions breaching all notion of civility. 'I had to hear it from Ed that you were concerned about me enough to ask him to intervene. Why not come to me and ask me what I need from you instead of going behind my back?' Georgiana hadn't realised how much it had hurt to hear that until just now. All that time she'd been here believing she was all alone in her recovery, her parents had kept up that façade of cold indifference to cover their concern. At a time when she'd needed comforting, needed them, more than ever.

Her mother was fidgeting with her hands in her lap, unwilling to meet Georgiana's eye. 'You didn't seem to want us anywhere near you and you're so strong we knew you'd pull through.'

'That didn't mean I didn't need you to tell me you loved me, that you'd be proud of me no matter what happened.'

'It goes without saying, Georgiana.' Her father wasn't any better at understanding her point than her mother.

'No, it doesn't. Did you ever say that to Freddie? No. None of us did. He took it as confirmation we were ashamed of him and his sexuality. To the point he believed we wouldn't miss him if he took his own life.'

'It's not our way to be demonstrative with our feelings. You know what's expected of us, and you, in our position. Blaming us for whatever was going on in poor Freddie's troubled mind isn't going to bring him back.' Her mother was dabbing at her eyes now. Lord forbid she'd be seen shedding a tear over the son she'd lost. Georgiana was beginning to think she was fighting a losing battle instead of making reparations with her parents.

'What's more important to you? Keeping up appearances or your family? You've already lost a son because you wouldn't face up to reality. Freddie was gay and he killed himself because he knew you could never accept it. There, I've said it.' She was breathless as the words poured out of her on a tide of emotion. These were things that should have been dealt with long ago but she was as guilty of hiding from the truth as they were, when she'd joined the army and left the country rather than face this.

'I know, I know.' Her mother was openly weeping now and Georgiana's father went to comfort her.

'The loss of your brother was unbearable, Georgiana, and we didn't see the point in dragging his name through the mud by releasing the details. It didn't mean we were ashamed of him. We wished we'd done more for him, been more, but regret won't change history. Your mother has been worried sick over you too, aware that you're pushing us away. Tell us what we can do so we don't lose you too.' The plea from her father was more than she'd expected when she'd opened this dialogue, but she hoped it was the beginning of the healing process for all of them.

'This. Being honest with me. This is the first time you've acknowledged what happened to Freddie.' A huge weight lifted from her so she no longer felt that chest-crushing pain every time she thought of her brother and the betrayal they'd unknowingly taken part in.

'I think about it every day. I don't want to lose you, Georgiana. This will have to work two ways. You need to tell us how you feel. How we can help. It's going to be a learning curve for us.' The words coming from her mother's lips were everything she'd wanted to hear for so long and her father was nodding his head in agreement with every word. It was going to take time to build the sort of relationship most people had with their families but time she had. They owed it to Freddie to make this work.

'For me too. I'm making a lot of changes. I'm going to take advantage of the second chance I've been given at life. Freddie never got one.'

'We let you both down. Instead of trying to mould you into the people we thought you needed to be, we should have let you be the amazing people you are. I'm sorry we realised that too late for Freddie.' Her mother was sobbing now.

'I'm sure he knew you loved him in your own way.' They'd all made mistakes, none of which could be rectified now. All they could do was hold their hands up and move on. Something her parents were apparently willing to do.

'Our thinking and parenting came with the vision of what we should be as role models. Not what our children needed from us.'

Georgiana understood what her father was saying and realised they'd tried to be supportive even if they hadn't always known how to demonstrate that.

'I appreciate everything you've tried to do for my recovery here. It's really what set me on this path, helping out with the gala and thinking about my future again.' Along with the introduction her mother had engineered between her and Ed. Not that Georgiana was going to give her credit for opening up her heart again when there was every chance it would get battered the next time she met him.

'It's an amazing thing you're doing, helping those children.'

'Thank you, Father. It's not all my doing. Ed... I mean, Mr Lawrence is the one who put it all into motion.'

Despite promises to herself, her feelings for him hadn't diminished since she'd taken some time out from him. She'd justified the break in face-to-face conversation by telling herself she'd confused friendship and compassion for something more. Except she couldn't get him out of her head.

When it came to helping people, he was always first in the queue. A man who could be relied upon to do the right thing. That was exactly why he'd put an end to the fabulous kissing, regardless of how hot and bothered they'd been. They had to put the charity and the clinic before their own wanton needs. Unfortunately.

Now the gala dinner was only a matter of days away she would have to see him again, along with the rest of the world. The publicity was a necessary evil to get the charity off the ground, but she was willing to sacrifice her vanity for the future of their patients.

'You and the doctor seem to be close these days,' her mother said nonchalantly, not fooling Georgiana for a second that she wasn't interested in anything that might be going on.

'You know he's been opening the clinic for me at night and we've had stuff to sort out for the charity.' Georgiana brushed off any insinuation there was something more than professional interest there, but she was finding it impossible to maintain eye contact with the lie.

'He's a good man, I'm told. Very honourable.' That had to have come from her mother for her father to talk about someone he'd never met in such glowing terms.

'Yes, I'm sure it wouldn't have been his idea to sneak you out of here like a thief in the middle of the night.' Her mother's accusation was directed at her.

'Actually, it was a joint enterprise.' Ed had been the first to suggest sneaking her out, but she'd followed up on the idea. They'd both been complicit. It made her laugh to think of the absurd picture their exploits would have made to a spectator. At the time her freedom was everything and Ed had gone along with it all. Who knew what it would've cost him if anything had gone wrong? Yet he'd done everything she'd asked of him. Whatever it took to make her comfortable in a world she thought she no longer knew. He'd been her rock and she was missing him dearly when she'd been so enjoying their time together.

'My rebellious daughter.' Her father chuckled.

The build-up to the gala was exciting but also terrifying. It was going to be her big reveal to the country and she wanted Ed by her side for that. She could get through it on her own—she was strong enough to do anything after all she'd survived. The difference was she wanted him there with her. Everything was better when he was around.

'Is Edward escorting you to the gala, dear?' Again, her mother's astuteness astounded her. She wondered if this was a recent thing now her parents had decided to try harder to be involved in her life or something they'd both chosen to ignore until now.

'He'll be there. We haven't discussed the logistics of it yet.' Since it was being held in her family home, she wouldn't have to make a dramatic entrance. Therefore, she was under no pressure to have a plus one as she arrived at the event. Something she knew would've been under scrutiny and a strain on whatever fragile relationship they had left, if at all.

'Don't you think you should? It's only a matter of days away. You can't simply leave these things to chance. Have you even spoken to a stylist about dressing you for the occasion? You want to make a good impression.'

Georgiana read that as, 'You'll want something to detract from the ugly fake leg.'

'I've chosen my own outfit. I promise I won't embarrass you. This is too important to me.'

'We know. Be true to yourself, that's all we want for you.' Her father retrieved his tumbler of whisky from the mantelpiece and raised it in her honour.

Georgiana frowned. 'Okay, who are you and what have you done with my real parents?'

Instead of taking offence, her mother actually laughed.

'I know it's hard for you to believe, Georgiana, but you're not the only one who's had a life-changing experience. Losing your brother and not knowing if you were going to pull through really made us appreciate the time we have together. We'll do whatever it takes to make you believe that.'

'I believe you,' she said, her voice barely audible. If she'd given them a chance to prove themselves when she'd first returned, they could have had this conversation then. Instead of appreciating the changes they'd made, adapting the house, she'd shut herself off from them. Ignored the changing world around her to focus on the negatives she'd have to live with.

In the same way her injuries had made her reassess her life, they'd also caused her parents to rethink what was important. She was thankful she apparently topped that list. Not many had the support she'd taken for granted until now.

The emotionally charged family love-in was in danger of becoming awkward. She feared there was a group hug coming, or, worse, a mass sobbing. The attempt her parents were making to understand her state of mind and implement changes to their attitude showed they were doing their best to relate to her. Trying to break out of the old regime, which didn't fit with the modern world. That was all she could ask of them.

Ed was tearing his hair out trying to manage everything at once. With the gala only two days away he was attempting to organise his time better between work and family. He wasn't succeeding. His dad had been on the phone about the hospital appointment he'd promised to drive him to. He had patients queuing up for consultations, which was a good thing businesswise, but he was time poor at present.

It didn't mean he wouldn't give anything to be with Georgiana again. By kissing her he'd been playing with fire and he was the one left burning. He should've stopped it but he'd fed the fire. Now he was suffering the after effects. He was missing her and had even resorted to texting her an inane message asking what colour she'd be wearing on the night so he could co-ordinate with her. Just so he could have some sort of communication with her. Not that she'd replied.

He'd left himself the lion's share of the organising to do, with Georgiana doing her bit at a distance from him. Goodness knew he was out of his depth organising an event at the palace to kick-start a brand-new charity. Talk about pressure. Pressure he'd put himself under by not sharing the load with anyone. She was right, he had to learn to reach out to people where he could and stop doing everything by himself. It wasn't a weakness to ask for help and certainly didn't make him any less of a good son or brother if his every waking moment wasn't devoted to them. Jamie was a grown man now, living his own life Perhaps it was about time he did too.

He thought about Georgiana and what she was prepared to put herself through to help him and the charity and was humbled by her courage once more.

It was one of the many, many qualities he admired in her. If nerves were getting the better of him, he could only imagine how she was feeling. Yet he knew she'd come through for everyone concerned. He hoped, in being open about what had happened to her, she'd benefit as much as those they were raising funding and awareness for.

He heard some commotion out in Reception and attempted to ignore the increasing level of noise, hoping Giles or Security would take care of it. There was too much for him to do without getting into a row out there. When the sound of feet thundered down the corridor, he knew he'd have to go and investigate.

'What on earth is going on out here?' he demanded as he made his way through the growing crowd of staff and patients. Even though he'd been preoccupied he was sure he'd have heard a fire alarm going off. Although the gasps and excited whispers whooshing around the crowd led him to believe that nothing life-threatening had happened.

'Excuse me. Pardon me.' He eased his way through to the eye of the storm, where he was confronted by a mass of mobile phones vying for a photo op. Bewildered, he looked to Giles, who was grinning like a loon beside him. 'Have I missed something?'

'I think Christmas has come early for us.' He gestured towards the door, where everyone's attention was focused.

In that second Ed was as spellbound as all those around him. A smiling Georgiana was holding court, resplendent in a chic white trouser suit and surrounded by men in black with earpieces and walkie talkies.

She hadn't spotted him yet, busy chatting with a young man in a wheelchair who was clearly as infatuated with Georgiana as Ed. She always looked beautiful to him, but she was glowing as children lined up to say hello to her. He didn't know what had prompted an official royal visit but he was smiling from ear to ear because of it.

She was agreeing enthusiastically with whatever the teenage girl next to her was saying and gave her a hug before straightening up again. That was when Ed caught her eye. His breath caught somewhere between his lungs and his throat when she beamed back at him.

'Sorry about all the disruption, Mr Lawrence. I was coming to pay you a visit but the parents decreed I bring the circus to town with me this time.' She shrugged apologetically.

'No problem. We can go to my office if you want. I think there's room for your bodyguards.' After their last encounter he wouldn't be surprised if she'd brought them along for protection from him.

'I'm sure we can manage a conversation without them.' Her knowing wink said she knew exactly what he was referring to but she wasn't holding anything against him. More was the pity.

'You know where to find me when you're ready.' He began to make his way back to his office, expecting her to take her time with her appreciative audience. Those clamouring to meet her were sure to give her a confidence boost after her time out of the limelight. It was also a good trial run to stabilise her nerves before her big night.

'Thanks, everyone. It's lovely to meet you all. I hope to see you again soon,' he heard her say before following him down the corridor.

Her minders were herding the crowd back, giving her some room for a conversation in private. It was only on seeing her in action that Ed remembered who it was he was dealing with. Georgiana Ashley was a princess and he'd had the audacity to kiss her like a man possessed.

He kept a few steps ahead, so he was able to make some attempt at tidying his desk before she came in.

'Take a seat,' he said, pointing to the chair on the other

side of the desk, maintaining an acceptable distance between them.

She closed the door and sat down. 'This wasn't supposed to be a whole "thing". This is why I resorted to sneaking out. It's much less hassle.'

'But this is safer. I do think you've made everyone's day here. Including Giles. You know news of this visit is going to spread like wildfire?' So far she'd been so opposed to the idea of people even knowing she was back in the country they'd been playing hide and seek with palace security. This move was on the very opposite end of that scale.

'I'm aware of that. Why do you think I didn't turn up in my workout gear?' She rapped her knuckles on the prothesis hidden beneath her trousers.

'I suppose it will garner interest leading up to the fundraising campaign.' People were going to want to know why she'd come to this specific clinic and, as much as he didn't want her to get hurt, they needed the publicity. Every penny counted in helping these families.

'I thought that too.'

'Oh.' He was at a loss for words that she'd gone to all this trouble in person when they'd been conducting all of their conversations over the phone since the last time they'd been alone in here.

'I thought I'd pop in and say hello before the big night. I wasn't sure what you'd be wearing, though, when you said we'd be colour co-ordinated. I'm wearing blue, so does that mean you'll be in a blue bow tie and cummerbund or were you going to go the whole hog in a matching sky-blue tuxedo?' Teasing him with that mischievous look on her face wasn't doing anything to prevent him wanting to kiss her again.

'I was thinking head-to-toe blue. Maybe with a side split in the trousers.' One kiss and he was completely gaga over her. He was pretty sure he wasn't managing to hide it either.

'Should I come pick you up? Hire a limousine? Buy a corsage?' He hadn't been on the dating scene for a while and he didn't know the etiquette for courting a princess. Not that they were dating, but he would be escorting her.

She was laughing at him again. He obviously wasn't cut out for the escort business either. 'It's not the prom, Ed, and I live at the palace, remember? I'll see you there.'

'Right. I'll get there early to help with the catering or whatever else needs doing.'

'There's no need. My parents have everything in hand. They've been very supportive with regard to the event.'

Ed didn't know if he'd ever not be preoccupied again when in the same room as Georgiana, that kiss never to be forgotten.

'It sounds as though you're making real roads to getting your relationship back on track. Excellent news. I'm so pleased for you.' If she had her parents to turn to again the onus would no longer be on him to provide support and that was what he wanted, wasn't it? That he wasn't spending so much time thinking about her. Then why did he have a sudden sinking feeling in the pit of his stomach, thinking this gala night could be the end of something beautiful?

'Speaking of which, I should get back and help organise the flower arrangements, seating and all of those important details my mother will be freaking out about.' She rose to go and, as good manners decreed, Ed stood to open the door for her. Before she left she placed a hand lightly on his chest and kissed him on the cheek. A barely there, ghost of kisses past, which still managed to make a significant impact. She hesitated to move away and Ed held his breath. If she decided to kiss him again he was no stronger to resist than he had been the last time.

When she did step back and finally walk away all the oxygen in the room and in his lungs went with her.

He was in big, big trouble.

CHAPTER NINE

'I THOUGHT YOU might like to wear this.' Georgiana's mother placed the intricate silver tiara on her head. With delicate entwined vines and leaves, encrusted with tiny diamonds and sapphires, it wasn't as ostentatious as some of the crown jewels but none the less beautiful.

'Thank you. I look like a real princess now.' She thought about little girls like Hannah who would be expecting her to look the part and she had to admit this was one perk of the job.

'It was your grandmother's from when she was young and beautiful like you.' Her mother kissed her forehead and Georgiana felt the love radiating from her in waves. Being at home these days was so much more pleasurable now they were all doing their utmost to communicate and pull together as a family. Although tonight she was flying solo.

'I'm nervous.' This was her first official royal engagement but she also had the added pressure of introducing the charity for Ed. She didn't want to mess anything up for him.

'I still get stage fright about these things but such is the life of royalty. Anyway, I have great faith in you. You'll dazzle everyone in the room.' Her mother kissed

Georgiana on both cheeks once she'd finished her pep talk as her daughter prepared to go into battle with her insecurities.

Georgiana was grateful for the support and would never dream of taking it for granted again when it had played such a huge part in her recovery so far. When she'd first woken after the amputation, she'd never have believed she could walk out onto a stage in a room full of people to tell her story. She hadn't done it all on her own either.

'I really want to make you and Ed proud.'

Her mother pulled her into a hug. 'You're the best thing in our lives. We love you very much and you make us proud every single day just by being you.'

She released Georgiana from her grasp again. 'As for Edward, surely he's as smitten with you as you are with him. How couldn't he be when you're so amazing?'

'Mother!' she spluttered. 'I've told you, we work together, that's all.' Her conscience burned with the lie and the memory of their clinch.

'Uh-huh.' Her mother's arched eyebrow said she wasn't convinced by her protestation otherwise.

Deep down Georgiana knew what she was saying was true when she'd fallen hard for Ed.

'I should probably go down.'

As per her mother's advice she'd waited until all the guests had arrived before she made her entrance. Along with being protocol for the royal family to be the last to arrive, it meant all the gawping and gossiping would be over in one go.

After another hug and a deep breath, she descended the staircase and waited as her presence was announced to the assembled guests in the grand ballroom. She'd improved enough over the weeks that she was steady on her feet but she longed to be on Ed's arm for that extra security.

'Her Royal Highness, Princess Georgiana.'

She caught the end of the announcement, heard the clatter of chairs as people got to their feet as she made her way to the front of the room.

The number of curious faces staring back at her was overwhelming. She waved and smiled but she was close to walking back out. Then she saw Ed on the stage, handsome in his black tux and clapping her approach. She focused on him and glided past the round tables occupied by patients, veterans and possible donors. He met her on the steps and offered his arm, which she clung to gratefully.

'You look amazing,' he whispered into her ear, giving her that final boost before facing her demons.

'Did you change your mind about the blue suit?'

'I decided it wasn't my colour. It looks so much better on you.' He was full of much-needed compliments.

She took her place at the podium, her hesitation magnified at the microphone before she finally found her voice, 'I may look a little different from the last time I saw you. I've had some cosmetic surgery since then.'

To illustrate her point she stuck out her leg and the cloud of billowy fabric slid away to reveal her prosthetic to the crowd. She'd chosen the sky-blue, off-shoulder number deliberately. It was embroidered down one side with silver flowers and sequins, which spilled down onto layers of chiffon. The intentional, sexy side split was on the right-hand side, effectively revealing her prosthetic leg to the world and facing the last of her worries. There was no going back now.

The combination of awkward laughs at her joke and gasps was better than dead air. This wasn't about feeling sorry for herself and she didn't want people to do it for her either. The event and the charity were about improving the lives of the children like her. It was supposed to be an uplifting speech so she remained positive about the things they could do for children who'd lost limbs due to accident or illness. She kept it short with only a small reference as to how she'd lost her leg to prevent any speculating.

Between her and Ed, they'd agreed she would give a brief introduction to the charity and her involvement, before the dinner. He was in charge of the later presentation complete with moving footage of patient stories and their plans for a national sports competition. So as she came to the end of her spiel she'd be able to enjoy the rest of the evening along with everyone else.

'If there's one thing Mr Lawrence and his clinic have shown me it's that missing a limb doesn't have to mean missing out on life. With your financial support, Love on a Limb can make this a reality for dozens of children who otherwise might not have the opportunity to explore their full potential. A donation tonight could be the making of a sports star tomorrow. Please give generously and support our children's right to a future of hope. Thank you.'

Her mouth was dry as she gave a bow and walked back across the stage to thunderous applause. She was exhilarated by the reception she'd received and Ed almost had to catch her before she floated off the side of the steps. He gave her a glancing kiss on the cheek.

'You were amazing out there. A real asset to the charity and a credit to your family.'

'Do you think so?' She was no longer so concerned

with the reaction to her physical appearance as how that would translate into donations. Without those she wouldn't have achieved anything worthwhile.

'I know so. You're an amazing woman, Georgiana.' The deep timbre of Ed's voice reached inside her soul and she trembled beneath his admiring gaze.

'You're not so bad yourself, Mr Lawrence. As I'm sure you'll prove to me later tonight. I mean, to everyone here.' Her thoughts strayed somewhere where they weren't being watched by an audience.

Catching her wayward train of thought, Ed gave a wry smile. 'Just give me the word and I'm all yours.'

Georgiana was glad the guests were too preoccupied with the arrival of their first course to witness the flirty exchange going on backstage. As Ed escorted her to their table food was the last thing on her mind. His touch, all consuming. She didn't know how she was expected to get through the night without throwing herself at him. Especially when he kept looking at her as though she were the main course.

Even without knowing the final total raised or the number of sponsors signed, Ed considered the night a success. They'd delivered the message about the families who needed help, appealing to those who could afford to do so, and outlining the things they hoped to achieve.

Georgiana had enchanted those with fat wallets using her natural charm and elegance. Going from veterans with her own tales and engaging with the children and their families, letting them know they were very much a part of the event, she was everything everyone needed her to be. Only he got to see the real Georgiana in her workout gear, full of insecurities and, at times, innuendo and he considered himself damn lucky.

From what he'd seen everyone had had fun. Fantastic raffle prizes had been donated and won, dinner eaten and conversation had flowed. With the business aspect of raising money out of the way, it was time for him and Georgiana to enjoy what was left of the night.

They'd brought in a band to end the evening on a high. As they began to play their soft, smooth melody, Ed reached out a hand to Georgiana, who was about to take her seat after another round of schmoozing.

'Would you care to dance?'

'Pardon? Are you sure you're asking the right person?'

'The only person I want to dance with here. I'm sure you know how to do it better than I can.'

'I haven't done it since my operation. I'm not sure I can.' There was panic in her eyes but she took his hand all the same. That display of trust in him touched Ed's heart. He didn't want to do anything with the potential to embarrass or hurt her, but he thought she should enjoy every second of the night. It was as much hers as the charity's.

'I hear it's like riding a bike.' It was the sort of comment guaranteed a sardonic response but it was designed so she'd be too busy slamming his joke to worry about anything else.

He was right—they were on the dance floor before she was mid eye-roll.

'Is everyone watching?' she asked as he took her in his arms.

'I hope so. I didn't put on this tux to be ignored.'

She slapped his shoulder but she was laughing, the last of her anxiety slipping away.

Once they'd led the way, others followed until the floor was full and they were lost in one another's arms without a care.

'It's been a good night.' She was resting her head on his shoulder, the sweet scent of her perfume invading his senses and filling his lungs.

'I'm glad you've enjoyed it and that I was here to share it with you.'

'You know, it doesn't have to end here…'

He looked down at her to make sure she was saying what he thought he was hearing. 'Are you sure?'

There was no point in denying he wanted nothing more than to spend the night with her any more. They'd gone past that and with the gala out of the way they might be able to spend more quality time together. He didn't know where things would lead to, only that he wanted to give it a try.

'I've handed back the crown jewels, I've chatted with my old army buddies and stopped hiding the truth of who I am from them and everyone else here. I think I'm ready for bed now.' The nibbling at her bottom lip gave away something of her nerves but she nodded her head regardless. He grabbed her by the hand and led her off the floor.

'In that case, let's get these people their coats.'

The one thing he could hear above the roar of blood in his ears was Georgiana's giggle. It only made his heart beat twice as fast and his patience last half as long.

He didn't know what was happening to him, but for the first time in his life he was making himself and his needs a priority. It might seem selfish but Georgiana was the only good thing to come into his life in a long time and he didn't want to lose her when a few days without her felt like an eternity.

This could be his one chance at happiness and nothing was going to get in his way when she'd made it explicitly clear she wanted him too.

'What do we have to do to get these people to leave?' Ed was a warm breeze in Georgiana's ear but he still made her shiver.

'Shh. They've paid out a lot of money tonight. We can't very well tell them to clear off because we have better things to do.'

'Like each other,' he growled and made her melt at the animalistic tone of his desire.

As time went on, her bravado was beginning to ebb away, letting anxiety flow back in. She wanted to sleep with Ed; it was the next step for them. It was the personal significance she was having trouble with. This would be the first time she'd been naked with anyone since her life, and her body, had changed for ever. Though she wouldn't want it to happen with anyone else, it was nerve-wracking having sex with someone for the first time and this was so much more than that. There were other things to consider besides her desire for him. Not least how she would adjust to her new lopsided body during the act.

'Princess Georgiana would like to offer her gratitude and say her goodbyes,' Ed announced to those still congregated in the foyer.

'Goodnight, everyone. Thank you all for your support,' she managed to say before being whisked off back towards the ballroom.

The room was thankfully empty now. It had been a lot to go from isolation in her room to hosting such a large crowd in a few weeks. Although it hadn't been as scary on the night as she'd imagined. Most people simply wanted to know how her prosthesis worked and whether or not it was painful. Given the reasons they were all here tonight, she'd been only too happy to engage in those conversations.

Ed closed the door behind them and before she had a chance to speak he had her pinned against the closed door, kissing her the way she'd been imagining all night.

She groaned against his lips with the satisfaction of tasting him again, of having his body pressed tightly to hers. He moved his mouth across her cheek, kissed her neck, and sucked her earlobe into his mouth. *Oh.*

'Are you sure it's okay for me to stay? I don't want to cause you any problems,' he said, kissing the spot behind her ear that sent tiny electric shocks to every one of her erogenous zones.

'I'll just say you had too much to drink and couldn't drive home. There are dozens of bedrooms you could've stayed in if anyone asks.' They hadn't done much to hide their blossoming romance and she was sure tongues would be wagging about the princess and her handsome surgeon, but she didn't care. She'd spent too much time worrying about what people thought and Ed had shown her how much more fun she could be having if she concentrated on what it was she wanted. Tonight, it was him. In her bed. With her.

'As long as you're sure.'

'I love that you're being a gentleman but you should know by now I'm a woman who knows her own mind.' She reached up and tugged on his bow tie, loosening it along with her inhibitions.

He grabbed her wandering hands with his before she started undoing his shirt buttons.

'I get that, but I think we'd be more comfortable in the bedroom. I don't want to rush this in case someone finds us. I want to take my time with you.'

It had crossed her mind that it might be less awkward as her first time since the amputation to do it here, clothed, standing and quickly but his promise to take things slowly was too much to resist.

'Do you think they've all gone yet?' She was breathless with desire; all social etiquette faded into insignificance when he was kissing her all over.

'I bloody hope so.'

The ache inside her was so great she could only agree with his statement.

They checked the coast was clear and, with only catering staff zipping about collecting their stuff and the band loading their instruments into the van parked outside, they'd got their wish.

'Bedtime?' Ed slipped his arms around her waist and claimed her, setting off fireworks in her belly.

'Bedtime,' she confirmed, entwining her fingers around his so he knew this was a joint decision. He brought her hand to his mouth and kissed it. This was going to be all right. Ed made everything feel good.

Georgiana didn't remember climbing the huge staircase hand in hand with the man in front of her. The promise of what was to come propelled her in a daze, so she practically glided to her bedroom with him. The place where she'd been seeking solace for the past few months was now going to be the site for another historic event. One she hoped was going to be more positive and fun to look back on.

He tilted her chin up and placed a kiss on her mouth. A long, tender, swoon-worthy display of his intentions for the night. She was already a puddle of arousal before they'd even got naked.

With her help his jacket hit the floor. She whipped the loose bow tie from around his neck and tugged his shirt free of his trousers. All the time not taking her mouth from his. She needed that contact to stop her from worrying about what was coming next. As long as he was kissing her, wanting her, everything would be all right.

She heard the rasp of her zip and felt the air on her bare skin. Her breathing, which had been shallow and rapid, now seemed to have stopped altogether. This was the moment she'd thought she'd never be confident enough to experience. She'd thought she'd never be attractive to another man again. Ed's body, pressed so tightly against her, was disputing that for her.

Her hands were frozen, still clutching his shirt as he eased her dress away. She watched his eyes follow it to the floor. Not once flinching or showing anything but appreciation and lust. She could breathe again.

'You're beautiful.'

Once she let the compliment sink in she saw no reason not to repay the favour, unbuttoning his shirt and tossing it on the floor.

'In a hurry, are we?'

'Only to get you naked.' Her bravado was returning full force as she exposed him piece by piece.

'Be my guest,' he said, letting her strip him completely.

It was important for her to have some control of this moment and divesting him of his clothes was the best way to do that for now.

She'd seen him at the pool, yet the taut muscle and smooth contours of his body were still a revelation. While she was busy ogling him, Ed undid her strapless bra and buried his head between her bare breasts. If he wasn't careful, he was going to render both her legs useless when she was becoming a liquid mess beneath his touch.

'Ed, you're killing me here.' It was all she could do to remain upright, giving her no chance to explore his body as much as she wanted.

His response was to knead her breasts and suck hard on her nipples until her knees finally buckled. He caught her and carried her over to the bed. His every gesture, their every interaction since they'd met had been building to this and she was ready to burst with the heady anticipation of the night ahead.

He slowly inched her silky knickers down her legs until she was completely naked and open to him. There was only one thing spoiling everything for her. At this time her prosthetic seemed ugly and unnecessary but she didn't know how to remove it without spoiling the mood. Ed slid a hand there, attempting to remove it for her, but that was a humiliation too far. She tried to stop him but he silenced her with another kiss.

'Let me. I've done this a hundred times. Not in this scenario but you know what I mean.' They broke any potential awkwardness with their laughter. Ed's touch was so deft and gentle she hardly noticed what he was doing until he did the unthinkable. He kissed his way along her injured leg as though it was simply another part of her to be explored and appreciated. Those ridges and bumps where the surgeons had sewn her back together were now a map for his lips to follow. So gentle, so loving in a place more intimate than any other part of her body. Somewhere no one else had ever touched her so tenderly. Ed turned the most damaged part of her into something beautiful. A part of her she no longer needed to be ashamed about.

Tears burned behind her eyes but only for a second as he kissed his way towards her inner thigh and made her forget what was making her so emotional. Her head and her body now just a mass of sensations to enjoy.

The quick darting motion of his tongue along her sensitive skin made her quiver, her limbs trembling more the closer he came to her most sensitive spot. When he found her wet and waiting, he met her with his tongue, sending shudders of exquisite satisfaction wracking through her whole body. She was completely at his mercy, waiting for his next touch. He delved deeper, pushing the limits of her restraint, seeking only her pleasure.

The bedsheets were bunched in her hands as she clung to the last of her sanity. Then he hit that perfect spot that made it impossible to hold back the flood any longer.

She cried out until her throat was raw as Ed created wave after wave of pure pleasure at the tip of his tongue. He didn't stop his pursuit until he'd wrung every last drop of her climax from her.

When she came back down to earth she was dazed and unable to move a muscle. 'My body's like lead.' She giggled as the man between her legs raised his head.

'Is that a good thing?' He gave her that cheeky grin of his, full of pride at his accomplishment.

'You know it is.' She was sapped of all her strength, weak from the sheer force of her climax, and she couldn't have been happier about it.

'You're looking particularly smug, Princess.'

'So are you, Doctor.'

'And we haven't even had the main event yet.' He crept further up her body, completely covering her with his, bracing himself either side of her.

At the promise of more, certain parts of her came back to life, reawakened by the tender, loving kiss he left on her lips. She wrapped herself around him and he buried himself inside her with a satisfied grunt.

Her gasp as he filled her was only the beginning. Each stroke as their bodies collided again and again, all the accompanying kisses he gave her, were met with a satisfied moan.

Ed was so attentive to needs she wasn't aware she had, spoiling her, giving her everything she wanted and more. She'd never felt more like a princess in her life.

They hadn't discussed the future beyond tonight but she didn't see how they could carry on as though nothing had happened after this, when he'd changed her whole world.

Until tonight Ed had told her he hadn't wanted to mix business with pleasure. Family came first, work a close second and relationships didn't even make the list. Yet Georgiana knew when she was with him, she wasn't a misfit with no place in the world. She was a mentor, a medic, an ambassador, and along with all that he made her feel like the most desirable woman in the world.

As she and Ed reached that peak of absolute bliss together, their cries of ecstasy echoing each other, she knew she'd lost another piece of herself. Her heart.

CHAPTER TEN

GEORGIANA'S FIRST INSTINCT when she woke up was to reach for Ed. She had a smile on her face, remembering their conscientious exploring of the limits and logistics of an amputee's sex life. Until she was confident it didn't make the slightest bit of difference about her leg when making love with him. She was awestruck to discover that she still had a fully functioning sex drive and he made her feel as though she was the most important person in the world every time he'd kissed her during the night. Her body was thoroughly ravished and pleasantly numb this morning.

'Morning, sleepyhead,' she said, trying to rouse the naked figure sprawled across her bed. As pleasant as the sight was, they couldn't lie here all day.

'Hmm…?' A drowsy Ed rolled closer to her, his eyes still closed. It was no wonder he was exhausted after she'd put him through his paces last night.

'We should get up.' Her sigh was filled with longing and regret that their night together had to come to an end.

'Why? We still have some time before we have to go to work,' he mumbled into the pillow.

The way he said it so casually made her smile. As if they were any other couple about to start their day together. It had taken some time and soul-searching but she had a role now. One that was about more than just making personal appearances and news headlines. She had a purpose again. The talk with her parents and, later, the gala had given her so much hope about her place in the world. Okay, it wasn't the one she'd had, or had expected to have, but she wanted to capitalise on her sense of achievement.

Ed had given her the platform and confidence to address her issues in public but it was down to her to continue the momentum. There was so much more she could achieve using her position. She saw no reason why she shouldn't become an advocate for other charities and use her voice to get recognition where it was needed. As a representative of injured veterans and the amputee community she could do a lot to raise the profiles and funds for those who needed it. After months of floundering, not knowing where she'd be wanted and accepted, Georgiana believed she'd found a new path that would incorporate the princess and the soldier in her. She was keen to embark on this new life outside these walls. The one she'd been avoiding for so long.

'With everything that happened last night, I'm going to have to release a press statement.'

Ed snapped awake, his big blue eyes sparkling with mischief. 'There's really no need. I know I was good but you don't need to tell the whole world about it.'

Georgiana rolled her eyes. 'You've every right to be full of yourself this morning. Last night was…amazing. But I was talking about the gala. Word will be out about my injuries and I'll have to work with the palace to give an official statement about what happened and what it means to my position as Princess and next in line to the throne.'

'Surely you have a little time to fool around first?' He slipped his hand under the covers and swept it over the curve of her hips.

She groaned, tempted to surrender to her libido in place of her common sense. 'I really wish I did, but I have an appointment with my aftercare team first thing too.' Something her visits to the clinic had prompted her to do. She'd seen the importance of having regular check-ups and maintaining contact with the team who'd taken care of her. Her appointment today was to check out some recent discomfort she'd been experiencing. Probably the result of the extra workouts and busier lifestyle putting more strain on her body. No doubt they would tell her to take it easy.

Ed immediately sat up and cupped her face in his hands, his eyes searching her face for the truth. 'Is everything okay?'

The concern she saw and heard from him sent her heart fluttering and she leaned into his touch.

'I'm fine. It's just a check-up.'

'Do you want me to come with you? I could move a few things around—'

'Honestly, there's nothing to worry about, but I don't want to miss the appointment. We really should get moving.'

'You want me to go?' He pulled her in for another one of those deliciously long and passionate kisses she was trying—and failing—to deny herself.

'No, but if you don't I'll never leave this bed.'

'Is that such a bad thing?' He was kissing his way down her throat now and nibbling away at her defences.

She gave it considerable thought and came to the conclusion that she'd quite happily spend a lifetime in bed with Ed.

But could he spend a lifetime with her?

Georgiana wished she could live in his arms for ever and the pang of longing lasted after he'd dressed and left her bedroom looking dishevelled and gorgeous.

The news from the hospital sent her into something of a tailspin.

'Complications…bone spurs…further surgery.'

One appointment reminded her that nothing was permanent and an amputation didn't mean her health problems were over. Resuming her royal duties, training for a new job and a future with Ed could be in jeopardy and she didn't think she'd recover from losing everything again.

It wouldn't be as serious an operation as before. The abnormal bone that had grown around the end of her amputated limb was causing pressure points where it met her prosthetic. If refitting didn't help, she was going to have to have surgery to remove the excess bone. The reality meant she was likely going to have ongoing problems and pain for the rest of her days.

She'd gone straight to the clinic to find Ed when her test results and X-rays had not been favourable. He was the one she wanted to go to. In keeping with their agreement, she'd let her parents know too but Ed was the one she needed to comfort her and tell her everything would be all right.

Although, this latest information might alter everything between them. They already had things to work out, when he seemed to have so little time to devote to a relationship. She didn't know what this latest development would mean to them as a couple. So determined was she to speak to him on the matter that even when she was told that Mr Lawrence was at his parents' place, Georgiana got her driver to track down the address.

'I think I'll be fine on my own,' she insisted to her team when they pulled up outside the unremarkable detached cottage far enough outside the city she was sure she wouldn't be spotted.

There was no sign of Ed's car outside the house but she made her way up the path regardless. If someone was at home, perhaps they could tell her where to find him.

It took so long for someone to come to the door after she rang the bell she'd convinced herself the house was empty. Then a dark shape behind the frosted glass moved slowly towards her.

Thankfully she recognised the senior Mr Lawrence who opened the door even if he'd aged considerably since she'd last seen him. His body was thinner, his complexion paler and his bent posture gave away the deterioration in his health in the intervening years.

'Mr Lawrence, I'm so sorry for intruding into your afternoon but I was looking for your son. Is Edward here?'

'Miss Georgiana. How lovely to see you. Come in, come in.' He shuffled back to make room for her so Georgiana didn't see a choice but to follow him inside.

He pointed her towards the door down the hallway, presumably because she'd get there faster than he would. She saw the stairlift as she passed inside and wondered why on earth they wouldn't move somewhere all on one level when he clearly had mobility issues.

'Marg. Miss Georgiana has come to visit,' he called ahead to warn of her appearance.

When Georgiana walked into the unbearably warm

lounge she found Mrs Lawrence struggling out of her armchair. 'There's no need to get up. I just came to see if Edward was here.'

'Sit down and I'll go and put the kettle on. You just missed him. He was over earlier doing a few errands for us. We can't get about as much as we used to. Edward's a good boy. He's gone to pick up our prescriptions from the chemist.'

'Will he be back?' Georgiana followed her into the kitchen, where Mr Lawrence was pulling laundry out of the washing machine into a basket. The effort making him wheeze breathlessly.

'Let me do that for you,' she said, unable to stand by and watch without offering a helping hand.

'It's fine. I'll leave it there for our Edward. He'll peg it out for us when he comes back.' He straightened up as much as he could.

'Edward clearly takes very good care of you both.' She knew Ed wouldn't consider helping out a chore at all. It was apparent how much he loved his parents and he would do anything for them. But care for two elderly parents was a lot for one person to take on—could she really add to that?

'Oh, yes. He's always here for us. I wish we didn't have to rely on him so much, but age is getting the better of us these days. He's such a good son.' Mrs Lawrence fussed around getting her best china out and piling a selection of biscuits onto a plate.

Georgiana nodded as sadness wrapped her in its embrace. Ed had a full life. There for anyone who needed him but it didn't seem fair asking him to make room for her too. Especially when she was facing another surgery and an uncertain future. What if he was with her, caring for her, and something happened to his parents? Would he ever forgive her for diverting his focus? She wouldn't be able to live with herself knowing she'd caused him any unnecessary pain.

Mrs Lawrence let her husband carry the tea tray into the lounge. Georgiana followed with an even heavier heart than the one she'd arrived with.

She made small talk with his parents while they drank their tea and even forced down a biscuit to keep them happy. Though it was hard to swallow down along with the realisation of the situation. Ed was a man devoted to his parents and his patients. He had precious little time as it was and, when she faced potentially numerous health problems for the rest of her life, as much as it pained her, she couldn't expect him to dedicate any of that time to her.

'It was lovely to meet you both. Sorry I missed Edward but I really should be going.' She got to her feet, ready to escape the suburban life Ed enjoyed and she knew she could never have.

When Ed's father made an attempt to get up from his chair she held up a hand to stop him. 'Don't trouble yourself. I can let myself out. Thank you for your hospitality.'

They said their goodbyes and she promised to pass on their best wishes to her parents before she was able to finally make her way out. Only to find Ed pulling up outside the front of the house.

He got out of his car clutching a paper bag and wearing a smile on his face that unfortunately Georgiana couldn't replicate.

There was no way of knowing how long recovery would take after her surgery this time around. She might have to adjust all over again. Now she'd met Ed's parents, had confirmation he was stretched to breaking point already, it made sense for her to bow out of the picture. Especially when she was going to be incapacitated again for goodness knew how long. He already took care of everyone, his parents, his siblings, his patients; he didn't need someone else to look after. She couldn't add to that and she wouldn't ask him to. He'd already given her so much. She was stronger and more confident in herself because of him. But she couldn't keep relying on Ed to get her through. Some things she would have to do alone.

Ed was over the moon to see Georgiana. Leaving her bed this morning was one of the hardest things he'd ever had to do. Last night had been amazing, more than he could ever have dreamed of. Passionate, loving, experimental were all ways he could've described their first time and he certainly didn't want it to be their last.

Once she resumed her royal duties they were going to have to find some way of carving out some quality time together if this was going to work—and he wanted it to work.

Until meeting Georgiana he'd thought a relationship meant taking him away from his family, but he could see now he'd conditioned himself to be indispensable to everyone when they could survive perfectly well without him by their side twenty-four-seven. It could've been residual tendencies from his youth or a desire to spend the time with his parents that he'd missed out on when they were caring for Jamie, but he knew things had to change. It didn't mean he loved his family any less. Georgiana had gone to a different country to get away from her parents, but with some space and honest conversations their relationship seemed to be stronger than ever.

He realised he'd fallen for her and these days he lived for the moments they had together. It didn't mean he had to neglect anyone, he just had to make some changes to give them a chance as a couple. He'd begun with asking the pharmacist to deliver his parents' prescriptions from now on, taking advantage of a service he'd never considered before.

He was also planning to speak to his parents about hiring some home help. Choosing non-essential errands over the potential of a new relationship with Georgiana wasn't an option. Granted, good sex alone didn't equate to anything long term, but if he wasn't honest with himself about wanting a future with her he'd lose her.

He hadn't realised that until today. If he didn't take a long hard look at what he was doing with his life he could end up alone. He'd never been happier than when they were together. She represented parts of his life he'd neglected for too long—fun, companionship and love.

'Georgiana? What brings you here? Did you need me for something?'

'Nothing important.' She didn't seem as enthused to see him even though she must have come here to find him.

When he went to give her a hug she shrank back. It was such a change from last night when the only place she'd seemed at home was in his arms.

'Is something wrong?'

Her expression shuttered. 'We can't do this, Ed. You can't clone yourself to be in two or three different places at once. I knew the score from the start. Relationships come at the bottom of your priorities and now I... I'll put a strain on you even more. The clinic and the charity are too important to let personal issues interfere with your work.'

She sounded so cold, as if she'd already made her mind up that this was over, that Ed didn't know how to fight back. 'Why don't we go inside and talk?'

Georgiana shook her head. 'I've just taken tea with your parents and, if anything, it's made me see how much they need you. You'll be better off without me making demands on your time too.'

'My relationships in the past didn't last because it wasn't you I was with. I'm going to make changes, to make time for us. You know we could have something good. Last night was proof of that.' He went to reach for her again but Georgiana stepped back. For the first time in adulthood he had a real taste of how it felt to be alone.

'How much of a future do we really have, Ed? I'm next in line to the throne. When the time comes are you really going to give everything up to come and live my life? How can I even ask you to do that? How can I ask you to care for me if…?' Her hand swept down to her prosthesis as she trailed off. For the briefest of moments, he thought he saw pain in her eyes, but then her cool demeanour returned. 'We're dreaming if we think one night together means we're compatible.'

This time he did manage to catch hold of her arm and pull her to him. 'Do you want me to kiss you again and remind you that what we have together is amazing?'

His eyes were glittering with determination as she wrenched her arm from his grip. 'Don't make me call my security.'

'Oh, right. You're going full princess now, are you?

Now you've got your confidence back I'm surplus to requirements?'

'Something like that,' she spat at him and shattered what was left of his heart and his dreams of a future together.

'So, this is it? You're ending this on the doorstep. No discussion?'

'We've had the discussion. You don't need me being a burden any more.'

'You mean you don't need me any more.' He'd watched her transform from that defensive, spiky injured vet to a confident princess in her rightful place. She'd always been strong, she just had to believe in herself. It felt as though he'd been hit by a truck, which then reversed over him to finish the job, discovering that she wasn't as invested in him and their possible relationship. All the time he'd spent convincing himself it was in his best interests to stay single seemed laughable now when Georgiana was the one who'd decided she'd do better on her own. With his past relationship history he didn't even bother to disagree.

'You're right. I don't.' She swept away from him, taking the whole new future he'd planned with her. Now he was the one who didn't know where he belonged any more.

It had been days since Georgiana had broken her own heart. She'd put on a stellar performance, pretending to Ed she didn't care enough to continue with their relationship, until she'd got home. Then she'd locked herself in her bedroom and cried until there was a possibility of her drowning in her own tears. She'd wept for another life taken away from her and for the pain and hard work she knew she'd have to go through again in recovery. Most of all she'd wept for the man she knew she'd loved. And lost.

In the spirit of their new, open relationship she'd confided in her mother about the operation she was due to undergo and what had happened with Ed.

'It's a shame things didn't work out. Mr Lawrence is a lovely man but it's important that you're happy, Georgiana. Although, at this moment in time you don't look particularly happy,' her mother had said when she'd literally cried on her shoulder over the break-up.

However, she'd picked herself up and thrown herself back into work even if she'd lost something of her pep in the aftermath of breaking up with Ed. No, she wasn't happy but she couldn't carry on simply doing as she pleased. What she wanted wasn't necessarily in Ed's best interests. Yeah, it would be nice to have him by her side for her operation and recovery but at what cost to him? She'd get over him. Eventually.

Today she was setting up a new LGBTQ charity her parents had suggested to honour Freddie. Another new milestone in their continuing evolution into the modern world.

She was surprised and not altogether pleased to find out she had a visitor to the palace. It soon transpired her mother hadn't been entirely transparent about her recent dealings and had set this meeting up before conveniently going off to make an appearance anywhere other than here.

'You're Ed's brother?' Now Jamie had introduced himself she could see the similarities in their build and colouring.

'Don't hold that against me.' He laughed at his own joke. That cheeky sense of humour apparently ran through the rest of the family too. He was a good-looking guy and clearly had the family charm, but he wasn't a patch on his older brother in her eyes.

'What can I do for you? You said you'd been speaking to my mother?' Georgiana's heart was racing with desperation to find out what had brought him here but decorum decreed she play it cool.

'Yes, sorry. I don't usually do this kind of thing. You know, casually turn up at palaces and expect an audience with the princess in residence, but the queen thought it would be a good idea. I mean, do I need to call you Your Highness or bow or anything?' He pointed at the crutches he was currently resting on, having declined her invitation to sit.

'I don't think we need to stand on ceremony if you have my mother's ear.'

'That's only because I begged and pleaded with my father to make the call. It was a family emergency.'

That pricked her ears up and, anxious for the news that had brought him here, she asked, 'Is Ed all right?'

'It depends what you mean by all right. He's still breathing and working as hard as ever but I think you've broken him.'

'What do you mean?'

'Usually all he talks about is his work and his patients. Then there was the charity and of course, yourself. Now we can barely get a grunt out of him. He even took time off to show our parents around some sheltered accommodation. This should be the happiest time of his life, getting some independence back, but he's as miserable as sin.'

'I'm not sure what you want me to do.'

'I love my big bro to bits. I don't know what we would

have done without him growing up. He spent so many years taking care of us yet refuses to let us take care of him. Our Ed has a white knight complex. For him to make this change is a major deal. It's not a decision he would've made lightly and I'm sure he's done it for you.'

'I know he does a lot for your parents. I didn't ask him to stop.'

'No, but clearly having you in his life made him think differently about how he prioritised his time. I don't know what happened between you but I'm asking you not to give up on him.'

'It's complicated—' Her surgery was already scheduled. She wasn't going to tie him down by expecting him to take on the role of carer for her next.

Jamie rolled his eyes. 'I'd talk to him but he's stubborn. Short of staging some sort of intervention, pinning him to a chair and forcing him to open up about how he's feeling, I don't know how to fix him.'

'I'm not sure I'm in a position to do anything.' Georgiana didn't know where the surgery would leave her in terms of physical recovery and her future. Her circumstances since their last conversation hadn't changed, even if his had.

'My brother gives so much of himself to others, I think it's only fair you give him a chance to prove himself to you.'

Georgiana admired Jamie's devotion to his brother. She wasn't sure he'd approve if he knew, but it was touching nonetheless to see his love for his family was returned tenfold.

'I'm going to be incapacitated for a while but I think we do both need some closure.' By the time she'd had her surgery he'd realise what the road ahead held and any thoughts of beginning a carefree life with her would be well and truly put to rest.

CHAPTER ELEVEN

IN HINDSIGHT, Ed could have arranged driving lessons with an instructor for Jamie but he had nothing else to do with his time these days.

Until meeting Georgiana he'd thought a relationship meant taking him away from his family, but he could see now he'd been using them as an excuse not to get too close to anyone. It was too late now.

He groaned as he pulled into the car park and marched through Reception to his office, where he was picking Jamie up. Mad at himself and everyone else because he wasn't with the one person he wanted to be with.

'Are you ready to go? I haven't got all day. Some of us actually have work to do,' he barked at Jamie, who was spinning in his office chair.

'Who took a bite out of your biscuit? I hope you're not this rude to your patients, big brother.'

'Not my patients, just family who take me for granted.'

'This was your idea, remember? I was going to take lessons and you said I'd save money if I let you teach me. Don't take out your bad mood on me.' He grabbed his jacket and his usual cheery expression had been replaced by a scowl.

'Sorry.' None of this was Jamie's fault. It was entirely his for not making space in his life for Georgiana sooner.

When they'd been together he'd had a life, an equal with a lot of things in common. He'd lost everything worthwhile now that she was gone.

'Why don't you go and talk to Georgiana, sort out whatever is keeping you two apart?' Jamie ruffled his hair, enjoying Ed's moment of discomfort too much.

Ed raked his hair back into place with a rough hand. 'I don't know what you're talking about.'

'Uh-huh. That's why you haven't been yourself lately.'

Ed couldn't deny it, so he said nothing. Jamie didn't need to know he was having trouble even building the motivation to get out of bed in the morning.

His little brother slapped him on the back. 'Oh, you've got it bad, haven't you?'

Losing Georgiana had been the wake-up call he'd needed to put things into perspective. To see that he was allowed to make a life for himself. He didn't love his family any less now, they simply didn't need *him* twenty-four hours a day. Arrangements had been made for help and he was always on the end of the phone if they really needed him. It was ironic that after making all this extra time for a relationship, he had no one to share it with. He'd waited too long to make the changes.

'See? It's this bad mood, the dejected look on your face, that I can't bear to put up with for another second. Sort yourself out.'

Jamie was right, he couldn't go on like this for ever. Georgiana had left him, and he was supposed to accept it. However painful.

The problem was, he didn't want to accept it.

He loved her.

Not that he'd told her so. He hadn't been clear about his feelings at all or honest with himself about what he wanted. His determination not to make room in his life for a new relationship meant that he'd let her slip away. She hadn't known how important she was to him. He only had himself to blame for that.

And only he could make things right...

Georgiana's eyes were as heavy as the rest of her body and she struggled to open them.

'What's happening?' she slurred, her tongue stuck to the roof of her mouth because it was so dry.

'Do you need some water?'

There was a shuffling beside her as she tried to focus; she could see someone was at the side of her bed. 'Yes, please.'

'Just take enough to wet your lips for now,' instructed a familiar male voice.

Once she'd taken a sip and the effort of lifting her head proved impossible to sustain, she lay down again. It was difficult to think with the fog in her head but she eventually remembered where she was and what she was doing. 'I had an operation...'

'Yes, you did. Everything went well. You need to rest now.'

The voice comforted her. She didn't have anything to worry about. 'Sleep is good...' she mumbled and drifted happily back to oblivion.

When she awoke again, everything seemed less fuzzy and she had a vague recollection of her last foray back to consciousness.

'Ed?' She was sure it was him she'd heard in her hospital room. Unless it was wishful thinking during her delirium. The room was empty of visitors when she glanced around, although there was a chair pulled up by her bed. There was no reason Ed, or anyone else, would be here. She hadn't told him about the operation and she'd asked her parents not to visit for the simple reason she saw no need to upset them. When she was recovered enough she'd go home and recover there with their support. It didn't mean she wasn't feeling sorry for herself now, groggy, in pain and alone. Missing her mother, father and Ed.

'You're awake.' As Ed walked into the room carrying what looked and smelled like vending-machine coffee she wondered if she was still half asleep.

'I thought I dreamed you,' she told him as he resumed his place by her bed.

'I was here. Waiting for you to come around. How are you feeling?'

'Tired and sore. How did you know I was here?' After their last encounter and ghosting him since, she'd never expected to see him again. Much less at her side when she came around post-op. Whatever his reason for being here, she was glad to see him. Ed was the boost she needed when she was in the doldrums.

He took a slp of his coffee and grimaced before setting it down on her nightstand. 'Will you kill her if I tell you your mother called me?'

'Yes.' She was even more curious now about the background to this visit if he'd spoken to her family.

His laugh was like medicine after these weeks spent without him. 'At least you're being honest. For once. I suspect you might have fibbed during our last conversation.'

She squirmed on the rustling hospital sheets, under his knowing gaze. 'What do you mean?'

He leaned closer to the bed. 'I hear you and my brother spoke too.'

'So? People are allowed to be concerned about you even if you don't listen to them.'

'Am I supposed to believe it's a coincidence that you're told you need further surgery and you decide being with me is the wrong thing to do?'

She wanted to say yes and front out the lie but couldn't. A change of subject would have to suffice. 'Why did you come, Ed?'

'In case you had some stupid idea in your head that you didn't want me to think I *had* to take care of you. That you would steal time from my family if I wanted to be with you.'

'It's not an unreasonable assumption that you're the kind of man who'd volunteer for more charity work.'

He swore then, startling her with the ferocity of his expletive. 'What do I have to do to convince you I want to be with you? Faced with the prospect of losing you, I went back and took a good hard look at my life. I got help for my parents and talked to my brothers and sisters about sharing any responsibilities. All to show you I was serious about making a go of things with you and you wouldn't even take my calls.'

She was trying not to cry.

'I thought it was best for you.' For her too, when she'd been scared of becoming too reliant on him.

His smile gave her hope it wasn't too late to start again.

'I'm as much of a fan of people making decisions on my behalf as you are.'

'Point taken.'

He got up, squeezed onto the bed beside her and put

his arm around her shoulders, pulling her close to his body; it was all the pain relief she needed.

'In case you were in any doubt, Princess, I'm mad about you. I wanted to be here when you woke up to make sure you were all right and to tell you I'll be here for as long as you want me. I love you.'

Georgiana tilted her face up to him and saw the truth in his words for herself. 'I love you too. Can we start over?'

She knew she could live without him, but the fact she didn't want to said everything about her feelings towards him.

'No. This means we can learn from our mistakes, be honest with each other and face the future together.' He kissed her on the lips, convincing her everything would be all right if he was there for her.

For once she was letting someone else control her narrative. After all, it was exactly the one she'd choose for herself.

EPILOGUE

Two years later

GEORGIANA WRAPPED HER arms around Ed's neck and let him carry her the short distance she needed to go. 'I hate this.'

'I know, but it's only temporary. It's to make things a little easier on you. Your body needs a rest and now so do I.' Ed set her gently into the wheelchair, with that mischievous grin of his firmly in place.

'Ha-ha. This is all your fault, you know.'

'I think it took two of us, sweetheart.' He dropped a kiss on her lips then moved behind the chair so he could push her. Georgiana had no choice but to sit back and let him. She was tired, sore and cranky but the extra weight she was carrying these days had taken its toll.

If she didn't want to stop working altogether this was the only way for her to get about the clinic. It had been a busy couple of years for them as a couple. Not only because the Love on a Limb charity had proved to be a resounding success and they were realising Ed's dream of hosting a national sports event, but Georgiana had also completed her training course and was helping with the hydrotherapy sessions at the clinic when she could. Her current condition hadn't been factored into their schedule but, as usual, they were facing it together.

'I suppose it'll all be worth it in the end.'

'Of course it will. It's everything we didn't know we wanted.' She could hear the smile in his voice and it went some way to alleviating her discomfort. Things were going to change again very soon but she had no doubt Ed was going to step up and be there for her as always.

She toyed with the chain around her neck where her engagement ring hung. Her fingers were too big to wear it any more but it meant as much as ever. As soon as things had settled down again and she was back to her old self they were going to set a date for the wedding. She couldn't wait to make it official and become Mrs Lawrence. He was living with them at the palace for now, since it was already adapted to suit her extra needs. Hopefully they'd have their own place soon.

'I can't wait until he's here.' Georgiana stroked her belly, willing little Freddie to come and meet them soon. She'd taken her folic acid religiously, had all the checks and their baby boy was as healthy as could be expected.

'I can't believe I'm going to be a father.' Even after nine months Ed couldn't seem to quite get his head around it.

'I never considered I'd ever be a mother but here we are, only days away from becoming parents, so we'd better get used to it.' She laughed. If she'd harboured any last niggles that she was somehow not a whole woman, finding out she was pregnant put paid to them.

They were going to be a family soon, no longer content with the solitary lives they'd once held so dear. Now being together was all that mattered.

* * * * *

CAPTIVATED BY
HER RUNAWAY DOC

SUE MacKAY

MILLS & BOON

This story is dedicated to all my readers, especially as we cope with this strange time where the future is unknown. You make me happy with your support.

CHAPTER ONE

At eight forty-five Mallory Baine turned up her bumpy drive and huffed a relieved sigh. 'At long last.' A soak in a hot shower, then into PJs and a thick robe to devour the pizza sitting on the seat beside her while she unwound over a crime show on TV along with it.

Except there was a light on in her living room.

And a car parked by the garage.

Her heart lurched. 'Who the hell...?' No one had said they were stopping by tonight. Scanning back for anyone she might've told to make themselves at home, her memory came up blank. Yet it had to be someone who knew she left a spare key in the meter box. Didn't it? *It isn't an uncommon hiding place.* So, who was inside?

Parking next to the gleaming 4WD she didn't recognise, she snatched her phone from the console and shoved out to take a photo of the number plate. Just in case. She'd probably look like a fool when she learned who'd called in but, still, a girl had to be careful, even in Queenstown.

Woof, woof. Shade's 'Happy you're home, Mum' bark. Or it could be her 'I've smelt the pizza' bark. She obviously wasn't concerned about their visitor. Though any of her friends would've let Shade out of her run to go inside with them.

Crossing to her pet, she unlatched the wire gate and rubbed Shade's head, more for her own comfort than Shade's. 'Hey, girl. Who's visiting?'

Wag, wag, lick.

Some of the tension growing between her shoulder blades backed off. Whoever it was couldn't be all bad. Shade was savvy about people, though she was susceptible to meaty bribes. 'Come on inside. We've got someone to check out.'

A suitcase stood on the small porch near the back door and the key was still in the lock. A relieved sigh escaped Mallory. Woo-hoo. Typical Maisie. No warning, no checking if Mallory would be around for the weekend, her best friend would just fly in and hope for the best. She'd been promising a visit for weeks and after today, with their other close friend ending up in hospital, there couldn't be a better time. Mallory picked up the pizza and headed inside, down the short hall, calling out, 'Maisie, I hope you've brought the wine.' There wasn't any in her fridge, likewise much in the way of fresh food. 'Hello? Maisie? That you?'

A cough came from the sitting room. A masculine cough.

Mallory crashed to a stop in the doorway and reached down to hold Shade's collar with her free hand. A man was unfurling his long body from her couch, rubbing his eyes and yawning. Had he been asleep? Tough. More important was, 'Who are you?' she demanded through the pounding in her chest.

He stood tall, his woollen jersey half hitched up one side, the linen trousers creased and rumpled, dark hair falling into dark eyes. 'Hello.'

Hello? That was it? Not likely. Her hand slipped from

Shade's collar as she stood tall and straight, eyeballing him directly. He had no right to be here, no matter what he might think. 'What are you doing here? How did you find the key?' she snapped.

'Your brother told me where the key would be and to let myself in if you weren't home. He said you'd be back sometime tonight.'

He looked such a relaxed mess, and sounded so genuine, that her unease backed off a notch, only to be replaced by anger. *This is my house.* Not once had she come home to find a stranger lounging on her couch like he had every right to make himself comfortable. If he was a villain, he wasn't very good at it, lying around as though he had all the time in the world. Though why would someone with evil intent wait in the house with lights on and his vehicle parked in full view? 'I said, who the hell are you?' she snapped, using the anger to cover concerns about not having a clue what was going on.

'Josue Bisset.'

She stared at him. The tension began cranking up tighter. The name meant nothing. Neither did anything he'd said so far make sense. She kept staring at him.

He finally got the idea. 'The doctor about to start work at the local hospital where you're based as a paramedic? I'm going to board in your house until I find an alternative for the short time I'm here?' Doubt was creeping into his accent, and he glanced around the room. Was he looking for an escape route because it was dawning on him he'd screwed up?

He had. Big time. Continuing to watch him, Mallory drew herself even taller, all of one point six metres, and dug for a *don't fool with me* attitude. It came easily. No one did this to her. Her home was her sanctuary, her safe space. 'I don't have a brother.' With his stunned gaze now locked on her, she continued. 'I am not taking in a boarder. And I'm a helicopter pilot, not a paramedic.'

Something foreign escaped from his mouth.

French? The accent sounded similar to that of the girl from Avignon who worked in the bakery she frequented. 'You mind translating?' she demanded, not ready to play nice. 'Now?'

'I'd better not,' he said. He even smiled. 'It wouldn't translate politely.' He wasn't acting as though he might be on the back foot here and he damned well should be. He was still a stranger who'd walked into her house un-invited, despite what he believed to be a valid reason for doing so.

Beside her, Shade stood straight and firm, her head pointed at their intruder, her muscles tense. But she didn't seem too wary of Josue, more like questioning what was going on. Mallory resisted the urge to pat her because she'd probably relax, and she still knew nothing about this man and why he was in her house. She waited.

'*Désolé.* I thought I'd come to the right address. It's been a long journey from Wellington, crossing over on the ferry and driving all the way down here today.'

That was a helluva distance. Still, 'Don't you use a GPS?'

'I do, and it led me here. I was going to Kayla Johnson's house. Do you know her?'

One of my closest friends. All the air whooshed out of her lungs. Three hours ago, she'd flown out in the rescue helicopter to pick up Kayla from beyond the Cardrona ski field and taken her to the hospital in Dunedin be-cause Queenstown's hospital didn't do major surgeries. Her paramedic friend had two broken legs and was suffering from a severe concussion, having been lucky to avoid a small avalanche from taking her to the bottom of a rocky gully.

When Mallory had held Kayla's hand as she'd been unloaded at the hospital's emergency landing pad, Kayla had been talking gibberish, probably because of the concussion, but she'd said something about a doctor coming from Wellington. Was this man really meant to be staying in her friend's house? Was *she* supposed to go along and let him in because of a few whispered mutterings? It wasn't happening. At least not tonight. Hold on.

'GPSs are usually very accurate with street addresses. Kayla's house is another two hundred metres up the road.'

'Number 142. I have reached my destination,' he said in a monotone as if imitating the voice of his GPS. There was a suspicious glint in his eyes like he was laughing. Yes, his mouth was definitely twitching.

'Number 124. You have not reached your destination.' She retorted in a similar monotone, trying not to glint or twitch. He was beguiling to say the least. Great. Just what she needed at the moment.

'I must've muddled the numbers.'

'I'd say so.' It was getting harder by the minute not to give in to the smile trying to bust out from deep inside now that she was starting to relax. She didn't intend on making him feel too comfortable. Not yet anyway. That'd mean losing the upper hand, if she even had it.

Josue Bisset smiled slowly and easily. 'I'd better take my bags and get out of your way. I've caused enough trouble for one night.' His face softened further, making his mouth even more delectable.

He was probably used to winning over obstinate women. He was built, tall and broad with looks to match.

Women would lap up anything he said or did. But surely not a home invasion? Okay, a slight exaggeration now that she understood why he was here, but still. *Still what?* What to do next came to mind. *Nothing.* Let him get on his way and she could take that shower she'd been hankering for over the last hour. But she had yet to explain about Kayla.

Mallory walked through the sitting room to the double doors opening into her kitchen-dining space. 'It's not as straightforward as that.' With Shade nudging the back of her leg, she dumped the pizza on the bench and opened the pantry. Shade seemed to have decided to ignore Josue, which gave her hope he was all he appeared to be, a friendly, honest man who'd made a genuine mistake. Hopefully Kayla had had him checked out before offering him a room in her house. Hadn't he mentioned her brother?

'I take it you know Dean?' she called over her shoulder, and gasped when she saw Josue had followed her and was looking around the kitchen with something like hope.

He locked a steady gaze on her. 'I worked with him in Wellington.'

Fine. Dean wouldn't have sent him to his sister if he'd had any concerns. She filled Shade's bowl with food and placed it on a mat beside the water bowl. 'There you go, my girl.'

Her uninvited guest now stood with his hip against the kitchen counter, his nose crinkling as he breathed deep while looking at the pizza box. The mouth-watering smell of bacon and cheese and mixed herbs was probably getting to him. It was certainly reminding her how hungry she'd been before she'd seen the light on in here.

He said, 'Dean and I get on very well, and he showed

me around some interesting places during my time in the capital.'

It was a reference of sorts, Mallory supposed as she filled the kettle. It wasn't her place to change the arrangements, except they might not be the same any more. Kayla's parents would be on the road to Dunedin, if they hadn't already arrived, and they'd surely have contacted Dean about what had happened. But then the last thing that would be on Dean's mind would be the doctor moving into his sister's house.

'I know nothing about what you've organised but unfortunately things have changed. Kayla won't be coming home tonight, or for some weeks.' Kayla's parents would insist she stay with them until she was up on her feet again, and who knew how long that would take? 'She and two other people were caught on the edge of an avalanche this afternoon. Fortunately, they all survived but Kayla's injuries are serious. Both legs broken and a severe concussion at the very least. I was part of the team that airlifted her off the mountain earlier. She's now in a hospital in Dunedin.'

Shock filled those steady eyes. 'That's awful. I'm sorry to hear that. Have you heard any more about her condition since you returned to Queenstown?'

'No, but I'm unlikely to until her parents find out more. The paramedic thought Kayla would need surgery on her legs. They were in a bad way. She's going to hate being restricted by casts and crutches.' So much for getting back on track and recharging her energy, which had disappeared since her husband had died. 'Hopefully she'll be fine once she gets past the shock.' Mallory turned away to wipe a hand over her damp cheeks. Life was so unfair to some people. 'She's one of my closest friends.'

A light touch on her shoulder told her she wasn't alone, that Josue understood she was upset. It felt good, and totally out of place. She might have become a little restless with her life, due to not having anyone special to make a future with, but this good-looking Frenchman who claimed he was only here temporarily wasn't going to help one little bit. A short future was not what she intended next time she got involved with a guy. But it would have been good to download after today's drama. Drama he'd added to, she reminded herself.

He must've sensed her tension because he stepped back, putting space between them, not being intrusive. 'I do hope very much she's going to be all right. Maybe Dean's left a message to update me.' He pulled out his phone and shook his head. 'Nothing, but he's probably on his way south and, to be fair, there's no reason why I should be at the top of his list of people to tell.'

She was grateful for his small gesture of understanding and for not overdoing it. It made her feel she wasn't dealing with this completely alone, which was silly as she could talk to Maisie any time. 'I didn't know about you coming to stay, though Kayla did try to tell me something before the medical staff whisked her inside the hospital. She wasn't talking coherently and I'm only guessing it might've been about you.' *Now what?* Did she offer a complete stranger a room for the night? It wasn't in her to kick him out when he was new to town, though he could probably still go along the road to the other house.

'It was a last-minute arrangement after the accommodation I'd organised was withdrawn due to someone else now not leaving.' Doubt was filtering through the exhaustion coming off the man in waves. 'Maybe I should go into town and find a hotel for the night. I don't want to cause any more worries for Kayla or Dean.' Again, he locked his gaze on her. 'Or you. I am very sorry for this.' His apology sounded genuine.

'Don't worry about it.' She was shattered, her brain whirring all over the place. What were the choices? 'It's not up to me to say, but it sounds like there'd be no problem if you want to go to the house.' The guy was dropping on his feet, and obviously hungry by the way he kept glancing at the cooling pizza. Just as well she'd ordered an extra-large one. There went tomorrow's lunch. Shifting the box to the table, she collected plates and paper napkins, and nodded. 'Let's eat. Maybe you should try to get hold of Dean afterwards.'

'I will.' Hope was filling his eyes and lifting his drooping shoulders.

Mallory yawned, no longer able to hold herself upright, her whole body starting to sag with her own share of exhaustion. The need for a hot shower was becoming urgent, which was a normal response after a tricky rescue flight, especially when it involved someone she knew, something that happened quite often as she'd grown up here. Today's trip, flying Kayla to the hospital, had been particularly gruelling. Her friend was barely getting her life back together and then this. Now Mallory just wanted to unwind, but there was a foreigner in her house who needed help. And a lock on the bathroom door in case he wasn't as genuine as she'd begun to think.

Shade was happily chomping her way through her food, the tinny clicks against the bowl as she tongued up dried biscuits loud in the sudden silence. If she wasn't perturbed by their visitor, Mallory believed she was safe. After closing the curtains in the lounge and kitchen-dining area, she flicked on the heat pump that she'd forgotten to pre-set that morning, and said, 'Let's eat before we do anything else.'

Josue pulled out a chair for her. 'You are being so kind. As I said, I'm Josue, from Nice. I'm working at the hospital for two months before going home. I'm also joining the search and rescue outfit. Can I ask your name?' He held out his hand.

She hadn't told him? Of course she hadn't. She'd been too busy asserting herself. Slipping her hand into his to give a friendly shake, she ignored the heat that spilled into her and said, 'Mallory Baine.' She studied his face more deeply and nearly gasped. Talk about being blind before, or perhaps she had been too focused on him as an intruder and not a man, because now she saw good looking didn't begin to describe him.

A strong jawline, a hint of stubble darkening his chin and lower cheeks, generous lips and those big eyes that seemed to miss nothing. Wow. Then what he'd said dropped into her bemused head, and she tugged free of that warm grasp. 'I volunteer for S and R. That's why I was flying tonight.' So this man would be on her patch over the coming weeks. Seemed they had been destined to meet, which shouldn't be an issue, except for the sudden tapping going on under her ribs that wasn't about finding a stranger in her house, and more about how he was waking up her stalled libido. It had been a while since her last fling, and she didn't want another. These days she was more inclined to want the whole package. And Josue wasn't going to be that. Apparently, he was here short term, while she was looking for someone to share the bed *and* mow the lawns. Someone to have a family with.

'We'll be seeing a bit of each other then,' he replied, unknowingly agreeing with her earlier thoughts.

The accompanying smile went straight to her chest, spreading tendrils of warmth throughout the chill brought on by tiredness and the shock of finding a stranger in her house. Though she was getting used to him already. *Tap, tap*, went her pulse. *Shut up.*

'I guess we will. S and R can be busy.' This was getting out of hand. She'd met Josue less than fifteen minutes ago in the oddest situation and already he had her thinking about him in ways she didn't usually consider men. Two particular horrors having hurt her in the past had, until recently, kept her only wanting the occasional fling. Lately, though, she'd started wanting to find that one person to live with and love and share everything, even when there wasn't much time in her hectic life for a relationship, which was a deliberate ploy to keep her mind *off* what she didn't have and *on* what she did.

When she wasn't working, rescuing or keeping the property up to scratch, she was with her widowed mother at the dementia unit, painting her nails, combing her hair or searching for hidden possessions.

The worst thing Mallory had ever had to do in her life had been to admit her mother into full-time care. It had become necessary when she'd gone for a walk in the middle of the night last winter without a clue where she was. She'd been looking for Mallory's father, the love of her life. Not a safe thing to do under the best of circumstances, and a wake-up call for Mallory about her mother's mental state.

'Have you done search and rescue before?' she asked Josue, more to keep the conversation going than a serious need to learn anything about him.

'*Oui.* In France and then in Wellington. I think it might be physically more challenging in the Wakatipu terrain than anything I've done before.'

'The mountains are tough, the bush as dense as anywhere in the country and the rivers freezing even in summer.' She nodded at her German shepherd now happily curled up on a dog bed. 'Shade works the land searches.'

One brown eye opened at the sound of her name, and Shade thumped her tail.

Josue nodded. 'She has the strong build required to spend hours walking in all sorts of weather and terrain.'

'She loves it.' Opening the box, she nodded at the pizza. 'Help yourself. It won't be very hot now. Do you want me to reheat it?'

'*Merci.* This is good of you. I'm starving. It'll be fine as is. By the time I arrived in Queenstown all I wanted was to get to the house, but I should've stopped to get something to eat. I must've given you a fright, being in your house.' Again, that smile.

'"Fright" was one word for it.'

'What's another?' His smile widened. Used to charming his way through a woman's doubts?

'Disappointment.' Her return smile was tired but cheeky.

One eyebrow rose. 'Disappointment? You felt let down? How did I manage to do that by being inside your house uninvited?' He was still smiling at her.

Mallory surprised herself by laughing. 'I was shocked when I saw the lights on. I wasn't expecting anyone, but when I saw that case on my porch, I hoped my other close friend had decided to surprise me with a visit.' It would've been perfect timing after Kayla's accident.

They'd have talked half the night and convinced each other Kayla would be fine.

'Instead you found a sleepy Frenchman on the couch who'd messed up putting correct directions into his GPS.' He nodded. 'Yes, I can understand your disappointment.' His low laugh went straight to her blood, ramping up the pace and heat. 'At least I didn't scare you into considering doing something dangerous to me.'

'You wouldn't be sitting here munching on pizza if I'd had any serious qualms at all. Instead, Zac would be hauling you down to the police station by the scruff of your neck.'

'Zac?'

'A local policeman who lives around the corner.' The advantage of knowing many people in this town was having their numbers just a touch away. 'I'm thinking we shouldn't bother Dean tonight. Obviously, you can go to Kayla's house, but...' She hesitated. What she was about to say seemed pointless when the other house was a minute away, but Josue was shattered and alone, and she knew from experience how debilitating that could feel. Rapidly squashing unwanted images, she drew a breath and said, 'If you want to doss down here for the night and move along the road tomorrow, you're welcome.' Shade would be more than happy to sleep in her room, just in case she was completely wrong about him.

'Doss?'

'Grab a bed.'

'You'd trust a stranger to stay in your house?'

'If Dean's okay about you staying with Kayla then it's all right with me.' Kayla would've quizzed her brother for hours about this man. She took no risks about her safety. Except today she'd obviously got that wrong, but nothing would've indicated she was about to be knocked out by an avalanche.

Mallory knew about bad luck. Hers had come about because of her choice in men. Jasper had been bad enough, but they'd been teenagers, and she'd had a lot to learn. Whereas she'd been twenty-four when she'd moved in with Hogan, who'd turned out to be a right scrounger who had been enough to make her think twice for a long time about getting caught up with another man. A man she could trust with her heart again.

She did want to take another chance, and sometimes wondered if she was like her parents and would find the right match when she was older. In the meantime, she was cautious in a friendly way. But the restlessness over not having her own family was growing harder to deal with as the months went by. A loving man and kids were all that was missing from her life.

Her gaze went to Josue, who was watching her as he munched pizza. Waiting for her to retract her offer? He looked honest and decent, and there was a twinkle in his eyes when he wasn't yawning. Okay, so she might be too trusting, but better that than always being overly careful. Was Josue wondering how to answer her invitation? Had she put him on the spot somehow? 'Would you prefer to stay here or go along the road to the other house?'

'I'll stay, *merci*. I think you're right. It'll be best to get in touch with Dean tomorrow.'

'That's settled.' Taking a surreptitious look at her guest, she hoped she hadn't gone and done the wrong thing. Fingers crossed he was as decent as he looked.

When Mallory got up to make tea, she glanced down at her overalls. She never wore them inside, and certainly not while she ate dinner, even at her most knackered. She still had her boots on! 'I'll show you the room you'll use and then I'm taking a shower. There's an en suite bathroom attached to your room.'

She'd grown up in this house and still used her original bedroom, which had been enlarged when she'd been a teen. Her dad had died five years ago, which had been the catalyst for her mum starting to become lost in her own little world. Her parents had been so close they'd only functioned 100 per cent when they'd been together. It mightn't have caused the dementia, but her mum had never been the same since the day they'd buried Mallory's dad at the cemetery near Lake Wakatipu.

Mallory knew she'd been a surprise for her parents and, going by the loving atmosphere she'd grown up in, a very welcome one. They'd doted on her, even when she'd messed up big time and become pregnant, then depressed when she'd lost her baby due to an ectopic pregnancy. A stark memory flared of the physical and mental pain of losing her baby, while her boyfriend could only say with relief that they were too young to be parents anyway and that the surgical procedure had not only saved her life but their individual futures.

Her mum and dad had devoted all their time to her until she was back on her feet and then when she'd gone looking for a new career. The nursing course she had enrolled for had no longer been appealing, with thoughts of dealing with other people's pain dragging her down. Her mum had been disappointed as she'd wanted her daughter to follow in her footsteps, but she'd rallied and backed Mallory all the way when she'd decided on flying helicopters and, despite a fear of flying, had been Mallory's first passenger when she'd been allowed to take people up.

Now it was Mallory's turn to give her mother everything she could, including staying here in Queenstown for the foreseeable future, and spending time with her whenever possible. She'd already turned down with few regrets the dream job of flying rescue choppers in Nelson. Family came first, no matter what.

She led Josue to her parents' old room. 'Anything you want, just shout out.' She turned away. Bring on the shower. Nothing like a long, hot soak to ease the kinks in her back. The wind had been strong on the mountain, and along with the worry over Kayla, the thought of starting another avalanche with the downdraught from the rotors had been high on her mind, even though where she'd flown there had been little chance. Exhaustion always came after the adrenaline rush.

As the water pummelled the ache between her shoulder blades, relief at getting Kayla to safety finally pushed out the negatives, giving her that sense of satisfaction she got after a positive retrieval. Not that her friend would be pleased with where she was right now, but better that than at the bottom of the gulley with tons of snow on top.

As Mallory's body warmed, her mind wandered to the man down the hallway. Josue Bisset. Funny how Josue sounded sexier than Joshua. Softer, as though filled with hidden anticipation. And he was sexy, now that she had time to see him not as a problem but a man who had come to her district to work and help those in trouble out in the wilderness. Tall men with broad shoulders tapering down to narrow hips did it for her every time. Throw in a dazzling smile and vibrant eyes and she was a sucker for trouble.

Unreal how quickly she'd gone from anger to this unexpected curiosity about him. It was as though he was pushing buttons hidden deep inside her, reminding her it was time to have some fun again and to nudge the restlessness aside for a while. But to do that with her intruder? She grinned. That might become his name for his time in Queenstown. The Intruder. A darned sexy, interesting intruder at that. She didn't throw herself at men and yet she felt she wouldn't be averse to spending time with Josue. Then again, maybe not. He wasn't staying here forever, and she was.

Having witnessed her parents' deep love for each other, it was inherent to want the same, and so far she hadn't come close. At thirty-two she was starting to wonder if she'd be waiting till her forties, like her mother. *Not till I'm fifty as dad was, please.* Her family had been close, so special, she dreamed of attaining the same for herself. Sometimes she wondered if she was just hoping for too much. She wanted another chance to have a baby and yet was terrified of a repeat of last time. What if she had another ectopic pregnancy? And what if she couldn't conceive at all?

Hogan had accused her of being ungrateful for what they had, saying she wanted her dreams of love to come true when life wasn't like that. He might've been right, but she wasn't giving up yet. She'd gradually fallen out of love with him and he hadn't taken kindly to that, saying she was selfish. When she'd asked him to leave the flat she'd paid for, he'd left the next day while she was at work, transferring online her savings to his account on the way. So much for trusting him.

The water ran cool. Damn, she'd forgotten to tell Josue not to have a shower while this one was in use. Turning off the shower, she reached for a towel. The system didn't work properly when more than one hot tap was on at a time. She really should get around to having the plumber come by, except it seemed like an expense she didn't need when mostly she was the only one living here. Josue was here for one night. He wouldn't be causing problems with the system much longer.

Josue. She stared into the mirror. What did he see when looking at her? Freckles, green eyes, and wavy hair tied back out of the way for work. He'd seen her in her overalls so did that mean he missed the feminine side she kept out of sight while at work because she didn't want the men treating her any differently? It never bothered her what anyone thought of her appearance in heavy duty boots and sensible clothes for all seasons, but when she wasn't at work there was an array of soft blouses and tight trousers hanging in the wardrobe to relax into, shoes with heels and fashionable boots in bright shades of red and mustard and blue.

At home the hair came down to spill over her shoulders, blonde against the sky-blue satin PJs she was about to put on. They probably wouldn't impress a classy Frenchman. His casual clothes might be messed up, but they were stylish. But again, so what? This was home and she was being herself, sexy Frenchman hanging about or not.

Slipping a thick white robe over the PJs, she unlocked the door and headed to the kitchen to make that tea she'd been hanging out for since pulling up to the house.

Josue pulled on loose sports trousers and a sweatshirt. He hoped Mallory wouldn't mind if he made coffee. Being one of his bad habits from the years studying medicine, it didn't keep him awake. Besides, he was exhausted after the long day travelling and needed a caffeine fix.

He'd been so happy about coming to Queenstown he hadn't bothered to stop for a night on the way down the South Island.

The scenery had been stunning, but then mountains always upped his pulse rate. They were magical, and dangerous, and he enjoyed any time spent on one. They were the reason he'd decided to spend the last months of his New Zealand trip down here. Getting more insight into search and rescue in such rugged terrain to take home to use if he found a doctor's position at a skiing location, as he intended, was a bonus.

Looking at the bed, he knew he couldn't go there yet. There was too much going on in his head. Mostly about the woman who'd looked ready to boot him out on his backside when she'd first strode into her house and found him on her couch. She'd been equally shocked and angry, and right away had appeared determined he wasn't going to get the better of her. Not that he'd had any intention of trying to best her. He'd been the one in the wrong.

But, wow, she was something else, standing straight, her eyes fixed on him, her voice strong. Intriguing, to say the least. And gorgeous. Those freckles sprinkled across her cheeks she apparently didn't try to hide under layers of heavy make-up like some women he'd known made him long to kiss her gently. They were like a sign saying there was a wonderful woman behind the stance telling him not to mess with her, and that there was another, softer side to her strength hidden away from prying eyes.

He'd messed up completely on arrival, but who'd have thought both women hid the keys to their houses in the same place? And that they were friends? Even then, he should've realised when he'd walked into the house and seen all those photos hanging on the wall he'd presumed

were of Kayla and her parents. He'd been so taken with
the love in everyone's faces he hadn't realised Dean was
missing in the pictures. Mallory and who he now presumed were her parents looked so happy cuddled together
that an old envy had filled his heart.

Growing up in foster homes, he'd never known anything like that. In fact, he often didn't quite believe people
who said they were so in love the world was permanently
rosy, yet those photos told him different. Love could be
real. But was it possible for the likes of him who'd been
left on a doorstep at twelve months old?

Gabriel always insisted it was and he had shown him
great affection since the day he'd taken Josue under his
wing to help sort his life out. At fifteen, Josue had been
going off the rails in the direction of a life of crime when
the policeman who'd arrested him for theft had given him
a talking-to like no other, basically saying he had two
choices in life and not to blame anyone else for which
path he took.

Gabriel and his wife had taken him in a few months
later and had stood by him as he'd fumbled his way out
of trouble and into study and work, eventually making it
to medical school and into a career the boy whose mother
had abandoned had never imagined. The policeman and
Brigitte had been the first to love him unconditionally
and he had given the same back, warily at first and then
with all his being.

But he'd never found that kind of love with a woman.
Perhaps because he always backed off before they could
reject him, like most other people had in the past. He
wasn't counting casual friends. They came and went and
that was fine. It was the ones who could have loved him,
and hadn't, that had him fearful of being hurt again.

Gabriel and Brigitte had been the first to show him un-conditional love and he had to learn to return it. Twice he'd started to get close to a woman before fearing they wouldn't give him the love he craved and so he'd run.

Josue hauled air into his lungs and sighed slowly. It was an old story and he really should let it alone—especially now when he was in a wonderful country where he'd been welcomed with open arms and was having a great time. He didn't have to juggle emotions over a relationship because he wasn't getting into one.

Looking around, he sighed. This house wasn't where he was meant to be, wasn't number 142. A simple mistake with no serious consequences. If he had reached the right destination he'd probably still be lying on a couch, snoozing or awake, wondering where his hostess was. At least he had the answer to that question. He'd call Dean tomorrow to find out how his sister was and make sure her house was still available. If not, he'd look for some-where else, no problem.

He took another glance around. It'd be great to stay here but Mallory wouldn't want him hanging out in her space. She came across as independent and not need-ing company in the evenings while winter raged out-side. Then again, she might be a complete softy on the inside. After all she had given him, a stranger, a bed for the night rather than sending him along the road to a cold, empty house.

He was daydreaming. At the moment he had ar-rangements in place and wouldn't be changing them on a whim. A fascinating, gorgeous whim, though. Mal-lory hadn't flinched when she'd found him in her house, hadn't been fearful or stroppy. Not that he'd have wanted to push her good nature. He suspected she'd have had him on the floor with a foot on his back while she phoned the police if she'd had any doubts about why he'd come to be here. How embarrassing to be found in a stranger's home, looking like he was meant to be there, though that was probably what had saved him from having his backside kicked.

Mallory might be small, but she was strong. Not once had her shoulders dropped while sussing him out, her gaze had never wavered, and her tone had pierced him with a warning that he'd better be genuine or watch out.

'Josue,' a gentle, kind voice called from the kitchen, showing yet another side to Mallory. She straightened up from petting Shade as he joined her. 'I'm making tea. You want one?'

He gasped internally. Mallory wore pyjamas, the summer-sky shade making her eyes gleam. They drew him in. Dampness, no doubt from the shower, made her blonde hair darker. It fell in thick waves down her back and over her shoulders to her breasts. Her white robe was tied tightly around a tiny waist. Was this the same woman who'd been wearing shapeless overalls and thick work socks inside heavy boots? This version was feminine and lovely.

His breathing stuttered, as though his lungs were confused over taking air in or huffing it out. The other version had been gorgeous, but this Mallory? Gasp. Out of this world. His finger and thumb pinched his thigh. Reality returned through a sudden haze of lust. Why had he put the wrong damned number in the GPS? He was in for a sleepless night knowing this woman was in the same house.

'Josue?' Confusion scrunched her face. 'Tea?'

Tea? What? Shaking his head, he finally got his act together. 'Would you mind if I have coffee?' He crossed his fingers. 'As in real coffee?' Glancing over the benches, he smiled. 'It's okay. I see you have some.' Instant coffee was worse than none at all.

'Help yourself.'

'Merci.' Mallory was already treating him as though he fitted right in, moving around him in the small space as she prepared her tea. It made him feel good, like he mattered in a relaxed way. Even though it was casual and not deep and meaningful, that warmed him throughout. It wasn't something he'd had a lot of. None of the foster families he'd been placed with had been so quick to accept him, if they'd ever even got there. Only Gabriel and Brigitte had right from the get-go, and that had been massive as at the time he'd been the worst kind of brat possible. They were the reason he was heading home after this job, to be there when Gabriel had his heart surgery, to support both of them.

Yet, despite all they'd done for him, the memories remained of how every time he'd met a new family his hopes of being liked and cared about had been dashed. It was as though he had to prove himself every time he met someone, and as a kid he'd turned his anger to hurting others by stealing from them. Gabriel had soon talked sense into him, saying he was hurting himself more than anyone else. It was true, but he'd never quite got over being on edge when he first met someone.

Of course he mattered, as a man and as a doctor. He did believe it, but there was a hole inside that he just couldn't fill. In the two instances when he'd thought he'd come close with women he'd cared for, Colette and Liza, he'd continually questioned his feelings and their reactions to him, eventually leading those relationships to failure. So why was he feeling like he mattered here with this woman in a way he'd not known before? As though he just might be able to find that settled life he craved? It was a foreign sensation. Because she'd shared her pizza? Offered him a room? Or because she wandered around her kitchen as though he'd always been there?

No doubt he was overreacting to her kindness, but a rare warmth was spreading throughout him, surprising and confusing him. Should he be pleased or worried? He obviously wasn't having the same effect on Mallory. Which had to be good, he supposed, if he wanted to get to know her better, as he liked to do with locals wherever he was working. That way he learned more about the area, where best to ski, hike, eat and drink.

Right now he'd like to do all those things with Mallory. Already he knew that? *Oui*, he did, if that's what this unusual sense of anticipation meant. But, like everything he did, if he acted on these sensations waking up his manhood, it would be short term. He knew too well that the itch to move on would strike, as it had done all his life, after going from one foster family to the next, a new school each time, new people to get to know and try to impress.

Gabriel and Brigitte were the people he returned to often and kept in constant contact with when away from Nice. As a teen he'd had his own room in their house, and it was still his. Only with them did he have a complete sense of belonging. There was no family history to hold on to.

The only information he had was that his father had died when he was twelve months old and his mother had never replied to any of the letters he'd written to her as a child. *If she ever got them.* He'd met her briefly when he was fourteen. She had told him she'd started taking drugs soon after he was born and by the time she'd left him, she'd got deeper into the criminal world to feed her habit.

She believed she'd done the right thing by her son and to have visited him at all would have been worse than staying away. After that meeting, she had gone again and not many months later he'd learned she'd died of an overdose.

Mallory brushed past him, steaming mug in hand, as she headed for the lounge.

He was being gloomy. His life had moved on, improved, and there were all sorts of opportunities out there if he let go of the past. Letting the coffee stand, he joined Mallory, settling into a large leather armchair. 'Tell me about flying helicopters. What work do you do?'

A tired smile stretched her mouth wide and lit up her equally tired eyes. 'My full-time job mostly involves flying sightseeing trips up to the snow slopes or around the mountains, out to Milford Sound. Sometimes there are other trips, taking business people to cities up and down the South Island. It keeps me busy, and volunteering for Search and Rescue is an added bonus. My boss is happy for me to help out, but it has to be in my free time.'

Josue could listen to her voice all night. The Kiwi accent was sharper than European ones, but he liked its clarity, especially mixed with Mallory's softness. *Careful, Jos.* It was strange to be feeling a woman's voice, looks, attitude as warm and encompassing so easily. Could he finally be moving past the doubts that usually blocked him from believing anything was possible? Yet he was still overthinking everything. Though he was feeling more relaxed and comfortable than usual, none of that meant he could suddenly settle into a stable life and always be there for a woman he might fall in love with.

'As an S and R volunteer I also do some of the rescue flights, though I'm only the back-up pilot when others are unable to attend.'

'Like today.'

Her mouth dropped, and she blinked rapidly. 'Yes. Any rescue that involves seriously injured people, or worse, upsets me, and not only when it's someone very close to me.'

He wanted to hug away that pain, but they didn't know each other well enough. She might misinterpret the gesture. 'I understand, but those sentiments are why we do the job in the first place.' Was she completely relaxed with him? *Why question it, Jos? Just accept Mallory for who she appears to be.* His heart softened. Not many people in his past had been so accepting of him so fast. They'd wanted to know his history in other foster homes and schools before they'd asked if he liked eating beef, if they asked anything personal.

As an adult, he still looked for that reaction, and found it hard these days to accept that it was normal curiosity that had people asking questions about his job, family, past. His fault, but another old habit hard to let go. It stopped his expectations getting away from him, and stopped him from even beginning to wonder if he could be a good father if he ever got into a permanent relationship.

The TV remote Mallory had picked up remained still in her hand. 'There's also the adventure of heading out on foot into the bush or up a mountain to look for people who've got into trouble.' She spoke faster, higher, and the spark was back in her gaze.

'You're an adrenaline junkie?'

Now a grin came his way. 'As long as I operate safely and carefully, yes.'

He usually liked quiet women, not ones who attacked the world, but here he was, enjoying Mallory's company a lot. Was he more tired than he realised? Or was this the attraction? 'Remind me not to have an argument with you.' He didn't know if the adrenaline junkie ever took over from the careful, safe woman at the controls.

Her laughter filled the room, and his chest. 'Think I'd toss you out of the chopper?'

'Not a chance. I'm not going for a ride with you.' His grin came automatically, as though he was totally at ease with Mallory. At this realisation, his mouth flattened and he went to pour his coffee, trying to stifle the sudden sense there was a storm coming his way, one that would pick him up and shake out the past, open the gates to hope and something far more foreign—happiness. And stability.

His over-tired mind was playing games with him. He really knew nothing about this woman, and certainly not enough to wipe away everything that had kept him strong and safe over the years. Glancing around, his gaze landed on one of the photos that had caught at his heart earlier. Mallory sitting on the sofa she was on now, with her *maman* and *père* beside her, smiles splitting everyone's faces and love filling their eyes. Did she know how lucky she was? Lucky they had been there for her, had kept her with them and loved her so much?

For once he didn't feel the bitterness that rose when he saw families together like this. The air of confidence clinging to Mallory suggested that her family's love had made her strong and kind; the reasons he was staying here tonight and not along the road in an empty house. Envy touched him before it disappeared into a fragile happiness over being with a woman who demanded nothing of him he wasn't prepared to give. Too early to be thinking that, maybe, but he couldn't deny she was getting under his skin, touching him in a way that was foreign to him, but he still seemed to understand.

Tomorrow he'd wake up and realise he was an idiot and that this was all to do with exhaustion and wishful thinking. Not reality with a kind, sexy woman at the centre.

CHAPTER TWO

MALLORY'S PHONE INTERRUPTED the comfortable silence stretching out between her and Josue as they sat in the sunny conservatory the next morning, drinking coffee. Dean had called him to say he could still use Kayla's house as it would be a while before she was back to something like normal and able to get around the house.

Seeing the incoming number on her screen, she said, 'Uh-oh, looks like you're on your own for the rest of the morning. It's Jamie. He's from Search and Rescue, and Chief Fire Officer here.'

'I'm available if an extra body is required,' Josue told her.

She nodded. 'Hey, Jamie. We got a job to do?'

'Two young lads wandered away from their fathers in the hills near Gibbston nearly two hours ago. They were beside the river. You available?'

Why did the fathers wait so long to call for help? It was winter and it would be freezing out there. 'Yes.' She glanced at Josue. 'I've got Josue Bisset here. He's going to join S and R. He's done rescue work and is a doctor.'

'Bring him along.' Jamie gave her details of their meeting point. 'See you ASAP.'

'Got it.' She put the phone down. 'Guess learning your

way around Kayla's house will have to wait. Jamie wants
you on board.'

'Great.' He was already standing.

'Get changed into weatherproof gear. We'll get on the
road in five. There's some way to travel to join up with
the team. Shade, here, girl. You're going to work.'

Three hours later they were climbing through dense bush,
following Shade's lead as she headed higher and closer
to the river that was pouring down the ravine. 'Come on,
girl. Find them,' Mallory said quietly, so as not to distract
the dog, who was a little way ahead of them.

Howl.

Mallory stopped in her tracks. 'Shade?'

Howl.

It was what Mallory had been hoping for. Turning to
the man behind her, she fist-pumped the air. 'Shade's
found something. Hopefully the boys.' Her heart went
out to her four-legged girl. *Please have found them.* Mallory strode out, ducking under low branches, following
the rough track through the dense bush.

'I can hear the river.' Josue was directly behind her,
not faltering in the rugged terrain that was foreign to
him. 'Hopefully the boys haven't tried to enter it anywhere dangerous.'

'I doubt it, or Shade wouldn't have found them.' No
one wanted to find bodies, not even her girl. 'It sounded
like Shade's happy howl, and, yes—' she flicked a glance
over her shoulder to her search partner '—she has happy
and sad howls.' The radio crackled on her belt.

'Mallory? Did we just hear Shade?' Jamie, the search
leader, asked.

'You did. Josue and I are making our way to her now.'

She'd given the dog her head when she'd started getting agitated, a sure sign she was onto something. 'I'll send coordinates as soon as we know what we've got.' Slipping the radio back on her belt, she called, 'Shade.'

Woof, woof.

'Through there.' Josue veered off track to the right, taking the lead, ignoring the undergrowth, elbowing branches out of his way, turning back to make sure he hadn't flicked them in her face. *Désolé.*

'I'm fine.' She knew not to walk too close behind anyone in the bush. Not even when it was a man with the longest legs filling comfortably fitted black corduroy trousers tucked into trendy hiking boots; trousers that accentuated a tight butt that had her stomach doing loops. They'd automatically been paired up since she'd driven him to the starting point.

Josue broke through into daylight and stopped suddenly. *Sacré bleu.*

Mallory banged into the pack on his back. 'Oof. What? Let me see.' Was *sacré bleu* good or bad? She shoved around the man and looked across the riverbank to where Shade stood over two young boys, one prone and the other crying while trying to cuddle his pal. 'Wow.'

She began leaping over the rocks, aiming straight for them, pulling the radio free at the same time. 'Jamie, we've found them. Sending coordinates now.' As team leader he'd call the rest of the searchers, and soon everyone would be here to ascertain the situation. Glancing around, she knew it would be safe to bring in the rescue chopper to hover and lower the stretcher. Because of the proximity of the bush the helicopter wouldn't be landing on the narrow stretch of rocks. She'd call Scott, today's rescue pilot, shortly and give him the necessary details but first the boys needed attention. She wasn't even thinking the prostrate boy mightn't be alive. It wasn't an option.

Josue was already kneeling beside the boys and reaching for the inert one. 'Hello, Timmy and Morgan, we've been looking for you two. I'm Josue, a doctor, and this is Shade. She found you first. And this is Mallory. Shade's her dog.'

Mallory rubbed Shade's head. 'Well done, girl.' Turning to the boys, she added her bit. 'I am so happy to see you two.' The one holding his friend was shivering violently and his little face was white in contrast with blue lips. He didn't talk, just stared at them, eyes wide, breathing rapid and shallow, tears streaking down his cheeks.

Josue said, 'I've got this little man. He's barely conscious, by the look of things. Can you look after the other?'

'Yes.' She reached out to the lad. 'Your clothes are wet.' Saturated. She'd have to get him out of them and wrapped up in a thermal blanket. 'Have you been in the river?'

He nodded once. Then pointed to the nearby edge where the water was flowing slower than out in the middle.

They'd been lucky. 'Are you Timmy?'

He gave a slow headshake from side to side.

'So you're Morgan. What were you doing in the river?'

'Timmy fell on the rocks.'

'And you rescued him. What a great friend you are. That's wonderful.' These two had wandered off while their dads had been making a fire to cook a barbecue and had presumably got lost. That'd be frightening for youngsters, and even for adults inexperienced in the bush.

'He appears hypothermic,' Josue said after a quick glance their way. 'This boy is, too, though he's not wet through like your lad.'

Midwinter in the lower mountains, sunny it may be, but these kids were scared and small so it wouldn't have taken much time to lose body temperature, and they'd been missing for nearly five hours. Mallory leaned close to Josue and pulled the thermal blankets out of the pack he wore. 'Hopefully that's all they're suffering,'

'This boy's got a head wound, and he's not responding to stimulus, though that's possibly due to the hypothermia.' Josue opened the thermal blanket she'd handed over.

'Morgan, I need to check a few things about you. Can you feel it when I touch your hands?' Mallory asked quietly.

Another nod. 'Where's Dad?'

'He's waiting for you at the place where you were going to have a picnic.' She prodded his feet after removing his shoes. 'Feel that?'

He nodded.

Josue said quietly, 'Hello, Timmy. I'm Josue, a doctor. Morgan's right here. You've banged your head but you're going to be all right. I'm going to wrap you in this silver blanket. You'll feel warmer soon.'

More like he wouldn't get any colder, Mallory thought as she tugged at the jeans clinging to her boy like a second skin. Glancing across, she saw Timmy staring at Josue blankly. She nudged Morgan lightly. 'Say something to Timmy so he knows you're here and won't be frightened.'

'Timmy, it's okay. They found us.' Morgan's voice was high and squeaky, but Timmy's eyes opened further.

Pride swelled through Mallory. They had found these

two in time. Thanks to Shade more than anyone really, but this was why she did these searches, to bring home the victims of the climate and terrain to their waiting families. Helping people who'd had a run of bad luck gave her a sense of being part of something bigger than herself.

'So,' she said, finally managing to get the jeans off and started to remove Morgan's jacket. 'Are you hurt anywhere?'

He rolled his head slowly from side to side. 'No.'

'That's good. I'm going to check your pulse to see how fast your heart is beating as soon as I've got you all wrapped up. What happened to you?'

'We went for a walk and got lost. We know to follow the river down but it was deep and fast so we stayed on the rocks, hoping Dad would find us. Then Timmy slipped.'

The radio crackled to life. 'Mallory? What have we got?' the incoming pilot asked. 'I'm fifteen minutes away.'

'In a minute,' she muttered as she tugged her jacket off to wrap around Morgan over the thermal blanket for added warmth. The chilly air immediately lifted goose bumps on her skin.

'Okay for them to have water?' she asked Josue. She'd been trained in treating hypothermia, had dealt with it in the past, but Josue was the doctor on the spot. There were water bottles in each of their packs, along with hot chocolate and sandwiches. The warm drink would help the boys' chilled bodies.

'Go ahead.'

Handing over a bottle to Josue for Timmy and one to her little patient, she called Scott and gave him the details he needed. 'See you shortly.'

Josue was talking slowly and quietly to the boys. 'Sip the water, don't gulp or you might cough it back up.' He had Timmy wrapped firmly in the blanket and was fingering the wound on the boy's forehead. 'Did you see Timmy fall, Morgan?' He was studying Timmy's wrist, which Mallory realised was at an odd angle.

The boy pulled a face. 'He was crying and not looking where he was going. He landed on his stomach and then his head banged the rocks. I had to get in the water to push him up. It only came to my ankles but then I slipped and got wet.'

'You're very brave,' Josue said, before turning to her. 'Warming Timmy up is going to cause the pain to return. At least he's a little more alert now so I can give him some ibuprofen.' Josue slipped off the pack and delved into it.

'What about a sling? Or will we be able to keep the arm still by wrapping the blanket tighter around his arm and chest?'

'Let's try wrapping him tight. He needs his whole body in that blanket. How's Morgan's pulse?'

'Low normal,' Mallory told him.

The boy stared at her. 'Why's Dad not here?'

'He's not far away.' Hadn't he heard her answer earlier? Or had he, too, banged his head? She ran her hands over his skull and found no damage.

'I want him now.'

'We're going to get you out of here very soon.' The boys were approximately four kilometres in a direct line from their picnic spot but would've covered a lot more zigzagging through the bush. The fathers had searched for them before calling in help and returning to the spot they'd started out from in case the boys returned of their own accord. That would've been hard for the dads, but sensible. Once the search teams had set out, they'd wanted to go with them, so a police officer had remained with them to keep either man from dashing into the bush to look for the boys and getting lost himself. 'Have you ever been in a helicopter?'

'No-o.'

'Well, guess what? You and Timmy are going to have a ride in one soon. Isn't that cool? Helicopters are so much fun.'

'Will Dad be in it?'

'There won't be a lot of spare room with you two, the pilot and Josue inside.'

'I want Dad to come with me.'

She gave Morgan a hug. 'I know you do. Now he knows we've found you he can meet you at the airport when the helicopter lands.'

Josue said, 'His voice isn't as slurred now, which is a good sign.'

Mallory dug out the flask of hot chocolate and poured Morgan a drink. 'Have you been in the bush before?'

'With Dad. It was scary today.' Morgan was crying now. 'We were having fun looking for weka birds, then we couldn't find our way back. We heard lots of awful noises.'

'Next time, if you get lost, stay where you are. That makes it easier for us to find you.'

'How?'

'We wouldn't have to walk so far in so many different directions. If not for Shade, we'd still be looking now.'

The sound of twigs snapping announced the arrival of Jamie and Zac, followed shortly after by the rest of the crew, relief the only expression on everyone's face. A good result all round.

'I've called Base. Scott's on the way,' Jamie told them, not realising Mallory had been talking to the pilot. 'Josue, you're to go with the boys. There'll be an ambulance waiting with a paramedic at the airport, and Scott will give you a lift to where you're staying or to join the rest of us for a beer when we get out.' There was nothing more they could do now until the helicopter arrived.

Josue glanced her way, disappointment in his eyes. Why? Did he like hiking in this terrain that much? 'You can let yourself into my house again, if that's what you want.' She smiled now the stress of the search had slipped away. 'It's not as if you don't know where I keep the spare key.'

'I do.' A return smile came her way, making her all warm and happy.

A smile did that? Showed how good those smiles were. Or how quiet her life had become lately. 'Your gear's still there. You haven't had time to go grocery shopping either.' It sounded as though she was trying to convince him to stay another night. Was she? He couldn't stay for ever and Kayla would prefer someone was in her house while she was away.

There was confusion in his expression, probably because of how she'd mentioned him going to her house and not Kayla's. *Welcome to the club. I'm confused with myself too. And with you, Josue Bisset.* He intrigued her when it would be simpler to stay clear. Safer, anyway. 'Let's see what time I'm finished with the boys and that beer Jamie mentioned. Are you going to the pub?' he asked.

'I am. It's always good to wind down and talk the talk

after a rescue. Otherwise I lie awake half the night, going through everything.'

'But today we had a good result.'

'I still like to go over it all, making sure there was nothing I could've done better.' Yep, she was a perfectionist.

'Do you discuss all this with Shade?' Another smile.

Another nudge in the stomach. 'Shade's usually happy to have a meal and lie down on her bed.' Or in front of the fire at the pub. 'She seems to think she does a perfect job and doesn't need to drag through the details.'

'Go, Shade.'

Hearing her name, Shade wandered over and rubbed her head against Josue's thigh.

Josue ran his hand down her back before returning his attention to Timmy's head wound and the reddened crepe bandage. 'The bleeding appears to have slowed to a trickle. *Merci.*' Then he added, 'I'll wait in town for you, Mallory, if that's all right? I'll hitch a ride with this Scott.'

'No problem. We'll sort you out yet.'

He gave a deep laugh that tightened her skin further than the goose bumps had managed to do. 'No rush.'

How long did he say he was staying in Queenstown? Two months? She should be able to manage some spare time to get to know him better, *if* she followed through on unravelling the puzzle that was Josue, making the most of the sense of excitement he caused in her.

Josue had an unnatural desire to hug Mallory before he climbed into the helicopter. It was almost as though he needed to say, 'See you soon,' because he didn't want to leave her alone to go back on foot to the vehicles they'd arrived in. Another overreaction, but he couldn't seem to stop them. She was lovely inside and out. And apparently a perfectionist.

Hearing her talk about needing to go through the details of a rescue regardless of a good outcome told him how caring and careful she was. As if he hadn't experienced that with her generous offer of a bed last night. She was refreshingly open and honest. Or was he being more open to her than he was used to being with other people he hardly knew? He and Dean had also hit it off straight away, and he'd found himself accepting people more readily than normal since arriving in this country.

Was that what getting away from his home turf had done? Or only Mallory? Had he started to open his eyes and heart to another way of approaching life after leaving France? Had he begun to change while living and working in Wellington, and now, with Mallory, was he beginning to realise it?

Just the thought excited him. If that was right, then he could finally be stepping into the sort of life he'd once dreamed of. A life of love, with a woman to share everything with. Children to give his heart to along with the things he'd missed out on, growing up. A life where he could trust himself with a home *and* a family. *No.* Not children. That was going too far. He knew nothing about being a good father, and he wasn't putting any kids through the hell he'd known growing up.

Laughter reached his ears from outside the chopper. Mallory stood with Jamie and some of the other rescuers, waiting for the aircraft to leave. She *was* special. Which should have him dancing on the spot. Instead his gut was cramped and his chest tight. Not coming from a steady background ultimately meant he wouldn't know how to achieve one for those he loved. Even if that woman was someone like Mallory, who readily accepted him as she saw him, how could she possibly understand his uncertainties?

While searching for the boys, they'd walked through the bush, up and down slopes, slipping in mud, and not once had Mallory checked to see if he was capable of keeping up, and therefore a competent part of the team. She took it for granted he was. When they'd reached the boys, she'd made way for the doctor and hadn't tried to show how competent she was as a first-aider.

Now he got to fly out, while she'd be walking back the way they'd come, though probably on a more direct route. The doctor in him accepted it was his role to go with the boys and he had no intention of arguing. As a man he'd like nothing better than to walk out of the bush with this woman who'd managed to open his heart a little after only knowing her one night.

Her easy acceptance of him in her home last night after she'd got over the shock and her annoyance had blown him away. She hadn't walked up and said welcome, make yourself at home, but she had taken his explanation and had obviously added it to what little she knew about Dean's sister having someone to stay, and had been okay with his presence. He shook his head. Unbelievable. Not because of his past, but because she'd had every right to tell him to leave and sort the problem out himself. He had erred when he'd put in the street number, but if the two women hadn't hidden keys in the same places, surely he would've finally worked out he was in the wrong place?

'Josue, the boys are strapped in and ready to go. You need to strap yourself in, too.' Jamie stood just beyond the opening on the side of the chopper, bringing him back to reality with a clunk.

Reality in that Mallory may be coming up on his radar as special, but he wouldn't be staying on after his months here were up. He had always intended to return to Nice, the place where he belonged even if his roots were vague and a big let-down. New Zealand had given him a visa for two years, but he'd only planned on staying for one, knowing the inability to settle would drive him away sooner rather than later. Besides, he'd promised to return home for Gabriel's surgery later in the year anyway. 'Onto it. See you shortly.' He reached out to slide the door shut and then focused on the boys in front of him. 'Morgan, are you feeling all right?'

'Why does the helicopter shake so much?'

'That's because the rotors on top are going faster and faster. Soon we'll be off the ground and you won't notice the shaking so much.' He turned to look Timmy over. The boy's eyes were closed again. 'Timmy,' he called quietly.

Timmy opened his eyes and looked around. 'Where's my dad?' he cried.

'Both your dads are heading to the hospital, but we're going to get there quicker. They have to drive all the way.' Hopefully the mothers were already on the way from their homes in town. These little guys were overdue some hugs and loving.

Looking out the window in search of Mallory, he saw her walking into the bush, being swallowed by the thick manuka trees, Shade right on her heels. 'See you soon,' he whispered, before turning back to his charges. 'Hey, Morgan, this is fun, isn't it?'

It was now they'd found the boys and were getting them out to safety. It gave him a thrill and made him happy to have helped. It was one of the best things he'd been doing in this country. He owed Gabriel for convincing him to come here.

'You need to get away and take a long hard look at everything that's happened to you from a distance,' Gabriel had said as he'd driven Josue home from visiting his mother's gravesite for the first time.

'What do you mean?' Josue had asked. 'Nothing would've saved my mother from the drugs but herself, and she obviously hadn't wanted to.' Seeing the grave had raised old emotions that had torn through him like a sharp knife, reminding him of what he'd missed out on.

'Everyone chooses their own path.' Gabriel repeated what he'd said the first time they met. 'It's up to you how you deal with life's obstacles.'

'True. But how would going away change anything?' Josue asked around the bitterness.

'You might find closure. You could see the world through lighter eyes, a calmer mind. You could be so busy enjoying yourself, you'll forget to haul the past along every step of your life.'

'You going to tell me where to go too?'

Gabriel shook his head. 'No, my man, that's entirely up to you.' Then he spoilt it by saying, 'Some place with mountains and not many people where you can be yourself.'

'Next you'll be naming a country.' Josue had laughed then.

'You've always talked about New Zealand.'

'I knew it. You can't help yourself.' Josue stared out the window at the passing traffic, the idea growing as they made their way home.

And here he was—enjoying himself.

* * *

'Shade won't be able to walk if you guys keep feeding her like that,' Mallory admonished gently, softness in her heart as she watched her pet lying in front of the large open fire. Shade was a trouper, and today she'd proved yet again just how clever she was at tracking. Now everyone was spoiling her rotten for leading the team to the boys.

'She deserves every steak she gets,' Josue called from the bar, where he was buying another round of beers for the group. Hopefully no more steak for her dog, though. 'She's not exactly overweight.' His French accent seemed stronger in here surrounded by so many Kiwis. Still as sexy, though.

Not that she'd given the doctor, whose black jersey and corduroy trousers covered a body more suited to a basketball player in his prime, a lot of thought this afternoon other than how he worked as a partner in the rescue. He'd known what he was doing, even when the terrain was foreign, though apparently he had done some time helping in searches out of Wellington, which was similar but not as difficult.

He hadn't hesitated at fording freezing creeks or trudging through mud that sucked their boots down and fought letting go. And, yes, she was lying to herself. When he'd gone ahead of her, she'd been fully aware of him as a man. But they'd been in unison about what they were out there for. 'You saying I starve Shade?' She gave him a smile.

'Not after what you fed her last night. Or this morning.'

She'd given Shade an extra meal once she'd heard they

were off on a search, as sustenance never went astray when the dog put her heart into finding someone.

Mallory had slept in that morning, which told her how safe she'd felt with Josue in her house, and how much Kayla's accident had affected her. She'd phoned her friend's mother and learned Kayla had had rods implanted in her right leg and that the break in the left one wasn't anywhere near as serious. The concussion was severe and only time would help that. Mallory had passed on her love, explained that Josue had stayed with her last night, and said not to worry about a thing. By the time she'd showered and dressed in trousers and a thick red, angora jersey, Josue had been pacing the kitchen, sipping coffee and talking to Dean on his phone and getting much the same news.

She liked how Josue had put his hand up the moment he'd heard a search was to get under way. He didn't put his needs first, didn't think he should get to the house and unpack rather than go out in the cold and hike through wet bush and mud. He'd also fitted in with everyone immediately when they'd got to the start point. Quietly impressive, came to mind.

He intrigued her with his looks and that accent. She was aware of him whenever he was nearby, which was something she hadn't felt for a long time. Since Hogan. This interest in Josue was different, more grounded in who he might be and how he just got on with whatever was required of him without question, as he had with the boys when they'd found them.

He hadn't expected her to jump at his word. They'd got down to work on the boys together, sharing the jobs, putting Timmy and Morgan before anything else. The past had taught her some painful lessons and yet she barely knew him and couldn't wait to spend time learning more. And getting closer physically? *Why not?* She wasn't disinterested. How could she be when he had her fingertips tingling with only a look?

There was nothing better than occasionally having a good time with a hot man, as long as she'd got to know him a little and felt safe. *Stop.* She didn't have the time for a fling. *Didn't she?* Of course she did. But she wanted more, and that wasn't happening with this guy. This nagging restlessness had come about because she didn't have her family to go home to at the end of the day.

But, in the meantime, what was more important? Looking after the house and grounds, or seeing to her own requirements, as in having fun and meeting a man? Wanting to find the man of her dreams didn't mean celibacy until he came along. Besides, if that didn't happen for another few years, gulp, then she'd be like a dried-up prune.

Josue strode across the room with his hands clutching a load of full glasses.

She couldn't take her eyes off him. Even though she should. He'd pick up on her interest too easily and she didn't need him seeing that. Not until she'd made up her mind—fling or nothing. Nothing was getting more remote by the minute. She tried to concentrate on the men seated around the table, unwinding and telling tall tales as the thought of what the outcome could've been drained out of them. Everyone had been tense, the urgency greater than even the usually high level due to it being two wee lads missing and understanding how desperate their families would've been. Every searcher's nightmare. It was one thing to be out there for an adult who'd had an accident or got lost; a very different story when children were involved.

Placing the drinks on the table without spilling a drop, Josue handed one to Mallory and took the recently vacated seat beside her. 'Bet those boys won't be dashing into the bush again in a hurry.' He stretched his endless legs under the table.

Mallory deliberately looked across the table at Scott to save herself getting redder in the face from sussing those legs for longer than was sensible. But there was no stopping the flush rising in her cheeks. Taking a deep breath, she got on with being friendly while staring at the wet circles left by glasses on the tabletop. 'I doubt their parents will let them out of their bedrooms for a month. They'll want to know exactly where they are every minute.'

'I thought Kiwi parents liked their children to get outside to learn how to manage nature and what it threw at them.'

She glanced at Josue. Shouldn't have. He was laughing softly, teasing her. Turning her cheeks from pink to flaming red. What was it about this man that got her in a flap just looking at him? Good-looking men were a dime a dozen around Queenstown, as they came to ski or partake in extreme sports in droves, so it couldn't be Josue's looks that were rocking her world. Lifting her glass, she took two large mouthfuls and set it back down on the table. 'Is it like that in France?'

'For those lucky enough to have access to the countryside and the mountains.' His face tightened briefly, then he was smiling again. 'I was born in the city, but when I grew up I headed for the mountains as soon as I could afford it. I'd read many books about mountaineers all over the world and I wanted to see what the fascination of mountains was all about. I loved the outside air, the freedom and fewer people being around. There's a certain excitement about just being able to walk a kilometre without meeting anyone else, but I never took to climbing. Didn't have the head required for heights. Staring over cliff edges, knowing I'd have to go back down there, would only turn my gut sour.'

Dipping her head, she smiled. Again. Hell, this man was getting to her. He talked about himself as though he didn't have to prove how great he was all the time, like some of the guys she met through her work did. Sometimes she felt that some of them had to shove out their chests and strut just because she was a female at the chopper controls and therefore in charge of their destiny. As far as she was concerned they needed to get over themselves. 'Anyone would have to be crazy to do that. I'd far rather rely on rotors than my feet in those places. I've airlifted enough injured climbers off mountains to know where I'd prefer to be.'

'I thought you were going to say you don't like heights either and that would've been strange for a pilot.' He was teasing her in the nicest possible way.

'I passed the sanity test for my licence.' She grinned— just in case he was worried she was strange. 'But I agree. There's something special about the outdoors without having to go to extremes, even here where the tourists swamp the place to get a taste of reaching for the limits in as safe an environment as possible.'

'I've been told there're still many areas to go to get away from them, if you're lucky enough to know where they are.'

'Working in the emergency department, you'll meet people who can tell you where to go.' *Keep talking, Josue.*

That accent sent warm shivers up and down her spine, and made her shuffle on her chair. Which meant she should shut up with the questions and put a paper bag over her head.

'What about you? Do you get away often?'

'My job takes me all over the district, so I see a lot but from the air, not on the ground, whereas S and R does get me out into country I love, though usually in those circumstances I'm too busy worrying about who we're looking for and not absorbing the countryside. My dad used to take me on overnight hikes to huts and the like when I was younger. I haven't been back to many of them for a long time.'

'Want to show me one or two?' The sizzling smile was again teasing her, sucking her into his aura.

'I guess I can if we've both got free days at the same time.' Would she or wouldn't she try to make certain she did? He was so tempting. This was ridiculous. She never lost her mind over a man so quickly. But she hadn't. Not really. He was hot and gorgeous and great company, but she wasn't going to allow herself to get in deep, knowing he'd pack up and leave well before Christmas.

Anyway, she didn't make rash decisions or actions, didn't ever lose her mind over any man. Since Hogan, she'd become the steady, check-it-out-first kind of girl, even when it came to planning an overnight trip to a town she knew. 'We'd have to do day hikes, not overnight ones.' She wasn't staying alone in a hut with Josue when just sitting here in a group made her blood heat.

'We'll make it happen,' Josue said with a determined nod.

He wanted to spend time with her on hikes? Time up close and personal? Was she warming his skin as much as he was hers? Or was Josue determined to see lots of the district and she was an easy target for a guide? She smiled. What did it matter? She wanted to spend time with him doing anything and everything. Where had the steady, check-it-out-first woman gone? But what was not to like about him? Apart from the fact she couldn't read men any more than she could a book written in Swahili—and that was when she was being cautious. Her track record was short and abysmal. She'd got it so wrong with Hogan and Jasper. Her gaze drifted sideways. She stared at her glass.

All men should be like her dad: honest and gentle. Working in a male environment, she'd met men like that, and some not, but that didn't put her off them. She just didn't always get it right about how their thought processes worked, and expected them to be open and straightforward like her dad had been. Maisie always laughed at that one, saying no woman understood men better than to feed them, love them and let them get on with things.

'I've ordered fries and chicken all round.' Josue spoke loud enough now for everyone to hear.

'No more treats for Shade, please,' she begged. 'I'll have to deal with the bloated stomach for hours to come otherwise.' Leaning back in her chair, Mallory sipped her beer and relaxed. Her legs ached, her head was getting light—beer mixed with the thrill of finding those kids safe—and physical exhaustion was taking over. It was a comfortable sensation, one that came from having done something good with a group of people all in sync.

Plates of hot food arrived, filling the air with delicious fatty, spicy smells that had everyone reaching for the chips and chicken. There was more than enough to go round. Josue obviously understood how ravenous the team got once they relaxed from the hard work of climbing up and down hills and cliffs, of wading through rivers or trekking through thick bush.

'You've gone quiet.' Josue spoke softly.

Nothing unusual in that. 'I'm an observer.' She was seeing too much of those legs again. What would it be like to have them entwined with hers in bed? Jerking her head up, she stared directly into his eyes. Vibrant gold flecks dotted through the dark hazelnut colour. Happy eyes, generous and sensual. Beddable eyes. *Jeepers.* She was way in over her head. After how many hours? She didn't do this. An occasional casual fling with someone she was mildly attracted to was her lot. The exciting physical package she could manage, but not this gnawing sense of wanting more. The getting close and personal was a worry. Something about Josue suggested a fling with him would not be half-hearted. She sensed he might take over her mind, her feelings and she'd become besotted. *Which would be fine, except he isn't here forever.*

Josue *was* different. He didn't rush to talk over her or push his interests before hers. He was genuinely interested in what she did and thought. More than anything she felt comfortable around him in a close way, almost as she felt with Kayla and Maisie, yet she'd known them most of her life and not just since yesterday. But she didn't want to be best friends with Josue. This need filling her, tightening every nerve ending, had little to do with friendship and everything to do with getting absorbed into his life and opening up hers to let him in. 'Damn it.'

'Problem?'

A great big one. 'Not at all.' Not unless she gave in to

the intense feelings gripping her. Straightening her back, swallowing hard, Mallory turned to Josue, and fell into the deep shade looking back at her. She was swimming in treacle, going nowhere fast, and so tempted to dive deeper. Snatching up her glass, she gulped a large mouthful, which promptly went down the wrong way and she had to suffer the indignity of having her back slapped by Beddable Eyes's large, gentle hand. More coughing. Time she went home and had a hot shower, and got comfortable in some softer trousers and a thick jersey. *Huh, a cold shower would be more appropriate.*

Something solid plonked onto her thigh. It couldn't be Josue touching her. There weren't any sparks. Anyway, he wouldn't make such a blatant move. Would he? Her hand found Shade's warm, hard head. 'How's my girl?'

This time soppy brown eyes looked at her, filled with love. How come dogs loved without reservation? Without question? They just gave it out and only asked for some in return. And steak and chips.

'How long have you had her?' Josue asked as he began rubbing Shade's shoulders as though nothing had happened. Perhaps it hadn't for him. He probably looked at women like that all the time.

'I got her from animal rescue eighteen months ago.'

'Guess you're into all sorts of rescues then.' His smile was soft, kind and making her stomach tighten.

'I couldn't look at those beguiling eyes and walk away. She had me from the get-go.' She'd better not do the same thing with Josue's own beguiling eyes. She'd never leave her mother to deal with the dementia alone. The nurses were wonderful, but she was the only family her mother had.

Shade lifted her head, nudged Mallory's thigh gently.

'Okay, I get it.' Mallory pushed her chair back. 'We'll be back in a minute.'

Outside Mallory shoved her hands in her pockets and stared through the murky air of the car park as she walked slowly after Shade heading for the trees. 'Damn it. I am so attracted to him.' Her lungs expanded, contracted, pushing air through her lips. 'Too attracted.'

She paused, waited for Shade to join her again. 'Do you like Josue?' Her fingers rubbed between Shade's ears. 'You do, don't you?' That didn't make any difference to the situation. She loved Shade to bits but she had no say in this. Kayla would point out she should have some fun. It wouldn't be hard. He was delicious. But there was more to him than the physical traits that had her enthralled. Enough to take a chance and have some fun? She already felt differently about him from other men. She couldn't let that get out of hand. Yet she was reacting to Josue like she wanted to learn more about him in every way.

Shade nudged her, wagging her tail.

'You're ready to go back inside?'

Wag, wag.

I'm not, because I'm reacting very differently to Josue than I've ever done with any man before, which could kick me in the butt.

Taking out her phone, she pressed Maisie's number. 'Hi, have you heard any more about Kayla?'

'Hi to you too.' Maisie laughed. Then got serious. 'I talked to her mum, and she's having a rough day after hours of surgery first thing. They didn't do it last night because the orthopaedic surgeon wasn't available. I'm still getting my head around what's happened.'

'Me too, though I've been on a rescue today so that

took care of some of my headspace for a while. Kayla's supposed to be getting her life back together, not having it torn apart by an avalanche.' So unfair. 'You won't believe what else happened last night. I thought you'd come to visit.'

'Sorry, can't at the moment. Too much work on.'

'I figured.'

'So? Who was visiting if not me?'

'A Frenchman. He's a hunk, believe me.' Mallory filled Maisie in on what had happened. 'It's kind of funny really.'

'Might be karma. It's time you met someone interesting, and hot.'

'He's not staying around for long.'

'Then make the most of him while he's in the country.'

'Thanks, pal. I just might, although I—'

'Blah, blah. I'm not listening to your excuses not to have some fun. Anyway, who knows what he might do if he thinks you're the bee's knees.'

'Time I went back inside,' Mallory said. 'You're not helping. See you.' She hung up before Maisie could add any more stupidity to the conversation. So much for downloading and sorting things out with friends.

Where would she be without hers?

CHAPTER THREE

JOSUE CHATTED WITH the remaining guys around the table, glancing across to the main entrance every few minutes. Mallory wouldn't have left unless she'd forgotten he needed a lift, and she was too focused to do that. There was still half a glass of beer at her place by the table that she seemed to have set aside.

An intriguing woman, with a heart of gold, who liked helping people. The way she walked through the bush without hesitation and was very sure about following Shade spoke volumes of her competence in a situation many people would struggle with. The local bush was so dense there was no way of seeing through the trees because of all the undergrowth. Dean had told him a story about a Canadian man who went for an hour's walk behind the motel where he was staying and was found three days later completely disorientated and dehydrated. Nothing Josue had seen since made him think his friend had been exaggerating.

The door swung open. Shade trotted across to the mat in front of the fire and lay down.

Mallory started his way, but stopped to talk to a woman who'd called out to her.

Josue studied her, while pretending to listen to Scott

talking about flying to a rescue in Fiordland. Mallory was far more interesting. Her wild, blonde hair had begun escaping from the tight knot it'd been in to flick over her shoulders and touch her cheeks. Colour in her cheeks highlighted her all-seeing eyes. Her lips were full and tempting. *Oh, l'enfer.*

He'd better focus on the conversation going on around him. Safer. Not that he was immune to having fun. A fling didn't hurt if both people were keen. He sighed. It had been a while since he'd finished with the petite nurse in Wellington who he'd had fun with and no regrets when it finished. But that had been a fling without attachments. That might not be possible with Mallory since she already had him in knots just thinking about her.

Though, especially following his previous failed serious relationships, he found it hard to imagine he could find a woman he might fall in love with. It wasn't that he didn't want to find a woman to love and cherish forever. He did. But his mother hadn't loved him enough to get her act together and raise him. And not one person in the foster homes had done anything to prove her wrong. Gabriel and Brigitte loved him, and that was the most wonderful thing that had ever happened to him. But they were special. Could a woman love him, faults and all, forever? And could he give the same back without question? Without doubting every move he made? Unlikely.

'Josue, any problems today?' Jamie moved closer to be heard.

'None at all. Once Shade got wind of the boys it was fairly straightforward, if you don't count the sharp climb and then the drop off the edge to the riverside where the boys were huddled together.' The sense of relief when he'd seen them, Morgan staring at Shade as though she was magic, had been overwhelming. He'd surreptitiously swiped at his face while rushing towards them, only to see Mallory do the same as she'd knelt down beside them too.

The air vibrated around him. Mallory was back, sitting down in the same chair next to him. He'd half expected her to take a seat further away. There'd been something crackling between them earlier and he hadn't been sure she was happy about it. Could be he'd got that wrong. *Hope so.* His skin warmed. If only he could bury his fears, he'd be up for a night with her sometime. If she wanted the same, of course. *Only a night?* Had to be, or a few, but no more. Heading home after this contract would save him if he started getting too close. 'Shade looks happier.'

'Shade always looks happy.' Mallory smiled. 'Though she does a good poor-me act when it's time to be fed. Or when *she* thinks it's time for food.'

He'd like to get a dog but with his track record of moving on from place to place it wouldn't be fair on any pet. It was the same with women. He couldn't guarantee loving someone if it would mean settling in one place forever. He didn't know how to do that, so he'd go with his default and make the most of any opportunities on offer. 'Do you ski?' Maybe they could take a day trip to Coronet Peak together.

'Love it, and snowboarding even more. Like I told you, I grew up around here so it's a foregone conclusion I spend time on the snow whenever possible.'

Josue stretched his legs further under the table.

Mallory's gaze shifted and her breathing rate lifted.

So that was how it went. She was interested. So was he. But he wasn't about to act like a jerk and rush in.

But—but he wanted to follow up on this attraction. *Slow down, Jos.* Get to know her better first. For a fling? Something was offbeat here. *Him.* His pulse was racing and it was impossible not to watch as she sipped her beer then pulled a face. 'Would you like something different to drink?'

She blinked, pushed her half-empty glass aside, and nodded. 'I think I'll get a lemonade. I have to drive home yet. Can I get you something?'

Josue was on his feet, reaching for their glasses. 'I'll get this.'

'You got the last round.'

'*Oui.* And I'll get this one. Want something else to eat as well?' She hadn't indulged much in the fries and chicken.

'I'm going to have a burger soon, then I'm heading home for a hot shower and some clean clothes.' Another rapid blink, and she was staring across at Shade.

Clothes? It'll be bedtime by then. Bed. Mallory. Josue mentally slapped his head. He'd seen those fancy PJs she wore. 'What sort of burger?'

'Josue, you don't have to do this.'

He loved the way she said his name. Gravelly, sexy. 'It's a thank-you for last night. Your turn next time if you insist.'

'Next rescue we're on together?'

'I was thinking more along the lines of next time we share a beer at the pub.'

Her grin got him in the gut. Hard. It was genuine, carefree, and with no hidden agenda that he could see, no doubts about him. *Impressionnante.*

He spun around and aimed for the counter, turned back. 'Would you like something stronger if I drive us home?' Home? *Non*, he had somewhere else to put his head down tonight. 'I meant back to your place.'

That grin got wider, and hit harder. She dug into her pocket, then her fingers were doing a number on his palm as she handed her keys over. 'A vodka and lemon, thanks.'

He couldn't say if her dancing fingers had been deliberate, but judging by the rose shade filling Mallory's cheeks they hadn't. Feeling confused, he slid the keys into his pocket and headed for the bar, needing to find air more easily breathed.

Leaning against the counter while waiting for the order, he watched Mallory talking to the guys. She was comfortable with them, but then she worked in a male environment so it would come naturally. As was how she made him feel—like a friend already. Except the sensations tripping though his body weren't those he'd feel for any friend. This was dangerous. He didn't do strong need for a woman beyond sex. Yet he suddenly wanted to know everything about her, what was her favourite breakfast, the colour she liked the most, what side of the bed she preferred. *It couldn't happen.*

Why were his lungs squeezing with disappointment?

There was so much to her. She was tough, hadn't been fazed with the men on the rescue when they'd taken over the heavy lifting of the kids on stretchers, wore dull work clothes that fitted neatly but didn't accentuate her sexy shape, and yet her nails were manicured, her curly hair highlighted with dark blonde streaks and her make-up light and perfect.

When he sat down beside her again, he muttered, 'Impressive.'

She stared at him, wide eyed. 'What is?' Eyes he was coming to know already locked onto him. She seemed to be trying to read his mind, that look boring into his head with the temerity of a power drill.

There was no way that he was going to let her know what he'd been thinking. 'Why did you choose flying for a career?'

She continued to stare at him. 'The freedom, which is at odds with how restrictive flying really is. It's like going on an adventure every day of my life. There are so many factors contributing to the job on hand, weather, terrain, the people I'm with.' She was telling the truth, but not all the truth. He could hear there was more behind her words, in the depth of her eyes that had darkened ever so slightly while she'd been talking, in the sudden stiffness in her body.

Knowing there were things about himself he didn't share, he left it alone. 'You've obviously found your niche.'

A thoughtful expression flitted across her face, disappeared as fast as it had come. 'I think so.'

Again, he wondered more about what she didn't say than her reply. Had she ever left Queenstown to work elsewhere, or was this the only place she'd lived? Why this itch to learn so much about Mallory? It was new to him and, frankly, scary. *So put it aside, enjoy the company. Stop overthinking everything.*

Mallory led the way into her house, saying over her shoulder, 'Josue, you're back to where you were last night.'

That low sexy laugh came across the gap between them, turning her stomach to water. 'Nothing new for me.'

She turned to look at him. 'Meaning?' He was used

to finding himself in places he hadn't planned on? If so, quite the opposite of her steady life.

Josue shrugged. 'Nothing.' Then he added, 'I'm not obsessive about making plans and sticking to them.'

Again, unlike her, though not obsessive about keeping her life on track, she was careful and focused. If she'd been more in control when she'd been a teenager, she wouldn't have got pregnant and lost her baby, and been left with the fear of never becoming a mother. She would've been a nurse, not a pilot. No regrets about that one. Flying was the best job out there. But losing her baby had left a hole in her heart she'd never completely filled. He or she would've turned fourteen last month, a teenager finding their way in the world.

Sudden longing for a chance to go back and rectify her mistakes swamped her. She understood it was impossible, that there'd been nothing she could've done to save her baby, but there were moments when the yearning was unavoidable. It still gave her occasional sleepless nights, and a desperate need to stay safe and not fail anyone again.

'Mallory? Where have you gone?' Josue stood in front of her, worry flattening his mouth.

Shaking her head abruptly to banish the sadness, she lifted her face to look at this man who'd arrived into her life without warning and was tilting her so far off her heels it was scary. 'I like knowing where I'm headed and how to get there.'

'You're not just talking about a day trip, are you?'

Her mouth dropped open as she stared at him. He seemed to understand her, or parts of her, that most people weren't aware of, as far as she knew. Again—scary. Only last night she'd found him in her lounge, and even then she hadn't been overly uncomfortable around him. 'Not entirely,' she admitted.

'Come on, let's have coffee.' He took her arm to lead the way to *her* kitchen.

'Tea for me,' she muttered through the thickness in her mouth. 'Shouldn't you be getting along the road to Kayla's house?' *And leaving me alone to get a grip on my emotions.*

'I've got all night.' He was taking over, making their drinks as though he'd been here forever. As though he belonged here.

Strange, right? Certainly not something she was used to, or even encouraged with anyone except her closest friends. This was her sanctuary from the world, a place where she'd always felt loved and cared for. No one hurt her within these walls. But the way Josue fitted in *did* feel good. Almost from the start he'd begun causing her to look beyond her hectic life to see if she could make room for him—for a while.

'Milk with your tea?'

An ordinary, everyday question, and she smiled. 'Please.' And went to close all the curtains. At least today she'd set the heat pump to come on when the sun went down before she'd left for the rescue.

'You okay?' He slid a mug over the counter in front of her when she returned.

'I'm fine.' Locking her gaze on him, she added, 'Truly.'

'Good.' He came around to stand beside her, coffee in hand, and looked at the framed photos of her and her parents on the nearest wall. 'When I saw those last night, I was a little envious of the love glowing between the three of you. Your parents?' Then he took another look. 'Or grandparents?'

A common query. 'Mum and Dad. They married when they were forty and fifty and to their surprise I popped along very soon after.'

'They obviously didn't mind.'

'They adored me. Being an only child, I grew up being treated older than I really was, and that was fine, though often I found I was mentally ahead of my peers. And Kayla and Maisie are like my sisters. We get on so well about most things, so probably better than sisters.'

'You're lucky.'

Yes, she was. There was a hint of sorrow in his voice. He'd also said he felt envious looking at her family pictures. 'You didn't have such a loving childhood?'

'No.' He sipped his coffee, suddenly deep in thought. Then he faced her and said, 'Don't feel sorry for me but I grew up in foster care. When I was fifteen and headed for trouble, I met a police officer who took me under his wing. He saved my butt, and hasn't stopped since.' His smile was wry. 'I'm supposedly grown up now but it's still good to have Gabriel in my life. He's my go-to-for-advice man.'

Mallory tucked her arm through his and hugged him lightly. 'We all need one or two people to download on,' she agreed. 'That must've been hard, growing up in care. Did you get a nice family to live with?' Was the French system similar to the New Zealand one where some kids stayed long term and others moved around a lot?

'There were four families in total and I didn't fit in with any of them.'

Ouch. Not good. In her book, being surrounded by a loving family was the most important aspect of growing up, but then she'd been very lucky and didn't know any other way. 'This cop? You get along with the rest of his family?'

He went quiet for a moment, then put his hand on her shoulder and looked down at her. 'Brigitte, his wife, took me under her wing from the beginning, and wasn't as strict as Gabriel. I loved her for that alone. They never had children so they were very busy with their careers, yet there was always time for me, something I'd been looking for all my life until then. I got lucky with them, though I still struggle with it all after the way those foster families treated me.'

'To be expected.' Standing still, she watched emotions flit across his face: worry, care, tenderness, fear. 'I can't imagine what any of that was like. *Is* like.'

Placing his mug on the bench, Josue tentatively wrapped her into an embrace, his chin resting on the top of her head. 'We're getting along well so quickly. I hadn't expected anything like this.'

'Neither did I,' she whispered, as her heart thumped once, hard. This togetherness warmed her deep inside. A sensation that didn't happen often. Tightening her hold around him, she laid her cheek against him and breathed deeply, inhaling the masculine smell of his body.

Josue's hands were spread across her back, gentle and endearing. His fingertips began tracing small circles, winding her skin tighter and tighter.

Mallory raised her head, looked up at the strong jawline and on to the dark shadowed chin and on to those eyes that saw so much and were watching her with kindness and a sparkle. She drew a wobbly breath.

'I'd better get along to the house.'

'I guess you should.' Disappointment filled her head,

but he was probably right. It would be rushing things to follow through on the urge to kiss him. It wasn't her way. But there was no stopping the heat flooding her, the longing to feel his mouth on hers. What was going on? She liked to know who she was getting close to, know him better than she currently knew Josue. But there was no stopping these sensations knocking at her chest. He was wonderful, and gorgeous, and exciting.

'But before I go…' Josue lowered his head close to hers, his lips seeking hers, covering her mouth gently. Pressing into her, still gently, not demanding.

Mallory was lost. No stepping away from him. 'Yeah.' She was returning the kiss. Not so gently, but opening under his mouth, tasting those lips that had tantalised her since first meeting him. Against his chest her breasts tightened, peaking slowly. Her hands tightened against his back, pushing into him, feeling the tight ripple of his muscles under her palms.

She felt the instant Josue lifted his mouth away. *No. Come back.*

'I'll see you tomorrow.' There was a hitch in his voice.

'Okay.' She couldn't say any more through the disappointment engulfing her.

'Just one more,' Josue whispered, his mouth reclaiming hers.

Then he took her face in his hands, and pulled back barely enough to look into her eyes. 'Mallory?'

'Josue.' She nodded, running the tip of her tongue over her bottom lip. Her body melted at the desire filling his gaze, desire that matched her own and that she could feel right to the tips of her toes. Everything was happening fast, and it felt right. This had been coming ever since the night before when she'd come out of the bathroom in her PJs and robe and had seen Josue's eyes light up, sending her body into a flurry of desire. What made one man's reaction to her feel so different from others'? Not that she had loads of experience with men's reactions but enough to know Josue was different towards her. He looked at her as though she was spun gold. He touched her as though he'd never touched a woman before—carefully yet firmly, making her feel sexy.

The ensuing kiss was deeper, filled with passion, more demanding, and she gave back as much as she received from this amazing man. His lips were strong and demanding, soft and pliant, hungry—for her. He was getting to know her through their kiss. Tasting her, touching her mouth as though he could read her through his tongue.

Her hands touched him everywhere, feeling muscles through his shirt, ribs under her palms as she slid her hands from his back to his chest. Her mouth couldn't get enough of Josue's as she tried to return the intensity of his kiss, getting sidetracked by the desire firing throughout her body.

Strong hands were on her waist, raising her onto her toes against his full length. And still his mouth didn't leave hers.

Was this paradise or what? She felt as though she'd found a place she might never want to leave. A man she might not be able to walk away from. Ever. Her mouth froze.

Then cooler air crossed her lips. 'Mallory? Are you all right?'

Josue read her too easily. Or perhaps he didn't, because she couldn't be happier. Or more confused, but confusion wasn't getting in the way of sharing a wonderful moment—or more—with this man who seemed to know how to wake her up so gently she almost had to pinch herself to see if it was real.

'Do you want me to stop?' he gasped.

He would stop just like that if she said so? Wow. But it wasn't happening. She couldn't pull away. Not when her blood was pulsing through her veins and her head spinning. 'Please don't.' She raised her mouth to his again, felt him smile under her lips.

'Merci.' The word was drawn out long and slow, and did nothing to dampen her longing to feel his skin under her palms.

Deep down her stomach tightened and heat poured throughout. Her fingers quivered as she slipped her hands under his shirt and onto his back, feeling the tension in his muscles, the warmth of his skin. Then she forgot what she was doing as Josue placed his strong, large hands on her waist again, his palms like rough, cool satin on her hot skin.

Who was this man who was waking her up with a reciprocating need pulsing though his touch to connect with hers? Josue Bisset. French in his looks, in the way he wore his clothes, in that divine accent, and now she was starting to learn French in his touch. *Oui.* She needed him. Now. Pushing his trousers down those muscular thighs sent a shiver through her body as her palms grazed his hot skin and tense muscles.

Another shiver followed as her trousers slid down her legs, assisted by those large, strong, hot hands she already recognised. And he never stopped kissing her.

With his hands on her butt, she wound her legs around that incredible body, raised herself higher. Then she was being turned to lean against the wall as she kissed Josue, kissing as though her life depended upon it. Which it did at the moment. This heat, the need filling her veins, the gripping sense of falling off a ledge into a dream—this was what she'd been looking for, for so long. 'Josue,' she whispered around the need filling her mouth as he touched her, filled her and retreated, filled her, retreated, until her mind blanked except for the explosion that erupted throughout her with sensations she'd never known before.

What happened to taking things slowly? Of learning more about Mallory before getting to know her so intimately? Listening to her gentle breathing, Josue tightened his arm around her waist as they lay spooned under the covers on her bed, where she'd led him after their earth-shattering sex in the dining room. It seemed to have come out of nowhere, even when the atmosphere between them had been winding tighter and hotter for hours. He had meant it when he'd said he'd head away to the other house, and seconds later had returned to kissing Mallory instead. Because he'd been unable to stop. He'd had to kiss and taste, again and again. She'd reacted similarly, returning his kisses with a passion that undid any resolve not to get too involved—too soon, at least.

No. He had to remind himself that there could be no involvement other than a fling. He would be leaving soon and that was that. Unless… Unless nothing. Stopping in one place was alien, and to do that in another country that was not his homeland would overstretch his need to fit in. Or it might work perfectly.

Almost from the moment he'd stepped onto the ground in this country he'd had a sense of having found that something he felt had been missing for as long as he could remember. So far, he'd felt more and more at home wherever he'd gone in New Zealand, as though being so far from his previous life had lifted the self-imposed restrictions on his heart, but that still didn't mean he would settle permanently even if he found a reason to stay. Being constant, stable wasn't in his DNA. Only constantly moving around was.

Mallory snuggled that wonderful body even closer. She was something else. She was strong, focused, and appeared to know what she wanted from life, but underneath that he sensed a need. For what he had no idea, but she intrigued him, and had just blown his socks off with generous and demanding sex. Wild curly hair tickled his face with every breath he took. Those firm backside curves pressed into his groin.

A woman so different from any he'd spent time with. Or was he exaggerating in the heat of the moment? Though the heat was cooling and he still wanted her and liked what he'd experienced with her. Or rather had been stunned by it. Here was a woman he didn't want to roll away from in order to get on with the day, unlike the other women he'd got close to—and he wasn't even close to Mallory. *Yet.*

This new longing to stay put, to find out more about Mallory was taking over his usual safety mechanism of pulling down the blinds on his emotions. She made him feel as though he should let go for once, to try to find out if he really might be able to take a chance on love. *After only knowing her for twenty-four hours?* This was a far cry from when he spent weeks getting to know a woman and constantly looked out for difficulties and found them even if they weren't there. Dread slammed into his mind. This was going too far, too soon. It must never happen, he could not let himself get close. He was returning home soon. *Think, Jos. Back off now.*

But even as he berated himself, he splayed his hand across her stomach, felt the warmth transfer from her to him all down their bodies where they touched and breathed in her scent of sweat and exhaustion and sex.

'Josue?' That sharp accent cut through his meanderings.

'Oui?' How could he deny himself this moment?

'Merci.' Mallory rolled over in his arms and splayed her leg over him, her knee touching his manhood, awakening him when he'd barely recovered.

Sinking further into the bed, he allowed her to spread across him, smiling freely, without question. Happy. 'Don't thank *me*,' he gulped. Then swallowed. *He was happy?* Yes, incredibly happy. Unusually so. And it was scary. Yet his arms tightened around her.

Mallory lifted away enough to lean on an elbow and fix a gentle gaze on him. 'Problem?'

Oui. Toi. This woman read him too well. He did have a problem. She made him happy without trying, which made her a danger. Looking at her, a wave of sadness rose at the thought of leaving. He swallowed it. She was waiting for an answer, concern starting to fill those beautiful eyes. 'None at all,' he fibbed, then realised it wasn't a complete lie. Everything was perfect if he didn't think about what might happen beyond tonight and into the coming days. Taking her head gently in his hands, he pulled her down for a kiss.

Just a kiss. That went on and on, until their bodies were hot and tight and he was pushing into her as she sat over him, her head tipping back so that crazy mane swung across her shoulders and her fingernails skidded across his nipples, tightening them until he thought he'd explode. Driving into her, holding her waist to keep her with him, Josue forgot everything except Mallory and himself, joining together, coming together, dropping into a bundle of damp limbs and falling into safe oblivion.

CHAPTER FOUR

MALLORY GRINNED TO HERSELF. Her body ached in places she hadn't known existed before, and it had nothing to do with yesterday's search in the rugged hill country. The reason was singing in the shower down the hall.

Something in French that sounded off-key and hilarious because it made no sense to her. She'd nearly done the same when she'd been lathering the soap over her body under pummelling hot water fifteen minutes ago, but her singing would've scared the birds out of the garden where they were currently digging for worms amongst the weeds.

She never sang if anyone was around since her friends always gave her grief about the appalling racket she made, and there was no reason to expect Josue would react any differently. She couldn't be good at everything.

She also hadn't wanted Josue to know how alive she felt this morning. He'd probably bolt for Kayla's house, never to be seen again. But it was true, she felt more cheerful than she did normally. It wasn't unusual for her to bounce out of bed, but this morning she'd been walking on air. What a night. Josue was the man dreams were made of. Good looking, hot, tender and he'd put her first when they'd made love.

More than that, he'd been good with the boys in the bush, kind and caring, medically competent. He'd fitted in with the search team like he'd always been around. He wasn't egotistical. He wanted to be accepted, but didn't try to put it out there that he was clever. Which was all good and well as long as when it came time to finish with him she could do so without getting hurt, and she suspected it mightn't be quite that simple.

There were other men out there who had similar characteristics, but they hadn't pushed her buttons and set her tingling with anticipation. Unable to put her finger on what made him different, special even, the sort of man she'd hoped might be somewhere out there for her, was not a worry at the moment while she was still in the afterglow of a wonderful night. But she knew eventually it would creep in and set her to wondering if she'd made another misjudgement, if Josue would turn out to be all wrong once the glow faded. The only thing she knew for certain was that he wasn't staying around forever, and that was paramount to how, or if, she went about spending more time with him while remaining uninvolved.

Yet here she was, grinning like an idiot. How could she not? Her feet did a little tap dance on the spot. After finally having a shower to wash away the day's grime and the evening's fun, she'd gone to bed and had been joined by Josue, damp from his shower and ready to cuddle her to him as they'd fallen into an exhausted sleep, only to wake and make love again. Spooning together as they'd lain waiting to fall back to sleep once again had been as wonderful as the amazing sex. She'd felt comfortable with Josue, relaxed and carefree.

Hard to believe she'd found him lying uninvited on her couch the night before. The Intruder. A lot could happen in twenty-four hours. For her it had been a lot of fun and excitement. Even the hours spent searching for those boys and the drinks afterwards to wind down had been different, having Josue beside her. A bit like he was meant to be with her, and that she'd finally found someone who understood how she loved to use her skills to help people.

Her stomach was complaining of starvation, grumbling loudly, sending signals of hunger up her throat. Breakfast was urgently required, starting with tea for her, coffee for her guest. Guest? Not really. Another grin spread her mouth wide as she hummed out of tune. 'Bacon and eggs, hash browns and mushrooms.'

'Sounds good to me.'

Mallory leapt out of her skin. 'Don't creep up on me like that.'

'There wasn't any creeping happening.' Josue laughed. 'You were completely absorbed in your thoughts.'

'Always lots going on in my head.' Breathing slowly to still the rapid beating going on in her chest, she turned around to drink in the sight of the man who'd given her such a wonderful night of sex and cuddles and just being with her. She felt small beside him, but not weak or incapable. He didn't take anything away from her, instead he gave of himself for her pleasure and made her feel secure in his arms, made her stronger.

Despite his relaxed manner with people, he appeared to be a solitary man, keeping aspects about himself close, which made sense since he'd spent his childhood in care and not knowing family love as she had. That made it doubtful he'd want to get too involved when he was only here for a short time. Which was good. A couple of months of what they'd started last night? *Yes, please.* She began rising onto her toes, about to tap dance again, then got a grip on herself. Amazing sex or not, this couldn't go on willy-nilly. He'd leave and then what? Another broken heart? Her heels landed hard on the floor. *No, thanks.*

Josue placed a light kiss on her cheek then stepped around her to reach for the coffee. 'What have you got on today?'

Thump. That was her heart hitting the floor bringing her back to the stark reality of the thoughts that were running in her head. Today was a normal Sunday, with the usual chores and routines to get through. 'Grocery shopping, a few hours with Mum, and calling into work to fill in some paperwork for Kayla's flight on Friday night that I was lax about because I was so tired at the time.'

There was a contemplative look on his face as he carefully spooned coffee grains into the plunger.

'Plus the lawn could do with mowing.' Though she'd put that last on the list. Leaving it another week didn't make any difference in winter.

'I'll go along to Kayla's house to get sorted out, and see what I need for meals, and so on.'

Silence fell. Was he waiting for her to suggest he stay here for the next few days—or longer? So they could have more nights like last night? *Oh, yes.* Her hands clenched, loosened. Why not? Her body was almost humming with anticipation.

Her favourite song suddenly rang loud and clear from the kitchen counter.

Josue blinked, looked around to see where the music was coming from.

Smiling, Mallory picked up her phone, then, seeing the caller ID, her smile dimmed. 'Hi, Megan. Everything all right?' she asked the nurse from the dementia unit as she walked over to the window and stared out at the winter-dulled, overgrown English garden that had been her mother's passion, and obviously wasn't hers.

'Everything's fine. Are you coming in to see Dorothy today?'

'I'll be there later this morning. I couldn't make it yesterday as we had a rescue callout.' The staff didn't usually check on her visits. Something was not quite right. 'What's up?'

'Nothing serious, but can you spare me a few minutes when you get here? We've had to up some of Dorothy's meds and I want to talk to you about that.'

Mallory's stomach tightened. She had thought her mum had been less aware than usual lately. 'I had to remind her who I was on Thursday.'

'You've had to do that before, Mallory.'

'I know. But…' The sound of mugs being placed on the bench reminded her she wasn't alone. 'All right. I'll be there about eleven if that works for you.'

'I'll see you then.' The phone went silent.

Mallory continued staring at the weeds and sad-looking plants in what used to be a picture of colour and shapes in the garden. These days only the sparrows and thrushes were interested in the area. She should get out there and give the garden an overhaul, except what was the point when she'd only let it go again? Her mother wasn't likely to see it again, or, if she did, wouldn't recognise it as what used to be a wonderful, relaxing place to sit in the sun.

'Everything all right?' Josue called from the kitchen.

Her chest rose and fell before she turned. 'Sure. A nurse wants a chat when I go to see Mum later, that's all.' That was information enough.

'Your mother's unwell?'

'Yes.'

'Here's your tea.'

'Thanks.' Talking about Mum wasn't easy since she'd become so quiet, spending hours sitting in her rocking chair, staring at the wall, when she used to be such an exuberant woman who knew so many people. She now barely recognised her daughter. Mallory felt odd having a man in the house making tea while she took that call. It had been a long time since she'd had a man in her life, in her space, like this at all, and this was something personal, almost too personal when she still knew so little about him. 'I'll make the breakfast.'

'You're sad.' Josue was sipping his coffee as he watched her.

Gathering herself together, she gave him a wobbly smile then banged the pan on an element, poured in some oil and dug in the freezer for hash browns. 'My mother has dementia.'

'That lovely lady in the photographs? Mallory, that's awful. How do you cope?'

The next thing she knew she was being hugged tightly against that wide chest she'd often run her fingers over during the night. A kind hug filled with concern. A hug that warmed her heart. The same, yet different from his sexy hugs. 'I just do,' she whispered, snuggling closer. She could get used to this. *Hello, Mallory? He's not staying.*

'You're one tough lady,' Josue said above her head. 'Come on, let's get breakfast done so you can get on with your plans for the day.' His arms fell away.

Leaving her feeling bereft. Which was ridiculous. They didn't know each other well enough that they'd shared everything about themselves. They'd worked well as a team of two on the rescue, they'd had an amazing night that had her wishing for more along with a whole lot of other things, but two days ago they hadn't known the other existed. Last time she'd met a man and fallen for him, it hadn't been so instant, and it still hadn't lasted a year before she'd realised she hadn't loved him and how little they'd had in common after all. So to think she might find something true and meaningful in a couple of days with Josue was strange, and unlikely to work out.

Sighing, she glanced into the kitchen and gasped, dashing across to turn the heat off and cover the pan before the smoke erupted into a flame. 'That was close.' She'd been too easily distracted, first by the phone and then by those strong arms. A timely reminder that she couldn't let Josue distract her from the day-to-day routines, and that he couldn't sneak in and steal her heart, if that's what was happening. Her mother needed her here, focused, not falling for a man who lived on the other side of the world.

'Here, I'll take that outside.' Josue took the pan, holding the lid in place to prevent a fire, and disappeared out the door.

Another pan and another start on breakfast. Oil splashed into the pan as her shaking hands gripped the bottle. Had she really started falling for Josue so fast? If so, she had to put a halt to everything while she still could. That phone call from Megan had been a timely reminder about where her life was—here in Queenstown, spending time with her mum, flying choppers and helping out with Search and Rescue. It could not be about falling in love with a man who wouldn't be able to become a part of her dream.

A familiar nudge on her thigh had her looking down

into a pair of soft chocolate eyes. The confusion dominating her thoughts disappeared in a blink. 'Hello, my girl.' She rubbed Shade's head. 'Be patient. I'll feed you in a minute.'

'Is it all right I let her in? She was waiting by the door.'

'Of course it is. She's hungry.' *Like me*, Mallory admitted. She was thinking food, right? She had to be. Nothing else was happening. Not until she'd thought through everything, at least.

'How much?' Josue was holding up a scoop of dog biscuits.

'That's fine.' She nodded.

He poured them into Shade's bowl, then looked around. 'Your smoke alarm didn't go off with that smoke.'

Another thing she hadn't got around to. 'The battery needs changing.'

'Where do you keep them?'

'Second drawer.'

Within a minute the alarm was beeping to show it was back in use.

'Thanks.' Mallory cracked eggs in the pan.

'You should never let that happen. It could have been serious,' Josue warned.

'I know.' She should have dealt with it the moment she'd known the battery was flat, but she hadn't because it had been another exhausting day at work earlier in the week and she'd come home to shower and eat and had fallen asleep on the couch in front of the widescreen TV.

'I thought you said you liked to be in control.'

Drop it, will you? She'd stuffed up but nothing had gone wrong. 'I made a mistake. How do you like your eggs?'

Breakfast was quiet, almost as though neither wanted

to say anything else in case they fell out. Except she couldn't see that happening. Or was that wishful thinking? Because she knew how easy it was to get on the wrong side of someone, no matter how wonderful the night before had been. Her last short fling had finished in a disagreement about Shade and how she allowed her dog inside. Pathetic, but real. She put down her knife and fork, picked up her tea and watched Josue over the rim of her mug. She wasn't enjoying the quiet between them. 'Have you talked to Dean again?' He'd rung Josue while they'd been out looking for the boys and the call had been brief.

'Not yet. I'll do that shortly. I'm thinking I'll drop by the hospital later and introduce myself.'

'What about your plans to check out the skiing and tourist hot spots?' At one stage in the pub last night he'd been talking enthusiastically about bungee jumping and paragliding too.

'They'll keep. It's not as though I'll be working seven days a week.' Josue was watching her with a hint of hope reflected in his eyes.

What did he want from her? She wasn't offering for him to carry on staying here. Not after last night. She'd never get him out of her mind then, or her bed. Used to living on her own, she liked her space and the quiet times. Of course, there were plenty of hours when she wished for someone to be here, talking and sharing a meal, but the moments alone were mostly easy for her.

She slumped in her chair and picked up her tea and glanced across at Josue. Hell, he had her in a turmoil, with her mind throwing up questions about what she wanted. What to do about him, when usually if she met a man who interested her, she got on with spending time with him and letting the fling—if it came to that—run its course? Why not let go of all the concerns about her and Josue and just have a great time? It would be great, no doubts at all. He was sexy as. And fun. And interesting. Those three aspects made her wriggle with happiness.

She gave in—a little. 'We could go skiing next weekend, if you like.' She pointed out the window to snow-covered Cecil Peak on the other side of Lake Wakatipu. She never got tired of the stunning winter view, where the mountain appeared to be within arm's reach, the crisp white reflected on the mirror-like lake. Growing up here, the mountains were in her blood. The months she'd spent with Hogan in outback Australia where the view was brown and dry and flat compared to here for as far as the eye could see had made her feel she was on Mars.

'We can go to whichever ski field you'd prefer.'

His smile was devastating. '*Oui.* Coronet Peak first. I'm looking forward to it already.'

First? There'd be other times? Showed what offering to join him on one trip led to. Excitement tripped through her. Leaping up to get away from that smile destroying her need to remain sensible about Josue, Mallory tipped out the cold tea and started making another one. 'Let's hope we don't get called out to a rescue.'

His smile didn't dim a fraction. 'Then we'll do that and go skiing another time.'

Good answer. Except wasn't she supposed to be drawing back from the temptation that was Josue? The only way to do that was to put some space between them so she could think clearly without distractions like that damned smile. 'Right, guess I'd better get a move on.' *Wasn't I making a mug of tea?* She could drink it while applying her make-up. 'I need to be at the rest home by eleven and there's no such thing as a quick call into work. There're always wannabe pilots hanging around, wanting to talk the rotors off the flying machines.'

'I'll get out of your way,' Josue said. 'See you later?'

It would be so easy to say yes and have another wonderful night. Too easy. Drawing in a deep breath, she told him, 'I'm not sure what time I'll be done with Mum or the other chores I need to do. Maybe another day?' She was consumed with thoughts about what the nurse had to say about her mother. Fingers crossed Mum's placid persona hadn't started changing to something more aggressive, as the doctor and nurses had warned could happen. The last thing imaginable was her mother being aggressive. Not once in her life had Mallory seen her get so angry that she would lose control and hit out verbally or physically, and yet the medics had warned of the possibility.

'Yes, of course.' Josue's smile was gone. The light in those amazing eyes had flicked off. His relaxed stance had tightened. He started walking away.

Somehow, she'd hurt him. A lot. 'Josue?'

He waved over his shoulder and kept going.

No, damn it. Whatever she'd done had not been with the intention of hurting him. It had been about protecting herself. She caught up to him at the front door. 'Stop, Josue. Last night—well, it was wonderful.'

He nodded.

Now what? Try being honest, whatever that was in this case. 'I have never rushed into bed with a man so fast before. I have no regrets.'

Another nod. He wasn't making this easy.

Did he see her words as rejection? Possibly. It was, in a way, because she was afraid where this might lead. 'It's early days, Josue. We don't know each other very

well, though I trust you and like what I've seen so far.'
You can do better than that, Mallory Baine.

'It's all right, Mallory, I understand.' He ran a finger
down her cheek so softly it sent whispers of heat throughout her body.

How was she supposed to walk away from that? 'I
don't think you do,' she growled through the longing
building up inside. 'I'm not saying no to having anything
to do with you, but I need to take things slowly.' Heck,
when she got honest there was no stopping her.

Now he smiled. 'Bit late for that, don't you think?'

Warmth broke out, pushing away the chill that had
begun creeping over her. 'True.' Where to from here? 'I
have a busy life that I can't put on hold all the time. Besides, you're not here for ever, Josue.'

'I'm not usually anywhere for long, Mallory. I move
on a lot.' The seriousness in his voice was matching a
darkening in his eyes. He was giving her a warning. 'I
never stop still for any length of time.'

She should be grateful. It matched the warnings she'd
been trying to raise within herself. They could continue
having a fling and there'd be no expectations of more to
follow. While flings were supposedly short term—her
few had been—she already felt deep inside that nothing
with Josue would be short term for her. Already she'd
seen a sensitive side to him that called to her to share
herself, to open up to him about her needs and dreams,
and hopefully encourage him to talk about his in return.

'Thank you for your honesty.'

Had she just got herself into a deeper quandary? Nothing was going to be solved while standing here talking
awkwardly, so it'd be best to get on with the day and let
her mind quietly mull over everything. In the meantime,

she smiled, she couldn't just walk away without acknowledging he had affected her, and she did want more. Up on her toes, she kissed his cheek, and said, 'It *was* a wonderful night. But...'

'But what?' Driving away from Mallory had Josue grimacing with reluctance. He'd rather be back in her house, talking and sharing another coffee, making plans for going skiing or staying in and cuddling up in bed with their bodies entwined. Except for the sentence she hadn't finished.

Last night had to be one of the most amazing times he'd experienced with a woman, and that came from the way she made him feel so at home with her—if this unusual sense of having found his niche in the world was anything to go by. Not once had she made him feel out of place. *Wrong.* There had been that moment when he'd been lumbering to his feet from her couch that first night to face her steady glare and demanding questions.

But that had passed quickly and last night she'd been as ready for his kisses as he had hers, then when they'd let down the last barriers and he'd lifted her into his arms and up against the wall she'd been more than ready for him.

'But...' she'd said.

Not once had he questioned what they were doing in terms of what Mallory's expectations might have been. Was this to be a one-night stand? Or the beginning of a fling? A relationship? His stomach pulled inwards. That wasn't happening. They'd both end up hurt if that was her expectation. She'd been happy to share their lovemaking. Not that there'd been time to think about anything once they'd started kissing.

He had hauled on the brakes briefly, worried she would change her mind, but his concern had quickly been doused with more hot kisses followed with opening their bodies to each other. It had happened in a flash of need and heat that had scorched the air around them and blanked everything from his mind except Mallory and what she'd been doing to him.

The house he was making for appeared in his vision within moments. No wonder Mallory had been startled when he'd said where he'd been heading the other night. He had been so close. No regrets, however, or he might not have got to know Mallory so well so quickly. The chances of going out on yesterday's search would've been remote as no one had known he was in town, and even if he had and had ended up at the pub with everyone, he doubted he'd have spent much time with her.

Parking in the driveway he looked around at the neat lawns and tidy gardens. Obviously, Kayla spent more time working on her property than Mallory did, unless she paid to have it done. Everything was in its place, not a blade of grass too long, no weeds had dared raise their green heads between the shrubs, which meant inside would be as immaculate. And impersonal, he sighed.

But, then, he wasn't known for making his apartments anything more than somewhere to put his feet up. It might be why he'd felt oddly comfortable at Mallory's with her photos and shelves of books. It was cosy and friendly. With Shade's basket, rug and toys everything felt warm and homely. As far as he understood homely to be, that was.

At the front door he inserted the key he found in the meter box and let himself in. *Oui*, spick and span, not a dust mote to be seen. Hopefully Kayla had someone come in and do the work or he'd be busier here than at the emergency department. Chuckling as he made his way through the house, he found the bedroom obviously allocated to him with a pile of towels on the dresser and extra pillows stacked neatly on the end of the bed. Everything was too perfect, but he had no complaints. He'd have hated to find the home grubby and unkempt. It was the warmth of Mallory's home, as well Mallory herself, that had him looking twice here.

Get out of my head, Mallory Baine.

Like that was going to work. Not even before last night, and now there wasn't a hope in Hades. At first, she'd tickled his interest, and then she'd exploded into his head and shaken him to the core. Throughout his life he'd looked for love—mostly from foster parents because there hadn't been anyone else to expect it from. He'd made two close friends at medical school, but guys didn't admit that a close friendship had an element of love involved. What he'd presumed love to be with the two women he had got into serious relationships with had fallen by the wayside as he'd fought his demons. He'd wanted to fall in love but conversely had kept questioning himself about whether he'd finally found love, pushing away from both women when he'd begun overthinking his inexperience with emotional commitment. He'd hurt them both, and himself, due to his lack of confidence.

Now he'd met Mallory and the same questions were beginning to haunt him, only there was a difference. Never before had he felt anything near the warmth and sense of belonging he already felt with Mallory.

Which was why you warned her you don't settle down anywhere long term. He'd been looking out for her, didn't want to hurt her at all. Yes, and he'd been thinking of himself because he would not be staying on in New Zealand once his time at Queenstown Hospital was up. Would he be able to walk away from here as per normal when there wasn't a lot to hold him in Nice?

When he'd been preparing to fly out of France, Gabriel had told him to be open to opportunities, to grab them with both hands and see where they led. As if Gabriel believed he should be open-minded to another country, another language and a different lifestyle, and to a wonderful, caring and fun woman who might creep under his skin so fast it would be impossible to understand and accept as what he wanted, and needed.

He wouldn't.

He'd get on with what he'd come here to do, and see Mallory when they crossed paths in work or with Search and Rescue. She'd said she was unavailable tonight, but he didn't believe her. She was putting distance between them and he should be grateful, not feel let down. She was doing what he normally did. It felt as though she had rejected him. He was used to doing the rejecting long before his heart was involved, because that kept him safe. But last night had been wonderful, exciting and heartwarming. If Mallory thought they should take things slowly, then what had last night meant? There'd been no slowing down whatsoever.

Hades, but he really didn't know what he wanted. *Yes, you do.* What he didn't know was what to do about it. Risk-taking was not his thing, and getting close to Mallory would be the biggest risk of all.

One day at a time, *mon ami.*

She'd turned down his suggestion of getting together tonight. Rejection stung. What now? Go slowly, spend time with her whenever possible, take the risk she might turn him down again? Was working here and then return-ing home to France without getting to know Mallory even a viable option? Or would it be best to spend time with her and take whatever consequences arose on the chin?

One day at a time. It was possible. If he wanted this.

Right now, he had his bags to unpack and a depart-ment head to meet.

His phone vibrated in his pocket.

His chest expanded as warmth stole through him. *Mal-lory?*

Dean's name flashed on the screen.

Josue grunted a laugh at himself. Served him right for getting so excited over a phone ringing. '*Bonjour.* How's everything?'

'Come in, Shade.' Mallory's mother's eyes lit up as the dog bounded into her room. 'How's our girl?'

Shade laid her head on Dorothy's knees for the cus-tomary pat while Mallory placed the caramel chocolate and oranges she'd brought on the table, before giving her mother a kiss and then a hug she didn't want to stop. This was her mum. 'How's things, Mum?' At least she'd remembered Shade's name.

'I can't find my pyjamas anywhere. Did you take them home to wash?'

'No, I didn't. I'll have a look around, shall I?'

'Megan's done that, and she didn't find them. Some-one's taken my slippers too.'

Mallory sighed. This wasn't how she liked the day to start off, though to be fair her mum was sounding quite lucid today. Opening drawers and lifting clothes, she searched for any of the three sets of pyjamas usually there and came up blank. They were most likely hidden somewhere in the room, though Megan had said she couldn't find them anywhere when they'd had their talk. This was not an uncommon problem. Her mother often hid items like a pair of earrings or her favourite books and they inevitably turned up behind other books on the shelf, or in the back of a cupboard behind towels or shoes. 'I can't find them either. Let's do your nails now and I'll take another look later.'

Megan had also told her how her mother had started going for walks in the middle of the night. She'd been found in the staff kitchen, and out in the gardens, sitting watching the stars with only a thin dressing gown on in the bitter cold. It wasn't unusual with dementia and the staff had only wanted to keep her up to date with everything, but it had knocked Mallory. Knowing this was coming and actually hearing about her mother's wanderings were two different things and it upset her. There was nothing she could do to prevent her mother from doing this, and had to accept the staff were doing their best to keep her safe.

Mallory sighed and got out the nail polish remover and a bottle of polish before placing a stool by her mum's feet, ready to get on with making her mother happy.

'What colour this week?'

Mallory rubbed the wriggling feet before her to warm them. 'I've got blue with sparkles.'

'Goody. Reminds me of summer skies.'

It was one of her mother's better days. Despite the missing clothes, she was more alert and there hadn't been an awkward moment when she didn't know her daughter. Mallory smiled softly.

Of all the moments of forgetfulness and agitation the one that always got her in the heart was her mum forgetting her daughter's name. Sometimes it was only her name she forgot, other times she didn't even know who Mallory was. Mallory ranked them together. Hard, painful lumps of sorrow always filled her heart and stomach and brought on a load of memories of growing up and being laughed with, growled at, teased and encouraged by her mother's strong yet sweet voice. *Mallory, you mustn't. Mallory, yes, you can go. No, Mallory, don't do that. I love you, Mallory.*

Her heart swelled. She'd had a wonderful childhood that had followed her into adulthood, giving her the grounding for who she'd become and what she'd wanted for the future. Her future had to contain love. Deep and abiding love. She had plenty to give. It wasn't wrong to expect some in return.

Josue popped into her head. They'd clicked from the beginning. Yesterday's rescue showed how well they worked together. Last night in bed they'd been almost one, had read each other like a book. Already she felt he had a place in her life, as though she couldn't let him go. But he'd warned her he didn't settle anywhere for long, so backing off a bit would be wise. She glanced at her mother, who was watching her paint a nail. She wouldn't be leaving Queenstown to follow Josue anywhere. 'I've met a man I like, Mum. He's staying at Kayla's house and going to work at the hospital.'

'Handy for you.' Her mother's smiles were crooked since having some teeth removed, as though she was trying to hide the gaps.

Mallory had arranged an appointment in a few weeks with an orthodontist in Dunedin to sort out getting false teeth for her. 'He's French, from Nice. And he's gorgeous.' She kissed the tips of her fingers on one hand and spread them wide.

'Les Francais s'embrassent comme le diable.'

'What did you just say?' Her mother didn't speak French. Or so she'd believed.

'Frenchmen kiss like devils.' There was a twinkle in her eyes unlike any Mallory had seen in years.

'You know this how?'

'I kissed a Frenchman once. More than once really. When I was nineteen and went to France with my sisters. We met some men at the camping ground we were staying in. I fell in love with him.'

'What happened?' Mallory asked, the nail-polish brush hovering in the air above the middle toe. She'd never known her mother had once gone to France, let alone fallen in love while there. Was this true or a figment of her imagination?

'We had a good time and then I fell out of love and came home.' Her mother's eyes were flooded with memories. Good ones, judging by the soft smile lifting her mouth. A familiar smile she'd seen her mother give her father often throughout her life. It always softened Mallory's heart to know how in love her parents had been in their marriage. And now she was learning there'd been another man her mother might have smiled at like that. A Frenchman to boot.

But her mum had said she'd fallen out of love. *Like I did with Hogan when he started getting too demanding about how I did the housework or drove the car? Could I be more like Mum than I've ever considered?* Hey, that might mean there *was* someone special waiting around the corner like her dad had been for her mother. Josue? But he wasn't around any corner. He'd been in her house, her bed. She'd met him and they got on brilliantly. She was forgetting—or ignoring—the fact he'd be heading away again. Another thought brought reality to the fore. Even if she and Josue did get close enough to want to be together and she was free to follow him to France, she couldn't work. The language barrier would prevent her endorsing her pilot's licence there, so she'd be unemployable except for possibly a mundane job that brought her no excitement. It would be for the same reason she wouldn't be able to qualify as a paramedic either. The last thing she'd ever want to do would be to rely on someone else to support her, even for the time it took her to become fluent in another language—which could take years.

'Mallory, the polish is drying on the brush.'

It was. 'You surprised me about your Frenchman, and I forgot what I was doing.' Definitely one of her mum's better days. Almost how it used to be between them. 'What was his name?'

'Who? Tell me about your man.' Mischief twinkled out of pale blue eyes that had seen a lot over a lifetime of family and hard work, diverting attention from her past love.

'Mum, he's not my man.' And wasn't going to be if she remained sensible. If she decided to be less sensible, then he'd be her lover until he disappeared on a big tin bird and she'd get back to her normal, gratifying life. Alone. But not lonely. She had her friends and mother. Why did that suddenly make her feel despondent? She loved her job and being a part of the Search and Rescue team. Her home was comfortable, though there was always something needing to be done to it. Now that Kayla had returned home and was living almost next door, and Maisie was dealing with her own problems but with the potential of also coming home soon, she was happy.

Except it was time to find a man to settle down with permanently and get rid of this restlessness. Josue didn't fit her needs. He moved on a lot. She stayed put. So her heart would be at stake if she fell for him. She'd been there twice, and wasn't looking for a third mistake.

'Mallory Baine, when you get distracted like that, I know something—or someone—has got you in a dither. Now spill. Who is he?'

Forget losing her memory. This was the version of her mother when Mallory had been a teenager, testing her toes in the world of boys. She laughed. 'Josue, and, yes, he does kiss like the devil.' Too much information probably but she was so enjoying this rare moment with her mother that she didn't care.

'We clicked right from the start when I found him in my house, lying on the couch.' She went on to explain what had happened and how Josue had stayed the night. She didn't mention the next night and why he'd stayed then as well. That was far too much information. Not even at her most understanding would her mother have been hearing that.

'I'm glad you've met this man and you like him so much. It's about time.'

'You're rushing things, Mum.' Which was unlike her. Could it be that she wanted to see her daughter settled while she could still understand what was going on half of the time? Mallory's heart bumped. 'I am not falling in love and about to ride off into the sunset with him.'

If only it was that simple. But then nothing worth having was ever straightforward, or so her parents had repeatedly told her when she'd been growing up. So far, she'd chalked up one pregnancy that had ended disastrously and left her fearful of never having children. The relationship with Jasper, the baby's father, had ended equally badly, as had her relationship with Hogan, which, in hindsight, she'd been glad had run its course.

Career-wise, she had few regrets about not following through with the nursing course she'd signed up for as she'd been about to leave school, despite her having planned on becoming a nurse all her life—until the day her baby had died.

Being a pilot was wonderful and took her to places she'd never otherwise see. It also stretched her courage when flying in turbulent weather or retrieving people from rough seas or off sheer cliffs. It had taught her to be confident but wary, to be vigilant and focused. Now she wouldn't trade her career for any other, but she'd never quite let go of the idea of nursing, because it meant helping people. Being a first-aider was the antidote. In a way she was getting the best of both options, helping those in dire circumstances and feeding her need for action and excitement.

As she thought about Josue and her reaction to him, she finished painting her mother's fingernails. 'There you go. Done for another week.'

Dorothy held her hands up to study her nails. 'Pretty colour. Thanks, darling. What about yours? You were wearing that purple shade last week.'

Sometimes there was nothing at all wrong with her mother's memory. 'I'll do mine tonight. Do you want to come shopping with me at Frankton? Megan's okay with it.' As long as she watched her like a hawk. 'We could get you a new jersey to go with those navy trousers you're wearing.' Replacing the pyjamas was the real reason for the trip, but she didn't want to raise the subject and possibly upset her mother's good mood.

'I haven't got any money at the moment. It's gone. I think someone stole it.'

Okay, not a perfectly clear mind after all. 'That's fine, Mum. I've got my wallet with me.' She covered all her mother's day-to-day expenses, while the unit she lived in here at the rest home was covered by the family trust her dad had set up when he'd learned he was ill.

'Then what are we waiting for? Shade, we're going out, my girl.'

CHAPTER FIVE

'THE ONE THING I don't miss from here is this damned cold.' Maisie was curled in on herself in the passenger seat, wearing one of Mallory's woollen coats and a knitted hat. She'd flown down late yesterday from Tauranga so she could visit Kayla today, and had stayed the night with Mallory. They'd sat up talking for hours, catching up on everything they'd been up to, including discussing the Frenchman living in Kayla's house, and getting Mallory to fess up about spending the night with him.

'So you've said at least ten times since stepping off the plane last night. You be careful on the road with my car when you drive it later.' Mallory grinned as she blew warm air on her clasped hands while waiting for the heater to warm up. With a thick puffer jacket over a wool jersey and thick shirt with a merino body-tight top under those, it was still freezing outside her warm house. The temperature gauge read minus nine degrees.

It had been a long, cold week, and not only due to the weather. Deliberately avoiding Josue had been hard. Longing woke her during the nights, and it had been impossible to make sense of the need and emotions and warnings swirling through her head. But she'd felt she had to do it, to at least appear nonchalant, and not dropping at his feet with longing.

'I'm not that out of practice,' Maisie muttered through her glove-covered hands. 'Not like you and men.'

'You want to walk to Wanaka, by any chance?'

'It'd be quicker than sitting here, trying to get warm.' Maisie laughed. 'You know I get homesick every time I visit. No one gives me a hard time like you.'

'Maybe you should think about returning. You can't let the Crim wreck your life forever.' Maisie's ex-husband was doing time for ripping off old ladies of their hard-earned savings.

Maisie was quiet for all of twenty seconds, then blurted, 'I have applied for a job at the hospital. It's in a new department being set up and won't start until next year.'

'My day just got better.' Mallory unclipped her seat belt and leaned over to hug her friend. 'About bloody time.' Yes, the three of them back in town at long last.

Maisie sniffed. 'Glad you agree.'

'You didn't think otherwise?'

'Not really.' The doubt was new for Maisie. But after all she'd been through because of the Crim it was no surprise.

'Cheer up. We'll have the rose petals all over the drive when you arrive. You can stay with me.'

'You might have a Frenchman living with you by then.'

'If you've got nothing better to say, then shut up.' Mallory put the car into gear and began backing out the drive. Her girlfriends got away with saying things no one else could, but Maisie's words hit home, racking up the doubts—should she remain out of contact while she still could?

A yawn ripped through her. The late night was catching up already. Except she'd been tired before she'd picked up Maisie yesterday.

Glancing up the road to Kayla's house, she noted Josue's car parked outside. His headlights had lit up her window as he'd driven home earlier after a night at work and she again thought of him lying in her bed, his body wrapped around hers. Shaking her head, she headed for the intersection, taking her time as black ice became apparent the nearer she got to the corner.

'Watch out,' she yelled as two cars sped past the end of her road in opposite directions. The back wheels of one began to slide. 'Don't brake,' she shouted, even though no one would hear her.

Brake lights glowed red and then an almighty bang reached her inside the car as the vehicles collided. The larger four-wheel drive stopped with its engine crushing the front and driver's side of the car. Two people in the front seats had been thrown forward into the broken mess.

'There's never a dull moment being a nurse.' Maisie was already undoing her seat belt.

Pulling over to one side, Mallory picked up her phone and tapped the most recent number she'd added to her contacts. Climbing out of her car, she felt relief when Josue answered immediately. 'Can you come down the road to the corner? There's been a serious head-on collision and I saw two people being tossed about inside one vehicle.'

'On my way.' And he was gone.

People were coming out of their houses all along the street. Two men were rushing to the accident, phones to their ears.

'I've rung a doctor,' she said when she reached them. 'And Maisie here's a nurse.'

'I'm onto 111 for fire and ambulance,' her neighbour told her.

'I'll hang up then,' the other guy said. 'Holy crap. This is a mess. Did you see what happened, Mallory?'

'The SUV lost it on the black ice.' She approached the squashed sedan and could see it hadn't been a front to front hit, but the side of the sedan was also caved in. Other people were gathering, some already trying to open the doors. Maisie pushed through. 'Excuse me, I'm a nurse.'

A familiar black vehicle braked to a halt beside them and Josue climbed out, a small leather bag swinging from his hand.

It was as though she'd been on a diet for days and now someone had handed her a plate of dessert. He was as stunning as she remembered, and as tall and broad as her body remembered, too. Gulp.

'Has anyone called an ambulance?' he called to her.

'Yes. And Maisie's here, over at the SUV. She's a nurse.' Mallory focused on the emergency as she made her way to the passenger side, where she could see a woman inside slumped against the console.

Josue was striding across to the mangled cars. 'Mallory, can you triage the passenger while I do the same with the driver?' he asked as he took in the details.

Pride filled her. He knew she was capable. 'Of course.' She smiled. Someone had brought a crowbar and was attempting to open the driver's door. At least the passenger door wasn't stuck. As she leaned in towards the woman, she called, 'Everyone, this is Josue Bisset. He's a doctor.'

Josue looked around. 'Anyone injured in the other vehicle?'

'Two tourists and they're are upright but complaining of pains in various places,' Maisie called.

'The fire truck's on the way,' someone else informed him.

Mallory squatted on her haunches, kneeling down to see what had happened to the passenger. 'Hello, I'm Mallory, a first-aid responder. Can you hear me? What's your name?'

'Pam. What happened?' Her eyes opened slowly, and she tried to look around but quickly shut them again.

'You've been in an accident. Can you move your legs?' From what she could see under the airbag it looked like Pam's left one was jammed solid.

The eyes opened again, pain reflecting out at Mallory. 'I can move the right a little, but it gets tight if I try to pull it up.'

'Best not to try any more. You might cause more swelling. I'm going to check your pulse and then look for any other injuries. Is that all right?'

Pam nodded. 'I think I banged my head on the side of the car. The seat belt dug into my chest hard.' Blood was oozing down the side of the woman's head.

'Josue, have you got sterile pads in your bag?' Mallory asked through the smashed windscreen. 'We've got a head wound here.'

'Yes. Help yourself. I'll take a look at the wound as soon as I can.' He hadn't looked up from examining his patient's face and was lifting her eyelids to check her eyes.

'I've got them,' a man called over the car. 'How many do you want, Mallory?'

'Two, thanks.' The wound reached from Pam's forehead to behind her ear. 'Any dizziness, Pam? Is your eyesight clear?'

'My eyes are a bit blurry. My head's throbbing.'

Her speech was strong and clear, despite the shock that must be setting in. The hit to her head can't have caused concussion then. 'You're doing well.' Fingers crossed. Mallory dabbed at the bleeding area on Pam's head with a pad before placing the second one over the whole wound. 'Right, let's see what your pulse is doing.' She reached for Pam's wrist.

'The fire truck's arrived,' someone announced from behind her. 'Ambulance is nearly here.'

Mallory continued counting the beats under her finger and timing a minute on her watch.

'Need you here, Mallory.' There was an urgency in Josue's voice that didn't bode well for the woman he was attending.

Mallory placed Pam's wrist on her thigh and leapt up, said to the closest person standing by, 'Hold her hand and talk to her, will you?' Then she dashed around to the other side of the car, where the door had been wrenched wide, exposing the injured woman. Mallory gulped at the carnage confronting her, but she didn't have time to stop and recover her breath. Josue had his fist pressed hard into the woman's inner thigh, blood everywhere. 'What can I do?'

'We need to get her out of here so I can put more pressure on this. The femur's fractured and torn the artery. Get those men to help you while I try and keep pressure on this.'

Looking across to the firemen, she called out, 'Jamie, over here fast. We have to retrieve this woman urgently, and Josue can't step away for a moment.'

Jamie instantly issued orders, at the same time surveying the situation. 'Ryan, get a stretcher. Joe, with me. We'll take the shoulders and head. Nick, you take her legs. Josue, I'll tell you when to move and how. Mallory, you squeeze beside Josue and place your arms under her waist.'

She slipped into the minuscule space hard up against Josue and waited for Jamie to give the instructions.

'Take it slowly,' Josue warned. 'If I lose pressure, we have a problem.'

'Right. Ready. Everyone, slow lift now.'

Mallory's legs tightened and pinged with pain as she started to straighten, her arms taking the weight of the woman's torso as Josue struggled to stand up in the confined space while still pressing into that thigh.

'Keep lifting.' Jamie was watching everything like a hawk. 'Higher, Nick, counteract Josue pushing down. That's it. Right, everyone, one step away from the car. Another, another. That's it. She's free. Ryan, where's that stretcher?'

'Right here.'

'Okay, everyone, lower her onto the stretcher. One, two, three.'

Within moments the woman was lying on the stretcher and Mallory was on her knees beside her. 'Josue, want me to take over so you can do whatever else that's needed?'

'Yes. It won't be easy swapping places. We can't stop the pressure or she'll lose more blood. Clasp your hands into a fist like mine.' He nodded when she did so and said, 'Now put them hard against mine and push down at the same time as moving with me to replace my hands. Good. Keep going. Great. Stop. Now hold that pressure in place. Do not let up at all. Understand?'

'Yes.' She'd learned to do this in her advanced training, but actually doing it and having someone's life relying on her getting it right was frightening.

'You're great,' Josue said quietly.

Surely he meant *doing* great? It didn't matter. He made her feel special whatever he meant. 'So are you,' she replied equally softly. As a doctor, a lover and a man she already couldn't get enough of.

'Let's hope you're right.' He raised one eyebrow slowly and smiled. Then he straightened and looked around. 'Where's that ambulance?'

'Right here. Two more on the way,' Jamie informed them, reminding her she and Josue weren't alone here.

Of course, she knew they weren't but for a moment there she'd felt there was no one else around, even when her hands were pushed into a badly injured woman's thigh to hold back the bleeding that threatened her life. 'You going to hospital with this woman?'

Josue was shining a torch into the woman's eyes and getting no response. 'We need to fly her to Dunedin urgently.'

'Scott will be on standby at the airport.'

'Who calls him in?'

'You can. Or Jamie. My phone's in my pocket.' She held her breath at Josue touched her hip as he found the phone. 'There's a direct number under Emergency Rescue in Contacts.'

'Got it.' Josue punched the number and held her phone against his ear.

Mallory said, 'Tell Scott there's an empty section fifty

metres from the intersection. The cops will keep everyone away for him to land.'

He nodded. 'Will do. Scott? This is Josue Bisset. We have an emergency out on the corner of Mallory's road.' He rattled off the street names with a quick glance her way. Checking he was right? Or remembering how he'd got the address wrong the other night? 'I have a woman needing to get to Dunedin Hospital fast—like yesterday. Good. Thanks.' He shoved the phone back in her pocket. 'He's lifting off now.'

Josue placed a hand on their patient's carotid artery, checking his watch. After a minute he lifted his fingers off the artery, a frown between his eyes. 'Low pulse here. And there was no response when I shone the torch directly into her eyes.'

'Head injury?'

'There's a soft area on the forehead I don't like.' His hands were spread over the scalp, his fingers careful as he searched for more damage.

Mallory glanced sideways through the car to Pam, who was now being attended to by the paramedic and first aider from the ambulance. 'Pam's pulse was normal five minutes ago,' she called across to them.

'Thanks, Mallory. Did the doc give her any painkillers in preparation for the engine being lifted away?'

'Not yet.' There hadn't been time, and she doubted if Josue carried restricted drugs with him. Checking she hadn't lightened the pressure on the wound beneath her hands, she looked over the thigh for any indications of other bleeding. Nothing, but there was a sharp shape to the trousers where the femur had broken. She shuddered at the thought of the pain that would've hit the woman at the moment of impact. In some ways it was best she was unconscious.

The heavy thumping of rotors filled the air, announcing Scott's arrival.

'At last,' Josue muttered as he wound a wide crepe bandage around his patient's head that a paramedic from a second ambulance had supplied at his request.

Mallory felt a similar relief, even though Scott had been fast getting here.

Within minutes the woman was being loaded into the chopper, Mallory still applying pressure until Josue could take over for the flight to Dunedin. With the other ambulances having now arrived, a paramedic was accompanying him. As Josue placed his hands over the still-bleeding site he said again, 'You're great.'

Straightening as far as the cramped interior allowed, she smiled and repeated her earlier reply. 'You too.' They were so in sync it warmed her throughout. He was a great doctor, and as for the man, great didn't begin to describe how she felt. If not for him, this woman's chances would be even slimmer. If not for him, her heart would be lying quietly, not beating a little harder and more erratically every time they interacted. 'We work well together.' Along with the other things that they did so well together. Her skin heated, and she had to resist the urge to reach out and take his hand. Wrong place, wrong time.

'Catch up tonight?' A hint of longing flitted through his eyes, quickly replaced with a nonchalance she didn't believe.

'I'd like that.' She'd restrained herself from calling in on him all week and suddenly she was more than ready to spend time with him again. 'I'll text you. I have to take Maisie to the airport.' Then she dropped out of the chopper onto the ground and rushed over to the wreckage without looking back, taking that smile and the warmth in his eyes with her.

'Mallory, I understand you witnessed the accident.' Zac was standing by the wreckage in his police uniform. 'I'll need to get some details when you've got a moment.'

'You can ask me too.' Maisie appeared from behind her. 'Hello, Zac.'

He must've cricked his neck at the speed he turned to stare at his best mate's sister. 'Maisie, how the hell are you?' And he stepped up to wrap her in his arms. 'Long time no see.'

Maisie grinned and leaned back to look up at him. 'If you didn't go bush so often, maybe you'd see me when I come to town.'

Mallory feigned a yawn. 'All right if we get on with this? Maisie and I are on our way to see Kayla in Wanaka.' If only these two would get over themselves and get together, she thought, but they were both stubborn as mules. 'This is what I saw happen, Zac.'

Josue parked outside Kayla's house and leaned back against the head rest. So much for a day off. First Mallory's call about the accident as he'd been about to drop into bed after a long night in the department, and then the flight to Dunedin, where their patient had immediately been admitted for urgent surgery. Despite the woman's heart stopping once due to blood loss and low blood pressure, she'd survived that far, and he was hopeful that once the surgeons had got her in Theatre her chances would rise. They'd promised to let him know later on today how she'd got on and what else they'd found.

He'd been dropped off at home by the paramedic after

they'd returned to Queenstown. *Home?* Not the house necessarily, but he still felt comfortable in this town, with the people he worked with, and especially with Mallory. It was as though he belonged here, which he couldn't really. He didn't belong anywhere much except in Nice, and even there he tended to stay on the periphery of the group of friends he'd made through medical college and working in various hospitals.

As much as he'd hankered for caring friends and people to love him, as soon as he'd started getting close to anyone the old fears of being found lacking would start to haunt him.

Had he left some of his hang-ups behind when he'd come to this country? It was almost as though, because no one knew him, he could relax some of his fears of being rejected and therefore felt accepted.

Then there was Mallory. She added to, or was, the main reason he felt as though he'd found someone special that he could bond with. Like with Dean, he'd felt close to Mallory from the beginning. Unlike with Dean, there was a lot more in the closeness than just friendship. She was sexy and gorgeous and kept his veins bubbling just thinking about her.

Was she the reason Queenstown felt comfortable in a way nowhere else had for him? That couldn't be true. He had to be exaggerating the hunger for more to life than work and an occasional fling that had begun filling him from the night he'd met her. Hard to believe only one week ago she'd woken him on her couch, her eyes filled with questions and a warning not to be a smartass with her.

For two nights and two days he'd enjoyed her company over pizza and coffee, out in the bush, and getting very close in her bed. Then he hadn't set eyes on her until this morning. She was as beautiful as he'd remembered, as confident and capable dealing with the accident victims as she'd been with the boys last Saturday.

A sigh escaped. He'd missed her all week, especially when he hadn't been busy at work and had time on his hands. Twice he'd picked up his phone to call her. Both times he'd stared at her number, finger hovering above the screen as he'd thought hard. Should he call when he knew the day would come when he'd walk away? Already he knew he must not hurt her as he'd done Colette and Liza. She deserved better.

One evening he'd even debated walking down to her door and having a chat, sharing a coffee, catching up on what she'd been doing since they'd gone their separate ways after that amazing night in her bed. But she'd said no to seeing him last Sunday night, making him back off and give her some space. His heart had picked up when he'd suggested they get together tonight, and she hadn't hesitated to say yes. Relief had swamped him, quickly replaced with excitement. There was no stopping the sense that this time he might get it right.

As though there was more to come and he couldn't wait for it to unfold. Unbelievable. He hadn't done this in a long time, having decided it was best for everyone that he not get deeply involved. An occasional fling was one thing, safe and easy. This sense of knowing Mallory, of her knowing him, of wanting to find out more was new and exciting, but still scary.

A sharp wind rocked his vehicle, reminding him that his life at the moment included staying in this house while he worked at the local hospital, going on emergency medical flights to various cities and helping search for missing people. And perhaps even making friends, especially with a fascinating woman who lived only two hundred metres down the road.

There were a couple of hours to get through before Mallory turned up. It took only minutes to take off the filthy clothes he was wearing from working with the injured woman and throw them into the washing machine.

'Now what?' he wondered, looking around the immaculate living area. He could go for a drive along the lake and take a look around, but the idea didn't grip him. The day was getting on, cooling down rapidly, and he couldn't find any enthusiasm to go out. Was Mallory flying tourists around the mountains? He hadn't seen any sign of her at the airport when he'd got out of the rescue helicopter. But another woman had been with her at the accident so she could be anywhere. More likely she was probably on a tourist flight somewhere. What a fabulous job, flying around mountains and over lakes and taking people up to the snow-covered slopes.

Grr. He should be doing *something* instead of thinking about Mallory. Hadn't she mentioned mowing her lawn last weekend? It hadn't been done. Was that something he could do to ease this new restlessness winding through his veins?

He now had Kayla's number in his phone, so he texted her.

OK to use your mower to cut Mallory's lawn?

She came back in an instant. Help yourself. It's her mower anyway. You'll be her best friend forever. K

He laughed. Now, there was a good idea. Friends and then lovers? But they'd already made love. And he wanted to do that again, to hold Mallory and kiss her and run his hands over her satin skin. Friends next? Friendly lovers? Time to start on the lawn.

The mower in Kayla's shed was a ride-on and seemed to have as many gadgets as the helicopters Mallory flew. Typical of what he was getting to know about her. She certainly had a mechanical side to her brain. Plus a very feminine one, judging by the soft blouse and trousers she wore when not working, and the sexy lace panties and bra underneath that he'd had fun removing from her soft, warm body.

After a couple of minutes checking out the controls Josue got on board and started up, rode down the road and onto Mallory's lawn. He only hoped he'd got the settings right or there was going to be some explaining to do about chunks missing in the lawn. He hadn't used a ride-on before but it was a simple process once he figured out all the levers and buttons and soon he was driving around the massive lawn, quickly learning to dodge branches of trees strategically placed to take his head off if he wasn't vigilant.

The sun had almost disappeared behind the mountain when he finally rolled the mower into the shed and shut off the motor. The air was cold and crisp with the promise of another frost in the morning and yet Josue was warm with exhilaration. He'd enjoyed being outside in the crisp air and saving Mallory a chore this coming weekend. It also made him feel more at home than ever.

Careful, Jos. A mown lawn didn't make this his home or future. The warning didn't wipe the smile off his face or out of his chest, though. He fist-pumped as he headed inside for a sandwich. The fresh air had made him hungry.

* * *

The small stone-walled pub with a large open fire was busy as Mallory and Josue made their way up to the bar. 'Hey, Julie, how's things?' Mallory asked the girl pulling a beer.

'Great. I hear you went on the search for those boys last weekend. A good result.'

'It was.' She nodded to Josue. 'This is Josue Bisset. He was on the rescue too.' *By the way, he's wonderful.*

'Hi, Josue. Let me finish this order and I'll be right with you.'

Josue nodded, then looked at Mallory. 'You always know someone wherever you go.'

'That's what happens growing up in a small district, going to school and then working here. So many people are a part of that.'

'Have you done any travelling? Been overseas at all?'

'Once.' Not one of her favourite topics of discussion, her only trip abroad. She looked around. 'Shall I grab a table while there's one available?'

Josue's eyes narrowed a fraction, but all he said was, 'Sure. What do you want to drink?' So he'd noticed her reluctance to answer his questions.

Hopefully he wouldn't push it. 'A vodka and lime, thanks.'

She moved through the people crowded around tables and snagged one against the wall and hauled herself up onto a stool and rested her chin in her hand, trying to look dignified. The down side to being short was not being able to slip onto a bar stool with aplomb. She crossed her legs. The red leather ankle boots were her favourite winter accessory. They went with most of her outfits, and especially tonight's black fitted trousers and red-and-white shirt and black short jacket.

'Here you go.' Her vodka appeared in front of her.

She looked up into those intense eyes and smiled. 'Thanks.' Josue was so good looking she wanted to tighten her arms around herself and dance on the spot. He was with *her*, and he'd held her hand as they'd strolled through the town from his vehicle to here, making her feel special. Making her regret staying away over the week. It was time she'd never get back and she'd missed him. Strange, but it was how it was.

'I wouldn't have found this place without the GPS app on my phone.' He sat on the stool beside her. 'It's tucked away in such a narrow alley it's as though the owners don't want visitors finding it.'

'We know how good you are with your GPS.' She winked. 'Out-of-towners do find it, believe me. But it's a favourite with locals and we tend to crowd it out on certain nights of the week.'

'I'm glad you brought me here, though I probably won't be able to come back without you to lead the way.' He grinned and once again sent her blood heating. He did it too well.

How had she resisted calling him? Or going along the road to see him, sticking to her decision to take it slowly with him? Her restlessness over the need to find something more to her life had evolved into a need to spend more time with Josue and that had made her back off a little. 'I'll bring you again, promise.'

'*Merci*. I didn't even have to beg.' Josue laughed. 'Are you flying tomorrow?'

Anticipation began rising. 'I'm working tomorrow, but Sunday's mine. At this time of the year I usually do six out of seven days taking tourists on sightseeing flights or up to the ski fields with those who can afford it and prefer not to drive. What about you?'

'I have Sunday free too.'

'I want to go see Kayla again, take some things she asked for today. Would you like to come along and meet her? I could show you around the area afterwards.' It was the first she'd known she was going to make that suggestion. *A damned good one, Mallory.* It was time she got over holding out on having some fun with Josue. One week had been wasted already, and if he turned out to be as wonderful as she already hated to admit she thought he was, then she didn't want to lose any more time. She should get on and make the most of his time in Queenstown and deal with the consequences when they happened because she could no longer pretend she wasn't interested.

Josue leaned over and brushed her cheek with his lips. 'Count me in.'

His aftershave was spicy and light and set her aglow inside. Sipping her cool drink did nothing to chill the heat. Neither did the sudden need to open up to him some more. Wasn't getting to know him meant to include sharing herself and to take some steps towards risking allowing him to know more than she usually put out there?

'About me and travel, I've only been to Australia and then only to the outback. I did spend a few days in Brisbane on the way over, which was exciting, but most of my time was spent north of there on stations or farms.'

Surprise had slipped into Josue's gaze. Not expecting her to return to his earlier question? 'What did you do over there?'

'Crop dusting with a helicopter, and I took cattle owners out over their stations to find stock. The stations are huge, endless really, and flying is the easiest way around when they're not herding cattle, though they sometimes use choppers for that too. The dust can be horrendous and the heat is way beyond anything I'd ever experienced. The flies drove me crazy too.' It'd been an interesting six months, but she wouldn't be repeating it, and that had nothing to do with Hogan even when he'd been the reason she'd come home.

Josue was shaking his head and laughing. 'Anyone else I've asked about their overseas trips has talked about cities and historic buildings or sights like canyons or mountains, not flying in dust and dealing with flies. Mallory, you are something else.' He leaned in for another kiss, this time on the corner of her mouth.

She laughed with him. 'Maybe one day I'll get to travel to your part of the world and be the tourist with a camera around my neck as I take in all the sights I've heard so much about from the tourists I fly around here.'

'Let me know if you want to do that and I'll be your guide.' He stared her, then took a large gulp of his beer. 'I guess you won't be leaving Queenstown in a hurry with your mother here.'

Laying her hand on his thigh, she squeezed lightly. *Too intimate, Mallory?* Or was she getting on with letting go the restlessness? 'You're right. I'm not going anywhere as long as Mum's around. And to be fair, I've not thought a lot about travelling. It's never been something I've wanted to do.'

'So what made you go to Australia?' The steady look coming her way said he knew there was more than a straight-out job offer from a company that did helicopter work, and he'd have picked up on her abrupt answer the first time he'd mentioned her travelling.

Her glass was cool in her warm hand as she turned it in a circle on the table. Hadn't she wanted to let Josue in a little? In that case, she should tell him about Hogan. *All of it?* In order to trust Josue, she would see how it felt to tell him what she'd told no one else except Kayla and Maisie about Hogan's betrayal. 'I followed my boyfriend.'

Josue tipped his head to the side a little. 'This sounds interesting.'

Her smile surprised herself. 'Actually, it was.' As well as infuriating. 'I met Hogan when he worked a summer here on the river jet boats. We got on brilliantly so when he asked if I'd go to Australia with him when he went home, I was thrilled. I got a job and everything was wonderful.' So far so good. She sipped her drink.

Josue was watching her quietly. His hand covered hers for a brief moment. 'It was easy to get work?'

'Hogan's family helped by putting out the word in their district and soon I was busier than I'd ever been. It's an amazing place, being beyond the cities and towns, where everyone has to be strong and rely on each other to get through all that nature throws at them. I did like it, but it would never be somewhere I'd want to live forever.'

'Not even for love?'

'We never got far enough in our relationship for me to have to decide. Yes, I loved Hogan, but he'd often said he wanted to move to the coast and work in the tourist industry. He applied for plenty of positions but he couldn't get one he liked. He didn't want to start at the bottom. That's when his frustration started growing and I became the target for criticism. I didn't cook his favourite meal properly, made the bed wrong, was always at work when he wanted me. I started falling out of love and decided to come home.'

'I'm guessing you've been here ever since.'

She nodded. 'Yes, and no regrets.'

'There's more, isn't there?'

Mallory gasped. 'You're too clever for your own good.' Why not tell him? Usually she locked down on what Hogan had done because it made her feel and look stupid. But really it was no big deal and if she told someone, like Josue, then she might finally forgive Hogan. 'Hogan didn't take my leaving very well. He was furious. When I returned to our flat to pack up I discovered he'd emptied my bank accounts of every last cent.'

'He had your details?'

'We were in a relationship. I trusted him, otherwise why was I there?' Her mouth flattened. 'I won't do that again, I was stupid.' She'd given her trust and expected it to be reciprocated. It had been a painful lesson, and one hard to forget. She doubted she'd be quite so trusting so readily again about anything close to her heart.

Her hand was suddenly in Josue's, his fingers between hers. 'Not at all. You did what you believed was right.'

'That's fine until it went belly up. I didn't see it coming and I should've. He was always complaining about not having enough money for projects and yet spent all his earnings very freely.' She smiled at Josue, feeling happy about having told him. He seemed to understand why she felt so bad about herself, except now she didn't any more. She had made a mistake but it was in the past and she'd recouped her savings by working long hours and had had fun while doing it.

Josue leaned in and placed a kiss on her lips. 'Why am I the first you've told?'

Another gasp. 'How do you do that? Read me like a pamphlet advertising a trip on Lake Wakatipu?' It should be frightening, but it wasn't. She accepted his ability to understand her. Did that mean she was accepting him as more than a man to have a fling with? And why wasn't *that* scaring the daylights out of her if it was true? He had already warned her he'd move on regardless.

'I honestly don't know,' Josue admitted, looking a little confused. 'But I feel I know you. Strange when we haven't known each other long, but it's been like that from the beginning.'

He was admitting that? Did he understand how that was pulling her further into him? Mallory shook her head. There were no straightforward answers and she was tired of thinking too much about Josue leaving. She just wanted to get on and enjoy his company. Get closer and share their free time doing the things they both liked.

'Want another beer?' Then food, a walk around the town, and home to bed. It sounded like a good plan to her, one that warmed her throughout, including her heart. *Careful, Mallory.*

He said, 'Think I'll have a wine and order a steak, then take you for a stroll down to the wharf. After that we'll go home for some rest and recreation.'

Mallory was still laughing at his mind-reading skills when he returned with another round of drinks.

CHAPTER SIX

THREE WEEKS OF shared meals and bed, of laughter and in-depth conversations about everything except where they were going with this fling, and Josue was still smitten. More so. It seemed he couldn't get enough of Mallory.

Now at the top of the ski slope, Mallory looked gorgeous dressed in bright red skiing clothes and matching helmet and gloves. She was grinning like the cat with the cream as she studied the slope in front of her.

Until he tapped his glove-covered fist against hers and said, 'Last one to the bottom buys dinner.' Then he was gone, not waiting for her to agree or even turn to face in the downward direction. She could easily outrun him given half a chance, which he wasn't doing.

'Cheeky bugger,' she called.

'*Oui*, that's me.' He hadn't had such an enjoyable day in a long time. Seemed whatever they did together was fun and made them closer still. The skis skidded under him as he spun around and lunged his poles into the snow to push for more speed. 'I'm not buying dinner tonight.' But he was talking to air, or the other skiers standing around who he had to zigzag through to avoid crashing into someone. A quick glance behind showed Mallory having the same difficulty and had slowed up to dodge an accident. *Good.*

He aimed for the side of the slope where it was less congested, concentrating on keeping his skis parallel and his hips moving in unison with them as he swerved left then right down the steep slope. They were on the top field, where only experienced skiers went, and with fewer people up here and no young children learning to ski it gave a freedom he relished. Up here he could forget everything but the cold air rushing past his face and the glitter of the last of the sun on the snow. It was magic, made even more so today because Mallory was with him. Not right now, though. He was still ahead but not by much.

The urge to let rip and speed straight down, to whizz away, gripped him. Only the thought of losing control on the sharper slope coming up made him hold back and continue as he was.

Whish, whish. That wonderful sound of the snow under skis came from the left. Mallory was closing the gap. He squinted ahead. There was some way to go to the bottom. No way dinner was going to be on him.

Whish, whish. He pushed harder to the other side where the snow was less churned up. He didn't see the small rock until almost on it. Jerking sideways, his balance went from under him and, splat, he hit the snow hard. His skis snapped off his boots, his body sprawled wide.

'Josue?' Mallory swept up to him. 'Are you all right?' Her eyes were full of worry.

Shoving upwards, he stood, clipped his boots onto the skis. 'I'm fine.'

'Are you sure?'

'Two broken legs and a twisted arm.' He grinned as he reached for his poles. 'You going to help me?'

She pulled a face at him. 'You might as well order the pizzas now.' She was off, aiming for the markers for the end of the run now less than two hundred metres away.

'Make mine a Hawaiian with extra pineapple, will you?' Josue swept past her right before the line.

'That sweet tooth won't do you any favours,' she muttered through gasps of air.

'Bad loser?' He stood before her, dragging in air through his smile at a similar rate to her. Good. It hadn't been a doddle for him either. Not after he'd taken that fall.

'Not a bad run for an old bloke,' she quipped.

'An *injured* old bloke.' He laughed.

She suddenly went serious on him. 'You didn't hurt yourself, did you?'

Wrapping an arm over her shoulders, he pulled her close and kissed her cheek. 'Doubt I'll even have a bruise to show for it.' She wouldn't be able to kiss him better. Damn.

'Let's head on down and go home. I'm thinking a bowl of hot soup and steaming bread rolls sound especially good now. Better than pizza.'

The air was cooling rapidly now that the sun was dropping behind the mountain. All around them skiers were making their way down the lower slope to the main buildings and the car parks. 'It's been great having a day to ourselves, no calls from S and R.'

'No emergencies where I was needed at the hospital. *Oui,* a perfect day.' Josue hugged her again. 'And it's not over yet.' He did love being with Mallory. *Whoa.* His arm dropped to his side. *Getting too involved, Jos.*

Then Mallory was leaning into him, those bright eyes

twinkling mischievously. 'You want another race down the next slope?'

He couldn't stop the laughter bubbling up and out. Reaching for her, he wound his arms around her lithe body and kissed her long and hard, drinking in all that was Mallory. To hell with everything else. Right now, out here in the fresh, crisp air on the side of a stunning mountain he was happy beyond belief.

Mallory looked up at him, a twinkle in her eyes. 'I like it when you smile like you don't have a care in the world.'

'So do I.' And he truly did.

A shout came from behind them.

Reluctantly Josue broke their eye contact and looked around. He held his breath as he watched a skier speed down the slope too fast, his body hunched in a racing pose, poles sticking out behind him.

'Why do I think this is going to end badly?' Mallory muttered.

Suddenly the skier twisted abruptly and tumbled, rolling over and over, the skis flicking off one at a time as cries were heard. Then the skier slammed deep into the snow on his back.

Josue headed for the person, Mallory right beside him. 'So much for a day off, huh?' He dropped to his knees beside the skier. 'Hello, I'm Josue. Can you hear me?'

'Yes,' a male voice answered. 'What happened?'

'You lost control on your run and fell. I'm a doctor. What's your name?'

'Ian. My leg hurts.'

Mallory was opposite and already checking for signs of injury. 'Josue.' She pointed to the man's thigh. A broken ski pole was sticking into the muscle.

'This where it hurts?' Josue asked Ian as he gently

pressed around the pole entry. The pole had gone in quite a way. Best to leave it there until the guy was in the sterile environment of a hospital. Pulling the pole out could also cause more serious bleeding.

'Yes.' The guy was pushing himself up on his elbows.

'Careful. You might have other injuries.' He might have done damage to his spine with all that rolling.

'I'm good.' Ian looked at his bloodied leg and gulped. 'Oh.' He flipped backwards.

'He's fainted,' Mallory said as she continued feeling both legs for more injuries.

People were gathering around. Then a woman stepped up. 'I'm Jane, an instructor here. Do I need to get medical help?'

'I'm a doctor. Mallory here has first-aid skills. We're going to need assistance moving this man down to the main building, where he'll need to be transported to hospital.'

'Someone got lucky, crashing right in front of you two,' said the instructor. 'I'll be back with the mobile sled.'

'I guess he was.' Josue smiled at Mallory before looking for evidence of any other injuries. He found nothing, then ran his fingers over Ian's skull. No signs of injury there either. 'Hey, Ian,' he called. 'Wake up.'

'What happened?' Ian croaked.

'You fainted. Now, tell me, are you hurting anywhere else? Your head?' There could be a concussion or an internal bleed from the trauma of slamming into the snow.

'A bit wobbly, that's all.' This time he sat up slowly, looking everywhere but at his thigh. Lifting the opposite leg off the snow, he grimaced. 'Something not right with my left ankle.'

Mallory began undoing the laces of Ian's boot. 'I'm not taking the boot off, just trying to relieve the pressure. You've got some swelling going on. Whether it's broken or just sprained won't be apparent until you've had an X-ray.'

'Whichever, I won't be skiing any time soon, will I?' Ian grunted. 'My own fault, I suppose, but that run was too good not to race down.'

'You're not wrong there, mate.'

Another man had slid to stop a couple of metres away. 'Is Ian all right?' he asked. 'We're together,' he added quickly.

Josue was saved from answering when a four-wheeled, covered bike with a sled hitched to the back arrived and Jane leapt off. 'I've got a stretcher we can load the man onto and then lift him onto the tray,' she said to Josue. 'One of you want to ride with him? There's room in front for one of you and your gear.'

He'd forgotten about his skis and poles. 'Thanks. I'll go on the sled, keep Ian from moving too much. Let's get him loaded and down to the warmth of indoors.'

'I've notified the on-site medical crew at headquarters and they're arranging for the ambulance to be ready when we get down.' Jane was laying the stretcher beside Ian.

'I don't need that,' he grumbled and tried to stand up on one leg, and sat down abruptly with a groan.

'Let's do it our way.' Josue put a hand on the man's arm. 'Shuffle your butt across.' He looked Mallory's way. 'I'll see you down the bottom?' At her nod, he moved to sit on the bike.

Ten minutes later Jane pulled up beside the waiting ambulance, Mallory and Ian's friend joining them moments later. 'Just in time to help us get your mate aboard,' Josue told him.

With Ian inside the vehicle, Josue and Mallory gave a short account to the paramedic of the extent of the injuries they'd noted and headed towards the car park. Josue reached for Mallory's free hand. 'It was still a great day.'

'I never count helping someone as bad. Even when it disrupts a perfect day.' She grinned and leaned in to kiss him.

The alarm went off at five thirty. Monday morning once more. Another week about to kick off. Mallory groaned as she rolled over and tapped off the irritating buzzing, then yawned hard. She'd been doing a lot of that lately, but then there'd been plenty of nights in bed with Josue and evenings out for S and R meetings and meals at the pub. Her life had gone from busy to busier and she was loving it.

A large hand was splayed over her hip, kneading softly. Her legs were entangled with Josue's. Another amazing night. She'd thought it couldn't get any better after the first time they'd gone to bed yet every time was better than before. 'Why can't it be snowing and howling a gale?'

'You don't want to go to work?' came a low growly question from her shoulder, where Josue had tucked in his chin.

'Can't say the idea's enthralling me even when I'm only doing half a day. I've got my medical this afternoon.' The regular check required by the pilots' licensing board seemed to have come round fast. Hard to believe a year had gone by since the last one.

She tossed the cover aside and sat up, legs over the

side. If she didn't move now she might never get up. Not that she had a lot of energy left for getting up close with Josue, but this was more than her body aching from yesterday's skiing on Coronet Peak with this wonderful man. It was odd because she didn't usually feel too bad after a day on skis. Might ask her GP, who did the pilot medicals, if there was anything doing the rounds she might've caught from one of the many people she came into contact with through her job.

'Hey, that's cold.' Josue grabbed back the cover.

'Sure is.' Goose bumps were rising on her skin now that she wasn't curled up against Josue. 'I'm having a shower.' But first she'd put the kettle on.

In the kitchen she paused at the sight on the floor by the bench. The last of the pizzas from last night had disappeared except for some crumbs. 'Shade, naughty girl.' It was her own fault for not tidying up before going to bed with Josue.

Shade lifted her head from her bed and wagged her tail.

'Come on. Outside while I get ready for work.' No point making a fuss about the mess now. Shade would've forgotten what she'd done, or that she'd been naughty. It had been a golden opportunity and she'd taken it. Mallory laughed. Couldn't really blame her girl for that. She'd have done the same.

Holding the back door open, she stared at Shade until she grudgingly got up and walked out. It might be the morning ritual but in winter Shade never leapt off her bed with any exuberance.

In the shower, standing under hot water, arms crossed over her tender breasts, Mallory tipped her head back to wash the sleep away. 'Damn, forgot to put the kettle on.'

The bathroom door opened and Josue strolled in, definitely the man of her dreams in all his naked glory. What a body, with not a gram of fat—he was all muscle. Elbowing the door wide, she moved to one side to make room for him.

He was eyeing her with tenderness.

Her throat clogged. That tenderness for her was…was special and growing on her. She felt as though she was melting into a puddle at her feet. Her eyes were wet, not only from the shower but from the emotions he created within her. This was what she'd been looking for. She looked up at him, her insides all mushy with love. *Really?* Yes, really. It was fast, but everything felt right about this man, different from her previous experiences. He just fitted with her focus on work and caring for people and how he relaxed at home and shared the chores. The list was endless. Regardless of his warning about not staying around, she hadn't been able to avoid falling for him.

'Josue,' she whispered, and reached up to run her fingers over his chest.

He stood still, looking into her as though he was reading her heart. Though his eyes were light, not grave as they usually were when he spoke about leaving, so she hoped he had no idea what was going in on her head.

Her lungs were still, her heart beating in erratic little patters like it was trying to kickstart her breathing. Yes, this was love. Though where could it lead? She had no idea and was afraid to ask in case he ran from the shower and she never saw him again. She'd always known this could happen and she'd chosen to accept the consequences, whatever they were, right from the outset.

'Mallory.' Josue placed his hands on her arms, his

gaze still caught in hers, and he leaned in to place a kiss on her chin. 'Turn around.'

She stared at him for a moment. He meant everything to her. It had happened fast. *Now what?* They would carry on regardless, making the most of the time they had together. She turned around.

Josue began soaping her skin with gentle strokes, starting at her shoulders, easing the kinks out of her muscles, and slowly working lower down her back and over her backside.

She began relaxing under his touch. Was this Josue saying how much he cared for her? Showing, not telling her? Had he seen her love in her eyes? Or was he avoiding her truth? Not wanting her to love him?

His hands were on her waist, bringing her around to face him so he could start again on her breasts. His eyes were still light and his mouth soft. Then he stopped and leaned into kiss her.

She was so confused. What did Josue want? Glancing down, she saw he was ready for her, but when she reached for him, he smiled and shook his head. 'We haven't got time.'

Now there was a challenge if ever she'd heard one. Her hand wrapped around him. 'You think?' Josue was ready for her, wanted her, and despite her confusion she was going to show him how much she cared for him.

Josue laughed as he drove into the hospital car park. 'Never say that to Mallory unless you've got spare time, Jos,' he said to himself. Not that they'd needed long, they knew how to bring each other to a climax in an instant. Now he felt on top of the world when he was literally at the bottom of the globe, talking to himself out loud. But how was a man supposed to act when he'd just had another amazing night with a woman who turned him on with a look and followed through with so much more it was almost unbelievable? Almost but not entirely, because time and again he'd experienced Mallory's lovemaking and knew it was for real. And the feelings he had for Mallory were growing all the time. Truly. They were. It felt like love. Not that he had experienced it like this before, but if he was to fall in love this was how he wanted it to be. It felt real. Was he ready? How did he know?

There'd been a moment in the shower when Mallory had gone quiet on him, her eyes darkening as though she'd had something big to say. When she hadn't, he'd felt relieved and disappointed all at once. To hear what might fall from those lips could change his world forever. What if Mallory had come to care for him? Even love him? His heart began racing. Did she? It would be beyond his wildest dreams.

Then she'd smiled, her eyes lightening as she'd laid a hand on his chest. A loving gesture that had softened him. He'd begun soaping her body and they'd made love and he'd been happy. He was fitting in so well with Mallory, with his work and the search and rescue mob that he might really be finding his place. He wanted that, and he was beginning to think this time he just might be able to give as good as he got—with Mallory.

There was so much more than the lovemaking that was special with her. Lying spooned together, his arm around her waist, hearing her gentle breaths as she slept, sharing a hastily put-together meal, yesterday on the ski field, challenging each other. It gave him a sense of homecoming, of having found what he'd been looking for all his life, and that had struck him so deeply he might not be able to let go again.

Mallory was at the centre of everything happening to him. Should he be protecting himself or letting go and diving in? He'd spent his life looking for love and not finding it, Gabriel and Brigitte being the exceptions. Theirs was the sort of love a child required, bringing with it guidance and support and kindness. Until now he'd believed he was too unreliable, wouldn't be able to give stability to any relationship. And now? There was the thing. He had no idea. Except now he wanted to try, wanted to let these loving feelings take over to the point he was starting to think he could do it, could be there for Mallory through all the hurdles that life would throw at them.

The air was cold outside his car. Josue hunched his shoulders and headed inside to the department, his phone pressed to his ear, wanting to hear her voice.

'You've reached Mallory Baine. Please leave me a message and I'll get back to you.' Josue pressed off and then phoned again to listen to her voice, his gut turning into a tight ball as he left his message, 'Hey, it's me. Have a great day. See you later.'

'Josue, you're early,' the department head called from the centre desk as he made his way along the row of empty beds. 'Didn't you sleep last night?'

'No.' Not a lot of sleeping going on where he'd been. 'I woke up early so figured I might as well make myself useful.'

'Your timing's perfect.' John stood up. 'Feel like a coffee?'

'You have to ask?' What did John want to talk about at this hour?

John headed for his office where there was always coffee to be had. 'We've been quiet all night so I've had time to catch up on some paperwork.' He filled two mugs and passed one to Josue before closing the door. 'Grab a seat.'

This was shaping up to be a serious conversation. 'What's up?'

'This is confidential, all right?'

'Yes.'

'Jason's had a cancer diagnosis.'

The older doctor had been looking a bit jaded over the past month. 'I am sorry to hear that. I've heard so much about his cycling exploits it doesn't seem possible.'

'It's been a shock for those in the know. Jason's decided to step back from work—to resign, in fact. It's a serious diagnosis and he'd prefer to spend the time with family and doing a couple of things he's not got around to before.' John sipped his coffee thoughtfully. 'So I'm offering you a permanent position. I know you intend on returning to France next month but you've mentioned that your visa runs for another year. If you accepted the offer and wanted to stay on longer than the twelve months we'd be your sponsor for a resident's visa.'

Josue's chest tightened. Him take on a permanent position? He enjoyed working in this small hospital and had integrated with everyone easily. The work was stimulating so what more could he want? If he said yes it would be for at least a year, and possibly more. Excitement began fizzing in his veins. Then stopped. This would mean settling down, staying put in a town where Mallory lived, even if he got cold feet and called off their relationship. That's how he'd stayed safe in the past. Being able to leave. What if he were to take a chance and let Mallory fully into his life? If she was about to tell him she loved him then this was perfect. She was all he needed, wanted.

What? All I want? As in she really might be the one?
Yes, wasn't that what he'd been trying to tell himself?
He loved her. He stared around, looking for a distraction
from this blindside, and came up against John's steady
gaze as he waited for an answer. He had a job offer that
went some way to making this easier. Though it was as
if the decisions were being taken out of his hands. A job
offer and Mallory seeming to have something important
to tell him. He still had to return home for Gabriel's operation, but he could return afterwards, and make a go of it
with Mallory. Sharp pain squeezed his chest. If he'd read
her correctly, and so far he'd always got it right with her.

'Josue?' John finally asked. 'Are you all right?'

Not at all. Why did the idea of Mallory being the
love of his life feel more right than anything he'd ever
known? This was too much. He couldn't concentrate,
couldn't make any decisions right now. 'I'm surprised.'
Surprised didn't begin to describe his emotions. He was
overwhelmed, grateful, happy, *terrified.* Not of the job
but of finally falling in love. Darling Mallory. He had
to get out of here. 'Thank you for the offer.' *Be sensible. Don't rush it.* 'But I do have to be back in Nice next
month.'

'Are you at all interested in a permanent position?'

'There's a lot to consider.' He'd love to stay if he could
get past the constant fear of rejection when it came to settling down. *Give it a go.* Did he have it in him? He might
lose his heart. But anything worth holding onto took effort and determination. Or so he'd been told.

'How about you take the rest of the week to think
about it? After that I'll have to start looking further
afield, but I'd like you to come on board. You've fitted
in well with everyone and our systems.'

Josue nodded agreement. 'Sounds fair. I am keen, but there're things I have to look into.' *Give it a go. Stop overthinking.* He drained his coffee. Fresh air would be great even if it was freezing cold, but walking around the streets wasn't going to bring any answers. Only talking to Mallory could do that and he wasn't quite ready to lay his heart on the line and tell her about this offer. It was his decision to make. And he needed to absorb the knowledge he was falling for her too. Two hits in one go.

The caution he held close had kept him out of trouble before and it could save him from making a complete fool of himself this time. Was he really falling for her? If so, then, yes, he wanted the job. If not, he had to get away fast so as not to hurt her. And himself. *Too late for that one.*

John's phone rang.

Josue stood up. 'I'll get out of your way.'

'Sure.'

Josue's phone beeped as he stepped into the corridor and it took all his control not to rip it from his pocket. It had to be Mallory. No one else would be texting him. Unless it was S and R but they knew he was working today. He reached for the phone and smiled as happiness filled him. Happiness or love? *Both.*

S and R training tonight. Eat out first?

How could he have forgotten the training meeting? Oui. Pick you up at 6.00.

Damn. He'd needed time to work through everything that had happened but he'd answered without thinking. *See?* A knot formed in his gut. Staring at the phone, his heart squeezed. If he admitted to loving her it couldn't be a dabble in the water, he'd have to dive right in. He still had to go to France and help Gabriel. He owed that man so much. But once home would he be able to come back to Mallory, or would he stay away, letting the old fears of failure and rejection win? The knot tightened painfully. He swore.

'Josue, we've had a call.' A nurse appeared from a cubicle. 'The ambulance is on its way with a woman kicked in the stomach by her horse.'

Time to get on with why he'd come to Queenstown in the first place. He put his phone and Mallory back in his pocket where he could reach either of them in an instant. If only he could shove these sudden doubts away as easily. 'I'm coming.'

'Everything is in perfect working order.' Sara folded the blood-pressure cuff. 'I wish all my patients were like you.'

'Then you wouldn't have any,' Mallory retorted around a smile that quickly faltered. 'I'm glad I've passed. But there's one thing.' She hesitated. This was silly. What was a bit of exhaustion here and there? Except it had become so constant over the last few days she was starting to worry something serious was happening.

'Go on.' Sara was typing in her notes.

'I'm so tired all the time. It's getting worse. I have to drag myself out of bed every morning. I went skiing yesterday but most of the time I wasn't exactly speeding.' Except for the last run, trying to outrun Josue.

'Any other symptoms?'

'Like what?'

'Pain, aches, nausea, headaches.'

'None of the above.'

'You're eating all right?'

'Yes.' Ah, no. 'I didn't have breakfast this morning, and last night only two pieces of pizza. But that's no big deal.' She stared at the doctor. 'Come to think of it, I felt queasy on the drive to the mountain yesterday.'

'When was your last period?'

Her eyebrows lifted as she stared at Sara. What was Sara saying? No. She couldn't be. Nausea rose fast. 'Where's the bathroom?'

'Take deep breaths. It's through that door if you need it.' Sara sat back in her chair, waiting as Mallory sucked in lungfuls of air then huffed them out.

Her hands were tight balls on her thighs, her head spinning. This had to be a mistake. Deep breath. When did Josue arrive? He'd been here over a month. It was possible, but they'd taken precautions. A memory of the first time rose in her mind. 'July. Early July was my last one.' As the words spewed out her body slumped in the chair. This was not happening.

'Then we'd better find out if you're pregnant, don't you think?' Sara asked.

Mallory could only nod as despair took over. She couldn't have a baby on her own. It wasn't right. What would Josue say? If he wasn't interested in staying around for a relationship then he'd hardly want a baby to hold him down.

'Mallory, first things first. Let's do the urine test and find out if it's positive.'

She was. The blue line mesmerised her. A baby. *Her* baby. 'Is this real?' She'd dreamed of this day, and had feared it wouldn't happen. But she wasn't in a relationship. Josue was leaving.

'Yes, it is. I'm going to take a blood sample for an

HCG to find out how far along you are.' Sara looked over at her. 'One step at a time, okay?'

'I had an ectopic pregnancy when I was eighteen.' Josue was leaving.

'That doesn't mean you won't go full term with this one if that's what you want. It's rare for a woman to have two ectopic pregnancies and you haven't mentioned any symptoms that suggest this is anything but normal. You'd have known something was wrong well before now if your dates are right. However, I'll arrange a scan for you at the earliest possible time. It'll mean going to Invercargill.'

Mallory's head was spinning with the speed at which this was happening. She'd come for a pilot medical and was now pregnant and going for a scan. What had just happened to her day? Her life? Within minutes everything had changed radically. 'I'll go. I'm only going to worry myself sick until I know for certain this is a normal pregnancy.' Mallory gasped. Pregnant? Her? 'Am I really having a baby?'

Sara nodded. 'You are. Is that good news?'

'Yes.' The answer was out without any thought. It was true. It might be unexpected, and she had no idea what lay ahead with Josue, but, yes, it was the best news. She was already accepting it. But of course she would. This was what she'd wanted in her future—but her dream had included a man to love too. Not a man who said he wasn't staying around, who didn't believe he was capable of settling in one place and being happy. If that meant she'd have to raise a child on her own then she would. There was already a warm protectiveness for her child growing inside her. Her life had changed in the last few minutes. *Josue.* Her heart squeezed with love. How was she going to break the news to him? He cared for her, she knew he did whether he admitted it or not. Yet having a baby was a game changer. Josue would probably take the next plane out of the country, leaving her as Jasper had done with her first pregnancy. Despite his upbringing in foster care she didn't trust him not to make sure his own child never went through that anguish. He might want to, but staying around to be there all the time was a big ask for him. She sank further down the chair. She had to find a way to convince him to stay, to work at being a dad, to accept her love. Could she trust him when Jasper had run in this same situation? What if it *was* an ectopic pregnancy? Would he be relieved, just like Jasper had been, released from his responsibilities?

'Mallory, slow down. I can see the questions spinning through your mind. Take it easy. It's only been minutes since you found out. Let me take the blood, and then I suggest you go for a walk, get some air and just absorb the fact you're pregnant. One step at a time.'

'Sure.' That easily?

It was freezing cold outside and Mallory's nose felt numb within minutes of stomping along the path. A baby. Her hand lay over her belly. *Hello. Who are you? Are you comfortable in there?* At least it'd be warmer in there than out here.

How *was* she going to tell Josue? It would be a huge shock. She'd just been hit with the news and was slowly coming to grips with it. This wasn't something that could be put on hold until she felt ready to deal with it. Josue avoided issues by leaving, it was his go-to reaction. The real question was how to make him pause and consider everything. Her teeth were grinding, making them ache horribly. She didn't have a damned clue how to deal with any of this. Why spend time wondering about what Josue would do? Because she needed him at her side. More than that, she needed him to love her—for herself, not only as the mother of his child.

She stamped her boot on the hard ground and broke the ice covering the grit. *I'm pregnant.*

Unplanned, unexpected and a whole new beginning. Would this really shut down her restlessness now there was something—*someone*—to plan for? Yes, a baby was a wonder. One she'd begun to think she'd never experience when she hadn't found a man to love and be with forever. She'd finally met Josue, and loved him. As for the rest of that picture, that was nothing but a blank at the moment. She had to talk to him. First, she'd need to get used to the fact she was having a baby.

A gust of icy wind slapped her, sending shivers through her. What if the pregnancy *was* ectopic? She hadn't experienced any stomach pains like the first time so it couldn't be. *Don't get ahead of yourself or you might tempt fate.* Enough. She headed for her car. She'd go and see Kayla, picking up Shade from home on the way.

Checking her phone, she saw three texts from Kayla. Apparently she was going stir crazy with boredom.

I'm on my way, she texted, and headed towards Wanaka, where she might tell Kayla her news and have a good old talk about everything.

That didn't happen. Kayla wanted to get out of the house, said her parents were driving her crazy by not letting her do a damned thing during her recovery. Her concussion was long gone, but the left leg ached all the time and the other with a compound fracture gave constant stabs of pain giving cause for her parents insisting on her staying put on the couch. 'I've done nothing but rest for weeks and I'm going to become less active than a statue if I don't do something. Get me out of here.'

After cramming Kayla and her crutches onto the back seat of the car with her legs up and a seatbelt twisted across her body, and leaving Shade at the house, Mallory drove into town and a bar where they eventually sat drinking juice while Kayla vented and Mallory tried to listen and not think about Josue and the baby. When her song started playing, she stared at the name showing on her phone. What did she say? *Hi, having a great day? Wish you were here?* Reluctantly she picked it up. 'Hello, Josue.'

'Mallory, thank goodness. Where are you? I'm waiting to pick you up but there's no sign of you at home.'

She swore. The S and R meeting. Josue had said they'd go for something to eat first. 'I'm sorry. I'm with Kayla. I forgot all about the meeting.'

'You forgot? What's wrong?'

Everything. 'Nothing. Kayla was having a bad day and I came over to cheer her up. That's all.'

'Really?' Silence hung between them. He obviously wasn't satisfied with her answer.

She'd let him down. 'Really. I won't be going to the meeting now. I'll let them know.'

'You sure there's nothing wrong?'

She was hardly going to tell him over the phone. 'Josue, I am sorry.' Yet she'd forgotten they were going for a meal. Not surprising, but he didn't know why. 'I'll make it up to you, I promise.' *With the news that you're going to be a father.* She swallowed hard.

'I'll hold you to that.' His laugh was strained. 'Will you be home tonight?'

She couldn't tell him tonight. She wasn't ready. Once

he knew, there'd be no turning back. If he couldn't handle the idea of being a parent because it meant settling down, he'd leave Queenstown early and she would lose more time with him. 'If I do it'll be late.'

'I see.' It was clear from his voice he didn't. 'See you later in the week.'

Mallory dropped her phone back on the table with a sigh. That hadn't gone well. It didn't bode well for the discussion lying ahead of them. Would this be like before? Everything going fine with the men she fell for until the going got tough?

'Problem in the works?' Kayla asked. 'I take it that was Josue?'

'It was.' It would be too easy to spill the truth, put it out there and pick everything apart. It also wouldn't be fair, she realised. Josue deserved to be the first to know. 'I forgot he was going to pick me up for a meal before we went to the S and R meeting tonight.'

'Blame me for wanting you to stick by my side tonight.'

'I will.' Mallory picked up her orange juice and drained it. If only it had been something stronger, but then too many drinks had got her into this situation in the first place. It had to have happened the first night they'd had sex. It had been after the rescue of the two boys when she'd had a couple of beers and vodkas and hadn't thought about protection when she and Josue had got it on. 'When do you intend moving back to your house?'

'After Dad takes me in to see the surgeon next week, I'd rather hobble around on crutches in my own place. Whichever, I'm going to suggest to Josue he might as well stay on as there's not long to go before he leaves anyway.'

Mallory winced.

'If there's a problem with that I won't mention it. He can find somewhere else.'

'No, it's fine. Anyway, he's a dab hand with the mower now.' Tears streaked down her cheeks.

'Mallory?'

Josue should really be the first to know, but she needed a shoulder to cry on and she could trust Kayla not to say anything. 'I'm pregnant.'

'Come over here so I can hug you.' Kayla shuffled up the couch, awkwardly shifting her legs out of the way. 'Josue?'

Mallory nodded. 'Of course. He's leaving in a few weeks.'

'He might change his mind.'

If only it were that simple. She leaned back to look at Kayla and shook her head. 'It's going to take some work for that to happen.'

'Then you'd better get started. Tomorrow. Tonight you're staying here and we'll drink copious quantities of tea and talk just as much.'

CHAPTER SEVEN

'MALLORY, YOU'RE NEEDED to fly into the hills behind Arrowtown for a retrieval,' Pete called through from his office. 'The rescue chopper's already on an emergency flight so we're up.'

Leaping up from the desk where she'd been filling in paperwork for the tourist flights she'd done earlier in the day, she snatched up her yellow weatherproof jacket and slid into it. Funny how now she knew why she got so tired it didn't affect her as badly. 'Fill me in, boss.'

'A conservation department worker was felling trees by the Kawarau river when he slipped on unstable ground and dropped a tree on himself. He's also sliced his calf with the chainsaw. You're to fly the doctor and Jamie in to collect him and take him to Christchurch. They'll be here in five.'

Josue being the doctor? She hoped so. Even the impending news she had for him hadn't succeeded in downplaying the need he brought on, not only for the amazing sex but spending time with him, talking or not, just being in the same space. It never failed to surprise her. She'd dozed on and off throughout the night, the joy of a baby in her belly going around her head and battling with the fear it might be an ectopic pregnancy. Add Josue and what his reactions might be, and sleep hadn't got a look in. The sooner she told him the better, for both their sakes. Sara had phoned to say her scan was booked for tomorrow morning.

Mallory wouldn't relax until she'd had the scan and the result was good. But right now she had to focus on someone else and getting the man to care as soon as the men flying with her arrived. 'Who's with the forestry worker?' she asked Pete.

'Two other guys from the department. It was one of them who called for the helicopter.'

She'd tidied the chopper at the end of the last flight so all was in order. 'I'll get on board and file flight details with the tower.'

'I've flicked the coordinates through so I'll go and load the stretcher and other medical equipment for you.' Rescue gear wasn't stored on the helicopter they used for back-up emergency flights.

'Thanks,' she called.

Within minutes Mallory had the route and destination coordinates on the screen and was pressing the button on her headset to talk to the tower. 'Queenstown Tower, Tango Juliet Romeo.'

'Come in, Tango Juliet Romeo.'

'I'm filing a flight plan for an urgent retrieval of an injured forestry worker.' She gave the coordinates, their estimated time of departure, number of people on board and the destination after retrieval, which today was Christchurch due to availability of theatre space and surgeon.

'Roger, Tango Juliet Romeo. We'll facilitate your departure as soon as we hear you're ready for lift-off. Over.' As Mallory sighed her relief, the air controller came back. 'Stay safe, Mallory.'

'Will do. Thanks.'

A loud thud told her the men were boarding and then the door closed. Josue popped his head through the gap between the front seats. 'We're good to go.'

She breathed deeply, taking in his presence, feeling the warmth having him near brought on. 'Great.' She began the start-up procedure. 'Want to sit up here?' she asked, without taking her eyes off the dials as they recorded pressure, heat and the increasing rotor speed reaching the levels safe for lifting off the ground. He'd get a fantastic view of the region they were going to fly over to the foothills where their patient was in dire straits, and having him there right beside her would be an added bonus, despite the problem hanging between them. It might even help break the ice.

'Love to.' Josue slid into the seat beside her and buckled up.

Sighing with relief, Mallory focused on starting the flight. Pressing the button on her mouthpiece, she gave her call sign to the tower and said, 'Ready for lift-off.'

The tower came back immediately. 'Cleared for take-off. The A320 at the west end of the runway is standing by for your clearance.'

That had been done because this was an urgent flight otherwise she'd have had to wait a few minutes after the bigger plane took off so as not to get caught in the turbulence caused by the plane's engines. 'Cleared for take-off,' Mallory repeated, as she began increasing the collective and beginning to lift the cyclic for a 40-knot attitude. 'Here we go, guys.'

Another rescue underway. Her eyes skimmed the dials in front of her, then she glanced outside, scanning the area in front of the chopper as it left the ground, moving forward and gaining altitude. Her hands firm on the controls, her mind focused on flying and looking out for dangers, her heart was tight with longing for Josue's acceptance of her and the baby.

He was interesting and exciting, dedicated to his work and when he wasn't in her bed he kept her awake late into the night with the memories of their nights together. Loving him was never going to be easy. Only now she knew those memories weren't going to be enough. She wanted to spend a lifetime making more with him. A long-distance relationship would not work, wouldn't make anyone happy long term. If she couldn't leave Queenstown then she had to find a way to tempt Josue into staying here. That should be as easy as flying the helicopter over the ranges in a blizzard. At least it was possible, she sighed.

Thinking about why Mallory had brushed him off last night and how that had hurt, even when he should've been relieved, Josue couldn't quite believe the smile she'd given him as he'd settled into his seat. He was fully aware of the helicopter lifting smoothly off the ground and rising to the approved height for their thirty-minute flight. He had no qualms about Mallory's ability to fly, even though he'd not been up in the air with her at the controls before. It was just a feeling that anything Mallory did, she did well and with complete focus. As she had on the searches they'd done together before.

He'd never thought about it before but being in an aircraft meant depending on the person or people behind the controls and today that was the woman he was coming to like and respect more and more, and to care about to the point he believed he had fallen in love. She'd got to him like no other and his heart had got involved, whether he'd wanted it to or not. He'd like nothing more than to spend all his spare time with her, be a part of the daily jobs, doing the little things that made up a full, exciting day. Could he stay permanently?

When she'd said she'd forgotten about their date last night, he hadn't believed her. There'd been something in her voice that had said there was a lot more to her being unavailable than merely forgetting. 'Why did you avoid me last night?'

'I told you. Kayla was restless. I went to spend time with her.'

'When you'd already said you'd join me for a meal before the meeting?' He wasn't buying into this.

'I didn't deliberately avoid you. I did forget we'd arranged to get together. And I forgot about the meeting.'

He had to admit she sounded genuine. 'That's not like you.' Mallory was always organised and on the ball. 'Did you leave Shade at home too?'

'No, she came with me.' She placed a hand on his knee and squeezed lightly. 'Josue, I am really sorry for screwing up. I never meant to hurt you, I promise.'

Genuine again. It was what he wanted to hear. Had he been hasty in his reaction to her not being there for their date? Because he'd wanted to see her so badly when he was supposed to be careful? He took her hand in his and kissed her knuckles. 'Okay.'

She smiled and took her hand back to place it on the controls. 'Thanks.'

Sometimes it was still hard to believe how well they got on. The other day they'd had a wonderful time together skiing, totally in tune with each other. So much so that last night he couldn't accept she might've had a change of heart even when it would've made it easier for him to step back.

'You ready for this?' Mallory sidetracked him.

'I understand I'm to do a quick examination of the injuries, access how cognitive the patient is and decide if we need the stretcher.'

'You're on it. Hopefully it's a quick turnaround. We don't want to be hanging about too long at this time of day, and the other two on the ground still have to make their way back on foot. Luckily it's a benched track but it'll be freezing in the dark.'

Getting out of an aircraft when it wasn't on the ground always felt like a strange thing to be doing. He still didn't know what last night had been about. He understood Kayla's frustration at being stuck on the couch all the time, but not Mallory's reaction to his phone call. Was she gearing herself up for something? Did she also think that they were getting on well and that their fling was coming to mean more? Did she want to tell him she was falling for him?

He growled. This deeper sense of needing her when he couldn't guarantee to be there for her had his hands tightening into fists on his thighs. She gave him hope that he wouldn't always be alone, might finally be able to let go of some of his distrust issues. Was he hiding behind his past? Using it as an excuse to stay alone and remote and safe? If he was then Mallory unknowingly held power over him already, because the questions were rising thick and fast. Could he chance a relationship that might go further than any he'd had before? Go beyond short and fun to forever and happy? To do that he'd have to return from France with his mind fixed on letting his heart rule and not his past.

Josue shivered. If only he had the guts to drop the past and move forward to a future that might hold all the loving scenarios he'd dreamt about as a youngster. It wasn't easy when he'd so often laid his heart on the line with foster families only to have them send him away or treat him like he wasn't there. There'd only been so many times he'd been naïve enough to believe next time would be better. Only so many times he'd let them hurt him before he'd wised up and accepted he wasn't going to find the love he needed. This was why he'd walked away from Colette and Liza. One day they'd have woken up to the fact they didn't love him. Better to get in—or in his case, out—first.

'Nearly there.' Mallory's voice came loud and clear through his headphones, reminding him they were all on a mission to save someone.

Get a grip and stop thinking about yourself. Start focusing on the rescue of a seriously injured man who needs you fully alert to his requirements. But it had been a long time since he'd got so wound up about the past and it had all started when he'd met Mallory. Throw in the job offer, and it looked like his life could come together as he wanted—if he took the chance. 'I'll go back and get prepared.'

'Get that harness ready, Josue. If we have to lower you, I don't want to be mucking around.' Jamie hunched over and squeezed through the gap into the cockpit.

Josue slipped into the harness and altered the straps to fit snugly, twisting his shoulders left and right to make sure there were no snags. Then he got the medical pack

ready to put on if they weren't landing. Excitement began
streaming through his body. Rescues hyped him up as
he prepared to use his skills to help someone. Add in the
possibility of stepping off the side of the chopper with
only a winch to keep him safe and the excitement was
even greater.

'I'll return to the front and be a second pair of eyes
for Mallory.'

The moment he appeared beside her she said, 'Look
out your side and towards the front.' Her flat tone suggested she was concentrating on flying as much as looking for any signs of the men on the ground. It had to be a
lot to contend with and she was so calm about it.

Two minutes later he pointed towards the rocky area
in front of the chopper. 'There. Straight ahead.' Relief
and excitement filled him as he stared at the waving men.

'Got them,' Mallory replied. 'I can't land there. I'll do
a loop to see if there's somewhere close by that's clear of
trees and the river.'

Immediately the helicopter banked and began turning
in a wide circle. Josue could see down to the river and
the high bank on one side. The other side sloped down
to the water's edge but there was a lot of scrub curtail-
ing the option of landing. As they flew round, an area of
grass and rocks came into view. Would Mallory use that
or were the rocks an issue? She coolly manoeuvred her
machine above the up-reaching trees, her concentration
completely on the job in hand.

The helicopter straightened, slowed to a hover. 'Jamie, I
can put down here or we can go with lowering Josue where
the men were. What do you think? Josue, did you see a
way through that wouldn't be difficult with the stretcher?'

'No, I didn't.' Unfamiliar with such dense forest, he hadn't seen a track of any kind.

Jamie came back with, 'I didn't either.'

'Let's go with lowering Josue,' Jamie decided. 'Otherwise it's some haul up from the river to this spot, which won't be easy with a loaded stretcher.'

'Josue, you okay with that?' Mallory asked.

'Absolutely.' He'd begun heading into the body of the chopper but glanced back at Mallory, feeling a softness inside at her concern for him. He had the pack on his back within seconds.

Jamie attached the winch to the steel buckle on Josue's belt and checked the pack. He nodded once as he opened the door. 'As soon as you're on the ground unclip the hook. I'll lower the stretcher if required. Otherwise when you're ready to have the patient lifted let us know and raise your right arm and I'll return the winch to you. Keep us informed all the time.'

'Will do.' Josue understood it was important for everyone's sake he got this right.

'Ready?'

The helicopter was hovering above the spot they'd seen the men waving. Josue drew a breath and nodded. 'Yes.' Stepping onto the skid, one hand gripping the edge of the door, he looked down. The air whooshed out of his lungs. It wasn't a long way down, but he was going to have to step off the skid and trust the winch—and Mallory. He'd be fine. Another deep breath. 'Let's do it.'

Before he knew it, he was on the ground, with men grabbing the cable to steady him and get him unhooked. There hadn't been time to think about being in the air on the end of a cable. A smile split his face. Not bad. The noise overhead was deafening. Leaning nearer to the closest man, he shouted, 'I'm Dr Bisset. Josue.'

The guy nodded and pointed upstream towards the trees that followed the river and covered the hillside and set off.

Josue followed quickly, watching where he placed his feet on the slippery ground. It wouldn't do to go and break an ankle now.

Then they were at the edge of the trees, where it was damp, cold and a lot darker. There was a headlight glowing at them. 'This is Russell,' he was told. 'The chainsaw went through his leg above the ankle. We figured not to remove the boot. There's a lot of damage.' The guy pulled a face.

'You did the right thing,' Josue reassured the men. The injury had been described during the call to 111 and the details passed on to him. There was a high risk the foot had been cut off, leading him to ring the hospital in Christchurch to put the surgeons on standby. 'What other injuries has he sustained? I was told the tree landed on him.'

'He's complaining of chest pain on the side and in his right arm, which he can't move. If he says he's hurting, then he's in agony. He's a tough bastard at the best of times.'

Josue refrained from pointing out the obvious and knelt down beside the man they'd just reached. 'Hello, Russell. I'm Josue, a doctor. We're going to get you out of here fairly quickly but first I need to check you over.'

'Just do what you have to,' Russell grunted.

Josue looked at the boot-clad foot. What was left of the boot was helping slow the bleeding. He'd leave it in place. There was nothing he could do to improve the situation out here anyway. Once on board he'd apply tight bandages to help keep the blood flow to a minimum. From what he could see, he didn't like the chances of it being saved, but who knew? Surgeons could work miracles given half a chance. 'What's under that strapping?' he asked over his shoulder. The lower leg had been bound with what appeared to be a shirt torn into strips.

'Russ was bleeding all along the calf muscle up to the knee so we did what we could to stop it,' one of the men answered.

'You've done an excellent job looking after him.' At least Russell's neck and spine appeared to be uninjured by the way he was moving his head and shoulders, though Josue suspected the movement would be causing him some pain. 'Stay still if you can.'

'Reckon the arm's broken. My ribs hurt a bit too.'

Interpret 'a bit' to mean hurt like hell, Josue mused as he carefully felt along the ulna and radius of Russell's right arm. 'Movement won't be helping either your arm or your ribs.' Under his fingers he felt an inconsistency on the bones. 'You've fractured both bones in your lower arm. I'm going to look at your chest. Tell me about the pain there.'

'Only when I breathe too deep. Reckon that frigging tree got me fair and square.'

'I know this will hurt but take a long slow breath for me.' With a stethoscope Josue listened to Russell's lungs and heart. 'Good. You can stop. You may have broken some ribs but your lungs haven't been ruptured.' He pressed the button on his headset. 'Jamie, we need the stretcher.'

'On its way.'

'How's it going down there, Josue?' Mallory's voice was soft in his ears, and he smiled.

Impossible to stay distant with her when his heart went soft when she was near. 'All good. We'll be out of here shortly. The sooner our man's in hospital the better.' Still smiling, he said to the men with him, 'Can you get the stretcher?'

'On my way,' one of them answered.

'Right. Russell, I'm going to give you a shot of painkiller before we haul you up and on board.'

'Would prefer a bourbon,' the man croaked.

'You can pretend I'm giving you one intravenously,' Josue joked as he filled the syringe. He hoped this tough guy could weather what lay ahead with as much nonchalance.

'They're ready.' Jamie's voice came through the headset.

Mallory brought the helicopter over the men on the ground and slowly descended to ten metres, then hovered. 'Go.' Looking down, she saw Josue standing bent over his patient, protecting the man from the downdraught. Her heart softened for his kindness. She'd seen others do the same thing but from what he'd said Josue hadn't had much experience with chopper rescues and yet doing the right thing by his patient seemed to come naturally. Yeah, he was a good bloke, as the guys in the search and rescue crews would say. But she already knew that.

She read the dials, checked everything was as it should be, looked out and around the location and nodded. All good. The sky was beginning to darken but they'd be well on the way to Christchurch before night took over completely. At least it would be all twinkling stars as the weather forecast was for minus six in the morning. No wind or rain this end of the South Island, but watch out on Saturday. Storms bringing snow and ice were predicted. She shivered at the thought.

'Coming up now,' Jamie warned.

Keeping a firm eye on everything, she waited to be told everyone was on board. The man had to be in a serious condition. When a chainsaw was involved it usually meant horrendous injuries, and then a tree had fallen on top of him too. The injuries wouldn't be pretty.

A light thump, then the winch was dropping the cable down again to Josue.

Leaning against her window, she glanced down at the man who had her longing for things she shouldn't. Josue was attaching the hook that would haul him up, looking well at ease. Why did *he* make her think about love and a long-term relationship? Why not the last guy she'd spent time getting to know, only to decide he wasn't worth the effort?

She hadn't felt this sense of having found someone worth putting everything into, of risking her heart again, in a long time. Not since Hogan, and he'd been quite different, expecting her to change to fit in with him all the time. Josue took her for who she was, and didn't knock her faults. Of course this was early days, when everything was generally rosy, but somehow she didn't think Josue was going to turn out to be a very different man from the one she was slowly—but surely—falling deeper and deeper in love with. Come on, there hadn't been anything slow about it at all. *More like slam, bang, here I am.* She sighed.

Josue had disappeared from sight below the chopper, meaning he'd be on board in a second. Mallory dragged her attention back to what was important right at this moment and focused on being ready to ascend the moment Jamie said they were set.

Josue would spend the flight caring for the injured man, utterly focused on watching for bleeding, making certain the man's breathing was all right and that his heart wasn't faltering, administering pain relief that wasn't going to affect being taken to Theatre for surgery. She knew all this from previous flights with other doctors. He would not come forward and sit beside her to Christchurch, but he might on the way back to Queenstown.

In the meantime, she'd make sure they had a fast but safe trip. 'All set,' Jamie called. He would watch Josue and help wherever he could. That was Jamie. She'd worked with him on enough rescues to know he was always sucking up information, learning what he could as often as opportunities arose. When she thought about it, he and Josue had a lot in common.

'Russell, open your eyes. Look at me.' Josue's sharp command came through the headset and she could hear his worry, like there was a problem going on.

Better not be, Mallory thought. *Our team doesn't like bad results. They cause despair and sleepless nights.* Turning the helicopter in the direction of the river, she flew downstream, ascending until she reached a safe height, and then headed for Canterbury and the hospital in Christchurch, one ear listening out for Josue.

'That's it, Russell. You're in the helicopter and we're flying to Christchurch. Understand?' A pause. 'Good.' Some of the tension had left Josue's voice.

Mallory relaxed. If Josue was comfortable with how his patient was doing, then she was content with flying them all to get help. She hated the trips that were touch and go every minute of the way. She felt pressured to push harder than was safe. Not that she ever did but she couldn't help wondering how she'd feel if that was someone she loved back there with serious injuries.

On today's flight there *was* a man in the back she was keen on. She'd spent a lot of nights with him in her bed now and still wanted more. Her hand slid over her belly. A lot more. Her rare flings had never amounted to more than a few exciting moments before they'd finished, no hard feelings.

Initially that's what she'd hoped she'd started with Josue, despite the niggling feeling that there was more to him than other men she'd dated. As the days had gone by she'd realised she wanted to be with him as much as possible and not only in bed or on rescues. Now there was a baby in the mix. She held her breath, searching for pain in her abdomen and finding none. Bring on the scan and hopefully she could drop this fear that was even stronger than telling Josue he might become a father.

'Feel up to some dinner?' Josue asked from right beside her seat in the chopper parked outside the hangar in Queenstown.

Mallory tugged her eyes open and turned to look at him. Looked right into those eyes filled with wariness. Dang, she was tired. 'Sounds good,' she said through a yawn. Flying to Christchurch and back had taken every last drop of her concentration.

'Sorry to wake you up.'

'Yeah, I know. It's hard to get any peace around here.' Even her smile felt tired. 'I wanted a few minutes to myself. I always do after a rescue flight.' She needed to remember the patient was in good hands and had been all the time. Needed to accept she'd done her best and couldn't have done anything more. Needed to let go and get on with the rest of her night.

'I get like that too,' Josue admitted.

'Where do you want to eat? I'd prefer to stay at home.' Right now, going home and heating something from the freezer was as much as she could contemplate. Pregnancy was turning her into a dull old woman.

His hand covered her shoulder, squeezed gently. 'No problem. I'll sort some food. Let's get out of here.'

Did this mean she was forgiven for last night? 'I'll finish checking over the helicopter and sign off the paperwork and then head home.'

'I'll see you there in a bit.' His smile looked as tired as hers felt, and he still held himself back a little.

A shower. That's what she needed to ease the kinks in her back and warm away the tiredness in her muscles. *'Merci.'* That and *oui* were about the only French words she knew. Might be time to learn some more. Like *touch me. Kiss me.* 'See you when you're ready.' Learn to say I love you. You're going to be a father. *If* this pregnancy was normal.

Josue leaned in close and kissed her cheek. 'You *were* great today.'

'Just doing my job.' She loved her job and put everything into it. Hopefully she'd be able to fly for a while before the baby got in the way. If the baby wasn't in her fallopian tube. Thud. Her heart stuttered. Tomorrow would reveal the answer she was desperate for. The right answer. Her teeth were sharp, digging into her bottom lip.

'Doing it exceptionally well, or so it seemed for someone not very experienced with being in a helicopter. And stop chewing your lip. I'll feed you, I promise.'

If only he knew. He could, if she got on with telling him. *Tonight?* Yes, it had to be. There was no reason not to, and it would be good if he could go to the scan with her, though he was probably working tomorrow. 'See you soon.'

Breathing deep, inhaling a combination of Josue and aviation fuel, she got on with the checks required at the end of every flight, aware of Josue as he chattered with Jamie in the back as they packed the stretcher and gathered their gear before leaving the aircraft.

Just hearing his accent had her tummy tightening like a small caress. Then she recalled him whispering in French against her skin during the nights they'd spent together and the caress became thick with heat and need. *You've got it bad, Mallory.* Yep, she did. Only one thing to do about that. Enjoy every minute she had, making the most of him while she could and to heck with worrying about what to do when he left because no amount of fretting could change anything.

If only it was that simple. She hoped he didn't walk away from the life-changing news she was about to load on him. She didn't believe he would. No, make that she didn't *want* to believe he would. Josue took responsibility seriously, and this was his child, but he didn't do stopping in one place long term. He had a lot of fears to overcome. She'd do everything possible to help him through those. That's what love was about. She'd seen it with her parents, the support and unbreakable love that had got them through miscarriages and loss of jobs, and knew that's what she would give Josue. If he'd accept her being a part of his life. *If*—such a small word, so many directions it could go.

She crossed her fingers and yawned. Damn, she was exhausted. She was more likely to fall asleep at the table tonight than talk to Josue about the future.

CHAPTER EIGHT

SHADE MET JOSUE at the door, tail wagging and her nose raised to the pizzas he carried in one hand.

'No, girl, they're not for you.' He tried to ignore the hope shining up at him but Shade didn't make it easy. 'Even if you are gorgeous.'

'Shade, behave. You've been fed.' Mallory stood at the other end of the short hallway with a wide but tired grin on her face. 'You're such a sucker for those big eyes, Doctor.'

Forget Shade's beguiling eyes. It was the pair watching him that were devouring him with warmth. Josue's mouth dried. Mallory was heart-wrenchingly pretty. Dressed in a white floaty blouse that had a light blue floral pattern that matched the blue on her nails and fitted rust-coloured trousers that were feminine and accentuated her shape to perfection, she had him in the palm of her hand.

Her wavy hair shone under the light and had his hand itching to touch it. She'd put on new make-up, a little more accentuated than what she'd worn to work. This was Mallory the woman away from the predominantly male environment she worked in. 'You look beautiful.' Nothing to do with the make-up either.

She blinked, shook her head and looked away.

So there was still something bothering her.

Then her focus returned to him, a crimson shade colouring her cheeks. 'Are you going to stand there all night?'

'You think?' Since both hands were full he closed the door with his heel and followed her into the family room, where she'd laid out plates. 'Do you like Pinot noir, by any chance?' He'd stopped in at the supermarket while waiting for the pizzas.

'I do, but then I like most wines. Central Otago's well known for Pinot noirs.'

'Just as well I bought a local brand then.'

Placing the bottle and the pizzas on the table, he went into the kitchen and took glasses out of the cupboard. He was so comfortable here, as though he'd always been doing this. He knew where everything was, and how Mallory liked things to look. He'd brought her a large bunch of roses the second week he'd visited her here and had replaced them every week since because she got so much pleasure out a simple gesture that he did from the bottom of his heart. He'd started believing he could make settling down work, that the urge to run whenever the going got rough might not rear up so quickly, and when it did that he'd be able to manage it.

When Mallory hadn't turned up last night, he'd begun to feel the pain that losing her would bring and already the shutters had started to come down over his heart. The old need to go before she kicked him out had begun ringing loud and clear, reminding him how he usually did things.

His reasoning had been about going home for Gabriel, when in truth if he wasn't afraid of rejection he'd surely find a way to make everything work. He couldn't necessarily offer security to Mallory but he could try his hardest. If she wanted it. Why would she? She was confident in her own life.

Despite the love for her slowly expanding in his chest that he desperately wanted to follow, so was the fear of rejection. It was bigger than before, which told him his feelings for her were also bigger than he'd ever experienced before. The time to make a firm decision to move forward or step back was rushing at him with an incomprehensible speed. As much as he loved her, he still didn't trust himself to do the right thing by both of them.

'Josue?' She was right beside him.

'Let's eat. I'm starving.' For a lot of things. That's what was leading him into trouble. He couldn't let Mallory go, and yet sooner or later he might have to. He *was* leaving. He had to be there for Gabriel's operation so it would be safer to walk away from her while he still could, in case he wasn't coming back. *If* he could. He had yet to tell John his decision. He knew he was stalling. Since when had he got so indecisive? Since his heart had got involved.

'Me too.' Mallory was watching him with a big question in her eyes. 'Will you stay the night?'

That wasn't what was darkening those eyes but he'd go with it for now. He rubbed her back where she often ached after flying. *'Oui.'* His answer had come instinctively from the heart. How could he not spend another night with Mallory? Could he make this the last one? Impossible. *Grow a backbone. You want to look out for her, you've got to make up your mind and stick to it. One way or the other.*

'Are you working tomorrow?' Mallory had moved away to sit at the table and open the pizza boxes, sniffing the air like a hound.

He'd never eaten so many pizzas, and they weren't even a favourite. Another example of Mallory getting to him. 'I've got two days off. Two whole days in succession.' Might be an idea to go away somewhere, stay overnight in another town, do some sightseeing in the name of giving himself some space from his heart's desire.

'What are you going to do with them?'

Quickly thinking of the places he'd been told were must-sees, he went with, 'I thought I'd drive to Fiordland and go for a boat trip. I hear it's quite something.' He sat opposite her and lifted the wine bottle. 'Yes?'

'Yes to dinner. No to wine tonight. It's late and it'll keep me awake.'

'That's the idea.' He smiled and filled one glass. 'You're sure you won't have a little?'

'No, thanks.' She got up to get a glass of water, sat back down and reached for some food.

Needing to fill the gap in conversation before he blurted something awkward, like he wanted to spend more time with her, he said, 'Sometime before I head home I'd like to see the albatross colony at Dunedin. That's more interesting to me than Larnach's Castle. Not saying it wouldn't be interesting but we have plenty of castles in France.'

'Far grander, I'd expect.' Mallory was chewing slowly and her gaze seemed fixed on the family photos hanging on the wall behind him. What was she thinking about?

'What's up?'

Shaking her head, abruptly she bit into her pizza. 'Nothing.'

He never believed her when she said nothing, but he didn't want to argue. He'd done enough arguing with himself to last the week. They finished up dinner and cleared away the dishes in a companionable yet not completely relaxed silence.

Then Mallory made herself tea and said, 'I'm taking this to bed. You joining me?'

'I'll take Shade for a quick walk first, shall I?' The dog had grown restless in the last few minutes. Mallory always took her along the road or around the lawn before she settled down for the night so it seemed odd she was going to bed straight away.

'Would you? I'm exhausted.'

When Josue and Shade returned to the house, he was surprised to find Mallory sitting on the couch, drinking her tea and flicking idly through a magazine. Warmth spread through him. This was just how he imagined couples to be. Sharing the chores, making everything easier for each other and then going to bed and making love. He sighed. He adored Mallory. It no longer shocked him that he felt this way. It was true. He woke most mornings with happiness coursing through his veins and hope for another wonderful day in his heart. Mallory had given him this. Leaning over, he brushed his lips over her forehead. Maybe he could make it work for them.

'I thought you were going to bed.' There were shadows under her eyes, and when he thought about it, they'd been there all day. Hadn't she been sleeping well? Had the tension between them not really disappeared and was causing her to lie awake at night? Had he wanted to believe her so much when she'd apologised for missing their date that he'd avoided hearing something he might not like? Something different to what he'd begun hoping for? He hoped not. 'What's going on?'

Silence answered him.

'The only time you've been distant with me was when you forgot our date yesterday.' He highlighted 'forgot' with his forefingers.

Her shoulders tensed. She was scratching at her trousers above her knee. Not a Mallory action at all. Unless she was worried. Then she looked up and faced him squarely. 'Josue, sit down.'

The last time someone had spoken to him like that had been when he'd been about to be kicked out of school. He folded his arms across his chest and leaned his backside against the back of an armchair. 'What's going on?'

If only they could go to her bedroom and make love, sleep spooned together and then in the morning get up and share breakfast before Josue got organised for a day in Fiordland.

Mallory breathed deeply. That wasn't happening. There'd be no sleeping for her until he knew, and probably none afterwards. She couldn't have one last night when the baby didn't come between them because it was already there, causing trouble for their relationship.

Once Josue knew, nothing would be quite the same. Naturally he'd be shocked, just as she had been. But for Josue there was so much more to contend with. His past would be a big part of how he reacted. He wasn't going to sweep her up into his arms and tell her it was the most amazing news he'd ever heard and that the three of them would make a great family, even if he wanted to. Not Josue.

She was going to have to be patient and support him while waiting, impatiently, with crossed fingers. She loved him, and for her that meant one thing: together forever, loving each other and their child.

'Mallory, what is going on?' he demanded in a voice she didn't recognise. Was he getting angry with her?

Pulling her eyes open, she stared into Josue's troubled gaze and bit her lip hard to stop herself from crying. He was the most wonderful man she'd ever known, and any minute now she was probably going to lose him forever.

'Talk to me.'

Wriggling deeper into the couch, she gave him a weak smile. Talk to him? *Yes, Josue, that's exactly what I'm about to do. I hope you'll still be able to hug me afterwards.* 'You...' Gulp. 'I...'

Worry was darkening that steady gaze. 'What about us?' He didn't blink, didn't move a finger, his breathing was tight.

I can do this. 'Josue, I'm pregnant.'

Silence answered her.

Shock widened his eyes, tightened his mouth, but he said nothing, didn't cross to touch her, didn't move further away. Nothing.

She waited, breathless, stomach knotted, heart barely beating. And waited.

Finally, 'Is that why you've been so tired?'

Of all the things she'd guessed he might say, that wasn't one of them. He'd put his doctor's cap on. 'I think so. Plus the fact I'm terrified I could have another ectopic pregnancy has kept me from sleeping these last couple of nights.'

'Another? You've been pregnant before?'

'I was eighteen. My boyfriend left me at the time. I'm having a scan tomorrow to make sure this pregnancy is all right.'

Josue winced. 'How long have you known?'

'I found out yesterday, which was why I forgot about the meeting.'

His arms unfolded and lined up with his sides. His gaze was still directed on her. 'You didn't think to tell me then?'

She stood up, moved closer. Reaching for his hand, she wound hers around it. 'I wanted to tell you, but I needed to get everything clear in my mind.'

His hand jerked away. 'Everything? Like what exactly?'

She'd known this wasn't going to be easy but it still hurt. At the moment Josue was turning everything back on her. Probably his way of working through the shock of learning he was going to be a father. She would give him time to get used to the idea. 'Firstly, I want this baby very much.'

Josue's arms went back across his chest, his fingers white against his green jersey. 'I'd have been stunned if you thought otherwise.'

That was a positive sign, wasn't it? Did he feel the same? 'Family is important to me. I'm sure it's the same for you.'

'I don't talk about how I've always done my utmost not to be in this position because, as you know, I don't stay around long enough to be a parent.'

Her shoulders sagged. *Here we go.* She waited to hear him out.

'I can't give a child—or a partner—the stable life they deserve. How can I when I haven't had the experience of a loving family?' He shoved both hands through his hair, leaving it sticking up on end. 'This is crazy.'

'I couldn't fly a helicopter until I was taught.' She glared at him. *Easy, girl. He's taking this hard.* 'You learned to be a doctor, Josue. You can learn to be a fantastic father. And partner. Think what Gabriel and his wife gave you, how they shared their lives to help you make yours better.'

Josue stared at her as though he didn't recognise her. 'You think so?' He snapped his fingers. 'Just like that they wiped away my fears and pain? I spent my younger life being rejected, only to turn it around so now I do the rejecting. Does that sound like an ideal partner or father?'

'What I know is that my parents raised me with love and care. They taught me to be who I am. I am going to do the same with our child. We can do this, you and I.'

'No, Mallory. You don't know what you're saying. You really don't.'

'You're about to walk out on us?' She was going for the jugular, but being tough was in her blood, and Josue was worth every bit of her strength. She was resilient and would not let him go easily. He needed to understand she'd be there every time he tripped, as he would be for her if he gave them half a chance.

'No, Mallory, I'm going to go along the road to my bedroom to do a whole lot of thinking. I cannot guarantee you or any child a settled life, living with me.' Suddenly he blinked. Tears appeared in his eyes.

'Josue, you don't have to leave next month.' Damn, she'd all but begged there. That wouldn't help her case. 'Your visa has another year to run.'

'Yes, Mallory, I do. I promised Gabriel I'd be there for his surgery.'

'What are you talking about?' Her heart started banging hard. This might mean she'd never stood a chance of winning Josue over.

'He's having a coronary bypass. It was meant to happen in June but he got flu so it was delayed until next month. It's not urgent but his surgeon wants to do it while he's still in relatively good health. After all Gabriel and Brigitte have done for me I have to be there for them. I *am* their surrogate son.' A tight squeeze of her hand and he was back on his feet and reaching for his phone. 'Goodnight, Mallory.'

It sounded like goodbye. 'Wait. Of course you have to be with Gabriel and Brigitte. I understand, but you can come back afterwards.'

'Have you heard a thing I've said?'

Despite his denial, she dredged up a weak smile. 'Yes, I have. All of it, and here's the thing. I believe in you.' Her heart spilled into her words.

He glared at her. 'Laying it on a bit thick, aren't you?'

'It's the only way to get through to you.'

'Believe me, you did that with the words "I'm pregnant". They're going round and round in my head like a broken record.'

Josue was a kind, gentle man who wanted love. Did he not realise how much he loved the couple who'd taken him in and that if he loved them so much, he could love others? Especially his child? And if only he could love her, then they'd have no problems with this.

'I'll see you later on.' He was at the door, looking at her as though he'd forgotten why he'd been here in the first place.

He doesn't love me. The thought slammed into her, took her breath away and stopped her heart. Her hands splayed across her abdomen. *Sorry, baby, but Daddy doesn't love Mummy. I love him, though. With everything I have.* Josue needed to know that. If he threw it back in her face, she'd falter, but she'd stand tall, take the hurt on the chin, and fight for him. What a disaster this was turning out to be. He held on to his feelings too tightly. But he had been relaxing more and more, becoming a part of her life. She'd never told him her feelings for him either.

'Josue, wait.' She raced down the hall and out onto the porch. 'There's something you need to know.'

'Something more?'

She strode up to him and looked into those sad, lonely eyes. 'I love you with all my heart, Josue. You, and only you.'

He swayed towards her, then straightened, all the while looking at her, as though trying to find if she was being honest.

She said it again, with all her heart in every word. 'I love you.'

Then he was gone, stepping quietly along the footpath towards the house he wouldn't be staying in much longer.

I love you.

Mallory's words echoed in Josue's head again and again as he strode up to Kayla's house. He believed her. No one had ever said that to him before, not as clear and unadorned. Not even the two people who'd taken him under their wing.

'I love you.'

He tasted the words, listened to them, breathed them in. They scared him. They warmed him, undermined his worry about not being good enough for Mallory or their child.

A baby. He was going to be a father. Him. Who didn't know the first thing about raising a child with his heart. As a doctor he knew all too well how to change a soiled nappy or feed a hungry tot. As a man—he needed a manual and that was hardly the way to go about it.

Letting himself into the house, he flicked lights on and stared around at Kayla's home, so unlike Mallory's warm comfortable place that had caught his breath the first time he'd opened her front door. He couldn't stay another night here when Kayla was Mallory's best friend. He was the odd one out. Did Kayla know about the baby? They'd had been together last night. Kayla had told him on the phone she was returning home and that he could stay on for the rest of his time here.

Right now he needed to get away from Mallory's friend's space, from Mallory down the road. He'd head into town to find a hotel room for the night. Or he could hit the road and head to Fiordland, get there before the sun rose. Except the last thing he felt like doing now was being a sightseer. There was more than enough to look at inside his head.

In the bedroom he sank onto the bed and tried to decide what to do, but all that came to mind was walking back down the road and climbing into bed with Mallory, to hug her and never let go. Which was irresponsible. He had to make some decisions before anything else.

He was going to be a dad. Yes. Incredible. Unbelievable. To think parenthood had never been a part of his thinking and yet here he was, a father-to-be, with the only woman he'd loved so deeply she had him looking at who he was and who he might become if he found the guts to do it. How was it that the deeper the difficulties the more he found he loved her?

Why not go to her now and say that? Express his love in words. He'd been showing her in small ways, but she needed to hear him say it. So did he. Except he knew if he opened his mouth the only thing that would come out was his fear of failing her, or her rejecting him. He'd tell her he was leaving.

She said she loved you.

He had to go. Grabbing a bag, he tossed in all his gear, locked up the house, put the key back in the meter box, and drove away, slowing as he passed Mallory's house, which was in darkness. *Bet she's not sleeping.*

I love you, Josue.

'And I love you, Mallory, but that doesn't mean I won't hurt you.'

In town, Josue pulled up by the lake's edge, got out and started walking. It was easy going with a full moon to light his way. He wasn't tired. Not enough to go to sleep anyway.

He might never sleep again if he didn't sort this out.

What was his problem? Apart from his fear of letting Mallory and his baby down? Of being rejected despite her claim to love him? Wasn't that enough? She'd said he could do this, but she didn't know how little he knew. She was wrong to believe in him. He had warned her.

Bending down, he picked up a handful of pebbles and one at a time threw them across the calm water to bounce again and again before disappearing underneath the surface. Like him: he bounced along, meeting women, getting to know them, liking them, and then he sank, leaving only circles of emptiness behind him.

He was about to do that to Mallory.

Turning back the way he had come, his steps were slow. What if he went to the scan with her? Supported her? And then walked away?

That would be worse than not showing up at all.

The scan was important for her. The pain in her face

when she'd mentioned the ectopic pregnancy had hit him hard. If this was another of those she'd be devastated. Someone should be with her. If she didn't ask Kayla to go with her, he should. He was in a relationship with Mallory, no matter how hard he tried to look the other way, especially if she carried the baby to full term. They had made this baby together.

If Mallory believed he could do this, then he had to believe in himself. She'd been fierce when telling him they could make it work. Then she'd been so close to tears when she'd said she loved him. Those tears had nearly undone him and had him on his knees, begging for her to take him on, fears and all.

What? Josue scooped up some more pebbles and began flicking them across the surface. *He wanted this child?* Splash. Yes, he did—if he could guarantee him or her a happy, loving life. One where he was always there, always encouraging and supporting.

It wouldn't happen. He would be doing Mallory and the child a favour by getting out of here sooner rather than later, and never, ever coming back or making contact.

He turned back to his vehicle and began driving out of town.

Early the next morning Mallory sat in her car, afraid to put the key in the ignition because the moment she started the engine her journey to the scanning wand would begin.

She couldn't bear to think this might be the last opportunity to be pregnant, to have a baby.

'Stop being negative,' Kayla had growled over the phone last night before offering to go to Invercargill with her. 'The doctor told you everything appeared normal.'

'I'm afraid to believe her,' Mallory had admitted. After

all, she had hoped there was a chance Josue would believe her when she told him she loved him. Round three in the love stakes had stabbed her in the heart and was even more debilitating than the previous two. She was on her own in this. Kayla and Maisie would be there for her any time she called for help, but *if* she was going to be a mother then she had to stand tall and strong right from the get-go. It might be the only chance she got and there was no way she was going to get it wrong.

She'd put on heavier than usual make-up to put some colour in her white cheeks and cover the dark shadows below her eyes. It had been a long, sleepless night as hope that Josue might love her faded to despair as reality returned. He'd been stunned by her declaration, but there hadn't been any love coming her way, only bewilderment and fear. Plus the need to get away from her. That had hurt, but she had been warned.

There was a light tapping on her window.

Looking out, she gasped. 'Josue?' She stared at him. He looked as dishevelled as she felt. What did he want? She had to get on the road. Pressing the button, she opened the window. 'Hello.'

'You look like you had about as much sleep as I did. That's not the way to look after yourself, Mallory.'

If that's all he'd come to say, he could go away. 'You think?' She wouldn't mention not being able to force a single mouthful of toast down her throat for breakfast, and that only tea had made it past the lump in her throat, and then not a whole mug full.

'I'm coming with you.'

'Really? Just like that?' She ignored the hope rising inside her chest. It might mean nothing more than he needed to see proof that she was pregnant. Anger began winding her up. He'd come along for his own sake and nothing to do with how she might feel. Then he'd pack up and leave town. 'I don't think so, Josue. This is more than a quick squizz at a scan to see if I am safely pregnant and not going to have a procedure to remove my last Fallopian tube.' This was about her future, whether he was a part of that or not.

'I understand.'

'Do you?'

'Honestly? I'm trying.'

She stared at him long and hard, trying to sort through all the worries slapping around her skull, but there were too many and she was already exhausted. There was a long drive ahead too. 'Get in.'

'Want me to drive?'

Her shoulders slumped. So much for being strong. 'Yes, please.'

Josue opened the door and helped her out of the seat, led her around to the passenger side. Like she was an invalid.

She swallowed that one. They were going to be crammed into her car for a while, no point in getting grouchy. As they buckled themselves in she tried for normal, and asked, 'Where did you spend the night?'

Josue's car hadn't been parked outside Kayla's house when the sun had come up.

'I've moved out of the house.'

If she'd thought there was any hope at all by his turning up to go with her to Invercargill it had just taken a dive. He *was* leaving.

'Warm enough?' he asked as he started up the car.

'Yes.'

'Where are we going for this scan?'

'Invercargill Hospital.'

Josue stopped asking questions and Mallory sank down and closed her eyes. There was so much to say but she wasn't in the mood. All she wanted was to know her baby was where it should be and was going to be fine. Whatever Josue would do had to come second for now.

CHAPTER NINE

'ARE YOU COMING in with me?' Mallory asked as Josue parked outside the hospital. It had been a silent trip.

'Do you want me to?'

'Josue, answer the bloody question, will you?' She vented her frustration. 'What do you want?'

'To be there for you.' He wasn't looking at her.

Did this baby mean nothing to him? Or was this his fear taking control? Well, she'd decided to fight for him. Might as well start now. 'Thank you. I'd like your company, especially if…' She swallowed, unable to go on.

Now he faced her, nothing but concern in his expression. 'One step at a time, Mallory.'

Was that how he was dealing with all this? One step at a time? She'd ignore the tiny bubble of hope that brought on. 'Let's go in.'

Half an hour later, after waiting for the scan and then having the wand run across the goo on her abdomen, Mallory held her breath and stared at the radiologist.

A broad smile on his face brought her another bubble of hope. 'Mallory, Josue, all is well. Your baby is where it should be and looking as it's meant to. That's about all I can say at this stage. But you can stop worrying about an ectopic pregnancy.'

'All is well.' The statement bounced around Mallory's head. *My baby's real. This is really happening.* Her heart was bubbling fit to burst. She was going to be a mother. Bring him or her on.

'That's wonderful.'

Josue. Mallory blinked, looked to him and saw relief mixed with bewilderment coming at her. He didn't know where this left him. He hadn't made any decisions. Swallowing her disappointment, she reached for his hand and held tight. 'Yes, it is. Thank you, Doctor. I've been so scared and now I feel as though I'm walking on air.'

'I understand. I'm glad to have been the bearer of good news.' His eyes flicked to Josue and a frown appeared on his brow. 'I'll leave you both to absorb everything. A copy of the result will be sent to your GP.'

Just like that they were alone in the small space. Mallory shivered in the suddenly chill air. 'Josue, come on. Let's get outside and back on the road.'

'Yes, of course. What a relief for you.'

For me? 'It is the absolute best result I could get.' Her pregnancy really was normal. Phew. Unbelievable. Exciting. She clapped her hands. 'Fantastic.'

Josue said nothing.

'What about you? Does this make you happy?' She watched him think up an answer.

'I was thinking how worried you were this might be a repeat. I am very happy that you're not going through that again.'

'That sounds as though you've decided you're definitely having nothing to do with us. You're heading home, never to return.'

'Is that what I said?' His head shot up, and he locked a fierce look on her.

That was so out of character that she knew she'd gone too far. But she was fighting for him, for the father of her baby and for the man she loved and wanted to spend the rest of her life with. 'You haven't said anything. That's the trouble, Josue. I'd like to know what you're going to do.' Her hands were clenched. 'Sooner rather than later.'

'I'm sorry.' He looked the other way while she got back into her clothes, then took her elbow and started towards the lift that'd take them down to the car park. 'Let's wait until we're on our own before finishing this.'

Finishing this? Not starting or continuing, but finishing. The thrill at learning her baby was safe had been shunted aside with the dread that Josue was leaving them. Knowing how likely that was didn't make this any easier to accept. It'd have been better not to get her hopes up but she'd already given herself that speech weeks ago and hadn't managed to keep him at a distance. She loved him with everything she had and nothing would change that. No amount of pleading, telling him she loved him, asking him to reconsider would change his stubborn mind once he'd made it up.

Outside she waited for Josue to say something.

Instead he headed for the car, head down against the sharp wind, and his hand still on her elbow as though she needed support.

It would've been childish to pull away so she upped her pace to keep up and pretended the slight pressure from his fingers was loving.

Inside the car he turned on the heater and started for the main road back to Queenstown, his shoulders tight as he drove. His lips pressed against each other and his eyes were dark.

Did she give him a break or push for his thoughts?

She leaned back, her hand touching her stomach. A wave of happiness rolled through her, quickly gone. But she'd felt it, knew it to be true. Now that she could relax about an ectopic pregnancy not being a problem she was thrilled about the baby. One step on the way to her future was underway. Funny how when she hadn't been looking for it, it had happened anyway. Now she had Josue to talk to and make him see her love meant helping him overcome his difficulties and be happy too. 'Josue…'

Josue drew a breath. 'I've been offered a permanent position at the hospital with help to get a resident's visa should I want one.'

Her mouth fell open. Obviously she hadn't seen that coming. Why would she have? He'd kept quiet about everything going on in his life.

'Is that a good thing?' she asked.

'I'm still headed to Nice next month.'

'Even now you know about the baby?'

'I don't make rash decisions.' Even to him that sounded like he was covering up his feelings. Which he probably was.

She snapped, 'Rash stopped when I got pregnant.'

'Mallory, it may be straightforward for you to accept you're having a baby, but as I've never contemplated the idea…' He hesitated. Even if he hadn't, how could he not be excited knowing he was going to be a father? First he'd fallen in love, then been offered a job that fitted in with being with Mallory and now they were having a baby. It was too much to take in. It was so far out of his norm he was stumbling. 'You know my story.'

'Tell me more. There're a lot of gaps.'

'I've never considered being a parent and now I've

been confronted with the fact that I might have to without a say in the matter.'

'Like me, you mean?' She didn't look at him, just sat watching the kilometres disappearing under the front of the car.

'I suppose it is exactly the same, regardless of our different backgrounds.'

'Background has nothing to do with this.' Breathing deep, she asked softly, 'Then tell me what you're going to do. Stay or go?'

If only it was that straightforward. Josue braked as a truck cut across his line of traffic. Pressing his palm on the horn, he yelled, 'Idiot.'

Mallory looked across to him. 'Easy.'

Which only made him madder. How could he take anything easy when she wanted answers about the future? Wanted commitment from him? More than anything he wanted to tell her he was here forever, would raise their child with her, would buy a house and settle down and get everything right. If only he could say the words 'I love you' without tripping over them, without doubting them. 'Sure.'

He concentrated on driving and let the tension grow because he didn't know how to stop it without letting years of worry explode out of him. His knuckles were white, his stomach tighter than a basketball. To let rip would drive a wedge between them that could take years to fix. Not the way to get into a permanent relationship or to welcome a child into the world. If he was actually going to do it, and he still did not know the answer to that. The doubts far outweighed everything else.

Somewhere during the ride back to Queenstown, Mallory fell asleep. Josue relaxed a little and glanced across at her regularly. Tiredness lined her face but the fear of losing her baby had gone, leaving her as beautiful as ever. *'Je t'adore,'* he said quietly. 'But I doubt it's enough to walk into your life and never leave.'

At her house he went and unlocked the door then returned to lift her out and carried her into the bedroom, where he laid her on the bed and pulled a cover over her. 'Bye, Mallory.'

Whether she heard him he had no idea, but she didn't move or blink so he guessed not. Which meant she'd probably be annoyed when she woke up and found herself alone at home.

But as he stepped out of her room he heard a call.

'Josue? Are you there?'

Returning, he stood at the edge of her bed. *Don't ask me anything. I do not want to answer questions I have no idea about.* 'You've been out for the count most of the trip. I thought it best to let you continue sleeping.'

She wasn't buying it. 'Dodging the bullets?'

Leaning closer, he tucked a stray strand of hair behind her ear and locked his eyes on hers. 'For now, yes. I have some calls to make. All right?'

She stared at him as though searching deep inside for the truth. Finally Mallory gave him a small smile. 'I guess.'

His legs were shaky as he stepped away. He didn't want to leave her even for an hour but he had to. He was not making any promises he could not keep. Neither was he going to let loose the anger that he'd been holding in all the way back from Invercargill. 'See you later.' *Maybe.*

Not having sorted new accommodation yet, he drove to the same spot by the lake and parked. After staring at the water for a long time he got out and strode along the water's edge again. The water calmed him, as did the view of Cecil's Peak on the other side of the lake. This was a beautiful place and he could see himself living here. After a few kilometres of walking along the lake shore and up onto the road where the lake was inaccessible, he turned back.

He picked up his ringing phone and saw a video-call from Brigitte. *'Bonjour, Brigitte.'* Why was she in a hospital room? His heart dropped. 'What's happened?'

'It's all right.' Brigitte laughed. 'We have a surprise for you.' She moved her phone so he could see Gabriel in bed attached to any number of tubes and cables.

'What the...?'

'Hey, Josue, you worry too much. I'm fine.' Gabriel's voice was croaky, like he needed lots of fluid to lubricate his throat.

'He had his surgery today and has come through very well,' Brigitte was saying.

'But it wasn't scheduled till next month.' What was going on? 'I was going to be there with you.'

'An opportunity come up on the surgeon's schedule so I took it,' Gabriel croaked.

'And you're seriously all right?' Josue asked, even though Gabriel did look fine from here. 'You should've called me. I'd have caught the first plane out.'

'He's tired and sore, but otherwise everything went well.' Brigitte continued, 'We won't talk long or he'll fall asleep on you. But we wanted to tell you so you don't have to come home on our behalf.'

The tension exploded. 'I wanted to be there. Don't you understand?' It had been his excuse for leaving. 'I can't stay here.'

'Why ever not?' Gabriel asked. 'I thought you were enjoying New Zealand.'

'I was.'

'What's happened?'

'Nothing.' Everything. He'd screwed up big time. 'I am coming home.'

'Talk. And stop yelling.'

He hadn't known he was. 'I miss you both.'

'That's good because we're visiting you when I'm up and about.'

'Gabriel, you can't travel for a while after surgery.' What if he got ill on the flight?

'Too late.' Brigitte laughed. 'I booked flights for Christmas to come down to New Zealand. Gab wants to do this more than anything and since he's had a scare I have to agree. Do what we can while we can.'

Suddenly Josue felt as though the world was ganging up on him. A job offer. A baby. And now no reason to have to go home. He couldn't take it all in.

'Josue? You haven't answered my question. What's got you in this state?' Gabriel asked.

'I've got into a mess.'

'And you don't know what to do. Time to stand up and be counted, by any chance?' Gabriel knew him too well.

Josue swallowed his anger. These lovely people didn't deserve it any more than Mallory had. 'I've fallen in love. We're having a baby. I've got a job here if I want it.' The words poured out like he had no brakes.

'Wow.' Brigitte laughed. 'That's our Josue. Doesn't do anything in halves.'

Our Josue. It went straight to his heart. These people *were* his family. 'I've never gone for something so huge before.'

'So what's the problem?' Gabriel croaked, reminding Josue he should finish the call. 'Exactly why are you wanting to return to Nice?'

Josue stared at his mentor and saw the strength that had got him through life this far. Saw the love that went with the strength. And he decided. 'I'm not sure. I'd like to take a risk with Mallory, to stay on and settle down.' Now that he'd put it into words he felt relief settle over him. Had he made up his mind to move forward as easily as that? Impossible, surely?

He had been touching on the possibility for the weeks he'd known Mallory. The time to make up his mind had arrived and he couldn't walk away. He didn't want to. He was ready to take on the future and hopefully enjoy it.

Did this mean he could admit his feelings to her? To take a chance on them as a couple? He had to, otherwise he might as well pack his bags and go. But he wasn't going to. He would stay. He really would.

Mallory sat on the couch with her feet tucked under her backside and Shade's head in her lap. Unable to face anyone, she'd called Pete to ask for the rest of the day off and thankfully he'd agreed. She'd lit the fire, made tea and watched a movie, but she had no idea what it had been about.

When Kayla had rung to see if she needed company and that her dad could bring her over in his campervan, she'd turned her down. There was only one person she wanted to be with and he'd gone off on his own to make some calls apparently. But how long could some calls go on for? It had been hours since he'd left her in bed, looking as though he'd had the world's problems on his shoulders.

He didn't promise to come back, Mallory.

No, he didn't, but she could hope he might.

Shade sat up, her nose pointing towards the front door. 'Who is it, girl?'

The dog leapt to the floor and trotted out of the room.

'Mallory, can I come in?'

Josue. Her heart pounded painfully. This was the moment. She could feel it in her blood. Josue was here to tell her he was going home, that he wouldn't take the job or risk a life with her and their child. He'd be thinking he'd let them down. 'I'm in the lounge.' She pressed Off on the TV remote.

'Hey.' Josue came in and straight over to her where he sat on the other end of the couch. 'You all right?'

She nodded, unable to speak for fear of talking gibberish.

He reached for her hands and enclosed them in his warm ones, his thumbs moving back and forth softly on her cold skin. 'I've had a triple whammy these past couple of days.' He was smiling.

She crooked her head to one side. Smiling. That warm-her-toes smile. 'Sometimes it's best to get everything over and done with all at once.'

His smile widened. 'I'm hoping nothing's over and that this is the beginning of everything I've only ever dreamed about.'

Was she hearing him right? 'You'd better talk in words of one syllable.'

'I love you, Mallory Baine.'

That she could understand. 'Truly?' she blurted. 'It was only hours ago you were telling me how this was a shock and how I didn't understand where you were coming from. That your life had been terrible and I couldn't expect to know why you do the things you do.' She paused, drew a breath. 'Okay, so I've exaggerated, but what I did get was that you weren't interested in staying for the long haul.'

'You kind of got all of that right. I'm sorry for hurting you. I know your trust has been broken before. You can trust me. I've made up my mind to move forward, and that's with you and our baby. I want to give this, and you, all of my heart.'

'Oh, Josue.' She blinked but that didn't stop the tears flowing. She'd waited so long for this moment. A man and a baby. Life couldn't get any better.

'With all my heart, I love you.'

Her skin warmed, her heart changed rhythm to light and zippy. 'As I love you, Josue.'

'Yes, just like that.' He held her gaze. 'I'm going to take the job. I'm not going back to Nice at all. Gabriel and Brigitte are coming out here for Christmas.'

'What about his operation?' There's no way Josue would not be with the man who'd done so much for him.

'All done.' He explained what had happened, and the more he talked the more relaxed he became.

Josue was happy, she realised. 'You're sure about this, aren't you?'

'I am, but there's one more thing.'

Her heart slowed. *Don't make me sad now.* 'Go on,' she whispered.

'Will you marry me? Live with me and raise our child together?'

Mallory flew across the couch onto his lap and wound her arms around him. 'Yes,' she shouted. 'Yes.'

And then they were kissing and pulling back to smile at each other, and the love coming to her through those eyes told her she'd finally got it right and had found the right man to go through life with. She'd found the romance and love her parents had known. 'I love you so much, Josue. I can't believe I found you right here on this couch. It's going with us wherever we live.'

'About that. You need to find a better hiding place for the key. I don't want any other man wandering in and making himself at home here.'

'There's only one Mr Intruder in my life.' And she went back to kissing him.

The early summer sun streamed onto the lodge's deck, highlighting all the beautiful red and pink roses in their planter boxes lining the carpet leading up to the love of Mallory's life standing watching her as she and her mother began the walk from her single life to the beginning of her shared one, followed by Kayla and Maisie in beautiful cream silk gowns.

The smile lighting Josue's face and the love in his eyes melted her inside. Thank goodness for keys in meter boxes, and a dear friend who hadn't made it home that night. Kayla still teased her remorselessly, saying she was owed plenty for bringing them together.

'Who's that man?' Mallory's mother asked. 'He looks handsome.'

'That's Josue, Mum. I'm marrying him in a minute. Isn't he gorgeous?'

'Yes, darling, he's a stunner. Have I met him?'

Flip-flop went her heart. But she wasn't going to let her mother's condition spoil anything today, and she was determined her mum would have a good time, whether she remembered it or not. 'Yes, you have. He came and asked you if you'd let me marry him.'

'What did I say?'

'When you learned he was from France you said yes, and he hugged you.'

'That's him? Now I remember.'

Some of it anyway. Or maybe Mum was making up bits and pieces. It didn't matter. She was smiling and there was a twinkle in her faded blue eyes. Mallory squeezed her hand tight. 'Love you, Mum.'

They reached the group waiting at the end of their walk and paused. She looked into Josue's eyes and let go of the breath she'd been holding all the way down the aisle. He was here and he looked full to brimming with love for her. This was really happening; it wasn't a dream she was about to wake up from. Josue was real, was the love of her life, and this time she had got it right. Now she understood why she'd stuffed up with the first two men in her life. They had never been the right ones. Josue had always been meant to come along and take away her heart, giving her his in its place.

'Sweetheart, you look beautiful.' Josue leaned in and kissed both her cheeks. 'Stunning.'

Her eyes filled and she couldn't get a word out around the lump in her throat. *I love you.*

He nodded, looked at her mother, gave her two small kisses on her cheeks too. 'Hello, Dorothy. You look lovely, too.'

'I keep telling Mallory Frenchmen kiss like the devil.'

Laughter erupted amongst the seated guests as Maisie took Dorothy by the arm and held her beside Mallory.

Next to Josue, Gabriel and Brigitte laughed too. They were standing up with him, Gabriel's chest pushed out with pride. 'This is the most special day of my life, Mallory.'

Beside him Brigitte cleared her throat, and winked. 'Second most special.'

'Yes, of course.'

The marriage celebrant took over the proceedings. 'Shall we get the ceremony under way?'

'Yes, let's.' Mallory slid her free hand into Josue's and leaned close. 'I'm done waiting.'

'I can't believe I'm here marrying the love of my life.' Josue pinched his skin. *Oui*, it was true. His heart had been blocking his throat from the moment he'd seen Mallory begin walking up the aisle towards him. Bringing him love and happiness, with their baby warm inside her. He'd never have believed that day he'd boarded the plane to fly to New Zealand that everything was going to turn around for him, and that he'd find the most wonderful woman to share his life with.

Gabriel leaned close, said quietly, 'This is real, Josue.'

The man knew him too well. *'Je sais.'* Right from the bottom of his heart he understood how real and true it was and he couldn't wait to marry Mallory and begin the next phase of their life together.

Breathing deeply, he stood tall and listened to the celebrant begin the ceremony. It went by so fast. He was placing the ring on Mallory's slender finger and feeling the band of love she slipped onto his, and kissing her and hearing Gabriel saying that was enough, all before he knew it. When he heard the celebrant declare them man and wife, Monsieur and Madame Bisset, he lifted Mallory up into his arms and kissed her again. *'Je t'aime.'*

'I love you too,' she said through the kiss.

Dorothy's excited voice cut through their kiss. 'See, I

warned you Frenchmen kiss like the devil.' His mother-in-law was a bit of a character despite her health.

Mallory stood against him as he held her around the waist. 'I am so happy it's unbelievable.'

'*Non*, Mallory. It's believable. It's real. We just got married.'

Maisie handed her back the bouquet Mallory had relinquished to exchange wedding rings. 'I'm so happy. It's about time one of us was married.'

Mallory laughed. 'I think you two should have another shot at getting hitched again.'

Kayla smiled. 'Not me. Not yet. I'm coming right, but I'd like time to get settled back in Queenstown before I even think of men and marriage.' She grinned at Maisie. 'Guess that means you're next.'

'Don't even think you can start hooking me up for dates with every male who lands a ride in your ambulance. I am so not interested.' Maisie shrugged her shoulders, but her gaze had wandered out to the groups of friends standing talking and sipping the champagne that was being handed round.

Josue couldn't figure out who she paused on, but he did notice the sudden intake of breath. So there *was* someone she was interested in.

Mallory whispered, 'Watch this.' Suddenly she tossed her bouquet directly at Kayla who had no choice but to catch it.

Kayla glared at the bouquet, and then at Mallory. 'No, thanks.'

She went to hand it back to Mallory, but her friend laughed and held Josue's hands tight. 'Sorry, but my hands are full.'

'Mallory Baine, I swear you are a sneaky piece of work.'

Josue locked eyes with her. 'Kayla, haven't I introduced you to Mallory Bisset yet?' He loved the sound of his wife's name. He spun Mallory up into his arms and kissed her and kissed her some more. 'I promise to kiss you like the devil when you wake in the morning and before you go to sleep at night.' He leaned closer and whispered, 'And to love you forever.' It wouldn't be hard to do. His heart was in her hands now. Safe.

* * * * *

MILLS & BOON

Coming next month

A FAMILY MADE IN ROME
Annie O'Neil

Lizzy drew in a quick breath. 'Are those...?'

'Public baths,' Leon said, his voice low to match the magical surroundings. 'Second century AD, they think. They would've been adjacent to what is now the palazzo.'

'And these other rooms, the tiles, the kitchen areas—those are all centuries old?'

'Around five hundred years,' he confirmed. 'The palazzo went through numerous renovations, of course, and as you can see...' he gestured to the walls soaring above them '...so has the rest of Rome.'

Lizzy shook her head in disbelief, leaning into Leon's hand, a movement that seemed so natural anyone around them would assume they were a couple. A movement that elicited a hundred questions for Leon, who knew they weren't.

'I can't believe we're seven metres below the rest of Rome!'

He laughed appreciatively. 'I couldn't either, when I first saw it. These elements of the palazzo were only discovered recently—and excavated this century—and the addition of the glass floors, so people can walk freely above the remains, is even more recent.'

'Palazzo Valentini...' Lizzy sighed. 'It sounds so romantic, doesn't it?'

Leon gave her hand a squeeze, and to his surprise received a small squeeze of acknowledgment in return. Tipping his head to give the top of her head a kiss, just as he would have five years ago, seemed the natural thing to do—so he did it. She leant into him again, then shot him a shy smile.

Perhaps it was being cloaked in the low lighting. Perhaps it was holding hands. Perhaps it was simply being with Lizzy. But standing amidst the remains of an ancient family's household, where lives had been lived and lost, filled him with a profound sense of longing.

What sort of history would the two of them leave behind? And, more to the point, what sort of future would they have?

He felt as if someone had taken the well-worn and very familiar carpet he'd been walking on his entire life, yanked it out from underneath him and—just like in this palazzo—uncovered metres and metres of memories and emotions to excavate.

Could he do that? Clear away the anger and the pain from his past to allow for a bright, loving future with Lizzy?

Continue reading
A FAMILY MADE IN ROME
Annie O'Neil

Available next month
www.millsandboon.co.uk

COMING SOON!

We really hope you enjoyed reading this book.
If you're looking for more romance, be sure to
head to the shops when new books are
available on

Thursday 15th April